A Life Apart

A Life

Apart

A NOVEL

L. Y. Marlow

B\D\W\Y
BROADWAY BOOKS
NEW YORK

Copyright © 2014 by L. Y. Marlow

All rights reserved.
Published in the United States by Broadway Books,
an imprint of the Crown Publishing Group,
a division of Random House LLC,
a Penguin Random House Company, New York.
www.crownpublishing.com

Broadway Books and its logo, B\D\W\Y, are trademarks of
Random House LLC.

Library of Congress Cataloging-in-Publication Data
Marlow, L. Y. (Lydia Y.)
    A life apart : a novel / L. Y. Marlow.
        pages   cm
   1. Families of military personnel—United States. 2. Pearl Harbor
(Hawaii), Attack on, 1941.—History—Fiction. 3. African American
soldiers—History—Fiction. 4. United States—Armed Forces—
Military life. I. Title.
PS3613.A7663L54   2014
813'.6—dc23   2013050620

ISBN 978-0-307-71939-3
eBook ISBN 978-0-307-71940-9

Printed in the United States of America

Book design by Barbara Sturman
Cover design by Ann Weinstock
Cover photography by Felipe Rodriguez/V&W/The Image Works

10 9 8 7 6 5 4 3 2 1

First Edition

I watched her as she sat in the chair across from me reading a book that I'd given her long ago. She looked so beautiful, her lovely caramel face framed by her delicate bald head, her readers perched perfectly on her nose. For a few weeks now, we'd been living in a hotel room in Houston, Texas, where I'd taken her to seek alternative healing, my last hope to save her—*my mother*—suddenly diagnosed with stage 4 lung cancer.

Every morning as she slept, her breath labored, I'd ease from the double bed across from hers, and make my way to a corner of the hotel lobby to immerse myself in the writing of *this book*—a story that would breathe life back into my deflated, broken heart.

A Life Apart is dedicated to her, my mother, who has been my greatest inspiration, my best friend. Every letter, every word, every sentence, every prose, was breathed into this book because of her. During those times when I didn't think *I could,* when this book would challenge me beyond measure, I was often reminded of those moments when I watched her slowly fade away. There is *nothing* more painful, I often whispered to my soul.

In *Color Me Butterfly,* I tell the story of four generations of mothers and daughters (my grandmother, my mother, myself, and my daughter) that survived more than sixty years of domestic violence. It is through that story that you come to know my mother and why she is so very precious to me. Had it not been for her, I would have never had the courage to do what I love to do.

This book holds a special place in my heart,

beyond the compelling and complex characters that found their way into my mental skies, and onto a page. I, too, have had to endure my very own *life apart*. And though she is no longer physically here with me, there's not a day that goes by that I don't feel her spirit, hear her voice, take strength from her.

Ma, know that you are and will always be my greatest inspiration, the reason I do ALL that I do. This book belongs to you!

Much gratitude,

L.

A Life Apart

You may think I got no right to be here, no right at all.

The room is dark, abbreviated by specks of light. I step inside, watch the door slowly close behind me. My legs are heavy, like bricks are tied to them.

I edge closer to the bed. When I get close enough, I look down at her, and my heart swells. I close my eyes, wonder if I should have come.

I look around, take it all in—the white walls, the white sheets. A strange machine that makes a noise that brings sorrow to my heart. I turn away, think back on the time I first met her.

Until six months ago, I would have had no reason to be here. Fact of the matter is that I have come to appreciate life in ways I would have never believed possible. Life has a way of revealing a side of itself that no rightful mind would expect. It's like a maze, or pieces to a puzzle, fitting together like the speckled tile beneath my feet—white blocks with spots of gray. In the end, all you are left with are random patterns, like my life for the last half century.

My life? That's a long story, one that's not so easy to explain with all that done happened. All that done changed.

I changed.

I hear the door open. Then I see her: the nurse, *her* nurse. She smiles at me. I back away, let her do what she needs to do.

She moves around—probing, touching, then pushing a thin needle in one of the tubes that hangs above the bed. I watch her, the same way a mother watches her child.

"You a friend of hers?" the nurse asks, not looking at me.

I'm not sure what to say, or how to say it. No one has ever asked me this.

I nod.

"Will you be here long?"

I nod again, wonder how long is long.

"Well, if she wakes, please ring the bell. I need to take her temperature."

"All right," I finally manage. And when she is gone, I ease back closer to the bed, watch her again—her face, her narrow arms, her frail body—but she don't open her eyes, she barely moves.

I feel my face go wet. The tears came before I had time to stop them. I cry a lot now. Not around her. Mostly at night, when I'm alone, sitting in my living room. Mostly the tears come 'cause of something that happened long ago.

I take a seat, watch her through the night, let the dawn settle around me. I'm tired. The kind of tired that comes with time, sixty-two years in the making. I close my eyes, think back again on the first time I saw her—many, many years ago. She didn't know I had seen her, she would never know.

After a while, I turn to the window, see the sun rise, and through squinted eyes, I look at it. There is something about its blaze that pushes my mind to a faraway place. A place that is sometimes painful to visit.

I am startled when I see her stir, her eyes flutter open. I feel my breath come to a stop. I rise stiffly and go to her. Watch her, watching me.

"I knew you'd come," she says, a whisper.

I quickly dry my eyes, step closer to the bed. "Of course I was coming." I force a smile.

She manages to smile back. And we just look at each other for a long while.

She reaches for me. I lean in closer, squeeze her hands.

She closes her eyes, thinks about something, then opens them again, and with her eyes holding mine, she says, "Promise me . . . Promise me . . ."

I feel my knees buckle, my heart sink, brace myself for her next words.

Part One

1941

1

December 7, 1941

Morris opened his eyes to the crammed surroundings, a collage of single bunks, *racks,* stuffed together in stacks of three. Outside, the sun rose cautiously into the fragile beauty of morning. He stood and stretched, grimaced at the faint stabbing in his back that reminded him of the restless sleep he'd had. He hadn't had a good night's rest since he'd received Agnes's letter.

Since arriving at Pearl Harbor more than a year ago he often thought of home—of Agnes and Emma, especially Emma—the way she'd clasped her little fingers tightly around his; the times he watched her sleep in her crib, her tiny fist balled to her mouth; the way she'd look up at him with her big blue eyes. Agnes wrote every week, sending photographs of Emma and telling how each day she seemed to grow, sprouting like new fruit on a vine.

He missed his family, but he was also glad to be free of the mundane life, the burden, the awkward silences. And he had always dreamed of travel, being in an exotic world, in a place where he felt needed, around the things he most enjoyed— the ships, the work, the camaraderie. Some days, he walked the ships' decks for hours. He knew every ship and carrier by name; couldn't believe his luck to be working on such magnificent vessels. He breathed a little easier here, felt a sense of purpose and belonging.

It pained Morris that he had returned home to Boston only twice since he arrived in Hawaii—once after his sixteen-week training when Emma was born and again for only a few days after Agnes reminded him about their first-year marriage anniversary.

Being away for so long made him feel terrible, but the thought of returning to his new wife and child petrified him beyond anything he'd ever known. They had rushed into things, been forced to face a new reality. Thinking of Agnes and Emma filled him with guilt and a shame that he often pushed from his mind. Occasionally, without prompting, he had thoughts of going home, had even made arrangements twice. Like the last time when he had phoned Agnes and he'd pressed the phone to his ear, listening to her sobs, and he had promised he'd be home soon, *real soon*. Now, he read her letter again.

> *Morris,*
>
> *It's been two weeks since your last call. I don't see why you can't make more of an effort. Although Emma keeps me busy, it's not enough to fill the lonely days and nights I spend thinking of you. I wish you had never volunteered to go so far away. I need you. Emma needs you, too. She's growing up so quickly. Already, her first birthday is only a few weeks away. I'm planning a small party. I wish you could be here for it. We miss you deeply.*
>
> > *Love,*
> > *Agnes*

Morris stared at the photos Agnes had enclosed in her letter—Emma in a jumpsuit, crawling. Emma standing in her Taylor Tot walker. Emma taking her first steps. He quickly tucked the photos under his pillow as Joseph, his best friend, came back into their cabin.

On the day Morris arrived at Pearl Harbor, all the men in his platoon had been put into pairs. He and Joseph had been told one was responsible for the other. For the next sixteen weeks, they dove into small cubbyholes, avoided cross fire, learned weaponry, survived unimaginable physical exhaustion, and studied together. They'd become nearly one soul, one man.

"Emma turns one today," Morris finally said, his back still to Joseph.

Joseph had his own wife and child, and had managed to see them twice in the previous months. "You should go and talk to the lieutenant, ask him for leave so you can see your family," he said, distracted, busily preparing for his morning shift. "What time do you have to report for duty?"

"Oh seven hundred."

"That's not for another hour, so why don't you go and see the lieutenant before you report?"

Morris finally turned to face Joseph, shrugged. After Joseph left, he quickly dressed in his white navy shirt and pants, a dark neckerchief, all perfectly cleaned and starched. He grabbed his white top hat, then put away Agnes's letter and made sure everything was in order—his bunk crisp, his storage bin organized and stowed properly. He left the quarters, passing by rows of racks, and decided to take a shortcut, past the boiler and engine rooms and a control room, and ascended the back stairwell to the galley. He did not stop when he heard one of the other sailors call after him as he passed through the mess hall, ignoring the smell of fresh bacon and eggs. He would skip breakfast. He had no choice.

He scaled the narrow corridors until he reached the officer's quarters, his lieutenant's door. He knocked, stood at stance, and waited, listening to the rumblings of the lieutenant inside.

The lieutenant hastily opened the door, a white undershirt clumsily tucked into trousers, his hair disheveled. "What are you doing in my quarters at this hour?!"

Morris stood at stance, his eyes meeting the lieutenant's. "Sir . . . I need to go home to see my family. I haven't seen them in a long while. And I . . . well . . . sir, I was hoping you'd grant me leave after the admiral's visit."

The lieutenant glared at Morris, bothered. "Well, whose fault is that?!"

"It's no one's fault but my own, sir. I've just been so focused, I nearly forgot my place with my family," Morris said, thinking about Agnes.

The lieutenant glowered at Morris, partly because he was perturbed for the disturbance, and partly because he was once Morris—a young sailor scrambling to find his place, his balance between the navy and family. He sized up Morris, took his time thinking through his request. "You come see me after the admiral's departure today and I'll see what I can do," he finally said.

"Yes, sir," Morris said, relieved.

"And, son," the lieutenant said, eyeing Morris. "Don't you ever disturb me again this early on a Sunday morning. You got me?!"

"Yes, sir," Morris said; and succinctly saluted the lieutenant, before the door closed on him.

An hour later, Morris pulled a white hanky from his pocket and wiped the sweat from his face, but the heat did not slow his pace. He mopped the upper deck with precision. The dense, sulfuric smell of cleaned steel was thick in the air. Off in the distance, a group of sailors descended the ship for early morning mass while pockets of men spread out every few yards working in a flurry, preparing the USS *Oklahoma* for the admiral's visit.

Morris took in the perfect peaceful morning. It was a remarkable view, undisturbed by the more than two thousand young sailors and navy and marine officers spread throughout the ship, some having early morning chow, others assigned to their posts, many still asleep in their bunks.

He had fallen in love with Oahu—day after day of sunshine and bright blue waters, and a lush landscape that never stopped evolving from one colorful tableau to another. It was December and it felt like summer, so different from Boston. Before the navy sent him here, he had no idea there were such breathtaking places. He loved his work, loved serving on the USS *Oklahoma,* one of eight massive battleships moored along Battleship Row—the most impressive display of mankind's power in the whole world.

The battleships were beyond what Morris could have imagined, so mighty and so much more remarkable than the model ships he'd built since he was a boy. Sometimes when he had liberty, Morris would revisit each one, mesmerized by their sheer girth and power, the way they dominated the other ships that surrounded them—cruisers, destroyers, minesweepers. By far, his favorite was the USS *Arizona,* the last model ship he had built before he left home. The *Arizona* was simply the finest battleship that Morris had ever seen. He had spent hours visiting her, had even talked to the fleet admiral one day, curious to learn that she had escorted two presidents—Woodrow Wilson and Herbert Hoover; that she'd served as a gunnery training ship during World War I; and that she was the ship that was featured in *Here Comes the Navy,* one of his favorite movies. Morris was simply in awe of her.

Morris looked at his watch, noticed the time: 07:50. He

wondered how much longer it would take him to scrub the entire upper deck. Even the tedious work that stretched ahead of him couldn't dampen his mood. From his assigned post, he could see Joseph applying a fresh coat of paint. They'd drawn the short straws to get duty this morning, assigned the last-minute tasks so everything looked shipshape for the admiral's arrival. Morris put the mop down and made his way over to his friend.

Joseph straightened up and rubbed his lower back when he saw Morris approaching. "Did you see the lieutenant?" he asked.

"Yes, he told me to come back and see him after the admiral's visit. He's gonna see what he can do."

"I bet you can't wait to see your family," Joseph said, and smiled when he saw a wide grin break across Morris's face. "Oh man, that's more like it. You have been such a sourpuss! You won't regret it. Every time I see my kid he's like a brand-new person. You can't believe how quick they change . . ." Joseph trailed off, frowning up at the sky. He grabbed his binoculars. "What the hell is that?"

Morris looked over toward the mountains, confused to see a mass of planes heading their way, the roaring engines growing louder by the second.

"Is there a flight drill?" Morris asked, watching the planes flying low over the horizon, not too hasty, not too slow, just a full throttle of power that glided over the calm waters, approaching them.

Joseph trained his binoculars on the planes. "I think they would've given us some sort of notice if a flight drill was planned," he said, gazing out at the planes, in clear sight now.

"Holy cow! There's a lot of them." Joseph passed the binoculars to Morris.

Morris adjusted the focus, took a closer look. "Those planes got red circles on them."

"Red circles?" Joseph hastily snatched the binoculars, observed the wave of planes approaching them. "Ho-o-ly shit! Those are meatballs!"

"Meatballs? You mean Japanese planes?!" Morris blurted.

"Yes! Japanese planes! . . . Japanese planes!"

Joseph sprinted to the nearby machine gun turret, slammed it with his fist. "Dammit. It's got no ammo."

Morris raised the binoculars again, took a closer look. The planes were in clear sight now, bright flashes escaping their wings. Fifty, sixty, one hundred, maybe more—flying in perfect formation, not one breaking its stride.

Morris turned to his friend, saw Joseph running back to him, pointing frantically at the sky. "Take cover! Torpedoes!"

Morris saw it then; a deadly torpedo dropped from one of the planes and skidded in the water, headed straight for the twenty-nine-thousand-ton USS *Oklahoma*.

The ship erupted in a blast, a giant fireball that sent Joseph hurtling into the air and Morris flying into a steel wall. With his vision blurred, ears ringing, Morris watched the chaos unfold: men cutting across the deck at breakneck speed. Some moved with purpose. Some scrambled for cover. Some did not move at all. Some were shot down right in front of him. One man was in flames, and leaped over the side of the ship. Morris lay dazed, disoriented, trying to grasp the barrage of planes with large red circles—*meatballs*—descending on Pearl Harbor, cutting men down in droves.

Morris looked up, saw more planes crisscrossing the sky, zipping past him. He ducked for cover as a sea of bullets showered the ship, debris and shrapnel flying in every direction. With both legs injured, he pushed himself up on his forearms, dragged himself to a nearby station. He struggled to hoist himself up and grab hold of the .50-caliber machine gun, took aim at two planes coming straight at him, torpedoes strapped to their bellies. His gut turned to lead as he saw the bombs drop into the water, heading toward the *Oklahoma*.

The ship shuddered, rocked with a terrifying force.

"Air raid! Air raid! This is not a drill! Man your stations! Man your stations!" All around him soldiers ran in a panic. There were so many wounded, many already dead. Morris scaled the deck frantically, and then he saw it: Joseph, his body twisted, his wide-open eyes mirroring the pale blue sky, pools of his plum-wine blood streaming from him.

Morris turned away and vomited as another torpedo ripped through the bowels of the *Oklahoma*. The ship bucked, threw him across the deck, and knocked him unconscious. Moments later, he came to, and tried to move, crawl to a safe place, steeling himself in between dozens of bodies that he passed. His legs were increasingly painful, but he strained to move them anyway. He had almost reached the broom closet when he heard a choking gurgle, felt someone grab his ankle. He turned around, took in the sight of a man grasping for him.

"Please help me! Help me."

Instinctively, Morris clumsily dragged himself over to him.

"Help me, please. Help me," the man pleaded.

Morris pulled himself closer. He could see the damage from the bullets that had caught the man in his chest and stomach; his hands shielded his wide-open belly, intestines spilling like snakes. "Don't let me die. I don't want to die." He quivered.

Morris noticed that the man was about his age, maybe younger. He tried to sort it all out in his mind, figure out what to do. He grabbed hold of him. "God help us! Help us!" he cried, as another torpedo slammed into the *Oklahoma,* forcing her to raise clear out of the water, turning her on her side.

Morris slipped across the slick deck, helpless to stop his slide into the ocean. He thrashed, flailed his arms, horrified by the chaos that surrounded him: fires burning like infernos; bodies floating like a river; the warships of the U.S. Pacific Fleet in shambles, decimated by waves of Japanese planes. With one last rending effort, he clawed at the water, desperate to stay afloat. The sea tossed him forcibly, filled his eyes, his nose, his mouth. Suddenly, blackness closed around him. Then light—white bright light—flashed before his eyes, twinkling stars that slowed him. An eerie, strange peace descended upon him as he closed his eyes and surrendered, with thoughts of Emma . . . and Agnes.

2

Dark gray clouds lurked in the New England sky, reflecting Agnes's mood—the dread she felt every morning when she locked herself in the small hall bath, retching up everything, including her secret. She had wanted so desperately to tell somebody, anybody, especially her mother. But the thought of her father kept her from it.

Every morning Agnes lay in bed, her stomach twisted in knots as she listened to her parents' footsteps, their routine like clockwork—water running, doors shutting, then the smell of the Irish sausage that triggered her nausea. She'd keep still, taking in every sound. Some mornings she'd tiptoe her way to the door and lean against it, straining to hear if they spoke of her. But they did not. They hardly ever spoke. So, she'd find her way back to bed and just lie there, waiting until she heard her father's car fading in the distance.

But this morning was different.

There was an unusual quickness, a crackling energy she couldn't contain that seemed to come from inside her belly and fill up their home. She hurried through the morning awkwardly, her anxiety increasing with every passing minute. She tried to calm herself, taking deep breaths, then returned to her room. Rain pelted her windows, crisp droplets tapping politely at first, then incessantly picking up their pace. She had smelled the rain before she saw it. She didn't like the rain; it made their home feel even drearier, the silence oppressive. Solitude had become a familiar part of her day as she did anything she could to avoid them, *him,* her father—immersing herself in school activities, staying in her room, sneaking downstairs in the wee hours to eat what little she could force down. When her mother would coax her to the dining room for dinner, a rare occasion, she would just sit at the bulky oak table—her mother timidly stealing glances at her father, then at her—and she'd push around her food, taking small bites, forks clanking against porcelain the only sound.

Reluctantly, Agnes now turned to her closet. Putting together a smart, pretty outfit was a talent of hers, and she used to feel great pleasure when she admired the results in her mirror. These days, the stress of finding something that fit was robbing her of even this small joy. She reached for the few clothes that had a looser cut—a plaid elastic-waist skirt, a yellow scoop-neck blouse. Instinctively, she studied her reflection. Her whole body was different. Her face pale, her breasts rounded out and tender, her petite waistline expanding, the baby filling her out in places that only she noticed. Well, she and Morris.

Morris was the first boy she ever loved. She had waited weeks before telling him she was pregnant, and then they'd kept it to themselves even longer, as Morris had asked. He immediately said he would do the right thing, and she trusted him, more than she trusted anyone. She would do anything to please him. They had rarely been apart since they first met when their eleventh-grade English teacher paired them together for a class project.

"I'm Agnes," she had said. She had been secretly pleased to take the seat next to this boy who she had noticed in the hallways. She hadn't even known his name, but his sandy hair and ocean-blue eyes had made an impression. He reminded her of

Gary Cooper, whose movies she never missed. In fact, she had imagined a great love affair with him before she even opened her notebook. She pulled a sheet from it and wrote her name next to his. She knew that he lived in her neighborhood. He was not much different from the other boys, she thought, but there was something in his manner—confidence mixed with sensitivity—that set him apart.

"So, where are you from?" Morris had asked her that the first day they sat next to each other.

Agnes rode out the inevitable wave of sadness. She looked away, embarrassed by the sudden change in her mood. "Connecticut. We moved here after the hurricane."

Agnes could see from the look on his face, Morris had read about it in the newspapers. The hurricane had been the most powerful storm ever to strike New England; hundreds of people died, thousands of homes were destroyed, whole towns swept away. As they worked on the class project together, Morris gently asked about her family. His interest was flattering. Though she hadn't spoken about it to anyone, she began to open up, telling her story. How they had been forced to flee their home with just the few things they could carry. How the ocean had taken over the land so quickly, so violently. The look on her father's face when he realized they'd lost nearly everything, and the way her mother had cried for days. Then the dark days that followed when they were reduced to living in a shelter, everything they treasured devoured.

Now, not even two years later, Agnes smoothed out the blouse over her skirt, pressed down on it as though it would flatten the small bulge. She didn't notice her mother standing at her door. Alice stepped inside the room, closed the door behind her. "I saw Morris coming up to the door," she said. "He's probably downstairs by now." She stood for a moment, just looking at her daughter. Agnes could not meet her eyes.

"You know you can talk to me about anything," the tone of her voice gentle, her small frame and dark coloring a contrast to her daughter's.

Agnes was silent, a fraction of time passing. She watched the rain drum against the window, slow, even drops sliding down the glass. "Ma, I . . . I'm . . ." She sobbed before she quickly brushed past her mother and rushed into the bathroom, relieving herself of the saltines and ginger ale she had stashed in her room.

Moments later, she rinsed her mouth, splashed cold water on her face, and found her mother still waiting for her.

Alice studied her daughter, then said, "You should be about three months along?"

Agnes slowly nodded, amazed she didn't need to say the words.

"Is this why Morris came today? To tell your father?"

"Yes," Agnes said in a thin voice. "I'm sorry, Ma. I didn't mean for this to happen."

"Shhhh. It's going to be fine. Morris is doing the right thing. It will all be just fine." Alice reached for her daughter, embraced Agnes as she slid into her mother's waiting arms. "Oh, honey, I've been waiting to talk to you about this for weeks. Why didn't you tell me sooner?"

Agnes pulled away from her mother. "What? You knew?"

"Yes, I probably figured it out about the same time as you." Alice delicately smoothed a stray strand of hair from Agnes's eye. "I noticed the strange way you were acting. And then when I heard you crying in the bathroom, I wanted so badly to talk to you about it."

"Why didn't you?" Agnes felt the urge to cry again.

Alice looked away, thought about the time she was a young girl and had met Oscar, and later when she had to face her own mother with similar news; and how quickly the years had passed, the way things had changed, all that they'd been through. "I don't know," she finally said. She put her arms around Agnes, pulled her close, rocked her as Agnes clung to her for a long while, not wanting to face what was waiting for her downstairs.

M orris studied the front door with utter intensity, the rain drenching him. He removed his cap and adjusted his tie, the icy fear of God rising inside him. It didn't seem possible. Couldn't be possible. They had been together only a few times, and the thought hadn't once crossed his mind. He remembered the day that Agnes had told him the news, the way the words filled his ears. They were sitting in the park, and she had been quiet, her round face flushed, her eyes threaded with worry.

"Is everything okay?" Morris finally asked her. Their eyes met and sudden tears filled hers. She turned away, and in that moment he knew. It wasn't her words that caused his stomach to tumble like a stream, it was the look on her face—a look of shame, fear.

"It'll be fine," Morris promised. "We'll be fine," he whispered to himself again, a sliver of doubt lingering. He liked Agnes a great deal. At times, he even thought he loved her. But he wasn't ready to be a father. Not like this. Not under the same circumstances that caused his father to turn against his mother.

He could still see the look on his father's face. It was a Sunday morning in the middle of an icy winter and Morris was just five years old, sitting at the kitchen table, his head down, too afraid to look at his father. His mother stood at the stove, wearing her old apron stained in all the familiar places, and Ben, only two years old, sat in his highchair across from them, oblivious.

"She treeecked me," his father slurred, his breath tarred with booze. "Go on, tell 'em. Tell the boy how you treeecked me. Tell 'em how if it weren't for 'em, I would'r been long gone," he said, the words barely out of his mouth when he bolted from the chair like a cat, his stride so sudden, so quick, that Gilda didn't know he had grabbed her until his hands were around her throat.

"Da, no!" Morris screamed, rushing to his mother's aid.

His father let go of her only long enough to grab Morris and sling him into the wall, his body too thin to withstand the impact.

Morris had crumpled on the floor, bruised, his head folded into his small arms as his mother's screams pierced the room, the same screams he'd heard for as long as he could remember. He closed his eyes, did what he'd always done—recited the song that his mother had taught him, words that took him to a faraway place: *Mary had a little lamb, little lamb, little lamb . . . Mary had a little lamb whose fleece was white as snow.*

And now, one sentence. One word. One fleeting thought and Morris could hear that *little lamb* again, and his father's syrupy Boston accent with its misplaced *r*'s and strange vowels—a memory so strong he felt transported back in time. *I woulda had a betta life if it weren't for you,* he would say. That's how it all began. The blame that rose suddenly from nothing into a fierce twister that swirled from the ground so big and dark and strong. Morris felt he was to blame whenever his father looked at him with disgust on his face. He'd take his frustration out on Morris and his mother, and when little Ben was of age and his two sisters came along, he'd take it out on them, too. It was no wonder that Morris had mixed feelings when he lost his father two years earlier to a bout of influenza. The last time he'd seen him in the hospital, his body, which had once seemed giant, was shriveled and weak. His father's voice was small and shrill, with a hint of self-pity, as he told Morris he was now the man of the house. Morris stood at the edge of the hospital bed, his fifteen-year-old mind as unsure of itself then as it was now. And he found himself wanting to run as far away as he could get.

He wished he could run now, wished he could go far away. He had made Agnes keep it to herself, telling her that he needed time to find a job, but what he really needed was for her to wait until he was ready to own up to it—and that meant only one thing: marriage.

"Maybe we should give it away?" Morris had suggested thoughtfully one day. He was startled to see the horror on Agnes's face. "You mean put it up for an adoption?!" Morris had nodded, and Agnes shook her head. "I can't do that. . . . We can't do that!" And he had agreed quickly, not wanting to hurt Agnes, a girl whose beauty and sadness fascinated him from the moment he laid eyes on her. And he knew that Agnes had grown to trust him, from the time he asked her out on their first date.

"Do you wanna grab a burger or somethin' after school?" Morris had said at the end of class one day, feeling awkward.

Agnes's innocent smile was all the answer he needed. "Yes," she said, and nodded. "I'd like that."

They walked the six blocks to the Charles Street Sandwich Shop, the place Vincent's father owned. Morris had told Vincent about Agnes, and it was his friend's coaxing that gave him the nerve to ask her on a date. "Bring her to the sandwich shop," Vincent had suggested. "I'll take care of you." Morris had agreed, partly because he trusted Vincent, and partly because he hadn't saved up quite enough money to take her on a proper date.

"You ever been here?" Morris asked as Agnes took the seat across from him.

"No, this is my first time." Agnes took in her surroundings—
the checkered tables that lined the picture windows, the oversized counter and eight stools, the photos on the walls.

"I come here all the time. The burgers are really good."
Morris spotted Vincent behind the counter serving up a milk
shake to a young boy and his father.

"I used to come here with my dad. I understand . . . you
know, about what you told me about your family," Morris
said suddenly. "I mean, about losin' your sister. I lost my father." He hesitated. "I mean . . . he died."

Morris saw a flash of hurt, then solace pass over Agnes, a
look he recognized from those rare moments when he conjured up thoughts of his father. He could tell that she had
learned to live with pain, too.

"What can I get for you two?" Vincent interrupted, a
mile-wide grin on his face, pad and pencil in hand. Agnes was
surprised, then amused as Vincent pushed Morris over in the
booth to make room for himself. "You must be Agnes. I've
seen you at school. And of course this buffoon won't stop talking about you."

Morris cringed, kicked Vincent under the table. "Agnes,
this is my best friend, Vincent, and this is his pop's place."

Agnes blushed. "I'm honored to meet you." She giggled as
Vincent kissed her hand and removed himself from the booth.

"Can I bring you two a couple of colas?"

"Yes." Morris gave him a nod. "And you can get back to
work now."

Secretly, Morris was glad Vincent had interrupted the conversation. What had he been thinking bringing up his father?

An awkward moment passed, and Agnes considered Morris thoughtfully. He was uneasy, unsure of where to take the
conversation. "What was your father like?" she asked casually.

"Actually, he wasn't bad . . . when he wasn't drinking."

Morris took his time telling her about his family, the way his mother couldn't wear a sleeveless dress for weeks or go out of the house without sunglasses. The way he was forced to protect little Ben and his two small sisters.

Now, he knocked on Agnes's door, ready to own up to the truth, and he couldn't help but wonder if, somewhere beneath the surface, his father lurked in him, too. He had to come to terms with the harsh reality: he was to marry Agnes, the girl he cared deeply about but wasn't quite sure he loved. He was to marry her anyway, under the same shaky circumstances his father had married his mother.

After the second knock, Oscar finally opened the door. For a moment, Oscar seemed startled to see Morris. He ushered him inside, gestured for Morris to take a seat.

Oscar sat across from Morris, his untamable salt-and-pepper hair and thick brows stark against his weathered face. He wore dark corduroy trousers, a plaid shirt, and suspenders. Morris sat still, avoiding Oscar's stare. He shifted uncomfortably in his seat, started to speak, but then stopped, realizing small talk was useless. He had slept restlessly for the past few nights, going over what he would say, how he would say it. "Just tell him," Vincent had suggested with casual ease. "Beating around the bush ain't gonna make him respect you more when you finally come out with it." Morris counted on doing just that—*saying* it—but now, sitting across from Oscar, he was struck dumb.

"What took you so long?" Oscar said, peering at Alice.

Agnes followed her mother into the living room, took a seat next to Morris on the sofa, briefly smiled at him. He noticed her soft face, her shining hair. She was beautiful, and she was about to be his. He dried his clammy palms on his trousers. Alice sat next to her daughter, and for a time, no one spoke.

"So, what is it?" Oscar demanded.

"Sir," Morris began, the lump in his throat pulsing. After a moment's silence he looked up at Oscar. "Sir . . . Agnes and I . . . Well, sir . . . You see, Agnes . . . Agnes . . . Agnes is . . . expecting."

Oscar cursed him, muttered a few words under his breath in a language Morris didn't recognize, but could tell from the tone, they weren't nice words. Oscar leaned forward, eyed Morris. "And how do you 'spose you gonna take care of my daughter?" he said.

Morris looked straight at him, having given this some thought. "I found a job at the shipyard. I want to do right by Agnes."

"You would've done right by my daughter if ya hadn't touched her in the first place! Shipyard jobs ain't gonna raise a family. My daughter deserves better."

Morris glanced at Agnes, afraid she might run from her father's shaming glare.

"Maybe we can help them," Alice butted in quietly.

Oscar shot a look at her. "Help them do what? The boy don't deserve her!"

"Daddy, don't!" Agnes sobbed. She finally raised her head, sat up straighter now. "Why do you have to be so mean? Why can't you at least try to understand? Ever since Emma . . ."

Agnes's words trailed off; the mention of Emma's name shattered the air like broken glass.

Losing Emma had changed them all—her mother, Alice, whose carefree and jubilant spirit was now meek, frail, going through the motions of daily life; and her father, Oscar, once gregarious, always ready to take his girls for ice cream and tell them stories about his upbringing in Ireland. He had lost his taste for ice cream and storytelling in the same way he had lost his taste for life; and Agnes, now their only child, their only daughter, had learned to live with her loss and their pain, too.

Agnes stole a glance at Morris, could see that he understood what she had never been able to tell him: that her little sister, Emma, had died during the hurricane. She looked away, suddenly embarrassed, and almost jumped when she felt his warm hand on hers.

Alice started to sob. Oscar glared at his daughter. "You want me to understand the disgrace you brought on this family?! What you've done is a sin against God! How dare you mix your sister's memory up with your sin?"

"Sir . . ." Morris interjected, apprehensive. For a moment, he glanced at Agnes, still in tears, and Alice, who stared at slightly shaking hands in her lap, and then tentatively turned back to Oscar. "Sir, I'm really sorry, and I know this isn't ideal, but I plan to take care of Agnes . . . and . . . and the baby. I want to marry her," Morris reasoned, searching Oscar's face. "I . . . I care about her. I want to do the right thing."

Oscar narrowed his eyes, like he knew Morris couldn't bring himself to say he loved her. He stood abruptly, shot a look at Agnes. "I guess you got no choice. Now, do you?!" he said, then stormed from the room.

Three weeks later, Agnes took her time undressing, caressing the small bulge, the life growing inside her. She made her way to the bathroom. A bath always calmed her, especially the early morning sickness. She set the towel where she could reach it, and stepped gingerly into the tub, then lay back and closed her eyes. She liked the way the water soothed her, forced her to shut her mind and slow her thoughts. These last days, as the wedding was hastily being arranged, she realized she was truly happy. No matter the impulse that led her to give herself to Morris, against all her Catholic upbringing.

The first time they did *it,* a Sunday afternoon, was only six months ago. Morris had come to her house after her parents had gone out for the afternoon. They quietly sat in the backyard, and then he surprised her with a gift.

"Close your eyes," he told her, a sheepish grin brightening his charming face, his hair parted on one side, flattened across the top. Agnes smiled as she softly closed them, felt something cool melt against her skin. She reached to touch a sequined butterfly on a gold chain around her neck. "For you," he mumbled.

"It's so beautiful," Agnes whispered, touching the butterfly. It was perfect. Then she leaned over to kiss him, longer and more passionately than she had ever allowed herself, at least in full daylight. She was filled with uncharacteristic boldness, with the overwhelming desire to know what came next. She was tired of being the good girl, the girl she was before Emma died.

She took Morris by the hand and led him quietly to her room, and with the sounds of a lazy Sunday afternoon, Agnes cried silently as she gave herself to him.

After that first time, they hadn't done it again for a while, both nervous about what happened. They had long since decided that they were a couple, but they had both been virgins, and something had changed for Agnes that afternoon. Her love for Morris had deepened. Morris was the closest person to her, always there when she needed him, telling her that things would get better. And they did. She did. Morris Sullivan, with his languid, laid-back ways, was everything she was not— carefree, sensible, grown-up. And though there was a short time after she told Morris she was pregnant that she wasn't sure

if he would do the right thing, he chose to build a life with her
and this child after all. And she knew then that she loved him
more than her father or anyone could ever know.

Agnes soaked awhile longer before toweling off. She
crossed the hall to her room, went straight to the closet, and
pulled out the simple, Celtic dress her mother had made for
her. She couldn't wait for Morris to see her in it. She slipped
on the dress and turned in the mirror from side to side, admiring how perfectly it fit.

"I can't believe today is already here."

Agnes was startled to see her mother standing in the doorway, watching her. "How long have you been there?"

"Not long. Your father's downstairs waiting for you,"
Alice said, joining Agnes.

They both stared into the mirror, mother and daughter.
Her mother sighed. "You look beautiful. Let me help you
with that." Alice fastened the butterfly necklace around her
daughter's neck. "There's one more thing," she said. She left
the room for only a minute, and returned with a small black
velvet gift box. "I want you to have these." She handed the
box to Agnes.

Agnes slowly opened it. "Oh, Ma, they're so elegant."
She smiled through tears at the vintage diamond-and-pearl
earrings.

"I wore them on my wedding day and now I want you to
wear them."

Agnes reached for her mother, embraced her. She wanted
to tell her mother just how much this day meant to her, but she
stopped. It was her mother who said quietly: "I know." Then
she helped Agnes put on the earrings, and gently pinned the
tiara to Agnes's hair. She handed Agnes the bouquet—white,
long-stemmed orchids peppered with lavender wildflowers,
their sweet fragrance filling the room.

Agnes glanced at herself one last time before she made her way down the stairs, her mother following. Oscar stood in the foyer, and when he saw his daughter, his eyes filled. Agnes and her mother waited for him to say something, anything. But he just stood there, tears falling down his cheeks.

Agnes wondered if his tears came from joy or shame.

3

Beatrice had left home a few years after Robert, when she was old enough to know there was no future for a precocious colored girl like herself. She had brains, she knew that, but back home they would have had her married off and making babies by now. She wanted to do something more with her life, to leave the South the way Robert had done.

Robert was three years older than his sister, and had talked about joining the navy ever since he was old enough to know what it was. *I'ma be a seaman,* he had said to Beatrice one day while he played with the first toy ship he'd gotten for Christmas. *A sea—man? What's a sea—man?* Beatrice asked. *They live on ships, and they fix them, and they sail them,* Robert said. Beatrice had pretended to understand. From that day on, Robert talked, read, and studied about the navy—learned everything there was to know. Sometimes, Beatrice would sit with him in their room and listen to him read books about the great American ships; she'd ask questions that sprung from her innocent, six-year-old mind: *Where they come from, Robert? Why they so big? How you gon' get in the navy as a colored boy?* Robert answered every question, convinced that he was going to do what few colored boys would ever have the chance to. He studied hard, graduated at the top of his high school class, and when the navy sent him his orders to report, he and Beatrice and their mother, Esther, all cried together.

Now, Beatrice anxiously listened to the conductor announce the arrival of her brother's train. She hadn't seen Robert since the last time he was home and she was leaving to
attend the teachers college in Boston.

She looked on attentively as the train lolled its way into the
station, watched countless passengers unload. "Robert!" she
called as soon as she saw him. She galloped into her brother's
arms, barely giving him time to step from the train.

Robert swung her around, her sundress and legs flying
freely in the warm summer breeze. "Sis, it's so good to see
you."

After he put her down, Beatrice stepped back to take a
look at him. "Heavens, look at you," she said, admiring his
white navy attire, how he seemed to have grown three inches
taller and a lot more confident since she last saw him.

Robert flashed his famous grin. "And look at my little sister, a college girl now."

"Gosh, Robert, it's been too long. Me and Mama been
worried sick."

"Ain't no need in all that worryin'. The navy treatin' me all
right. Learnin' a lot about them ships, more than I thought I
already knew."

Beatrice smiled, looked around for his bags. "You hungry?
I got a real treat for you. Some of the best southern cookin' in
Roxbury."

"Don't none of these folks in the North know how to cook
like back home."

"You just wait and see," Beatrice teased. She took her
brother's hand and led him toward the car she'd borrowed,
and drove the short distance to Ms. Salma's Place in Roxbury.

The minute Beatrice and Robert walked into Salma's
Place, heads turned and stayed turned at the striking colored
man in his navy whites.

"Wow, sis. You didn't tell me this many of our folks done found their way here."

Beatrice smiled. She'd had the same thought when she first arrived more than a year ago. Since the moment she stepped off that Greyhound bus, wide-eyed and curious, she knew she would like Roxbury, a place and life that was a whole different world to living in the South. "Where did all these colored folk come from?" Beatrice asked her best friend, Nellie. "I reckon they come from the same place we come from," Nellie had answered. It didn't take Beatrice long to fit in.

Some days, when she wasn't in school or studying or working, Beatrice would take the bus to downtown Roxbury, dazzled by the scores of colored people dressed in their Sunday finery, frequenting the pool halls and jazz clubs and theater houses and restaurants. It was beyond her imagination.

Roxbury, with its dainty homes and busy streets, was similar to the North End, but different only in the pattern of people—a few Jewish, not so many Irish, and mostly blacks. Beatrice noticed the way the colored people minded their homes, their children, their cars—working long hours during the week, washing their sidewalks on Saturday, and worshipping together on Sunday.

Their ways soon became Beatrice's ways.

Beatrice looked around the room, at all the familiar faces. "I really like it here, Robert. It's so different from living in the South."

"I see . . ." Robert paused deliberately and looked at a tall middle-aged woman who approached them. There was something about her. When she spoke, he could tell she was from the South.

"Well, you must be Robert. Beatrice has told everybody in Roxbury about her brother who joined the navy. Said you was gonna be the first colored admiral to sail his own ship. I'm Salma," she said, a wide smile on her face.

"Well, my sister has always believed that much more than I. But if she say so, I'll take it on a good day, Ms. Salma."

"Well, why don't we start with getting you the best seat in the house. Ain't nothin' too good for a colored man in uniform in these parts. Follow me."

Beatrice and Robert followed Ms. Salma to a table. "I'ma send my girl over shortly. You order as much as you want, Robert."

"Isn't this place great, Robert?" Beatrice whispered across the table after they were seated.

Robert leaned forward, lowered his voice. "This here real nice, sis. Who would've thought that colored folk were livin' like this here in the North. You sure we can afford to eat here?"

"Stop all that worrying, Robert! Ain't nothin' too good for my big brother. Besides, I'm working now. Got me a part-time job as a waitress at a diner downtown. The owner real nice, and I get to work as much I want. I've been saving what little I can to send back home to Mama. It's a little different up here. I like it here, Robert, and Nellie like it, too."

"Knowing that Nellie like it here too don't set my mind at rest. That girl's been a bad influence on you since day one," Robert teased, and Beatrice smiled back at him. She'd missed this, too.

Nellie had been Beatrice's best friend back home in Jackson since Beatrice was six years old. Nellie was two years older than Beatrice, and served at times as the older sister that Beatrice had always longed for: standing up for her at school against the bigger girls, helping her with her homework, even teaching her things that a girl her age was too young to know. The girls would spend hours in Nellie's room rummaging through her mother's makeup and jewelry box, dressing up like little women.

Years later, when Nellie had been accepted into the teachers college, she made a promise to see to it that Beatrice got into the college, too. And Nellie had kept her promise.

On the day Beatrice left for college, tears flowed down her mother's face. Before she knew it, they were both crying.

"Final call for Boston," the Greyhound driver had announced.

"You hush on up now, chile," Esther had said to her daughter. "Gon' and make me and your daddy proud. Ain't no sense in all that cryin'. You fitna become a teacher. And there'll be plenty of time for you to come back home. I'ma send for ya."

"All right, Mama," Beatrice had said, squeezing tighter. Before that moment, Beatrice had never been away from her mother long enough to consider how much she might miss her, but Esther's words mustered up enough courage for Beatrice to get on the bus.

It had been a long ride from Mississippi to Boston, slightly more than thirty-two hours. Long enough for Beatrice to toss her thoughts back and forth about whether she'd made the right decision. She often had regretted receiving the teachers college acceptance letter, and had changed her mind a thousand times about going.

But now, she couldn't imagine living anywhere else but Roxbury.

"Well, hello, handsome," Gloria, the waitress, said, interrupting Beatrice's thoughts. "What can I get for you?"

Beatrice gave her brother a pleased smile when he glanced over at her.

"Well, let's see. I'll have the smothered chops and mashed potatoes and a side of them collards I see everybody else got on their plates."

"Good choice. And what can I get for you, Miss Beatrice?"

"Just bring me the same, Gloria," Beatrice said.

"You got it!" Gloria gathered the menus and made her way back to the kitchen.

Beatrice turned to face Robert again. "Well, how long do I have my brother for? I hope you gonna stay a few days so I can show you off."

Robert suddenly cleared his throat, like he had something important to say. "Actually, there's a train leaving tomorrow mornin' to Norfolk. I need to get there to board the ship back to Pearl Harbor." Robert wouldn't make eye contact. "I came all this way because I have something to talk to you about."

Beatrice shivered, bothered by his serious manner. "What, Robert?"

He skimmed the room, to make sure no one could hear him, then looked Beatrice in the eye. "I heard some news that many of us colored boys at Pearl Harbor are going to be shipped to Europe to fight in that war."

Beatrice studied Robert's serious face. The ruckus in the background shadowed Robert's words.

"They make us pick someone," Robert whispered. "Someone who will be notified in case something happens. Next of kin."

"Oh, Robert!" Beatrice gasped.

"Look . . . . Nobody's coming for me yet. But if we do end up in that war, and if my time comes, I don't want Mama hearing the news alone in that house. She didn't look too good while I was there. I can tell she worried sick about me. That's why I came straight here before I headed back to Pearl Harbor. . . . I want you to tell her if something happens to me, Beatrice."

Beatrice had been frozen from the moment Robert started talking. It dawned on her what he was saying. "You want me to be the person they . . . notify?"

"Yeah, sis. It has to be you. For Mama. Okay?"

Beatrice's face went blank, bewildered at what Robert had just asked of her. "Robert, I don't like talking like this. I don't know what I would ever do if we lost you."

"But you got to be the one, Beatrice. There's no one else, and I don't want Mama findin' out another way. 'Sides, I don't plan on letting nothin' happen to me. I just want you to be the first to know. In case. Okay, sis?"

Beatrice looked away from the earnest expression that settled on Robert's face, her voice thick with emotion when she turned back to him. "All right, but you got to promise me you gonna come home. Promise me, Robert!"

Robert flashed that grin at her again. "I promise, sis. You can count on it."

That afternoon, they spent every moment together. Talking, eating, reminiscing about their childhood, their family. Robert told her everything about where he was stationed in Hawaii, how beautiful it was and how the ships were beyond anything that he had imagined. Beatrice had never before seen Robert's face light up the way it did when he spoke about the navy.

Later that night while lying awake in bed, Beatrice replayed their conversations in her head. Robert was always surprising her. But knowing her brother the way she did, he wouldn't have come all this way to tell her about the next-of-kin affairs unless things were getting pretty serious. She had heard about the war in Germany, but what did that have to do with her brother in Pearl Harbor, unless there was something Robert was keeping from her?

She often regretted moving so far away from her mother after Robert had left. She couldn't imagine her life if she had stayed behind with Mama in Jackson. But her newfound fulfillment had come at a price. She hadn't thought about how

lonely her mother must be. How strong she had to be to overcome her grief over their father's death, then see her son and
daughter go off, far away from home. And now that Robert
may be going off to Europe to fight in that war, Beatrice was
especially worried about her now.

4

Day of Infamy

A strong hand grabbed Morris by the scruff of his uniform, lifting his head out of the choppy water. "Don't let go! Don't let go! I got you, buddy! We got another live one!" he shouted, pulling Morris to safety.

He lowered Morris to the ground, near a pile of other men. To Morris, it felt like rebirth. He had been going under, preparing for the end. Now, he was on a boat, heaving up ocean water.

"Easy. Easy now, buddy." A firm hand pressed on his back, the deep voice melodious and calm. Morris felt his insides quiet as he finally gulped in the air. He became aware of the commotion all around him—wounded men, dazed, wandering; men stacking dead bodies on one side of him and live ones on the other; other men taking their stations, fending off the enemy.

He looked at the large colored man who crouched next to him. His lungs burned. The stench of burning flesh assaulted his nose. He grabbed the man's arm. "Are there more coming?"

"No way of knowing. Gonna get you inside and safe soon as we can. You gonna be okay."

Morris struggled to sit upright, felt the pain rushing back into his limbs.

"Whoa—you just lie there," the man said, easing Morris back down.

Morris still held his arm. "What's . . . what's your name?" he asked.

The man paused. "Robert . . . Robert Dobbins."

"Are you the one . . ." Morris choked on his words. "Are you the one who pulled me from the water? The one who saved me?"

"I wouldn't say I saved you. I just gave you a hand is all." Robert patted Morris on the shoulder and walked away.

Morris watched Robert make his way down the line, check on each man, then turn to a man who lay moaning, his body burned beyond recognition.

"It's all right," Morris heard Robert shout above the chaos, holding the man's hand. "It's okay."

The man gripped Robert's hand, his eyes wild with fear, trying desperately to say something.

"I'm here with you! Don't be afraid!" Strangely, even in the wild confusion, Morris kept watching Robert as planes roared nearby, zipping past them. Then Morris saw Robert grasp the man, before he shuddered and stopped breathing. Morris turned away when Robert closed the man's eyes and covered him with a tarp.

Morris lay there, unmoving. A heavy anguish settled over him. How many minutes had passed since he saw the first plane? How long since his life had changed forever? He closed his eyes, imagined being in another place, at another time, away from all the commotion, the burning ships, as he kept his thoughts locked on the Lord's Prayer: *Our Father who art in Heaven* . . . His faith . . . the only thing that gave him hope.

5

Agnes

Agnes assessed the house, admiring it. She had been at it since early that morning—blowing up balloons, hanging streamers, decorating the table perfectly with a pink-and-white polka-dot Minnie Mouse tablecloth and matching plates, napkins, and cone hats. Balloons in every shade floated around a cake that read *"Happy 1st Birthday, Emma."* While she worked, Emma followed her, taking careful wobbly steps, as the Miracle Merry-Go-Round rhyme played on a nearby music box.

Emma had just learned to walk, and all morning she'd been fascinated by the balloons that seemed to float like sheer magic, gliding through the room, tickles of string hanging from them. She had chased one that had suddenly floated above her, tempting her to stomp after it, her little legs sheltered in her white high-top walking shoes. Every streamer, every color, everything fascinated her. She reached for a streamer that had fallen from the ceiling and yanked it.

"Emma!" Astonished, Emma watched her mother rehang the streamer—the whole morning had been captivating. She turned and noticed the mysterious Minnie Mouse cups, and wobbled in pursuit.

"Honey, no. These are for your party. You have to wait." Agnes picked Emma up, kissed her on her forehead, and snuggled her close. She stayed that way for a long while, feeling desolate, her energy drained, wondering how she was going to get through Emma's first birthday without Morris. But her mother and father, and Morris's family and her friends, would all be there. She had wanted Morris to be there, and she had written a few times to remind him, but Morris had told her that the admiral was coming on that day. He promised to call.

The doorbell rang. Agnes put Emma down and rushed to check her face in the mirror before she opened the door.

"Look at you. You're so pretty. How's my little birthday girl?" Claudia smiled at Emma in her pink-and-white polka-dot dress. She gave the little boy standing at her feet a gentle push. "Go play with Emma, Harry." Then Claudia pressed past Agnes with an armful of bags. "I got the cheese spread and the ice cream, too. Oh, and I wasn't sure if you needed any more crackers so I picked up some. And I found a pin-the-tail-on-the-donkey game. It was the last one. Can you believe it?" Claudia suddenly stopped and noticed Agnes. "Are you okay? You're not dressed."

Agnes took the bags from Claudia and began to slowly unload them. She was embarrassed at how she looked. Claudia was fresh and pressed, as usual. The two women, next-door neighbors, had become fast friends when they discovered that both their husbands were in the military and they both had toddlers. Claudia's husband had been in the air force for three years now, and Claudia had long adjusted to the life that Agnes was still getting used to. "It was hard at first. Sometimes Jim's gone for months," Claudia had told Agnes. "But the time passes quickly. It'll get easier." Agnes had listened, and things did seem to get easier. Agnes liked Claudia, and it was a relief to have someone so close by that she could talk to, someone who understood her.

The house was scented with roast beef, roasted potatoes, a

green bean casserole, delicacies that Agnes could barely afford on Morris's salary, but she had managed to stash away what little she could for Emma's first birthday, and her parents and Morris's mother and brother also pitched in.

Agnes pulled the roast from the oven, placed it on a hot plate. She glanced over at Emma, who was enthralled with the colorful blocks that Claudia had given her. She and Harry were attempting to build a tower. Distantly, she could still hear the merry-go-round music and the familiar sounds of a Sunday afternoon outside her window.

"I know what you must be feeling," Claudia said.

"I just miss Morris and it's Emma's first birthday and he's not here," Agnes said, welling up.

"Oh, sweetie, it's going to be all right. You have to pull yourself together and be strong for Emma. I'm sure he would have been here if he could. These things happen sometimes."

"I just don't understand why he couldn't be here for Emma's first birthday. He hasn't been home in a long time."

"It's awful, I know," Claudia said. "But it's not his fault. You must know that, right?"

"I know," Agnes said. "But it still doesn't make it right." She wanted Morris to see how festive and happy she and Emma were—this first year of her daughter's life had, in some ways, been the best of her own life, but she could never shake the lingering disappointment that Morris wasn't there to experience it. Who else besides him could appreciate Emma's first word, her first tooth, the first time she stood on her own?

Agnes quickly sliced the roast, salted the potatoes, and skillfully arranged the meat and potatoes onto a platter. She prepared the last items for the children—slices of ripe banana, tiny sandwiches with cheese spread, pasta spirals. She stopped to glance over again at Emma, her heart filling at the way Emma tried to stack one block onto the other and chuckled when the blocks fell into her lap. These moments, Agnes thought, were the ones that years later she would remember, when Emma was smiling down at her own daughter, and the world was moving around her, so unpredictable, so unsteady and ragged. She stood for a moment looking at Emma. Then she went into the dining room and placed the number 1 candle in the center of the cake and two smaller candles on either side—one for her and one for Morris. She would have to blow out all three on her own.

"The salad is ready. Anything else I can help with?" Claudia joined her in the dining room.

Agnes looked around. "No, I think everything's ready."

"Then why don't I take Emma home with me and Harry for a little while so you can get dressed? You look like you could use some time to yourself."

Claudia scooped Emma up and grabbed Harry by the hand. Emma's big blue eyes were on her mother as Claudia carried her out the door. Agnes watched them disappear before she walked through the house, her footsteps hollow on the wood floors, picking up Emma's toys and the party wrappings, surveying the work she'd done. The house was so quiet, and she had rarely been alone since Emma was born. She had managed to avoid any moments of solitude, moments when her own thoughts became dangerous, working her into despair. Claudia's friendship had helped, but there were still times when Morris's absence came as an unpleasant surprise, as if she might wake up and feel him lying next to her.

It might have been different, if things had been better between them before he left. But his joining the navy had come as such a shock to her—how could he leave them like that? She longed for him when he was gone. Morris had promised to be with her, and then he had left and chased his silly dream anyway.

She went upstairs to their bedroom and stood at her closet, searching through the few dresses she owned. She thought about the time she had spent a Saturday afternoon in town at a dress boutique combing through a collection of pretty dresses that she imagined she'd wear one day and Morris would take her in his arms and tell her how beautiful she still was to him. But he hadn't said anything like that in so long. She often wondered if he still saw her the way he'd seen her not so long ago.

Agnes decided against a pretty lilac floral dress and selected a simple long-sleeved navy V-neck one instead. She quickly changed and pulled her hair back from her face, revealing her strong cheekbones, pleased at how she had bounced back since Emma. She brushed her lips with a little lipstick and pinched her cheeks to blush them. She slipped on some low-heeled shoes and checked herself in the mirror once more before she heard the phone ring.

"Hello . . . hello," Agnes said, hoping to hear Morris's voice.

"Agnes, hi, it's me."

Agnes recognized the voice right away. "Hi, Vincent," she said.

"I was calling to let you know I'm going to be late. I'm filling in for my dad and I can't leave the diner until he gets back."

Agnes pressed the phone to her ear, said nothing. She glanced at the clock. Already it was close to 3 P.M.; people would be arriving soon.

"Agnes, are you there?"

Agnes nodded into the phone. "Yes, I'm here," she finally said, discreetly wiping her disappointed tears as though Vincent could see them.

"Has Morris called yet? I'm hoping he calls when I'm there."

Agnes looked over at the clock again, thought about the

time in Hawaii. It was 10 A.M. Morris should have called by now. "No, he hasn't called yet, but if he does before you get here, I'll let him know you asked about him," she said.

"Okay. I'll see you and Emma soon. I got her something really nice."

Agnes could hear the smile in Vincent's voice. "That's sweet, Vincent. We'll see you when you get here," she said, then hung up.

The world was quiet for a moment, and she shut her eyes, closed out the things around her. *Why hasn't he called?* She went to her dresser, searching for the last letter Morris had written to her. She pulled it out and read it again, looking for clues that maybe he was going to surprise her. But there were none. The letter was no different from any other letter he had written.

> *Dear Agnes,*
>
> *How are you? How's Emma? I miss her and I can't believe that her first birthday is coming up soon. She's getting so big I hardly recognize her in the photos you sent. Things have been really busy here. We've been working around the clock to prepare for the admiral's visit. In fact, I just found out that it's the same day as Emma's birthday. So, I won't be coming home for the party. Please don't be mad. I'm really sorry about that, but I promise to call. Take care of yourself and Emma. I can't wait to come home soon.*
>
> *Love always,*
> *Morris*

Agnes closed the letter and tucked it safely back in her dresser drawer. She lay down on the bed for a long while, willing Morris to call, but the phone didn't ring.

Instead she heard the front door open and Claudia's quick stride moving through the foyer. "We're back," she heard Claudia call out. Then she heard more voices, and she recognized them right away. It was her mother and father, Morris's family, and a few of her neighbors. And she could hear music. Claudia must have turned on the radio. For a moment she wanted them all to just go away.

She kept her eyes closed and she didn't move, just stayed there in her own quiet thoughts. She did not want to go downstairs, just wanted to curl up right there and fade away.

"What are you doing? Everyone's here. Are you okay?" Agnes opened her eyes to Claudia standing at her bedroom door.

Agnes was powerless to stop the tears. "Morris still hasn't called and I'm worried. That's not like him to not call when it's concerning Emma," she said.

"Oh, honey, he'll call, but you got to stop worrying yourself like this."

"Something's not right, I can feel it."

Claudia took a seat next to Agnes, put her hand over hers. "Honey, I know how you feel. I've been through it, too, but you can't keep doing this. Morris is fine. You said the admiral was coming today. Maybe he can't get away to call until after the admiral leaves. He's fine, honey. Now you got to pull yourself together and come downstairs before you get everyone worrying about you."

Agnes nodded, pushed herself up from the bed, and wiped the tears from her face for what seemed the hundredth time that day. "You're right," she said, looking around for her shoes. "Just give me a few minutes and I'll be down."

"That's my girl." Claudia reached to embrace her friend. "I'll see you down there, okay?"

"Okay," Agnes said, then watched Claudia leave. She

smoothed her dress and went into the bathroom. Ten minutes later she emerged with a fresh face and spirit. She checked herself one last time in the mirror. Satisfied, she made her way downstairs and was surprised to find everyone in the living room, surrounding the radio.

For a moment, they did not notice her walk in. "What is it? What happened?" Agnes said, prompting them all to turn.

It was her mother who drew her eye. Alice was pale, her handkerchief clutched to her mouth. Agnes was transported back to the moment, all those years ago, after the hurricane, when her mother saw the spot where their house used to stand. She had the same look on her face now. "Mom?" Agnes said, flustered.

"It's Morris, honey."

Agnes went still. "What . . . what about Morris?"

The radio seemed to go silent, the room unmoving. Claudia spoke up. "It's Pearl Harbor. The Japanese bombed Pearl Harbor."

Agnes's eyes floated from Claudia to Morris's mother, and then back to her own mother. She felt her hand suddenly go over her mouth, before she heard the sound of her own cry, a harrowing croak from deep in her throat.

6

Beatrice

Beatrice stood at the door, a suitcase in one hand, her Bible in the other. She had taken the first train out of Boston to Jackson, Mississippi; had stayed awake through the night, unable to sleep. A sorrowful heartbeat drummed in her chest as she waited for Esther to open the door. She had called her mother the day that Pearl Harbor was bombed. They hadn't known then just how many had died, and she had reassured her mother that Robert was fine, words that comforted her own mind.

That is, until she saw two uniformed men approaching the house in Roxbury. She'd never felt hate in her life the way she hated those men, coming to give her the news. The same terrible news that she was about to pass on to her mother. Beatrice took a shaky breath, hugged her Bible to her chest, waited for the door to open.

When Esther opened the door and saw Beatrice, took in the grief on her face, her heart crumbled. "What are you doing here? Is it Robert? Did something happen to my boy?"

Beatrice looked grief-stricken. "Mama . . . he's gone. Robert's gone, Mama. He's gone. . . ."

"What—?!" Esther winced, her breath caught in her throat as she slipped toward the floor.

Beatrice caught her, rocked her mother in her arms until Esther's cries became a whimpering sob. They stayed that way for a long while, sheer grief stilling them. Esther did not speak, and Beatrice found there was a calm in not talking, a freedom in not bringing to light what felt so dark.

In the days that followed, Esther seemed content to let Beatrice be her voice, her strength, her will to live beyond the loss of her child. As time passed, Beatrice would often slip away from the house in the evenings, walking the long roads to let go of her own pain.

On good days, Esther and Beatrice would sit on the porch till late in the evening talking about Robert, and sometimes they'd pull out the photo album, smiles lighting up their faces. "He was a sweet chile," Esther would declare. "Sweet, sweet chile."

Later, when Esther retired to her bedroom, and the house was dark, Beatrice could hear her mother crying, too. She'd cry for her husband, Wilbert, whom she'd lost years back to a sickness that crept up and quickly stripped him away from his family. She'd cry for Robert, the son the navy took from her. And Beatrice knew she'd cry for her, too.

After a month, Beatrice clung to her mother at the bus depot. "I don't want to leave you, Mama. Not now. Not like this."

Esther lifted Beatrice's chin, cupped her face in her hands. "Shh, you go on back to that college 'fore you be done lost your place. I'm gon' be jus' fine. Jus' fine knowin' you gettin' your teacher's education."

Beatrice clung to her mother one last time before she boarded the bus back to Boston. As the bus slowly pulled away, she could see that losing Robert had already aged her mother.

7

Morris

Morris lay in a narrow cot, one leg propped on a pillow, the other hung from a sling. He had been awake for hours, alert to the sounds of the hospital ship *Solace*—doctors and nurses shuffling frantically up and down the corridor; urgent tin carts carrying morphine and saline solution; the moans of men, some near death, some burned beyond recognition.

He'd been there for little more than a week, yet it seemed longer. The morphine was wearing off now, ridding him of a deep, induced sleep. He remembered faces bending to him. The doctor. The nurses. Men who'd come to check on the wounded. And he remembered their voices, the talk of defeat, a planned victory, of war. *It all happened so suddenly,* Morris vaguely remembered one of them saying. So many lives lost. More than three hundred Japanese planes had attacked them. Most of the warships were sunk or damaged; thousands were dead, men buried alive beneath the *Arizona*.

Morris pulled his leg from the sling, pushed the sheet from his body. He wondered what time it was. Early afternoon, he guessed. His leg ached, his head pricked with pain, yet he knew the men who lay nearby in agonizing pain were worse off. The doctor had called for him to spend at least two more weeks in the hospital, maybe more, but he couldn't lie there for another minute. Not one more minute. He hoisted his wrapped leg to the side of his cot, used his strong arm to force himself up.

"Wait! What are you doing? Where are you going?"

Morris recognized the voice the moment he heard her. The nurse. His nurse. The one who'd dressed his leg and given him shots of morphine. She'd been there the whole time, attentively caring for him and all the men assigned to her ward.

"Let me help you," the nurse said, reaching out her arm for Morris to grab. "Where are you trying to go?"

There was something unfinished, something that nagged at him in the distorted dreams. The dream was always the same. He was alone in the middle of the ocean. There was a dense and powerful stench, a pestilent odor that choked him. *Burning oil.* Black smoke drifting above his head. With each passing moment, the water became hotter until it began to boil, the currents pulling him below. In the distance he saw a plane diving low, aiming for him. When the plane got close, he could see the Japanese pilot, a smirk on his face. He called for help, but no one came. *No one.* He shut his eyes tight and in the afterlight he could see Agnes and Emma standing onshore, reaching out to him, and he reached out, too. *Emma . . . Agnes . . .* he called to them, but the more he reached, the smaller they became, like tiny gnats in a tube. Then his head dipped below the surface, and suddenly out of nowhere, a man appeared.

A colored man.

Weak and disoriented, Morris grabbed hold of the nurse. "I . . . I . . . need . . . to find Robert . . . Robert—Dobbins."

"You're in no condition to go anywhere. You need your rest," the nurse said, forcing him back down.

Morris knocked her away. "No! I can't just lie here and do nothing!"

"You shouldn't be putting weight on that leg and you have a concussion. Please lie back down!"

Morris felt the yearning again, an urge stronger than anything he'd ever felt in his young life, and no matter how much the nurse insisted, there were things he knew for sure: he needed to find Robert Dobbins, but he was confined to this cot with his injured leg and a dizziness in his head, and everything around him seemed urgent, final.

The next morning, the nurse returned carrying a pair of crutches. "We don't have enough of these to go around," she said, laying the crutches on the cot next to Morris. "Your concussion improved so I swiped these from up the hall and they need to be back by thirteen hundred hours. You will not be leaving this hospital until you show me you can get up and down this hallway without falling over."

Morris guessed the nurse had taken the crutches at great personal risk. "Thank you," he said, and tried to smile. "I haven't even asked your name."

"It's Maude." She offered her hand. Morris took it, then grabbed the crutches, brought his cast leg over the edge of the cot, and leaned on the nurse's shoulder to stand, awkward and stiff.

Using the crutches, he made slow, clumsy progress through the cot-ridden, narrow space. It didn't take him long to figure his way around, but the effort was exhausting. By the time he got to the end of the hallway, he was drenched in sweat.

The nurse brought Morris a chair and some water. "No sense in going out there until you can be of some use. You'll do more harm than good. Let's give it more time." She smiled kindly. "Head back whenever you are ready."

Determined, Morris hoisted himself up on the crutches again and walked the hallway until he could take it no more.

When the nurse showed up at her usual time two mornings later, Morris was dressed and ready to go.

"Are you sure about this?" she said, seeing Morris sitting on the edge of the cot, his right pant leg torn over the cast.

Morris thought of his friend Joseph, his blood pooling on

the deck, and of Robert Dobbins, the way he had saved him. "I've never been more sure about anything in my life," he said.

Four weeks later, Morris stood outside Captain Shaw's office. He'd thought long and hard about what he planned to say to the captain, had made up his mind that he'd just be plain truthful. *No sense in being dishonest,* he'd told himself time and again. It would only cause him to have to answer more questions that he had no answers to.

"What is it I can do for you, son?" Captain Shaw said after Morris was escorted in.

Captain Shaw was a tall, stout figure, with a square face and dimpled chin. His eyes were bright and his hair sandy, combed straight as though every stitch was pasted in place. His uniform was pressed and immaculate, his shoes spit-shined.

Morris suddenly lost his nerve. "Sir," he said quickly. "Sir . . . I was just wanting to know how I might find out about one of our soldiers?"

"What is it you're wanting to know?" Captain Shaw said absently.

"Sir, he's a colored soldier."

Captain Shaw stopped shuffling through a stack of papers, looked up at Morris. "Why are you interested in knowing about a colored soldier?"

Morris looked straight at Captain Shaw, an expression of embarrassment on his face. Suddenly the story about wanting to thank a colored soldier seemed silly, inappropriate. He'd noticed how the colored soldiers served in segregated units, were hardly acknowledged for their work, considered *less than* their white counterparts.

"Well, sir . . . he . . . he saved my life, sir," Morris stuttered. "I mean, I wouldn't be here if it weren't for him."

Captain Shaw frowned.

"It's just something I want to do," Morris said. "I mean, I think it's the right thing to do . . . sir."

Captain Shaw studied Morris, took his time answering. "Well, son, I don't think I need to remind you that we got lots of work to do around here." Morris held his tongue, knowing better than to contradict the captain. "Besides, what do you think others will think if you go snooping around to thank a colored soldier when so many of our other boys saved lives, too?"

"Well, sir . . . I don't see why anyone would have a problem with it. We work alongside them."

"Well, things just ain't that way," Captain Shaw suggested tactfully.

Morris didn't say anything.

"Have you talked to anyone else about this?"

"No, sir. Not yet. I thought I should speak to you first."

Captain Shaw swiveled a half turn in his chair toward the small window, looked out at the ships.

"Well, if you have your heart set on this, then the first place I would start is at the hospital *Solace*. They should have records of all the soldiers."

"Yes, sir," Morris answered anxiously.

Captain Shaw stood, faced Morris, and smoothed his hair with his left hand, a habit that telegraphed uncertainty. "I don't want you spending too much time on this. And I also want you to keep quiet about it. Don't go around asking too many questions. Just find out what you can and be done with it."

Captain Shaw walked toward the small window, his back to Morris. "If something does come of this, you never spoke to me about it," he said. Then he turned and looked straight at him. "You understand what I'm saying, son?"

Morris nodded. "Yes, sir. I understand."

"Very well then."

Captain Shaw stood at stance, waited for Morris to salute him.

Morris wasted no time getting over to the *Solace*. He thought about what Captain Shaw had said: *you never spoke to me about it.* The words rang out as clear as the ship's horn that bellowed in the distance. If he couldn't use the captain's name, then how was he to explain why he was poking around about a colored soldier? Until now, he'd never much thought about the controversy this would bring.

The *Solace* was hot, had few windows. Electric bulbs made faint umbrellas of light throughout the dimly lit space. It looked no different than it had when Morris was one of its patients.

"Hello, ma'am," Morris said to a young, thin nurse behind a makeshift desk.

She took her time looking up. "What can I do for you?"

Morris paused, losing his nerve. "Well . . . I'd like to find out if you have any information about one of our soldiers."

"I'd be glad to check for you," she said, now standing to face Morris. "What's his name?"

"Robert Dobbins," Morris said quickly.

"All right then. Why don't you take a seat." She pointed toward two white aluminum chairs. "I'll get on this right away."

Morris took a seat and closed his eyes; the smells around him seemed to swell off the walls and swim up into his nose. He hated the lingering stench, a sickening reminder of the time he'd spent there as a patient only a few weeks ago. He'd managed to stay away from here, to keep his promise to himself never to return. But here, beneath the stench and the stark weariness could be the answers to lead him to Robert Dobbins.

"Excuse me, sir."

The voice pulled him from his thoughts. He rushed from his seat. "Yes, ma'am."

"Sir, are you sure about that name? I'm not finding anything on him. There seems to be no record of a Robert Dobbins."

"Ummm, well . . ." Morris felt his face flush. "He's colored."

"Colored?"

"Yes, ma'am." Morris stared down at the thick binder between them. "Do you have records on the colored sailors?"

They stood in silence, the quiet broken only by the voices of passersby rushing from one end of the corridor to the next.

"Well, you should have told me that before!" She scooped up the large white binder, disappearing again.

Morris took his seat, stared off into the distance. Down the hall, he noticed a man lying on a cot propped against the wall, his face covered in gauze.

"I found your Robert Dobbins," the nurse said, reappearing. "We don't have much information on the colored soldiers. Only thing I can tell you is that he was assigned to the *West Virginia* and he's deceased."

"Deceased!?"

"Yes, he died," she said, unconcerned.

Morris turned his face away from her, adjusting to the news, gazing at the much thinner binder between them. "Does it say anything about how he died?"

"No. We don't keep those kinds of records here."

"But you're a hospital. Wouldn't you know how your patients died!?"

"Not if they weren't treated here!"

"All right," Morris said. "Well, can you at least tell me where I might find more information?"

"No, sir. I'm afraid not!"

Over the next week, he visited the naval headquarters and

the *West Virginia,* but he was met with the same suspicious questions and very few answers until he finally visited the colored quarters, careful not to be seen as he entered.

The moment Morris stepped inside the barrack, an eerie hush descended on the room. The crowd of men turned, looked stoically at him. One of them finally spoke up.

"You need somethin'?"

Morris looked from one to the other, lost for words. "Well . . . I'm Sullivan. Morris Sullivan. I served on the *Oklahoma.* I mean, I was one of the ones that survived," he said, suddenly feeling foolish.

They stayed silent.

Morris looked around the room. "I survived because one of your men saved me." He paused, took in their faces. "Robert Dobbins. And, well . . . I just wanted to pay my respects."

They all eyed him. Another man stepped forward. "No need in paying your respects. What difference it gon' make? Not like that gon' bring him back."

"And what do you care?" another one said.

Morris held his eyes. "I care because I wouldn't be here if it weren't for him. I'm not looking for no trouble."

The men stared at him.

A short, stout man suddenly emerged, eyed Morris suspiciously. "What you say your name is?" he said.

Morris met his gaze. "Sullivan. Morris Sullivan."

"Sullivan, Robert was my best friend. He served on the *West Virginia.* Cleaned the quarters. All he ever wanted to do was to become a seaman, use the skills that he was trained to use. Serve properly on one of those ships. He died tryna save another white soldier . . . And it just ain't right that he died for his country and his country could care less about him after all those peoples he saved. They didn't even give him a proper burial."

Morris looked at the man as if they were the only ones standing there, as if the crowd of other men didn't exist. "What's your name?" he said.

"Bernard. My name Bernard."

"Bernard, do you know if Robert got any family back home?"

"Why you needin' to know 'bout his family?"

Morris paused, gave some thought to his own question. "Well, I . . . I'd like to write a letter to them, tell them how Robert saved my life."

Bernard looked around at the other men, waited for one of them to nod permission. "He got a sister," Bernard began. "She the one I wrote . . . the one Robert asked me to send a letter to if anything ever happened to him."

"Do you know where she lives? You think you can loan me her address?"

This time Bernard didn't seek the men's permission. He went straight to his bunk, came back with a small piece of paper that he'd scribbled something on, and handed it to Morris.

"She's in Boston?" Morris asked incredulously, staring at the brown paper that Bernard had given him.

"Yeah, she go to that teachers college for colored girls."

Morris shook his head in disbelief. "I live in Boston. That's where I'm from."

"Well, I reckon it be no coincidence then," Bernard said, and walked away.

After Morris returned to his quarters, things seemed different. There was something eerie, unsettling that pricked at his spirit. Just yesterday he had written a letter to Vincent to tell him about Robert Dobbins, how he'd saved his life, and he had reminded Vincent of all the times they had gawked at the colored people when they were little boys. *I don't know Vincent,* he had written. *I feel so bad about what we did, about how my father treated them.* He thought about the way the colored soldiers had opened up to him, about the things they'd shared. Morris quickly retrieved the small brown paper that Bernard had given him, studied it. *BEATRICE DOBBINS*—Bernard had written in large perfect print. Morris stared at it intently, recognized the address, and thought again about all the times he and Vincent had ventured to that side of town. At once, he grabbed the pad that he used to write letters to Agnes. The weight of it felt substantial, heavy, a force that matched his heart. He sat on his bunk, pushed way back against the wall, held the pocket light in his mouth, the tiny bulb reflecting toward the page as he wrote.

8

Beatrice

Beatrice trekked through the ice-covered streets, hands tucked deep in her pockets, a wool hat and coat cinched tightly against the damp. Two days of sleet and below-average temperatures had frozen the Roxbury neighborhood, making it almost impossible to move about. It was the kind of weather that made you wonder if things were nearing an end. That's what Mrs. Mary Baker said, the spirited colored woman who lived in the lower-level apartment of the two-story duplex where Beatrice and Nellie shared the top floor.

Mrs. Baker and her husband, Herbert, owned the small duplex. They spent their entire life's savings to afford it. They'd come to Boston more than ten years ago when Herbert had accepted a position teaching at the Teachers College of the City of Boston, a rare opportunity for any colored man from the South, but one that Herbert had earned through sheer diligence and excellence. Herbert had had two missions in his new role: to be one of the best colored professors in the country, and to help other colored students gain the best teacher's education. Both Mary and Herbert were very active in recruiting students from the South. Mary was a member of the League of Women for Community Service and the Boston School Committee. When Nellie told Mrs. Baker about her best friend, Beatrice, back home in Jackson, both Mr. and Mrs. Baker did everything they could to help Beatrice get accepted to the college.

Beatrice and Nellie's apartment was a quaint space with a tiny living room, a small kitchen with a burner stove, a large bedroom that was divided in half, and a bathroom not big enough for two. They both worked part-time to stave off the cost of their college educations. Beatrice waitressed, and Nellie helped out at church, each earning barely enough to get by.

Since returning after Robert's funeral, Beatrice missed her mother deeply and had written every week, as she'd promised, telling her mother everything—about Roxbury, her school, and her work, and always comforting words about Robert.

I miss Robert, Mama, but I know he's in heaven with Daddy. And we gonna be all right. You and me, Mama. I promise.

The letters always brought fresh tears, and often Nellie would stand outside their bedroom door and listen to Beatrice cry, and sometimes she would rock Beatrice in her arms, comforting her. One time as Nellie held Beatrice, she said: "You remember the time I spent the night with you so we can go to church together and we hid Robert's church shoes, and when Robert got dressed on Sunday morning and he couldn't find his shoes, your daddy got so mad at him? '*Boy, why you can't never keep no shoes on your feet? Why we got to be late for church every Sunday 'cause you can't find your shoes?*' We laughed so hard."

Beatrice smiled. "That was something awful, wasn't it?"

"Yes, it was," Nellie said, then turned and looked thoughtfully at Beatrice. "Those are the kinds of memories you need to hold on to Beatrice. Not all the other stuff you be worrying yourself about. Robert's in a good place now, and your mama is one of the strongest women I know. She gonna be just fine."

Now, Beatrice let herself into their small apartment, out of the freezing cold.

"I waited up for you," Nellie said when Beatrice finally came through the door.

Beatrice pulled herself from the damp coat. "You didn't need to do that," she said, shivering. "My God, it's cold out there. Ain't no buses running and I had to walk all this way." Beatrice barely noticed Nellie had pulled something from her housecoat.

"I wanted to be sure you got this." Nellie handed her a white envelope.

Beatrice became still, stared at the envelope. After a moment, she opened it, and her eyes moistened.

"What is it, Beatrice? Is it about your brother?"

Beatrice needn't say a word. After all, it was Nellie who often went to Beatrice in the middle of the night to quiet her sobs. It was Nellie who'd been there when Beatrice first heard the news about Robert. It was Nellie who had helped Beatrice keep her brother's memory alive.

"Robert didn't die in vain, Nellie," Beatrice finally said, looking up from the letter, sobbing. "He died saving people. My brother was a hero."

Later, while Beatrice lay in bed, she read the letter twice, savoring every word. She still had trouble believing it even as she held the proof in her hands. She could tell that the man took great care in the writing.

> *Dear Miss Dobbins,*
>   *My name is Morris Sullivan and I am stationed at Pearl Harbor and served aboard the USS Oklahoma. You don't know me, but I received your address from Bernard, who informed me about the loss of your brother. First, please accept my deepest sympathy. My heart goes out to you and your family. I know that losing Robert must be very difficult, but I wanted to let you know that your brother was one of the bravest men that the navy*

has ever seen. He saved my life, and the lives of many others.

Miss Dobbins, I didn't know your brother before that morning, but in the few moments I saw him, he shined his light on everyone he touched. Why God would choose to take a man like that, and leave behind a man like me, I don't understand. But I do know Heaven is a brighter place with him there. Had it not been for Robert, I would not be here to write this letter to you. I will not forget that. Robert will always be my hero.

With deepest sympathy,
Morris Sullivan

Beatrice folded the letter one last time, then dropped to her knees beside her bed and prayed. This time she didn't ask God to answer her prayers. This time she thanked Him. She thanked Him for answers to the questions that haunted her. She thanked Him for protecting Robert's memory. She thanked Him for *Morris Sullivan*.

And for the first time in months, she slept with some semblance of peace.

9

Agnes

The Morris who left more than a year ago was not the same man Agnes met at the train station, and Agnes knew it the moment she laid eyes on him. Morris looked fatigued in his white navy dress and top hat. The Hawaiian sun had tanned his skin, but somehow he still looked sallow, weathered.

"Hello," Agnes mumbled, suddenly shy, never taking her eyes from him. Without moving, they stared at each other.

Morris smiled weakly, put down his sack, and reached for her. "God, it's good to be home," he whispered in her ear.

Agnes smiled, embraced him. She had missed him more deeply than the words in her letters could express. She had thought about this moment often, wondering what it would feel like to hold him again. She didn't want to let him go after he kissed her softly on the lips. "This looks really good on you." She touched the lapels of his shirt.

Morris smiled, but there was something missing from his eyes. The spark seemed to be gone. He hadn't told her the details of what happened on that day, but somehow she knew that more than his leg had been injured. Agnes shook off the thought, glad to finally have him home. He needed care, love, and home-cooked meals. A few days of it and he would be more himself, especially once he saw Emma. Morris was staring at her face now. "You're as beautiful as ever," he said.

Agnes took Morris's hand in her own, squeezed it, and he

squeezed back. It wasn't until Morris picked up his sack and started to walk that she noticed his limp.

The Boston streets moved with the pace of a Saturday, a sense of gloom suspended in the warm midafternoon air. Morris was quiet, seemed to be taking in the faces of the people around him. Agnes fought the urge to fill the silence, decided to just let him be. But before she knew it, she was talking up a storm, and Morris barely grunted a reply the whole way home, where everyone was waiting—Emma, Morris's mother, brother, and sisters, Agnes's parents, and Vincent.

Once they arrived, Gilda reached for her son without words, took him into her arms. Morris took his time with each one of them—his mother, two sisters, his brother, Agnes's parents, and, finally, Emma. Morris lifted the sleeping child, studied her.

"Isn't she beautiful?" Agnes said.

Morris seemed unable to speak. He kissed Emma's forehead, and when she opened her big blue eyes and smiled up at him, he smiled back through tears. Agnes remembered how she felt after Emma had been born, watching Morris hold her for the first time. Forgetting about the many sleepless nights she had worried about him and their marriage.

"Can you believe she'll be eighteen months soon? Wait till you see her walk, and she can already say 'Mama.'"

Morris touched Emma's curly hair, kissed her pudgy fingers, struggled to hold her steadily when she began to squirm in his arms.

"Careful—she's strong. She'll throw herself right out of your arms if you let her," Agnes warned.

One of Morris's sisters reached for Emma. "Let me take her. She needs to be changed."

Morris handed the baby over immediately. He looked

around at all the faces that circled around him, and seemed to notice Vincent for the first time.

"Vincent." He smiled at his friend.

"Holy shit. Pardon my language, Mrs. Sullivan. I mean, look at you. The last time I saw you, you were a scared little boy." Vincent gripped Morris by both shoulders, eyed Morris's white navy attire. "Glad to see you, man. Damn glad," he said, becoming misty-eyed.

Morris grinned, and for a second, he was the boy Agnes had met that day in high school.

As Alice and Gilda helped Agnes prepare the early dinner, Morris and Vincent retreated to the living room. When Agnes checked on them, they barely looked. Morris had never talked to her like that. She felt jealous, but told herself she was being silly.

Agnes felt a hand on her shoulder. She turned to see her father.

"I don't mean to interrupt," Oscar said.

"Sir," Morris said, standing suddenly.

"I . . . I just wanted to let you know that I appreciate what ya doin'. You know, in the navy, and over there in Pearl Harbor and all."

Morris's stance was much different from the boy that once had to face Oscar. "I appreciate that, sir," he said, and extended his hand to Oscar. He seemed stunned when Oscar embraced him instead.

Later, after everyone had left and Agnes had put Emma down for the night, she found Morris sitting in the living room in the fading evening light.

"There you are," Agnes said.

Morris smiled at her. "Come sit with me for a minute." Morris patted the seat next to him.

Agnes snuggled close to him and they sat quietly for a long

time, the silence broken only by the clanking of the old radiator and by voices of passersby outside their window. The living room was now dark, flickers of light beaming through the curtains.

"You must be exhausted. Can I get you anything?"

"No, I'm fine." Morris seemed to be studying her. "I really missed you and Emma," he said.

"I missed you, too. I'm so glad you're finally home." Agnes's voice was close to breaking. "You need to rest. Let's go upstairs." She reached out to take his hand.

Agnes led him to their room, and watched as he slowly removed his shirt and pants and shoes, then lay back on the pillow, shutting his eyes and falling into a deep sleep almost right away. Agnes slipped under the covers next to him, breathing in his scent, letting herself feel something almost like contentment.

"It's me. I'm here. You're home. You're finally home," Agnes said, reaching for Morris. She held him tightly, watched Morris look around the dark room, trying to recognize his surroundings. That first night, Morris had seemed to be confined by a tiredness that left him motionless. But by the second night, he was torn from his sleep in a cold sweat. Agnes rocked him in her arms, and she could feel his body tense up, his breathing shallow and labored.

"Honey, are you okay? Please talk to me. Tell me what's going on."

Morris sat up on the side of the bed, his back to her. "I'm fine," he said, and walked out of the room.

The next morning, Agnes watched Morris from the kitchen. How content he seemed just to sit on the living room floor and play with Emma—helping her stack and knock down the colorful blocks, watching her play with Minnie

Mouse, chasing behind her. Agnes could tell how much joy Emma brought him. His daughter delighted him.

Alice seemed to know just what to say to her daughter when Agnes called her that morning and told her that she was worried about Morris, that he wasn't the same and he wouldn't talk to her. *A home-cooked meal would surely make him feel better,* Alice had said. And Agnes took her mother's advice and spent the next few days cooking all of Morris's favorite foods—lamb roast with chive potatoes, Boston baked beans, New England clam chowder, lemon meringue pie, a rare indulgence beyond the food they could really afford. One day for lunch, she even went to the Charles Street Sandwich Shop and got two medium-rare burgers, cooked just the way Morris had ordered them on their first date.

Now, the house was quiet as Agnes carried a sleeping Emma to lay her down for her nap. She stood at the crib watching Emma, her breathing slow and even, then glanced at the clock. Already it was four fifteen, and soon their family and friends would be arriving for the surprise dinner party that she'd planned for Morris. She walked from room to room, tidying up the house. It seemed very important that everything was in its proper place. At one point, she slipped into her bedroom and changed into a pleated scoop-neck swing dress. She inspected herself in the floor-length mirror, twirling from side to side, pleased with the way the dress molded to her figure. She styled her hair into an updo and expertly applied her makeup before she finally woke Emma.

"Let's get you all pretty for Daddy," she said, lifting Emma from her crib.

Agnes dressed Emma and brushed her hair, then took her downstairs, pausing to look out the living room window to see if anyone had arrived. She made her way to the kitchen and put the coffee on, and then covered Emma with a bib and fed her soft carrots and applesauce. Then she heated the food she'd spent half the day preparing, and washed the last of the dishes. She imagined the surprised look on Morris's face when he returned home, at precisely 7 P.M. *Take him out to do something fun. He really needs that—and promise me you won't tip him off,* Agnes had said to Vincent.

A half hour later, Agnes heard the doorbell, and she removed her apron, checked herself and Emma again, then rushed to open the door to Claudia and her son.

"Are you okay?" Claudia asked. "Something's wrong. I can tell."

Agnes looked at Claudia. "I'm just nervous. I hope he likes it."

"It's going to be fine. He'll love it," Claudia said.

"I know. I guess I just make myself sick with this sometimes, and he's not been himself. I just don't want to upset him."

"Agnes, you've got to stop this. Morris is fine. You're fine."

Agnes watched Emma chase after the little boy, suddenly reminded of Emma's ill-timed birthday party. Why had she planned this stupid dinner party anyhow? What difference would it make? She suddenly turned away from Claudia, reached inside the oven to pull a dish from it.

"Let me help you with that." Claudia took the dish from Agnes. "I saw your parents arriving. I'll take care of this."

Agnes went to the door to greet her parents.

"What time will Morris be here?" Alice asked her daughter.

"Vincent's going to have him here at seven."

"That's soon. Can I help you with anything?"

"Maybe you can keep an eye on Emma and Harry while I set the table."

Agnes made sure everything was perfect—the food, the house, the decorations. She fanned out Emma's dress and checked her hair once more; then herself, made sure her hair, her makeup, her dress were perfect. And when she saw Vincent's car pull up and park, she hushed everyone and turned down the lights, and they all waited quietly, not a single soul moving, except for Emma and her little friend.

Agnes froze when she heard Morris's key in the door, his precise footsteps in the foyer, and an innocent-acting Vincent following behind him. She held her breath.

"*SURPRISE!!!*"

Morris stopped abruptly, taken aback by the more than two dozen people in his living room. He displayed no pleasure at the sight of them, and great confusion, too. He looked at Agnes. "Surprise," Agnes mouthed. Their eyes met and she was shocked at the resentment she saw in his. She took him by the hand and led him into the living room, and for the next four hours, she tried to ignore the way Morris seemed to do just enough to appease her.

After the last guest left, Morris helped Agnes clean the kitchen, the two of them barely talking, and when they finally turned in for the night, they both pretended they were asleep, not touching, facing opposite walls.

The next morning, Agnes dressed Emma for church and then brought her down to Morris. "Can you take her while I get dressed?"

Morris was dressed in his full navy whites. He turned and looked at her. "I can't go with you this morning. I have to take care of something. I won't be gone long," he said, and left Agnes standing there, speechless.

10

Morris

Morris spotted the address on the small brown paper, aware of two little boys—one caramel with big brown eyes and dark curly hair, and the other with chestnut skin and coarse hair. They suddenly stopped throwing the ball, and the scraps of conversation halted, curious about the white man in uniform who stepped from his car.

Morris took off his hat and walked up to the door that matched the address that Bernard had given him. He could feel their eyes on him.

The woman who finally opened the door was well-kept, graceful, in an olive dress, her gray hair handsomely styled. She had on a half apron that was tied at her waist. The scent of homemade stew wafted from beyond the door and into Morris's nostrils.

"Ma'am, my name is Morris Sullivan and I was given this address for Beatrice Dobbins. Does she live here?"

The woman dried her hands on her apron, eyed Morris suspiciously. "What business you got with Beatrice?"

Morris had a sudden inclination to quickly make his way back across town. "I knew her brother at Pearl Harbor. It's a long story. Do you mind if I come in?"

Morris knew how he must look to this woman, standing at her front door, a white stranger asking to come inside her home.

The woman took in his dress whites, and seemed to decide

he was harmless enough. She moved aside, beckoning him into the foyer, and pointed for him to take a seat on the settee, a handsome piece of furniture adorning a tidy and tasteful living room. She introduced herself as "Mrs. Baker," and when she sat across from him, Morris explained how Robert had saved his life, and that Bernard had given him Beatrice's address. "I just want to let her know that if it weren't for her brother, I wouldn't be here," Morris said.

Mrs. Baker eyed Morris. "You ain't got no bizness in this part of town lookin' for my Beatrice," she said.

Morris spoke quickly, tripping over his words. "Ma'am, I realize how this must look. But I don't mean Beatrice any harm. I just want to thank her for her brother."

Mrs. Baker held Morris's eyes for a moment, then suddenly stood. "Wait here," she said, and disappeared into a hall that led to a staircase.

Morris looked around, took in the clean and comfortable home, the scent of lavender and cinnamon and home cooking. He could hear hushed voices drifting from upstairs. He sat quiet, not moving until Mrs. Baker appeared again, followed by a young woman about his age.

Beatrice stepped into the living room, dressed in a simple blue dress, her hair pulled back, her face fresh with no makeup. Two eyes that reminded him eerily of Robert's—the ones he sometimes saw in his dreams—looked quizzically at him.

Morris rushed to stand. "Miss Dobbins."

"Well, I'll leave you two alone," Mrs. Baker said, and gave Beatrice a careful look before she disappeared.

Morris reached out his hand. "I'm Morris Sullivan. I wrote you a letter. Did you get it?"

"I got it," Beatrice said, not taking his hand.

"Would you like to take a seat? I thought maybe we can talk."

"Mr. Sullivan . . ." Beatrice glanced over her shoulder, in the direction Mrs. Baker had gone.

"Please, call me Morris."

"And you can call me Beatrice." She smiled, and suddenly there were Robert's dimples.

"You really do favor your brother. I mean, you look so much like him."

"Thank you, Morris." She was still standing. "You will have to forgive my shock. When I got your letter . . . well, I never would have imagined in a million years that you were a *white* man." The smile came on her face again. "Mrs. Baker looked like she seen a ghost when she came up to tell me you were here."

Morris was surprised by her directness. "Please, have a seat," Beatrice said.

Morris sat down again, trying to remember what he had come there to say, still taken aback by her smile.

Beatrice perched on the edge of the sofa next to Morris. "What brings you to Boston?"

"Oh, I was born and raised in Boston. I couldn't believe it when I saw you lived here, too. I took it as a sign that I should try to find you." Morris couldn't believe the things this woman was pulling out of him. He stammered, afraid of what might come out of his mouth next. "I . . . I wanted to tell you how grateful I am to your brother for saving my life. He was a good man."

Beatrice nodded.

"I know losing him must have been hard for you and your family."

"It broke my mama's heart wide open," Beatrice said, tearing up.

Morris reached out to touch her arm. She flinched and he drew back, embarrassed. "I'm sorry . . . I mean, I just came

here to pay my respects. I know I probably shouldn't have
come, but I had to. I mean I wanted to. I made a commitment
to Robert. I mean . . . to myself in Robert's honor."

"I think it's amazing that you came here today . . . that
you see my brother as a hero. He always dreamed of serving in
the navy. It brings me and my mother some comfort knowing
he died helping others."

"He actually carried me to safety, with no concern for
himself. I've never seen that kind of bravery."

"Is that how you hurt your leg? I mean, at Pearl Harbor?"
she said after a moment.

Morris nodded. "Yes, but it's better now."

They sat, a comfortable silence between them. "Was he
scared, do you think?" Beatrice asked suddenly. "Do you
think he suffered?"

Morris closed his eyes for a moment, the intensity of imagining what Robert might have felt overwhelmed him. "No,
he didn't seem scared. But it was terrifying. Robert must have
felt that, too. The difference was he knew what to do about it.
I could only watch."

"You were injured." This time it was Beatrice who reached
out. Her hand was warm on his arm. Her eyes were lovely—
almond-shaped and the color of cinnamon. Her sensitivity
had brought him a sense of peace. He was as relaxed as he had
been since coming home.

"I was lucky your brother came along." He paused, and
saw how Beatrice looked at him. "I didn't see him die. Didn't
know about it until weeks later, when I tried to track him
down."

"That right there makes you special. A lot of white men
wouldn't thank a colored man for saving his life."

"Well, they'd be wrong." Morris realized then that he

hadn't thought about Beatrice's race once. In fact, there was an undeniable attraction.

"So, was Robert your only brother? Do you have other siblings?" Morris asked, eager to change the subject.

"No, it was just me and Robert. I guess Mama and Daddy just planned on us. What about you? You come from a big family?"

"Yes, I have a brother and two sisters. They all live with my mother, and I have a wife and a little baby girl named Emma. I got a photo of her, would you like to see it?" Morris reached to pull the photo from his wallet. "This is Emma," he said, handing over the photo to Beatrice.

Beatrice examined the photo. "She's a very pretty little girl. I bet she look just like her mama."

"Yeah, she does favor her mother, but I think she got my eyes."

Beatrice nodded thoughtfully, and for the first time she noticed his eyes, how pale blue they were against his face. She suddenly averted her eyes from his and handed him back the picture. "You must miss her something awful when you're gone." After a moment she asked, "Do you like being in the navy?"

Morris gave this some thought. "Yes, I do. I always loved ships. My father gave me my first ship when I was three."

"Robert loved ships, too. I used to sit with him all day watching him draw pictures of these big ole ships. He taught me everything there was to know about them."

"Did you like them? The ships?"

"I did. I didn't understand them as much as Robert, but I thought they were interesting. Robert loved the battleships the most. He was so fixed on them. Sometimes, he'd lie on the floor for hours with the first ship that my daddy gave to him for Christmas. He'd piece it all together and then break it apart and put it back together again. He got really good at it. That's what made him want to go in the navy."

"Me, too," Morris said. They looked at each other, and something unexpected passed between them. They both looked away, embarrassed.

"So, what about you? Bernard told me that you're in school to become a teacher?"

"Yes, I am. I've wanted to be a teacher ever since I was a little girl. Robert . . . he used to play school with me, too, let me be his teacher even though he was older than me," she said, smiling at the thought.

"Your mother must be proud of you. What else do you do in your free time when you're not learning about becoming a teacher?" Morris asked, genuinely curious about her life.

"I have a part-time job downtown at a diner. It helps with some of my living and school expenses."

"Where do you work?"

"At the Charles Street Sandwich Shop."

"Wait a minute . . . you mean the Charles Street Sandwich Shop on Charles Street?"

Beatrice laughed. "Well, it's not the Charles Street Sandwich Shop on Beacon Street!"

"You've got to be kidding me. My best friend, Vincent, works there. His father owns the place."

"You mean Mr. Vincent is your best friend?"

"Yes. We've been best friends since I was a little boy. We went to high school together, too, and he wanted to join the navy, too, but he couldn't because he has bad eyesight."

"What a small world," Beatrice said. "Mrs. Baker got me the job there. She and Mr. Vincent's father have a special friendship. She get him to hire all the colored girls from my school. In fact, she's responsible for me being here. She and

Mr. Baker recruit girls for the teachers college. Most of us are from the South."

"Mrs. Baker is a special lady. She's very protective of you, I see."

A soft smile broke across Beatrice's face. Morris noticed her beautiful eyes again, the way her smile softened her.

Suddenly, Mrs. Baker poked her head in. "'Bout time to tend to your studies, don't you think, Beatrice?"

Beatrice stood quickly. "Yes, ma'am."

Morris stood up, too, and followed Beatrice to the door. "Well, I guess I better be going," he said clumsily.

He stretched out his hand, and Beatrice took it with both her hands. "Now it is my turn to thank you, Morris Sullivan, for being a decent and kind man. I'm proud my brother helped you that day. You take care of yourself now." Beatrice released his hand and opened the door for him.

Morris put his hat on, gave her a long look, and smiled before he left.

11

Morris had been in his room for hours, piecing together the ship and his thoughts. He carefully laid out the tiny pieces—the hull, the deck, the keel, the guns—and used a trained eye and skill to craft the handsome ship. He made sure that every piece found its proper place, that nothing was awry. The ships gave his mind order, a solitude that allowed his thoughts to take shape alongside the steady progress of his work.

Tomorrow, he would be leaving to return to Pearl Harbor, and already his bags were packed. *We're going to miss you,* Agnes had said to him that very morning as they sat at the dining table having breakfast. He looked at her, and their eyes met, and then he glanced across the room, over at Emma, who sat in her high chair. *I'm going to miss you, too,* he had said. In the two weeks that he'd been home, he had finally gotten used to being there, and it troubled him that he had to leave again so soon. The truth was, he cherished the time he spent with Emma. He loved to read her stories, feeling her chubby little warmth in his arms, her head falling against his chest as she drifted into sleep. He loved to play on the floor with her and watch her sprawl into unabashed laughter as the colorful blocks fell into her lap. It pained him that he would have to be away from her for so long again. But he had no choice. The navy needed him, and he needed the navy. In fact, he was somewhat relieved to be ridding himself of the way Agnes tried so hard to fix him. He had never been able to tell her the truth about Pearl Harbor. He didn't know how to open up to her, and he didn't want to. Agnes was too fragile. But he enjoyed the time that he spent with her—the walks in the park, the dinners, the evenings when they would just sit in the quiet living room together. And then there was someone else that he thought about, too.

Beatrice.

Since they had met, he had played their conversation over and over again in his mind. He could see just how very hurt she was by the loss of her brother, and he could tell that she spent a great deal of time caring for her mother. He admired her for that. In a way, she reminded him of his own mother, the way she unselfishly took care of her family. She was smart, too, getting her college degree and working while she did it. And he liked the way she was not afraid to say what she was thinking. Until recently, he had not thought about how differently colored people were treated, the way they were forced to concede to the whim of everyone around them. But not Beatrice. She had a way about her, a confidence that he had never seen in any colored person, or any woman for that matter. And he could also see that she had a quiet spirit, an appealing softness to her.

He had to see her again.

Morris put down the hull and looked toward the window. The rain pelted, hadn't let up since early that morning. He could tell by the hush in the house that Agnes had put Emma down for her afternoon nap, and she was probably resting, too. He made his way to Emma's room to check on her, and then to their bedroom, where Agnes slept peacefully. He thought about waking her, but decided to leave a note instead. *Gone to see Vincent. Be back soon.* He left the note on the kitchen counter and grabbed his raincoat.

Morris walked swiftly, the collar of his raincoat pulled above his ears. The rain pounded the city with large silver drops. The winds pulled his umbrella in one direction and him in the other. After a while, he stuffed the umbrella under his arm and cut through the Boston Common. The park's trees shielded him as he neared Frog Pond, a kidney-shaped pond that nudged through the park, its stream serving as a place of serenity in the summer months and the best ice-skating in the winter. He inhaled slowly, taking the crisp scent of rain into his lungs. Clean. Cool. Fresh.

The Charles Street Sandwich Shop was in clear sight now, the rain slanting across its roof through the stodgy tree lines. A whiff of corned beef rose through the air and tugged at his belly.

The door to the sandwich shop opened and a man stepped out, holding the door for Morris. Morris stepped inside, sobered by the sights that sparked memories of the man he used to be.

Vincent moved quickly about, serving the patrons. He suddenly turned and blinked in surprise. "What are you doin' here? I was goin' to stop by after my shift ends."

Morris pulled himself from his drenched coat, hung it over a stool. "I thought to come see you instead," he said.

"Have a seat. Can I get you something, maybe a cola?"

Morris glanced nervously around the room. "Actually, I was wondering if I could sit in Beatrice's section."

Vincent gave him a strange look. "What?! Why?"

Morris knew he couldn't tell Vincent the truth—that he felt drawn to Beatrice as sure as gravity kept his boots on the ground. He was slow to speak. "I met her brother at Pearl Harbor," he said casually.

Vincent nodded, looking confused as he led Morris to Beatrice.

Beatrice carried plates on a platter, careful not to muss her immaculately ironed uniform. Morris stared at her—the red-and-white striped apron wrapped tightly around her waist; her hair pulled straight into a neat ponytail, accenting her eyes; her face with no makeup, just a tad of color on her lips.

She smiled at the family sitting at table four as she served their food. "Let me know if you need anything else." She turned to greet the single at table six, and was shocked to see Morris Sullivan staring at her. *Oh Lord, please tell me that white man is not here to see me,* Beatrice thought. She put a smile on her face and walked up to him.

"Hello, Morris. What can I get for you?" she said quickly, and pulled the pad from her apron.

"I just wanted to say good-bye. I leave tomorrow."

Beatrice glanced around the room. "You came here to see me? Are you out of your mind?"

"I couldn't leave without saying good-bye."

For the past few days, Beatrice had thought about him, too. She liked Morris, the respect he showed Robert, his modesty . . . his kind blue eyes. But she had put those thoughts aside, knowing better than to dwell on him. She didn't quite understand this Morris Sullivan. He seemed honest enough, beyond what she would expect. She had thought to talk to Nellie about it, tell her about their first meeting and how kind he was and the way he seemingly cared about Robert, but she had decided against it, concerned that Nellie might pick up on something more, the same thing that had brought him there.

"You shouldn't have come here," Beatrice whispered.

"I know."

"I'll bring you a coke. Then you have to leave." Beatrice scribbled something on her pad and rushed to the soda fountain, aware of Vincent's eyes on her.

Morris looked around the diner, noticed how Vincent eyed Beatrice and watched him, too.

"Here you go," Beatrice said, falsely cheerful. She handed him the bill. "You can pay the cashier."

Morris pulled out a piece of paper, stuffed it between two dollar bills, and thrust it at Beatrice. "Please take it. It's my address. I'd like you to write to me."

Beatrice took the money, smiling calmly. "I don't think that's a good idea."

"I like talking to you, Beatrice." But Morris's eyes smoldered and Beatrice knew he had more than talk on his mind. She felt her knees go weak.

"Morris, I don't need any trouble. You have a wife. Write to her," she said, and quickly walked away.

As she walked away, she saw Vincent approach Morris's table and she hoped Morris was smart enough not to tell Vincent what he'd said to her. Even if Morris was color-blind, as he seemed to be, he couldn't expect anyone else to understand.

She made her way into the kitchen and leaned against a wall, out of sight. She liked him—too much. It was good that he was headed back to Pearl Harbor, because she wasn't sure she was strong enough to push him away again.

12

Agnes

Agnes rushed to rescue a crying Emma. Emma had tried to follow a much bigger boy up on the sliding board before she lost her balance and fell.

"She's fine," Agnes said to an older lady who had also hurried over to Emma.

"I was beginning to think she was alone," the lady said, smiling blithely at Agnes.

Agnes politely smiled back, embarrassed that she had taken her eyes off Emma.

"I come here all the time, but I haven't seen you and your little girl. Do you come to this park often?"

"No, we usually go to the park a little closer to our home, but I had some errands to run in this part of town, so . . ."

"Well, it's lovely. It looks like your little girl is enjoying herself. How old is she?"

"She just turned eighteen months," Agnes said. "Not quite old enough to slide on her own yet."

"Oh, she'll be there in no time, you just wait and see. They grow up so fast. Faster than we have any time to enjoy them."

Emma squirmed to release herself from her mother's arms.

"You got yourself a feisty one, huh?"

Agnes smiled again and politely waved and walked away. The tulips were in full bloom, and the trees shielded her from the noonday sun. Emma sat on the grass with a little boy, enthralled by a butterfly that had fluttered onto the bottom of the slide. Agnes lingered on a nearby bench and intently watched Emma, so utterly absorbed by the little boy and the butterfly. The sunlight glinted on Emma's serious face. Other than her sky-blue eyes that she took from her father, Agnes saw herself in Emma, for sure.

"Agnes, how are you?"

Agnes turned to see Helen Clemson, her neighbor, pushing her newborn in a carriage, and Jonas, her three-year-old boy, holding her hand. Jonas was just a bit taller and a year and a half older than Emma, and Agnes often babysat Jonas when Helen had errands. Agnes had even watched Jonas the night that Helen had the new baby. Agnes didn't mind it at all. She enjoyed watching Emma's little face light up every time Jonas came knocking. She saw the same look on Emma's face now as Jonas pulled from his mother's hand and charged toward her.

"What are you doing here?" Helen asked.

"Well, I was in the neighborhood and I thought to stop by the park and let Emma play for a while," Agnes said, acutely aware of the way Helen was looking at her. Helen seemed almost confused by Agnes's plain white blouse and rumpled plaid skirt and no makeup. No matter where Agnes went, she always looked well put together. Always. She took pleasure in making sure she and Emma were perfectly dressed down to the last detail, even though they couldn't afford much. But not today. This morning, she just could not get beyond how awful she felt since Morris left two weeks ago.

Each morning, she tried desperately to rid herself of the sadness, sometimes going to see her mother, or taking long walks with Emma in her carriage—walking until she found herself in a different park or a different place. One day, she'd walked for so long and so far that by the time she finally realized it, she knew it was impossible for her to walk all the way back home, so she had no choice but to phone Claudia to come and get her. During those solemn moments, she thought of Morris, how far away he seemed now, more emotionally than physically. She tried not to think of it. It wasn't her nature to dwell on those things, or cling to sadness. Before Emma came, she was always full of joy, the one other girls turned to for advice.

Helen forced a smile. "You look lovely today," she said. But her eyes said, *What's wrong with you? You don't look like yourself.*

"Thanks. I . . . well, I rushed out today without noticing." Agnes fussily touched the collar of her plain white shirt. "Look how big Sarah has gotten!" Impulsively, she reached down and picked up the baby, all dressed up in a frilly pink outfit and matching hat. She was warm in Agnes's arms. Agnes felt a rush of pleasure, reminded of the way Emma still felt in her arms and of her scent, so pure and clean. She and Morris had barely touched each other while he was home. She wondered if there was another baby in her future. She glanced over at Emma and Jonas, fascinated by the butterfly.

"Sarah's three months now," Helen said. "Can you believe it?"

"Really? They grow up so fast."

Agnes fought the sharp pang of anxiety, envy. Helen had a perfect family, her children and husband untouched by the tragedy. Everyone was always telling her not to worry, that Morris was fine, that he would be okay. But what did they know? They could never understand what she was going through, how difficult it was for her. It wasn't just the war and Morris's safety that worried her. It was so much more. So much more.

Agnes managed a smile, and laid Sarah back in her carriage.

Helen looked over at the children. "Well, I guess we better

be on our way. I'm meeting a few other mothers here for our weekly stroll-and-roll walk. Would you care to join us?"

"Oh, no. Emma and I have more errands we need to get to. Maybe another time."

It pleased Agnes to reject Helen's invitation as though she had something so much more important to do. And she did. She followed Helen over to the sliding board and gathered Emma before she waved good-bye and put Emma into her carriage and walked.

When she reached the Charles Street Sandwich Shop, she pulled out her mirrored compact, and dabbed her face with powder and red lipstick, then she straightened Emma's clothes and smoothed her hair, too.

"Okay, that's better," she said, then waited until it was safe to cross. She greeted a man and woman who held the door for her as she wheeled Emma's carriage into the diner.

Vincent rushed over when he saw Agnes sit down with Emma. "How are you? What are you doing here?"

"Well, I took Emma to the park and I thought we'd stop by to say hello."

"I'm surprised to see you. I haven't heard from you since Morris's party. Is everything okay?"

Agnes fidgeted a bit, looked straight at Vincent. "Actually, I was hoping to talk to you. Can you get away for a few minutes?"

Vincent shrugged. "Sure thing, Agnes." He looked back over at the kitchen, and then over at Beatrice, who was taking the order from a table across from them. Their eyes met, and he could have sworn he saw something in her face, the way it changed when he looked at her. He turned back to Agnes. "Let me take care of a few things and I'll be right back." He laid the menu on the table and quickly made his way back to the kitchen.

Agnes lifted Emma from her carriage and sat her in her lap, then glanced at the menu. She had not come to eat, only to talk to Vincent, but suddenly she craved a burger, a shake, and maybe a slice of that homemade apple pie. From where she sat, she could see patrons coming and going. Most of the stools around the counter were empty, and the tables that circled the diner were nearly empty, too. She had noticed recently how much things had changed—people seemed tense, aloof. The tension had been building for months, and the newspapers were full of stories about war.

She wondered what Vincent must be thinking about her just showing up like that. She had never confided in Vincent before now, and Vincent never gave her any indication that he knew about the tension between her and Morris.

Consumed by her thoughts, Agnes didn't notice the young colored woman standing there.

She finally looked up. "I'm sorry. Did you say something?"

"Yes, I said your little girl is beautiful."

"Oh, thank you. She's very special," Agnes said.

"She has some beautiful eyes. What's her name?"

"Emma. Her name is Emma."

There was a sudden silence, a single missing stroke of time. Agnes saw the woman's face go slack, look closely at Emma. "Her father must adore her. Will he be joining you?"

"Oh, no. He's not here. He's in the navy. He was just home for a little while, and he had to go back. To Pearl Harbor . . ."

Beatrice noticed the way Agnes's voice trailed, the sadness in her eyes. She thought to say something else, then changed her mind. "What can I get for you?" she finally said, pulling the pad from her apron.

Agnes noticed something different in her tone.

"I'll take her order, Beatrice," Vincent said, appearing suddenly. "Why don't you see about the other tables?"

Beatrice gave Vincent a nod, and quickly walked away.

"Would you like a burger and shake?" Vincent asked.

"Yes, that would be good," Agnes said, intrigued by the way Vincent looked at the woman before he turned back to her.

"Okay, let me put your order in and I'll be right back."

Agnes watched Vincent disappear into the kitchen, then she looked over at the young colored woman, puzzled. She became a little embarrassed when the woman caught her staring. Agnes turned away quickly. At one point, Agnes noticed the woman stealing glances at her, too, and she mulled over her: She could have been about her age, Agnes guessed, maybe a year or two younger. She had soft, haunting eyes the color of cinnamon accenting her smooth almond face. She wasn't from Boston, Agnes could tell from the way she spoke—with a proper southern accent. She was pretty. Very pretty.

"All right, your order's in," Vincent said, glancing at Beatrice. "So, are you all right?"

Agnes put Emma back in her carriage, turned to him. "Vincent, I know Morris tells you everything. You know him better than I do. You must have noticed how different he seemed when he came home. Something's wrong, Vincent. Please, Vincent, tell me—"

"Whoa. Whoa. Slow down," Vincent said, putting up his hand.

Agnes stopped, looked around the diner, embarrassed. "I'm sorry," she said, lowering her voice.

"Now, I know Morris may not be the same—and, yeah, I noticed that he's a little different, but you have to understand what he's been through. It's been hell for him."

"I know, but he won't talk to me about it. He just seems so distant now, like he doesn't want to be here with me and Emma."

"He loves you and Emma, Agnes. You know that."

Agnes gave Vincent a long look, and then turned and looked down at Emma, now sleeping in her carriage. "I know," she finally said. "I guess . . . well, I just get so crazy sometimes with him gone, and I'm worried. Things are getting worse. What if they ship him overseas? I don't know what I would do if something were to happen to him."

"Nothing's going to happen to him, Agnes." Vincent looked at her. "I promise."

Agnes leaned back in her chair, relieved. "Okay, I guess you're right."

"Good." Vincent reached across the table and squeezed her hand. "Now let me go check on that burger for you."

Agnes smiled bashfully, then watched Vincent disappear, as she tried to convince herself to believe him.

13

Morris

S oon after Morris returned to Pearl Harbor, he was immediately assigned to the Salvage Division, commissioned to
recover the sunken ships. He wanted to be on the front line,
fighting in the war, but his injured leg kept him from it. He
and his crew worked long and exhausting hours, sometimes
around the clock, to refloat the capsized ships, retrieve human
remains, ammunition, and secret documents from the oil-
fouled ships that had been trapped underwater for months.
The smells of death and mold and loss sickened him.

The threat of a once-distant war in Europe and now the
Pacific had become a daily part of life at Pearl Harbor. No
matter their color, creed, or religion, they all just wanted to
feel safe again, the blurring of lines blended in worship, work,
and war.

In the past months, Morris hadn't missed a day of mass, always being the first to arrive and sometimes the last to depart.
Oftentimes after church let out and the crowd had thinned,
Morris would remain there, his mind wandering through a
jumble of thoughts. Sometimes he'd bring along his letters,
and he'd sit there reading each, always one from his mother,
one from Agnes, and now from Beatrice.

Today, as usual, after everyone stumbled slowly out of the
church, he stayed behind and thought about the first letter he
had written to Beatrice after returning to Pearl Harbor:

I felt foolish for showing up there like that, but I wanted
to tell you just how much I enjoyed talking to you.
You were so easy to talk to. I think of you and Robert
often and I would really like it if you would write to me
sometimes. Friends are pretty scarce around here. Maybe
you can tell me what Robert taught you about the ships,
that would be really nice. Or maybe you will tell me
more about you and your home and family. I hope you
will consider writing soon.

After that, he had waited for her to write back, but she
did not. He had not intended to keep writing, but something
lured him, something he didn't quite understand. Maybe it
was the way she spoke about the ships, an interest he had never
shared with anyone. Or perhaps it was the loss he saw in her
eyes, a loss that he knew she saw in his. Or maybe it was her
laugh, her smile, the way he felt free around her. Whatever
the reason, he just could not stop thinking about her, and after
two months had passed, he was elated when she finally wrote.

I've thought about you, too. But I just didn't think it
was proper for me to write to you. You have a wife and
a child, a very beautiful wife and child. I saw them not
long ago at the diner and I couldn't help but wonder
why you would want me to write. Besides which, I'm
colored, if you haven't noticed. What are people going to
think? No white man has so much as spoken my name
before now. I've never met anyone like you. You are so
different. I know Robert would have really liked you;
and for that reason, I find myself liking you, too.

Beatrice was right. It wasn't proper for him to keep writing. He did have Agnes and Emma to think about, but he

could never talk to Agnes the way he could talk to Beatrice. He realized that from the moment he met her. It seemed that she understood what he'd been through—she seemed to know that he was different. A difference he had come to understand as a young boy, and now he remembered it as vividly as the words in Beatrice's letter: he was just eight years old, and he was in the backyard playing with his colored friend, Charlie, when suddenly his father bolted out the back door, rifle cocked.

"What you doin' in my yahd?" he said, pointing the cold, steel object just inches away from Charlie's head, his eyes blazing.

Morris froze, watched the ball drop from Charlie's hand. A trail of sweat traced the boy's small neck, snaked down the length of his spine. Morris breathed slowly, taking in the pungent odor of alcohol and gun dust. "Suh, I . . . I was just playin' ball with him," Charlie finally said, pointing a trembling finger at Morris.

"Yah playin' with niggahs now, boy?! Is that what I'm hearin'?!" his father said, cutting his eyes over to Morris.

Fixated on the gun, Morris could feel his father's scrutinizing gaze, and his mother's, who peered out the window with a face full of worry. Charlie stood unmoving, moisture suddenly streaming down his leg.

"An'sah me, boy! Yah playin' with niggahs? Is that what yah doin'?"

Morris shook his head slowly. "No." He trembled. "I ain't playin' with no niggahs." He stole a glance at Charlie.

Ever since he was old enough to understand, Morris noticed the way coloreds were treated, how they stayed with their own kind, and the way his school had only children like him and no children like Charlie. But when Charlie showed up on his street one day and asked him to throw the ball, he didn't think about any of those things, just about Charlie and his ball.

"Yah got no bizness round hea'," his father had said. "Yah got two seconds to get off my property, and don't yah ever let me catch yah near my boy again."

Charlie glanced over at Morris one last time and slowly backed away, knowing better than to meet the white man's gaze.

Now Morris imagined his father gripping the rifle, the look on his mother's face, and the easy, hateful way that word rolled off his father's tongue. But most of all, he thought about Beatrice and the hard, fast rules about coloreds and whites. Mixing unlike kinds together was, in the eyes of many, just dead wrong.

It was a wrong Morris ignored again when it came to Robert's best friend, Bernard, the one who had given him Beatrice's address. The two of them had struck up an easy friendship. Bernard worked as an attendant—serving food, washing dishes and linens, disposing of garbage, laboring as many long and hard hours as Morris and the crew that was salvaging the ships. It had seemed the most natural thing in the world for Morris to talk to Bernard when he saw him working in the mess hall, but their friendship would have been unthinkable even to Morris before death and disaster had erased all the usual barriers. A few nights a week, they'd meet at the beach and Bernard would play the harmonica. Afterward, they'd talk. Sometimes for hours.

One night, several months after he returned from liberty, Morris spotted Bernard in the mess hall. He needed to talk to a friend, and Bernard was his only option. "I'll see you tonight?" he asked, his back turned to the other soldiers. Bernard refused to meet his eyes. He seemed to struggle with their friendship, visibly nervous about being seen by the other soldiers. "Okay," Bernard finally said.

That night, Morris met Bernard at their usual spot, near
the limestone rocks, one of the few places that were preserved,
untainted by the bombs. He was a little nervous. What had
been a secret was finally about to be revealed. He thought of
Agnes, who had been supportive, encouraging, patient, and
who had become so self-sufficient while he'd been away, running the household and tending to Emma, practically raising
her on her own. When he went home, there were only fleeting
moments when he recognized the young girl he had married.
But he could tell she hadn't forgiven him for joining the navy,
even now, when the whole country was at war.

Morris looked out toward the coast, and all he could see
was an eternity of blue-green waters, a vision so different
from many months ago. He took his time, taken by the sights
and the air and the memories. As he neared the limestones, he
could see a figure in the distance, sitting on an oversized rock,
chiseled like a piece of art.

Without words, Morris took a seat on a rock the same
width and height as the one Bernard sat on—two oversized
boulders carved from the same stone. They sat, each looking
out toward the coast. The envelope in Morris's hand felt light,
airy, a subtle reminder of why he was there. He closed his eyes
for a few minutes. The air was heavy with the mist from the
waves, and the scent of burning oil still masked the island.
When he opened his eyes, he saw a young family—a woman,
a man, and a small child—walking the beach nearby.

"I met somebody," Morris said suddenly. He briefly looked
over at Bernard, then turned his attention back on the family, who were now distant figures. "Somebody who I've been
writing."

Bernard turned to look at Morris.

Morris stiffened, held Bernard's gaze. "I've been writing

Beatrice . . . Robert's sister," he finally said, taking in the uneasy expression on Bernard's face. "When I went home, I went to pay my respects for Robert and I met her." He shifted to relieve the pressure that was building in his legs. A heaviness consumed him and he leaned into the hard surface, breathing in the cool mist. His body was sore from the overlong hours they'd worked, nearly around the clock.

"I have three brothers," Bernard said, stoically. "Got only two left now."

Morris looked over at Bernard, watched Bernard's face change.

"One of my brothers, James—the oldest one—got killed years ago," Bernard said, his voice flat. Morris studied him, then had to look away from what was there: Bernard's face expressionless, vacant.

Bernard focused on the waters that rose and fell with each fluid motion. But like the waves, the memories must have come full and turbulent. It was minutes before he spoke again.

"It was James's birthday." Bernard shifted on the rock as though he was trying to balance the memories.

"Mama had sent me and James into town. She needed flour and eggs to make a cake. Daddy had long since left. So James, the oldest of us four boys, was now the man of the house. Mama sent him everywhere.

" 'You go 'long with him, Bernard,' she said. I ain't think nothin' of it. Was just glad that I get to go and get me one of those Mary Jane candies. They costs only a penny and I'd saved up enough to buy me a heaping full." Bernard paused, his face raw with grief. He took his time.

"There was this white girl," he said, still drawn into the memory. "Real nice to coloreds. She'd talk to us sometimes. Not in a wrong kind of way. Just real friendly like.

"When she saw us that day, she waved, and me and James waved back. But this time I don't know what ail James. He did something he should have never done. He winked at her. We ain't know that Old Man Smithfield was watching. His family led the Klan. They organized all over Birmingham and on up through Montgomery, as far as Georgia. They known for the rallies and the hangings. One time they hang a ten-year-old boy. They say he slapped a little white girl for calling him a nigger. That boy mama cried for years. They say she die from a broken heart.

"If they be willin' to hang a child, I knew the moment they showed up in front my mama's doo' that they was comin' for James.

"Mama begged and pleaded with those men not to take her child. Promised she'd make him do anything they say. Just don't take him. Even offered up herself.

"But they wouldn't hear of it. Me and my brothers watched while they tied James's legs and arms with rope and catch hold of him to the back of Old Man Smithfield's truck.

"And you know what that old, evil man say to my mama?" Bernard glanced over at Morris, his face wet with tears. "He looked her square in the eye and say, 'We gon' teach your nigger boy a lesson. He ain't never gonna wink at one of ours again.' Then they all got in that truck and pulled away, dragging James from the back like he a dead dog. We ain't know where they take him. All's we know that wherever they take him there wasn't nary a thing we could do to save him."

Bernard paused, kept staring in the distance, his voice gripped with the memory. "We finally found James two days later. They beat him, hung him, and shot him full of holes. We ain't hardly recognized him. My mama let him hang there for a week. Said she wanted everyone to see what those evil men had done to her child. Then Mama took to her bed, unable to eat, barely sleep. Her heart broken in tiny pieces."

Bernard turned, met Morris's gaze for the first time. There was a long silence, and then he said, "You ain't see no grief till you see your mama bury her child. You fixin' to mix up in somethin' you ain't got no bizness mixin' in," Bernard said, then walked off, leaving Morris alone.

14

Beatrice

It had been two days since Esther had watched a taxi approach in the distance, slow and steady. When the car finally came to a halt and Esther saw a young woman in a bright yellow hat and matching gloves emerge, she almost couldn't believe this fine lady was her Beatrice. She hadn't seen her daughter in a while, had ached for the company of her girl. *I'll be home soon,* Beatrice would tell her mother in the letters. But as days turned into weeks, weeks into months, and months stretched into a year, Esther forced the longing in her heart to quiet down.

Finally, Beatrice had written to say she would be home for Thanksgiving. They had enjoyed quite a feast with Esther's church friends. And the next morning, a chilly one, Esther found Beatrice sitting alone on the front porch wrapped in a blanket, her notebook clutched in her hand.

"Good mornin'," Esther said, startling Beatrice.

"Good mornin', Mama. You sleep well?"

"I'se slept just fine. Been sleepin' well enough since that taxi pulled up to my front porch. Why you up so early? Ain't you restin' okay?"

Beatrice looked out toward the trees. "I'm resting just fine, Mama," she said quietly.

There were three things that Esther knew well: herself, her children, and the Lord. This morning, it didn't take too many words for her to know that something just wasn't right with Beatrice.

"You know, your father and I stayed together for as long as we did because we never kept things from each other." Esther looked straight at Beatrice. "Shoot, he had no choice but to tell everything, 'cause the man couldn't keep a secret if it was glued to him." Esther shook her head, smiling, as though she had skipped back in time.

"You right about that, Mama," Beatrice said with a smile. "I remember the time Daddy took me and Robert into town to pick out that old couch for your birthday and he made us promise not to share a peep of it with you. But no sooner did we come home than you asked him what took us so long, and Daddy blurted it out like an eight-year-old."

Esther laughed.

"Those were the good ole times," Esther said, basking in the memories.

Beatrice looked down at her notebook, pulled a letter from it, then quickly stuffed it back in the book. After a long silence, Beatrice looked over at her mother.

"Mama? You remember the nice man I told you about? The one Robert saved? The one who wrote me the letter?"

Esther nodded absentmindedly.

"Well, after he wrote a few times, I wrote him back, and . . ."

Esther went still, stared at her daughter. "And what?" she said, afraid to hear where this was going.

Beatrice gave her mother a wary look. "We been writing to each other," she finally said.

"What you mean, you been writin' each other? What's the sense in that," Esther said, more a statement than a question.

Beatrice looked at her mother. "I guess things aren't so good over there with that war," she said.

"Ain't he got no family he could write?"

"Yes, ma'am. He got family. He got a wife and a baby girl, and other family."

"Then if he got all that family, what's the sense in writin' you?"

"I think he feels like he owes something to me for us losing Robert. I think he feels that we have an understanding 'cause we both lost something."

"What he done lost?!"

Beatrice's voice shifted. "He lost a friend. Saw him nearly blown to pieces. Said it was something awful to see."

Esther's face clouded with sorrow. "There ain't never been no sense in no war. Just causes so much pain."

"At least we know Robert died with honor, Mama. And that there are good men like Morris who are fighting in that war."

Esther nodded in agreement. "Yes, I reckon you right."

"And Morris is a good person. I can tell from his letters."

Esther turned toward her daughter, gave her a look. "You be careful with all this talk about a good white man and writin' letters."

"Not all white men bad, Mama. Look at all the ones helping to get the colored girls into my school and the ones like Morris fighting 'longside our colored men."

Esther gestured toward the oak tree. There was a bitterness in her tone. "Them there good white men you speakin' of are the ones that be stringin' our boys up in those trees."

"Just 'cause some of them bad, don't make them all bad," Beatrice whispered, more to herself than her mother.

Esther stared at Beatrice through narrow eyes. "You done gon' up to that big city and forgot where you come from. Ain't no difference between good and bad white men. They all evil. No sense in you gettin' yourself all messed up over writin' some letters. He don't mean you no good."

Beatrice nodded, didn't say anything, just tucked the letter back into her notebook.

The train ride back to Boston felt long and tiring, void of the anticipation Beatrice had when she'd made her way home. She heard the whisper of her mother's stern tone: *Ain't nothin' but trouble in writin' to some white man*. Since their talk, there had been a quiet distance between Esther and Beatrice, as though their words had lodged a silent dispute between them—a mother who understood the strife of the South and a daughter who'd tasted the sweet promise of civility up North, a civility rarely seen back home.

Beatrice could still see the look on her mother's face, a look of warning and sheer distaste. For Beatrice there was no talking back, only listening, if not to her mother's words then to the wisdom beneath them. She knew her mother only wanted what was best for her. Beatrice even understood why she felt the way she did.

Beatrice had been there, and she'd remembered it more times than she cared to. It was the fall of 1934, and Esther and her husband, Wilbert, sat on the front porch watching the sun fade in the distance. Beatrice and Robert played nearby. It was a quiet Sunday evening, and they enjoyed sitting on their porch after church and an early supper. It was how they relaxed after a long week of hard work and worry, and how they'd spent the most precious time together as a family.

Wilbert and Esther heard the ruckus before they saw it—an old Ford pickup truck, black with a hatch that seemed to dip toward the ground. The driving was sporadic, reckless. There were three men inside. One sat in the back, on the hatch, one's body leaned out from the passenger window, and the driver swerved from one side of the road to the other.

Wilbert stood from his seat and covered the tips of his

brows, shielding what was left of the early evening sun. Esther stood, too, and strained her eyes to see their faces as they neared her home.

"Beatrice and Robert, get on up hea' on the porch," Wilbert warned.

Beatrice quickly grabbed her rag doll, her yellow sweater, and her sandals and rushed up onto the porch. Robert stood frozen, watching the truck approach them.

"Boy, didn't I tell you to get on up hea'," Wilbert shouted, his eyes never leaving the truck as it came to an erratic halt, nearly crashing into the ditch.

Beatrice could smell them all the way from the porch—a raw, pungent odor. Liquor. Something she had occasionally smelled on her father.

"What can I do you for?" Wilbert said, staring at them. He spoke casually, as if they might be lost or in need of a helping hand. Most likely it was one or the other, Beatrice thought. They wouldn't just stop on their property for no reason, let alone right in front of their door. Even at her young age, Beatrice knew they didn't mix in the same company, and the whites rarely came on a colored man's property unless they knew him, were invited, or there was trouble.

"Boy," one of the men said in a thick southern drawl. "Get me a cool drink of wata'."

Wilbert stared straight at the man, but Beatrice could see the way he held his jaw tight, the trickle of sweat that ran down his face.

The man's face was angry. "You hear what I say, boy!"

Wilbert didn't move. "Esther, please get the man a cool drink of water," Wilbert said firmly, never taking his eyes from him.

Esther shoved past her husband and rushed inside.

"Looky here," the other man said. "The little niggra got her a white doll." He reached his hand out toward Beatrice.

Beatrice looked up at her father. Wilbert nodded permission, and Beatrice slowly handed over the doll.

"What's your doll baby's name?"

Beatrice didn't answer. Sounds played in the background—the screen door latch slapping against the frame, Esther's footsteps against the wood boards, Robert's heavy breaths.

The man narrowed his eyes. "Gal, ain't you hear me talkin' to you?"

Wilbert shot a stiff look at the man. "Beatrice, answer the man's question," he said in an even tone.

Beatrice slowly lifted her eyes. "Maacceee Ann," she said.

The man smiled, revealing a mouth full of cocoa-colored chewing tobacco, a smidgeon of the juice creased in the cracks of his mouth. "Maacceee Ann, huh? My baby girl got a little doll, too. But hers ain't nearly as pretty as yours," he said, running his eyes from Beatrice's fearful face down to her scrawny legs.

"I think y'all need to be goin' now," Wilbert said, thrusting over the glass of water.

The man snatched it. "We gonna go when we good and ready!"

Wilbert looked toward the road, but if the neighbors took notice, they were staying behind closed doors.

"I see you done caught yourself a good-sized buck." Wilbert gestured toward the back hatch, making small talk.

The men laughed wearily and one of them slapped his thigh as if Wilbert had ignited a proud moment.

"Damn right we did," the driver said. "Shot down that buck like he was a runnin' niggra."

A gale of laughter squawked from the men's throats, the laughs breaking into hacking coughs.

"Speaking of niggras . . . You eva' catch you a buck?" the driver asked.

Wilbert shrugged. "Yeah. I done caught me a buck or two."

"Betcha he wasn't as stout as this one. Was he?"

"Can't say he was," Wilbert said, careful not to spark more trouble.

"You eva' tasted your buck? Made sure the meat was tenda' before you string 'em?"

Wilbert shook his head. "No. No, suh."

"Nor have I! But I been meanin' to have someone taste it for me."

Wilbert looked from the first man to the second and then the third. He turned and gave Esther a wary look.

"Beatrice and Robert, y'all come on inside with me," Esther said, reaching for the children. Beatrice ran for her mother, seeking the safety of her skirts.

One of the men lurched forward. "Where you think y'all goin'? Ain't nobody leavin' till I say so."

Wilbert stepped forward, forgetting his place. "Why don't you let my family gon' inside. Ain't no need in keepin' them out hea'."

An evil smile poured from the man's face. "Now, why would I want to let them go inside when I'd rather let them see their daddy eat some of the flesh from this hea' buck?"

The other men snickered. Esther glared at them.

"Now get on down here, boy, and taste this sweet meat."

Wilbert didn't budge.

"Don't let me tell you again, boy. If I have to tell you again, your family gon' be watchin' you be strung up in that tree over yonder."

Wilbert turned and glanced at his family. To Beatrice, it looked as if there was an uncharacteristic sadness in her father's walk, a new heaviness in his legs, as he came down off the porch and walked toward the back of the truck.

"What part should I give him, Homer?" the youngest man said to the driver.

Wilbert stared down at the deer. The deer lay stiff, its legs bound with rope, large marble eyes open wide. Blood dripped from a quarter-sized gaping hole.

"Cut 'em a piece right from the belly. I heard that if you make a niggra eat raw buck from the belly, his young'uns lava to turn up lookin' like one."

All three men burst into laughter.

Wilbert never took his eyes from the deer. Esther never took her eyes from Wilbert. Beatrice started to cry. And Robert turned and looked toward the tree, too afraid to look at his father.

The man pulled a hunting knife from his pocket and thrust it deep into the deer's belly, carving through flesh. "Now that's a nice size. That niggra liable to have two buck-faced monkeys when he finish eatin' this," he said, grinning. He pulled the meat from the deer and shoved it toward Wilbert.

"Take it!" the other man said.

Wilbert glanced at Robert, his eyes cloaked in shame.

"Niggra, you betta' take this meat fo' I string you and your boy up in that tree over there."

Wilbert reached out his hand slowly and grabbed the meat, bit into its flesh.

"Hot diggidy dog!" The youngest man slapped his buddy on the back. "Looka him go. That niggra tearin' up somethin' other, ain't he?"

The men burst into electrified amusement, their squawks cutting through Esther's heart.

Beatrice's face was full of tears when she turned from the window, the train lulling along. Sometimes the memory was distant, and other times it would resurface without prompt-

ing. She recalled the weeks and months and years that followed. The look in her father's eyes. Big, dark marble eyes.
Empty eyes.

"Mama's right," Beatrice murmured. "Ain't no sense in
writin' no letters. I'm fixin' to put a stop to this right now." She
pulled the notebook from her bag and opened it to a fresh page.

> *Dear Morris,*
> *I wanted to let you know that this will be my last*
> *letter to you. I just don't think it's right for us to write*
> *to each other. Besides, what will people think if they*
> *found out?*
> *Please do not send me any more letters.*
> *Beatrice*

Beatrice scanned the letter one last time. *I will mail this as
soon as I return home,* she thought. *Just felt grateful to him, is all.
Not many, colored or white, tend to other folks' dead.*

She closed the notebook, shoved it back into her bag,
and took a final look toward the Mississippi sky. As the train
moved toward Boston, jostling her with its gentle rhythm, she
drifted into a fitful sleep.

15

January 1943

"We are at war. Two wars, as a matter of fact. One in Germany and the other in Japan. World War Two, they done called it. Men, women, children, even whole families are dying every day. And for what? For what?!" Pastor Gilbert shouted from the pulpit. A thunderous round of amens, pounding fists, and stomping feet filled New Hope Baptist Church, causing the room to shiver. Nearly every colored man, woman, and child in Roxbury had turned out for the morning's service.

Beatrice clutched her Bible, mesmerized by Pastor Gilbert's words. She took no notice of Nellie, sitting next to her, or Mr. and Mrs. Baker, sitting two pews ahead.

Pastor Gilbert leaned in closer, gripped the pulpit, letting his striking figure settle in the minds of his congregation. He scanned their faces, holding on to every pair of eyes. Men and women listened intently, children stopped squirming in their seats, and the whining of babies faded in the distance. He waited until the room became still, the silence building.

"We ain't got long now. These wars 'bout to take us to our end. So many people disgraced. So many lives lost. Just yesterday the newspapers reported about how Hitler and those Nazis are killin' folk. Forcin' them into ghettos. Linin' them up and burnin' them. Burnin' God's children. Why?" Pastor Gilbert's tone rose with the flush on his face. "'Cause they say the Jews are taintin' their society. How they believe that the Jews are taintin' their society? How they figured that they have the right to take life? That they are any better than any one of you?"

Tears streamed down faces; sporadic cries of grief could be heard throughout the pews.

"Just this past week," Pastor Gilbert went on, "President Roosevelt announced the first bombings of German targets. A necessary evil, they claim. And then there's Japan. A war that done run rampant. I heard on the radio 'bout how we over there in the Pacific killin' just about anything that moves. Now, don't get me wrong. I believe it wasn't right for the Japanese to bomb Pearl Harbor. But that don't give us no right! No right to take matters in our own hands, to do God's work!"

Ummm-hmmm. Yessuh!

"And you know what else, church?" Pastor Gilbert lamented, his cadence melodic. "Many of you here today done suffered the loss of a loved one." Pastor Gilbert pointed a finger at faces stricken with grief. "Many of you done come to me and talked of your pain. Talked of your grief. Told how this war has taken your son, your husband, your brother."

A woman stood, shouted incoherently, and fainted.

"We done lost so many," Pastor Gilbert called out, his voice quivering. "Done took sons from their mothers. Husbands from their wives. Brothers from their sisters. We done seen how war don't do nothin' but rip families apart. How the hunger for power can make men lose their humanity. How one bad deed leads to another." Pastor Gilbert leaned in to the pulpit, lowered his voice. "When you go home this morning, I want each one of you to drop to your knees. Drop to your knees and ask God for mercy. Beg Him to forgive those who done brought such strife upon us."

Nellie glanced at Beatrice sobbing. She reached over and lightly covered Beatrice's hand. "Are you okay?" she whispered.

Beatrice nodded, touched the gold locket with a tiny photo of Robert that hung around her neck. Hearing Pastor Gilbert's sermon brought back painful memories. She sobbed, unable to speak, thinking of her mother, how very difficult it had been for her. She had been home just that past Thanksgiving and she had been so heartbroken to see the grief still on her mother's face. It pained her every time she saw her mother or heard her voice on the phone or read her letters; now seeing so many other grief-stricken mothers reminded her of her own.

After a while, Beatrice finally wiped the tears from her face, noticed she and Nellie now sat alone. "I guess we should get going."

"We can stay as long as we need to," Nellie said softly.

"I'm fine now. Really. I'm okay," Beatrice said. "Besides, we've got so much to do today. I got to write a letter to Mama, and we've got to clean the apartment, and cook Sunday dinner. And we both need to study."

Nellie drew her in for a closer look. "Are you sure?"

"Yes. I'm sure."

Nellie stood and reached her hand for Beatrice to take.

"Are you sure you're going to be okay?" Nellie asked again.

Beatrice turned and looked at her. "Yes, I'm feeling better now. I guess today's service really spoke to me."

They walked in silence, and after a while, Nellie looked at Beatrice and asked, "You get any more letters from Morris Sullivan?"

Beatrice was surprised by Nellie's sudden interest in Morris Sullivan. She had long since stopped talking about him, since she'd written the letter to tell him she would no longer be writing to him, that it would do them both no good. The more time Beatrice took to respond, the more suspicious Nellie became.

"Yes," Beatrice finally said. "He still send letters, but I haven't written him back in a long while."

When they finally reached the apartment, Beatrice fished in her purse for the keys and instead pulled out the worn letter, the one she carried with her everywhere, the first letter that Morris Sullivan had sent nearly a year ago. She held it, thinking of how she'd felt when she'd read it: layers of joy and relief and grief.

"You carry that with you. Have you got it that bad?"

"Oh, Nellie." Beatrice let out a moan. "It's so hard. I like him . . . a lot. He's sweet and smart. I like his letters."

Nellie shook her head. "You two are a regular Romeo and Juliet, aren't you? Well, don't forget—it's you they'd be coming for, not him. Don't give in, Beatrice. There's nothing but hurt waiting for you on the other side."

That night, after all the chores were done, and after Sunday dinner, in the quiet darkness of her room with a small lamp that gave off just enough light, Beatrice sat on her bed and wrote a letter to her mother, told her all about Pastor Gilbert's sermon. *It really moved me, Mama,* she wrote. *I guess I was so upset by my own pain that I'd forgotten about all the other families who lost loved ones, too.*

She was going to be okay now, she continued, and she had decided to talk to Mr. and Mrs. Baker first thing in the morning about what she could do to help.

I can't wait to come home again soon, Mama.

As soon as I am able.

She ended the letter in the same way she'd ended it every Sunday. *I miss you, Mama. I miss you more than you know.*

Beatrice stuffed the letter in an envelope and placed it on the windowsill next to two unopened letters that had been there for weeks. She gazed at the envelopes. There was something unfinished, something that nagged at her every time she looked at them. She picked up one of the envelopes, examined it closely. She missed reading his letters, and missed writing him, too. She wondered at times how he was doing, if he was okay. Every time she heard more news about the war, she said a silent prayer for him, found herself feeling protective and worried and sympathetic. She had never expected to care for a man like Morris Sullivan—a married white man, no less. Her emotions had suddenly taken a sharp turn, left her feeling so very vulnerable.

"Darn it," she whispered, and reverently tore the letter open. She took her time reading it. In the quiet, the moonlight brightened the room, reflecting the words on the page. Her eyes blurred as she searched the page for the words that brought her to tears:

December 7, 1942

Dear Beatrice,

Today is the one-year anniversary of the bombing. I can't believe a year has passed already. It's like it was only yesterday. We held a memorial to pay our respects to those that were lost. But everyone seemed torn up about it. It's still very hard. I said a prayer for Robert. Sometimes it's hard, but I do it for Robert, knowing that he gave his life for me and so many others. I hope you are doing good. I know today must be hard for you, too. I am thinking of you and your family. Please write soon—

She read the letter once and then again, even touched them, the dents where he'd pressed his pen on the page.

"*I do it for Robert*," she whispered to herself.

She didn't know who her tears were for: Robert, who died

a terrible death in a war that seemed to have no meaning. Her mother, who'd lost a husband and then a child. Her father, whose pride and spirit had been broken by hatred. Morris Sullivan, whose strength and comfort came from an unlikely source. Or for herself, whose memories were all mixed in with joy and pain and suffering.

After a long moment, Beatrice stood and reached for something under her mattress. When she pulled out the worn sealed envelope from a shoe box full of letters, she was reminded of her return trip home from Jackson and the last letter she'd written to Morris months ago, the one she never mailed.

In an instant, she tore the envelope in half, tossed it aside, and grabbed her notebook. And this time, she didn't think about all the pain, she didn't think about what others would say. She just pressed her pen on the page and wrote:

> *Dear Morris,*
>
> *I'm sorry I haven't written to you lately, but to be honest, I'd intended to never write to you again. I've been feeling so guilty about our circumstances. But I've been thinking of you a lot lately. In fact, all the time, and after I read your last letter, it made me think of you more. Your words about Robert really touched me, and made me realize just how much I have come to care for you. I know it's wrong. God knows it's wrong, and I feel terribly guilty about it. But I can't help feeling the way I do. My heart and prayers are with you always,*
>
> Beatrice

She folded the letter and looked out at the moon. As a little girl, when she felt afraid to sleep in her room, she would pull the curtains as far back as they would go and she would lie facing the window, looking up at the stars and the moon, and imagine that she was far away from there, that there was nothing that could frighten her. Tonight, as she lay facing the moon, the tears melting into her pillow, the pain that gripped her heart seemed to lighten and her thoughts became clearer.

This time she would mail the letter. Morris Sullivan would hear from her again.

16

Morris

Morris closed his eyes to the sweet sound of Bernard's harmonica, his mind numb to the fleet of ships that brought back countless men, their bodies and minds marred by war. Daily, he read reports of immeasurable atrocity. And he had looked into the returning soldiers' eyes, imagining what they'd seen—the bloody consequences of battle, the evidence of evil.

He looked up at the cloudless Hawaiian sky, and he could see tiny specs of bright stars, diamond dust. He took in the dusk, the calm waters. The beach was nearly deserted, aside from a young couple who lay quietly together in the far distance, and he was reminded of a time when he and Agnes shared similar moments together, not so long ago. He leaned back against the rock, closed his eyes again, and let the music still him.

"You know, I wonder what kind of person she is," Morris said after Bernard stopped playing the harmonica.

Bernard gave him a puzzled look. "Who you meanin'?"

"Mrs. Roosevelt. The first lady. Ever since we learned that she's coming tomorrow, I've been wondering what kind of person she is, and if all that stuff they say about her is true, about all the good she's doing?"

Bernard gave this some thought. "I reckon it is. They say she's real nice like and she got a soft spot for colored folk."

"Well, I hope she lives up to her reputation." Morris suddenly stood, picked up a stone, and flung it. The stone rippled against the water, causing a light to flare and subside.

Bernard watched the stone, and they were silent for a time until they heard the sudden commotion down the beach, a group of sailors walking toward them.

Morris immediately recognized the tall, skinny fellow with the lean face and green eyes.

The men surrounded them.

"What you doin' out here with this nigger?" Green Eyes said, staring down Morris.

Morris met his gaze. "What business is it of yours?"

Bernard quickly stood, quietly slid the harmonica into his pocket.

"Hey, boy, what you doin' out here this late?" one of them shouted at Bernard.

Bernard said nothing, just looked at Morris for an answer.

"His name is Bernard and he's with me. What's it to you?"

Green Eyes stumbled forward, and Morris could smell booze. "So what are you now, a nigger lover?!"

They all laughed. Morris recognized a few of them, men he'd worked side by side with every day. Men he thought were his friends.

Green Eyes turned to Bernard. "What's that you hidin' in your pocket? You done stole somethin', boy?"

Bernard kept his eyes down.

"You hear me talkin' to you, boy?!"

Bernard pulled the harmonica from his pocket, and Green Eyes snatched it from him. "So what kind of horn is this, boy?"

"It ain't no horn. It's a harmonica," Bernard said.

"You sassin' me, boy?!"

Bernard looked around at the others, then over at Morris.

"Since you so damn smart, nigger, why don't you play

somethin' for us?" He tossed the harmonica back at Bernard, gave his buddies a wink. "How about it? Y'all wanna hear this nigger play us a tune?"

"Yeah, nigger! Why don't you play something," the short one finally said.

Bernard glanced over at Morris again, watched Morris shake his head, bidding him not to do it.

Slowly, Bernard put the harmonica to his lips and closed his eyes, letting the sweet tune fill the warm air, soften the despair at Pearl Harbor:

> Amazing Grace, how sweet the sound,
> That saved a wretch like me . . .
> I once was lost but now am found,
> Was blind, but now I see . . .

The men watched Bernard, the silent grief surrounding them, and when Bernard finally removed the harmonica from his lips, they all stared at him.

"So you think 'cause you know how to play that nigger music you better than us?!" Green Eyes suddenly knocked the instrument from Bernard's hands, smashed it with his foot.

"Wait—a—minute!" Morris lunged at him, causing Green Eyes to fall back.

"You fuckin' nigger lover! How dare you put your nigger lovin' hands on me!" He swung a punch at Morris, knocking him to the ground. Two of the other men suddenly strong-armed Morris, hoisted him up. The others grabbed Bernard.

"I'm gonna teach you a lesson, nigger!" Green Eyes sneered. He rolled up his sleeves, looked over at Morris, and spit in his face before he unleashed his wrath on Bernard, drawing blood.

"Stop it! Stop it!" Morris squirmed to free himself.

"You think you better than us, nigger!" Green Eyes said,

his face enflamed with rage. Bernard moaned with each blow until he slumped to the ground.

Green Eyes shook out his hand and rolled down his sleeves. "I think we're done here." He signaled the men to leave.

"You motherfuckers!!! You motherfuckers!!!" Morris shouted after them, then turned to help his friend. "God, are you okay?"

Bernard knocked Morris away, struggled to get to his feet. His face dripped with blood as he gathered the scattered pieces of his harmonica. He didn't say anything, wouldn't even look at Morris.

"Bernard, wait!" Morris shouted, grabbing Bernard's arm to stop him from leaving.

Bernard pulled away, gave Morris a long, cold look. "No!" he said firmly, then walked away.

The next morning, Morris stood twelve deep in a row of men, anxious to see Eleanor Roosevelt. The first lady's brownish-blond hair, darkened with age, was pulled below a brimmed khaki sailor's hat that matched her single-breasted jacket, a sea pin fastened smartly to it. Morris eyed her—believed her coming there was for a purpose beyond her own knowing. He had barely slept all night thinking about what they had done to Bernard. He was to blame, had told himself if only he hadn't said anything to them, if only he hadn't pushed so hard to be Bernard's friend. And now, keeping what they had done to Bernard to himself, he thought, was the same as holding Bernard down while they beat him. He had to tell the first lady. She needed to know, someone needed to know.

Morris looked over at the first lady, watched her peer out at the thirty-six hundred men who stood in formation, many with stripes and stars draping their collars and cuffs—an indication of rank and stature. Beyond the USS *West Virginia,* flags fluttered in the wind, adorning massive ships that had been salvaged. It was September 21, 1943, and in the short time since the first lady had arrived, already Morris felt as though a solemn weight had been lifted. He turned and glanced at the eight rows of colored soldiers, searching for Bernard. Bernard stood ramrod straight, his whites immaculately cleaned and ironed, his face covered with bruises, one eye nearly shut. He wondered what Bernard was thinking, knowing the power the first lady carried. They'd heard the stories of how she had helped the Tuskegee Airmen when she insisted on taking a ride in an airplane with a colored pilot at the controls; and later when she'd forced the air force to allow the trained colored soldiers to enter into combat. And now, Morris wondered if she could help Bernard.

Morris took in Eleanor Roosevelt's blue and rather small, piercing eyes, shadowed by thick, uneven brows, watched her blink at the camera's flash, the image already materializing, concealing the exhaustion she must have felt from her tour to Australia, New Zealand, and seventeen South Pacific islands, visiting more than four hundred thousand soldiers.

A hush fell over the ship as she moved closer to the microphone, gazed at the crowd of men—Morris could tell she understood the despair that had touched the life of every man before her. Some had personally witnessed torture, or seen his best friend killed, or lived with the stench of rotting corpses and disease. Most had been scarred by war—a crippled leg here, a severed arm there, a mind that raced with horrific thoughts. Many worked aboard ships that still reeked of odors disinfectants could not smother.

"Good afternoon, ladies and gentlemen," the first lady said. "I come to you this day, a day that has marked a very critical time in our lives. I am honored to stand before you to express how very, very proud I am of your untiring commitment and courage. We have endured the worst that war has to offer, and for nearly two years, the knowledge that something· of this kind might have happened still lingers in our minds. It once seemed impossible that life as we knew it could suddenly be stripped away. But it is because of your courage and your unwavering commitment that we will prevail."

An electrifying applause moved through the USS *West Virginia,* sparking hope, uplifting deflated souls, bringing tears to eyes. Morris was mesmerized by the tall, wide-smiled, unpretty woman. He studied her face, her gestures, the way she galvanized the crowd.

"You boys are the heroes," the first lady continued. "You are the stitches in our country's fabric that hold it all together. You are the ones who deserve the most praise. It is because of your courage, your strength, and your honor that I am able to stand here before you today. You have protected our America. And it is because of you that She stands today so evermore strong."

The cheer swelled, then receded, and scatters of whistles and clutched fists filled the air. Mrs. Roosevelt spoke with candid assurance, with a confidence that Morris had seldom heard from a woman.

As soon as her talk was over, and the applause rose strong, then tapered off, Morris kept his eye on the first lady as she stepped from the podium. There were plenty of comments and questions—one from a colonel who stepped forward and thanked her for her remarks; another from a man who asked how the president was holding up; then a young sailor who had spoken up timidly. "So many have died. Some beheaded, throats cut, tortured, and starved," the young sailor said, ignoring the stares. "Mrs. Roosevelt, with all due respect, when will this war come to an end?"

The first lady looked at the young man with comforting eyes, and a stoic silence grew in the ripe fall sun. Her husband knew how to put words to difficult questions, while she knew only how to say what was in her heart.

"Young man, I want nothing more than to end this war and bring our boys home. I lose sleep at night worrying about the lives that are being lost every day. I can't tell you when this war will end, but what I can tell you is that we must continue to forge ahead. We must not lose hope."

The colonel rushed to the podium. "That will be all for now," he said, raising his hand to fend off any more questions.

Morris kept his distance as the first lady descended the stage and began making her way through the crowd, stopping to greet anyone who approached her. Morris waited for the crowd to thin, and with one swift movement, he found himself crossing the deck beyond his own volition. In the distance, he could hear voices, the laughs from the sailors who had collected around her; two of them he recognized from the previous night. His heart raced as he came within reach and was abruptly halted by Bernard.

"I know what you're thinkin'," Bernard muttered, blocking Morris's path. "Don't do it!"

"But what they did to you was wrong!" Morris's stare was as intense as Bernard's own.

"What's it gon' change?! What difference will it make? It ain't gon' do nothin' but make it harder on us."

"She needs to know what they did to you! The way they treat you all! It can change things! She can change things! She's the first lady. The president's wife!"

Morris and Bernard sized each other up, neither one wavering.

Bernard broke the silence first. "I can't tell you what to do, but all's I got to say is you leave me out of it. Leave us all out of it!" he said, and brusquely walked away.

Morris glanced over again at the first lady, standing just a few feet away. His throat seemed to dry up, sealing off the escape of words. He understood why he was standing there now, ready to approach this powerful woman. But he couldn't do it, didn't want to make any more trouble for Bernard. A sadness swelled in his chest, made him want to go against Bernard's wishes. It was inevitable that it would come to this. He had known so from the beginning. His friendship with Bernard had filled him with a false sense of hope, a hope that had grown steadily—at the same pace as his fondness for Beatrice. It had been like living in his own segmented world, in love with a version of the world that could not be. As he stood there, alone, he looked around like a newborn opening his eyes for the first time, squinting through the murkiness, seeing the truth that things would never change.

Later that evening, Morris wrote a letter to Agnes. He was sorry that he had not written sooner, he wrote. But he had received her letter, and was glad about her decision to take some nursing classes.

He'd hoped to make it home for Thanksgiving, as she wished. But he doubted that he would be able to since there was so much work, and no news of when the war would end. But he would try to be home soon.

As soon as possible.

He closed the letter the same way he had always done—with little mention of Pearl Harbor. No mention of the first lady. No mention of what had happened to Bernard.

He opened the notebook to a fresh page and started another letter, the second one this week.

Dear Beatrice,

    *Bernard was attacked last night and I felt so bad
that I couldn't do anything. The first lady came to Pearl
Harbor today and I wanted to tell her, but I didn't.
But it's just not right. Something has to be done. I
can't believe this stuff happens still, after all we've been
through. I can't wait until the war is over, and I get
to come home. When things get really bad, I think of
Robert, and how he risked his life for me and others.
And I think of you and your letters.*

He sealed the letter and tucked it away for safekeeping.
Then he lay down, closed his eyes, and turned his back to the
others.

17

Beatrice

For three days now, Esther had packed everything and anything that would set the pace for her long-awaited trip. Her train was to leave out of Jackson at noon and arrive in Boston the next day. Beatrice worried about her mother taking the train to a place she'd never been before. "Remember, Mama, I'll be right there waiting as soon as your train pulls into the station," Beatrice had said to her mother on the phone just that morning. Yes, Esther remembered everything her daughter had told her—about the need to pack plenty of food, a blanket for the chilly night, and her Bible to read along the way.

Esther was dressed in a well-tailored lilac-and-white dress, one that she had sewn herself, with a matching knit sweater and long silk gloves. A jaunty wide-crown hat trimmed with beads and soft feathers rested atop her head. Her shoes were white patent leather, closed toe, with a small heel. Inside a bag on her lap was a knitted blanket, a small sheet of paper with Beatrice's telephone number, an assortment of fruit and nuts, and a small white box with a gold chain and locket that held a photo of her family, taken years ago. The locket was a gift she planned to give to Beatrice.

Esther missed her family so much it sent a chilling ache through her, an emotion that she'd been able to suppress whenever she thought of her girl. Beatrice was what kept her going, what gave her the strength to turn from one day to another. As she thought of Beatrice, a single proud heartbeat drummed in her chest and throat, and she swallowed it, the way she swallowed the painful loss of Wilbert and Robert.

Esther gazed out the window at the country scenery that zipped dizzily past her. It had been a long time since she'd been on a train. The last time was more than twenty years ago, when she and Wilbert had taken the train to Shreveport, Louisiana, to attend Wilbert's mother's funeral. It was the first time Esther had ever met Wilbert's family, a family he rarely talked about. "Times ain't worth rememberin'," Wilbert often told Esther as though something dark, lurking, haunted him. He seldom spoke of his nine brothers and one sister, and a father who used to beat them for no rhyme or reason. "Mama stayed with him all those years. And he just treated us so bad. We ain't never saw a day with no grief," Wilbert told Esther one day as they sat on the porch and he stared off beyond the trees with eyes that showed no feeling. No sooner was Wilbert old enough to fend for himself than he left Shreveport, hiked and walked and begged his way for more than two hundred miles until he reached Jackson. A few years later, he met Esther and had promised her that he would never treat her and the children the way his daddy had treated him.

Esther leaned her head against the headrest and closed her eyes. She was tired, having worked two jobs six days a week—one cleaning white folks' houses and the other tending to Mr. Burke's shabby, old store. While she rocked along with the motion of the train, she glowed at the hard work with dividends that made it possible for her Beatrice to receive her teacher's diploma.

*

Nellie rushed into the living room, her head knotted in a scarf, a long gingham dress hugging her small frame. "You 'bout ready to hang it?" she asked, watching Beatrice press the last of the lace curtain.

"I sure hope Mama likes our place," Beatrice said, holding up the curtain, inspecting it one last time.

"Everything's just fine," Nellie said. "There ain't much more we can clean, or hang, or cook. Besides, your mama's gonna be so proud to see you with that diploma in your hand and so glad to take you back home with her."

Beatrice's heart sank. She'd been in Boston for nearly four years now, and things had changed. She'd changed. As her mother's arrival neared, Beatrice had worried, become exasperated by the thought of getting back on that train and watching the life she'd built in Boston gradually fade.

"Actually, I've decided to stay in Boston. Maybe find a teaching job like yours," Beatrice blurted.

Beatrice's words seemed to float in midair inside a lucid bubble and then burst.

"Beatrice, you can't do that! Your mama done come all this way to take you back with her!"

Beatrice hung the last curtain as though Nellie hadn't said a word.

"Train number 387 is arriving on track 8," a colored attendant announced, strolling up and down the corridor as the train puttered into the station and came to a halt.

A midafternoon breeze blew across the city and skated up Beatrice's back, cooling the heat that had collected from her nerves. *I wonder which car Mama's on,* she thought as the train attendants pushed open the doors and dropped the de-

parting stairs onto the ground. Beatrice and Nellie watched
and waited until finally they spotted a wide hat and saw an
inquisitive-eyed Esther step from the train.

"There she is," Beatrice said, moving quickly toward her
mother, Nellie trailing close behind.

"Mama, it's so good to see you." Esther held on to her
daughter for a long while, not a word passing between them.

Then Esther's eyes seemed to float over Nellie. "And look
at you. You ain't the same little girl who would show up at my
doo' with them skinny legs."

"No, ma'am, I ain't," Nellie said bashfully. "It's really good
to see you again, ma'am."

"It's good to see y'all, too, babe," Esther said, pulling them
both close to her.

As the car pulled in front of Mary and Herbert's house,
Esther saw them waiting. The Bakers reminded her of
her and Wilbert, the way they took pride in their home and
family. It took no time for Esther to warm up to them.

"It's mighty fine to meet the one who has raised such a
beautiful, kind, and respectful young lady. I can't speak highly
enough of your Beatrice."

Esther smiled, folded gently into Mary's arms. "I'm as glad
to make your acquaintance," she said.

"How was your trip?"

"Good, but things so different here," Esther said, looking
around, seeing the most colored faces she'd seen since the train
crept its way farther North.

"I know what you're thinking," Mary replied. "It takes
some getting used to, but it ain't all that bad. Roxbury is full
of colored folk and we mind our own."

Esther nodded, taking in Mary's words.

"Well, I reckon we better be getting you upstairs, Mama,

so you can rest up," Beatrice said. "Mrs. Baker, Nellie and I prepared supper for Mama. We'd be glad to have you and Mr. Baker join us."

"No, honey. You go on and enjoy your mama this evening. We'll have dinner together tomorrow after the ceremony. Besides, Esther needs her rest. We gonna have plenty of time to catch up."

E sther seemed surprised by the supper Beatrice and Nellie prepared: pork chops smothered in gravy, collard greens, macaroni and cheese, corn bread, and sweet tea. Nellie called it "good ole home cookin'."

Beatrice and Nellie set the table as Esther looked around the room at everything—the small sofa and chair, the polished secondhand coffee table, the plants accented perfectly in clay pots. "You girls really done made me proud," Esther said, admiring the room.

"Ma'am, that's the least we can do after all them pretty dresses and things you sent us over the years," Nellie said.

"Chile, those dresses didn't take no time. It helped me to get through my evenin's. Just imaginin' how pretty y'all would look in church every Sunday mornin'."

By the time Beatrice and Nellie cleared the table, the sun had faded, quieting down the evening.

"Mama, you're gonna take this room and Nellie and I are going to sleep out there," Beatrice said, leading her mother into the small bedroom.

"You girls don't have to give away your room," Esther said. "I don't want to put you out. We can all make do in here."

"No, ma'am," Nellie said, joining them. "We want you to be comfortable."

"All right, then," Esther said, seemingly content just to be near her girl again.

$\mathcal{R}$

Beatrice stood in front of the old mirrored glass, studying her image. In the past few years, her face had morphed from a girl's into a woman's face. She touched the corners of her brows and moved her fingers slowly down to her nose. The light in the small bathroom was dim, but she knew she looked beautiful and confident in her white dress, long white silk gloves, and white knitted shawl—the same attire that all the girls wore as they waited outside the auditorium doors.

Beatrice thought once more of how she was to tell her mother her news. With this decision on her mind, so full and powerful, she could see that it was the right thing for her, for both of them—both she and Mama. She loved her home, loved the memories that they had built there. But the South was no longer right for her. She just couldn't go back to that. And besides, Boston was so much better, offered things that weren't possible in the South. She had managed to carve a life for herself here. She had her friends and church and the work she did with the League. There were so many good reasons to stay in Boston, and so many bad memories back home—like the time when she was just seven years old and her father had taken her and Robert into town for ice cream. Mr. Jonathan, a mean, old white man, had made them wait in line for nearly an hour before he served them.

Then there was the time Esther had taken them to work with her at Mrs. Kimball's house. "You and Robert stay in the yard and play. I'll be done directly," Esther had told Robert and Beatrice. Esther had no choice but to bring them when she'd gotten word that their school had been flooded. While Beatrice and Robert played on the swings, out of nowhere, Janie, Mrs. Kimball's nine-year-old daughter, and two of her friends showed up.

"Look at the little niggers playing on my swings." Beatrice got down off the swing and took hold of Robert's hand. "What are you doing here? Playing in my yard?" Janie shouted.

"My mama's inside working. She told us to wait here for her," Beatrice answered, her eyes dropping to the grass.

"Well, you got no right touching my stuff!" Janie yelled, her friends staring at Beatrice, smirks on their faces. Then Janie did something that would stay with Beatrice for the rest of her life. She slapped Beatrice with a force that brought stars to her eyes. As if that wasn't disgraceful enough, she hauled off and spit on her. Beatrice felt Robert's eyes pinned on her as the gook slid down her face and soaked into her dress.

"You best remember your place, nigger!" Janie said, and walked away as though she and Beatrice had never played together, as if they had never been friends.

Beatrice watched this happening now in slow motion: the same house, the same swing, the same yard, the same grass, the same Janie, and the same spit. *I ain't going back to that,* she promised herself, the memory as vivid in her mind as the swells of exuberant voices that came from beyond the bathroom's walls.

"Beatrice, are you in there?" Mrs. Baker called out, her voice coming through the door.

Beatrice wiped back the tears. "Yes, ma'am. I'll be out directly." She took one last look before she opened the door to the voices, the music, and a crackling energy that engulfed her.

"There you are," Mrs. Baker said. "The ceremony is about to begin. Now hurry up and take your place in line."

Beatrice rushed to the front of the line and took her place. From where she stood, she could see out into the oversized auditorium. She looked around until she spotted it—the lilac-and-white hat, and underneath it, the pride that shone on her mother's face.

"All right, ladies, this is the day you've all waited for. I want you to march out there with your heads up high. You should be as proud of yourselves as we are of you. Now go and get that diploma!" Mrs. Baker said.

The feast that Mrs. Baker served up at her home that afternoon was nothing short of the best southern home cooking that side of Roxbury: fried chicken, potato salad, macaroni and cheese, collard greens, simmered cabbage, sweet potato pie, apple pie, chocolate cake, and lemon cake.

"Esther, would you like to bless the table?" Mrs. Baker offered as she took a seat at the dining table with her guests—Esther, Beatrice, Nellie, Pastor Gilbert and his wife, Josephine, and Caroline, two of the ladies who worked alongside Mrs. Baker at the Boston School Committee, and her husband, Herbert.

"I sho' would," Esther said. The group joined hands and bowed their heads. "Oh Heavenly Father, we come to You to thank You for this day—a day that's been a long time coming. A day that is one of the proudest of my life—to see my baby girl walk down that aisle and accept that diploma. We ask that You bless each and every life that has been touched by this day. We ask that You touch the lives of those who are suffering in that war. And, Father, I feel so blessed to be able to take my Beatrice back home. We ask that You bless this food and the hands that prepared it. In Jesus's name, we say AMEN."

"Amen!" they all said in perfect synchrony, except for Beatrice, who stared at her mother, a surge of sickness rolling through her.

"Y'all help yourselves," Mrs. Baker said, passing the dish of macaroni and cheese.

Nellie spooned a hefty helping of the collard greens onto

her plate and passed the dish to Beatrice. "Don't you want some greens?"

Beatrice watched the dishes being passed around, listened to the clamor. She shook her head without looking at Nellie, an anxiety building as she looked over at her mother, her face full of pride. She remembered Nellie's disapproving tone, and wondered what Mr. and Mrs. Baker and Pastor Gilbert would think of her decision. She stared at them, looking from face to face.

"Beatrice, you haven't touched your food, honey. Is everything all right?" Mrs. Baker asked.

"Everything's fine, ma'am. I just ain't that hungry, is all."

Pastor Gilbert turned to Beatrice. "So you ready to get back home soon?"

Beatrice stole a glance at her mother, felt the words leave her before she had time to think them through. "I'm not going back to Jackson."

Silence engulfed the room, interrupted by the clanking of a dish that Pastor Gilbert's wife dropped clumsily on the table, clumps of potato salad spilling. Beatrice only had eyes for her mother, watching her face blanch, shock merging with disbelief.

"Wha—What you mean, you ain't gon' back to Jackson?" Esther said, her breath caught in her chest.

Beatrice stared down at her hands in her lap. "I decided there ain't nothing left for me in Jackson. I want to stay here and find a teaching job," she mumbled.

Esther sized up her daughter. "How dare you talk about nothin' left in Jackson for you!" she said, her voice strained. "That's your home. Our home. The home your father broke his back for us to keep. I don't know what ail you, but you best be gettin' your senses back. I won't have no chile of mind disrespectin' the memories of her father."

Beatrice stared at her mother, tears rising. "Mama, I loved

Daddy and Robert, too. And I miss them. But we got to let them go. We can't just stay in that house mourning them for the rest of our lives. Daddy wouldn't want it that way."

"How dare you talk about what your daddy don't want. You may have that diploma now but that don't give you no right to talk down to me. That ain't how your father and me raised you!"

Esther pushed her chair back from the table. "Mary, I believe I done lost my appetite," she said, rising. Then stormed from the room without another word.

A steadiness quieted the room before Mr. Baker finally spoke up. "Beatrice, are you all right?"

"Yes, sir, I'm all right," Beatrice said in a small voice before she left the table and followed her mother.

Esther took no notice of Beatrice standing at the bedroom door. The room had been reassembled, with everything back in its place, as though Esther had never slept in it, as though she'd never been a guest in her daughter's home.

"Mama, you all right?" Beatrice finally said.

Esther did not look up, just kept on folding her things, placing them neatly into her suitcase.

"Mama, please don't be angry with me. I didn't mean to tell you like that. It's just something I've been thinking about for a long time. Something I need to do. Things will be better for me here, Mama, and for you, too. I want us both to stay and make this our home."

Esther froze. "I already got me a home!" she said, looking straight at her daughter.

"I know you already got a home and I'm not trying to take that from you. It's just that the South is no good for us. Things are really bad there. And ever since Daddy and Robert passed you've become so unhappy, just seem like you been slipping away with them."

Esther stared at her daughter, her face twisted. When she finally spoke, her voice was on the edge of breaking. "How dare you use your father's and brother's names in vain! You don't know nothin' 'bout what done slipped from me. The only thing that kept me goin' was knowin' that you'd come back home soon. Now you standin' there tellin' me what you need to do as though me and your daddy ain't raised you right!"

"Mama, that's not fair!" Beatrice cried.

"Fair! Fair? You don't know the half of fair!"

Beatrice shrank back. It took a moment before she could speak again. "Mama, please try to understand. This is something I need to do."

Esther suddenly stooped down and reached below the bed, pulled a box from beneath. She snatched the lid from it and dumped its contents. "Does *this* have somethin' to do with what you think you need to do?" Esther said, snatching a handful of the letters and tossing them at Beatrice.

"Mama, you got no right to go through my things!"

"I got no right?! You been writin' letters to that white man and you talkin' 'bout rights?!" Esther's words sliced through the thick air like a knife through butter, a tone so sarcastic it shamed Beatrice.

"Mama, we just friends. We write to each other to keep Robert's memory alive."

"How you keepin' Robert's memory alive when he say things like *your letters give him hope; he look forward to hearing from you; he glad you done come into his life?* That ain't got nothin' to do with my Robert, and don't you use my son's memory as an excuse to be tangled up with some white man!"

"I ain't tangled up with no white man! We just friends—"

"Don't you sass me! You done forgot how you was raised. Done gon' crazy messin' round with some married white man after all your father been through. I know Wilbert turnin' in his grave."

Beatrice felt a pain slice through her. When she spoke again her tone had softened, though the anger and hurt still showed on her face. "Mama, I didn't mean for things to turn out this way," she said, her heart pounding against her chest. "Please try to understand. Please don't do this."

There was a long silence, and this time when Esther spoke again, her suitcase was packed and her purse and sweater were on her arm.

"The daughter I raised done changed. Done turned into somebody I don't know no mo'." Esther paused and stared at her daughter, looked right through her. She hoisted the suitcase from the bed. "I'm gon' downstairs and stay with Mary and Herbert tonight and I'ma ask them to take me to the train station in the mornin'. You know where your home is if'n eva' you get your senses back," she said, and pushed past Beatrice.

The door latch clapped against the frame, a sound so eerie, so final.

Beatrice stood there for a long while, staring at the door. She could still hear her mother's voice in her head, see the pain on her face. She didn't mean to hurt her mother, never wanted to shame her. She felt so conflicted. She looked over at the letters that lay sprawled on the floor and bed, and she shut her eyes, shut out all the mistakes she had made. She never expected to fall in love with *him*, never intended to make a life in Boston. He wasn't the reason she wanted to stay, she had told herself time and again. It was so much bigger than that, so much more. Roxbury offered her something that she could never imagine in the South, something she would never have there—*hope.*

18

"This is worth everything we've worked so hard for," Morris said as he studied the photo of five U.S. marines and a U.S. navy corpsman raising the flag on Iwo Jima.

Bernard leaned over, stared at the photo, too. "Yeah, that's almost worth everything. I don't think I slept a wink in years."

Morris knew the strain on Bernard's face matched his own.

"You know what I think about when I can't sleep?" Bernard said, his voice flat. They sat at the tip of the beach, the water retreating beneath their feet.

"I think about what it be like when all this over. Whether things go back to bein' the way they were. Whether coloreds will have anymo' rights now that we done showed we deservin' of being treated equally."

Morris considered Bernard's words. He often wondered what things would be like when the war was over; whether the world would bend toward a solemn retreat, a kinship that led people to integrate rather than segregate, to reserve rather than retaliate, that employed altruism rather than aggression. In the year leading up to now, there had been more invasions and bombings, endless destruction.

The toll on the world had been devastating.

Back home, people wanted the war to be over, to return to a civility that seemed like a distant dream. Morris contemplated whether that life could exist beyond the words in his letters. He had come to expect a life outside of what he once knew, grasping at what little hope existed. In a way, they were better off than they were a year, a month, or even a week ago. They had long since become accustomed to the dwindling economy, food rationing, salvaging of steel and scrap, women bolstering the workforce for their sweethearts and sons who were fighting in the war.

"I hope things will get better," Morris said. "We can't be doing this for nothing. Things have to change."

"The war done been four years, and nothin' much seem to change! All's we got to account for is what done be, more death and dying, more people losing they's life. Sometimes I don't know why we here anymore."

Morris looked over at Bernard again. "I guess you're right. But we got our family to think about. We're fighting in this war for them, too. Besides, I think things are going to be different when we go home. I already got a letter from my boss at the shipyard. He wants me to come back there, said he got a big promotion waiting for me. What you gonna do when you get back home? You got a job lined up?"

"Not really. Ain't much promise for a colored man in Birmingham. I worked in a factory before I came here. But I hear they done got rid of most of the coloreds, done gave the jobs to the white men that be out of work. Things real bad in Birmingham." Bernard looked away, as if he was uncomfortable at the thought.

"How your baby girl doin'?" Bernard asked, changing the subject.

Morris's face lit up. "She's doing just fine. Growing up real fast. She'll be five before we know it."

"Good God almighty! I memba' when you showed me her photo. She wasn't no bigger than this." Bernard stretched his hands apart.

There was silence and Morris knew that another thought was brewing in Bernard.

"You know what I done decided?" Bernard's face became somber. "I done decided when I return home I'm gonna marry LouAnn, the girl I courted before I left. She be writin' me all the time, talkin' 'bout how she be prayin' for me. She a good woman. And she gon' make a good wife and mother. I done decided that I want a house full of chi'ren. A girl like you got and two boys." Bernard looked over at Morris. "Maybe you get to meet LouAnn someday. Come to Birmingham and meet my family."

"I'd like that," Morris said, his eyes moistened. "I'd like that a lot."

꩜

On a drizzly morning aboard the USS *West Virginia,* the flag fluttered briskly at half-mast in a cloudy sky that hung low over the usually sunny island, desolate now as Morris and the other men stood in formation, tuned in to President Truman's voice on the loud speakers.

"It is with a heavy heart that I stand before you, my friends and colleagues. . . . Only yesterday, we laid to rest the mortal remains of our beloved president, Franklin Delano Roosevelt. At a time like this, words are inadequate. The most eloquent tribute would be a reverent silence. Yet, in this decisive hour, when world events are moving so rapidly, our silence might be misunderstood and might give comfort to our enemies.

"In His infinite wisdom, Almighty God has seen fit to take from us a great man who loved, and was beloved by, all humanity."

As the new president spoke, Morris thought of the late President Roosevelt, the last photo he'd seen of him, the look on his face, the way he sat in his chair, his legs unmoving, just as he kept his pained legs at night. Without shame, Morris felt the tears collecting, as if a wave of emotion was lurking, waiting to pour out. Instinctively he blinked, but it was too late. The tears fell quickly with thoughts of their fallen leader and all the countless wounded and dead soldiers, their coffins draped in American flags. Day by day, he had worked on fleets of ships that came in and out and through Pearl Harbor, bringing daily reports of the Allies that launched assaults on Nazi forces, the discovery of mass graves and ghastly concentration camps, and of the soldiers who inched forward in the Pacific with intense, ruthless fighting and devastation. The mood across the world was dismal, overwrought with the sorrow that war had brought them.

One afternoon, Morris made his way to the colored quarters looking for Bernard.

"Have you heard?" Morris said, the moment he and Bernard were away from earshot of the others.

Bernard shook his head, said nothing.

"There's talk about the war ending in the Pacific. I even heard . . ." Morris looked around, made sure no one could hear. "I heard that we may drop an atomic bomb on Japan," he whispered.

"An atomic bomb?!"

Morris nodded. "It's top secret. Only a few people know."

"Good God almighty," Bernard said. "How you know there's any truth to that?"

Morris paused, looked around again. "I overheard one of my bunk mates who's been part of the briefings talking about it to one of his friends. They didn't know I was in my bunk."

"God help us all," Bernard said, more to himself than to Morris.

"If what I heard is true, the war may be ending soon," Morris said, preoccupied with thoughts of finally going home. He had often imagined what it would be like when he returned home, whether he and Agnes could start over, if it was even possible to do that. He had changed, and he could tell that Agnes had changed, too, grown beyond the young, frivolous girl who once adored him, into a woman who had been altered by the war. It seemed even the words in her letters signified a shift. Raising Emma on her own without him, Agnes had grown stronger, more independent.

And then there was Beatrice.

Theirs was a complicated friendship that had flourished into a kinship beyond his comprehension. It had not been easy for him, holding a special place in his heart for Beatrice, knowing, as he did, that he was betraying his wife and child. And he knew Beatrice cared for him, too. Though at first, it did not seem a feeling of want as much as kindness. A kindness that had developed steadily through words on a page, thoughts that they'd shared with only each other. He realized that Beatrice had written to him less and less lately, and that the few letters she did write had taken on a different tone, and he struggled to read between the lines to find her real meaning. With the war coming to an end, he had started to wonder: What would happen with them when he returned home? What if Agnes ever found out? What would his family think? He pondered these questions during many sleepless nights, and he couldn't help but wonder if Beatrice thought about it, too.

$\mathcal{A}$

Beatrice and Nellie sat behind Mrs. Baker and a group of women from the League of Women for Community

Services. The small church was filled with women from every corner of Boston.

They all had been members, volunteers, or admirers of the League, and they had done everything they could to help—volunteering their time with the Red Cross, shipping care packages to the soldiers, visiting the wounded. The women banded together—colored and white, young and old, wealthy and not—to ease the discomfort of the swelling number of families that had lost so much. Unity, which in different times had been carved only into niches of the city, had become commonplace.

Beatrice took notice of the long silences, broken by waves of sobs and tears from mothers and wives, their faces made hopeful as Mrs. Baker spoke.

"We all are here tonight to pray for all those whose lives were lost," Mrs. Baker said. She glanced briefly at Beatrice, held her eyes. "But no matter what, we've kept our faith because we know that God is still in control, that what has been taken from us will be restored, that there is nothing more important than family."

Beatrice touched the locket that hung around her neck, the one her mother had given to her. She thought of all that had happened over the past years. She was no longer the timid young colored girl who'd taken a bus on her own to Boston all those years ago. She was different, hardened in ways that made her stronger, and softened in ways that weren't possible living in the South. She suddenly thought of Morris Sullivan, *the letters,* and how they had become connected in ways she didn't quite understand.

"Always hold on to family," Mrs. Baker continued. "There's nothing more important than family. It's what keeps us grounded."

Beatrice's tears turned to quiet reflection as she thought of her mother, how very alone she must be, of the distance between them. It had been months since she had last spoken to her, and she missed her. She had tried time and again to phone her mother and she had written her, too, but Esther did not answer her calls nor return her letters. One day, she even asked Nellie to phone her and she worried when Nellie could not reach her, either. Knowing her mother, Beatrice understood that her decision to stay in Boston was something that her mother would never forgive. She knew it from the way Esther had looked at her, the pain she saw in her mother's eyes. In a way, she didn't blame her. She felt more ashamed of her actions than her mother had. Since her mother left Boston, she had stopped writing to Morris in an attempt to assuage her own guilt. But there was something more she knew she had to do.

Beatrice remained still, listening to the last of Mrs. Baker's words, and the words of all the other mothers, sisters, and friends who spoke about their loss or their families, or the day they prayed for their husbands or sons or brothers to come home. *Home,* Beatrice thought again.

Home.

She quietly gathered her things and made her way out of the room.

"Beatrice . . . ?"

Beatrice turned to Nellie rushing after her.

"What's wrong? Where are you going?"

Beatrice's face became slack. "I'm leaving, Nellie. I'm going back home."

"Let me get my things. I'll walk with you."

"No, Nellie. I don't mean our home. I'm going back home, to Jackson, to Mama."

Nellie gave Beatrice a careful look.

"Are you sure?" Nellie asked.

Beatrice looked away, her eyes filling again. "No, Nellie. I'm not. But I know it's something I must do. Mama needs me. She's lost her whole family, and I've been so selfish. I didn't mean to hurt her, Nellie. I didn't mean to hurt her."

Nellie pulled Beatrice close to her, held her as Beatrice cried, slow and steady whimpers that turned into hard sobbing. "It's going to be all right. You're going to be fine. Your mama's gonna be so glad to have you with her. She's gonna be so proud of you."

After a long moment, Beatrice released herself from Nellie's embrace, took the tissue that Nellie handed her.

"Are you okay?" Nellie asked.

Beatrice shook her head. "Yes. I'm fine. I just need to go and plan my trip. I want to leave on the next train to Jackson."

"Okay," Nellie said. "Let me grab my things and walk with you."

Beatrice watched Nellie quietly grab her things, saw her give Mrs. Baker a nod. And when Nellie rejoined her, they walked home in silence, not saying anything about the apartment they shared, or the job that Beatrice was supposed to start, or her work with the League.

That night, after Beatrice packed, she pulled out her composition book and opened it to a fresh page:

> Dear Morris,
>   By the time you receive this letter, I will be gone.
> I have decided to return home to Jackson. My mother
> needs me—

Beatrice stopped suddenly. *No, I'm not going to do this. This is why things are the way they are between me and Mama.* She abruptly ripped the letter from the book, reached beneath her bed, and retrieved the box full of letters. She took her time reading each one, savoring the words, the thoughts they had exchanged. And when she was done, she glanced at the letter she had begun to write and then gently laid it facedown inside the box, burying it along with her feelings.

19

Agnes, her mother and father, Gilda, her son and two daughters, and little Emma gathered around the radio, waiting for news. The war in Germany had long been over. Less than a month after President Roosevelt's death, victory in Europe had been declared, and Agnes had watched from her window as her neighbors danced in the streets. Her heart filled with hope that soon she would dance, too.

She had lain awake night after night, drumming up dire thoughts, wondering if she'd be next to answer the dreadful knock at the door. She would never forget the day the dark car pulled up and two uniformed officers straight-walked their way up to Claudia's front door. Claudia's low hurling wail broke through the quiet, a cry so piercing it caused Agnes's heart to drop.

Agnes tried hard not to think about it. And when her thoughts became unbearable, her mother and Gilda helped her through it. Their words consoled her, but still they couldn't fill the emptiness that had crept up since the day Morris left. With only occasional phone calls, letters that left so much unsaid, and the fleeting trips home, Agnes's loneliness threatened to invade her soul. She'd waited so long for her husband to finally come home, and she prayed that things would be different once they put the war behind them. But she couldn't help but think about how distant he was the times he'd returned home. And now, as she leaned on her mother and closed her eyes, something deep within her steeled her against the hollow uncertainty.

"*We interrupt this broadcast.*" Agnes looked intently at the radio as though President Truman were standing in her living room. She leaned in closer.

"*I have received this afternoon a message from the Japanese government,*" President Truman said, allowing a dramatic pause before he continued. "*Of . . . the UNCONDITIONAL SURRENDER OF JAPAN!*"

Agnes burst into tears at the news she thought she'd never hear: three years, eight months, and seven days after that fateful Sunday morning in Pearl Harbor, VJ Day—Victory in Japan—was declared, World War II had come to an end, and her husband, her love, was finally coming home.

ॐ

Morris came back from the war and avoided any talk about where he had been and what he had seen and was put at ease when Agnes didn't pry.

He was content spending countless hours with Emma, who'd grown beyond his imagination. She amused him with her childlike sense of self-righteousness, telling her father stories that only a five-year-old's mind could muster, singing him special songs that her grandmama had taught her. His little girl enchanted him and it was her love, and the love of those around him, that carried him from day to day.

Many of their friends and neighbors were shattered by the war—financially, emotionally, and physically. Morris was spared with a limp and memories that haunted him in the night, made him reach for Agnes. And Agnes would hold him, too, the same way she held Emma—rocking him in her

arms, wiping the sweat from his face—and for those few brief
moments, sometimes hours, Agnes would feel a closeness to
Morris that she hadn't felt in a very long time, a contrast to the
distance that had grown between them. For Agnes, the months
became an emotion-numbing blur. The days were dull and
long, and the nights full of relentless waves of fitful sleep and
silent grief.

Any hope of a change for the better in her marriage left
Agnes shortly after Morris returned. She felt more alone with
Morris home than when he was gone. He hardly noticed her
anymore. His moods shifted like rain drifting in wind. One
day he was fully alert, in tune to her every need, and the next
it was as if she didn't exist at all. Agnes refused to give in to the
feelings of desolation. To distract herself, she kept her mind
on Emma, telling herself that it would take time. The man
she fell in love with and married was still within reach. Often,
when Morris was in his room working on his ships, she'd
stand nearby watching him, remembering earlier days when
they'd gone out for long walks in the park, holding hands, the
air infused with the sweet smell of spring or the terse chill of
winter. It was those memories that comforted and consoled
her. Not this life, certainly.

Morris began the slow and deliberate merging back in to
life. He returned to the shipyard where he had worked before the navy. His old boss welcomed him like a hero, telling
him that he could have any job he wanted, encouraging him
to work as little or as much as he needed. Morris took his advice, threw himself into the mundane tasks of working long,
tiring hours that often stretched into late evening. On those
nights, Agnes would stand at the window, willing him home
to the plate of food wrapped in foil in the oven and the warm
bed left unmarked by his presence. But there was something
on Morris's mind, something he couldn't shake. He had tried

to shut it out, but he needed to hear from her, to see her face again.

A week later, Morris stepped inside the diner and spotted Vincent with his back to him, facing the cutout window that led into the kitchen.

"Where's my other plate?!" Vincent shouted into the kitchen. Morris watched, amused by how little Vincent had changed. He looked around. Everything was still as he remembered except for a collage of framed photos that covered the walls: men in uniform who'd served in the war. Morris scanned each photo until one caught his eye—a photo of him standing on the USS *Arizona*. He thought of the day the photo was taken, a memory that trembled on the edge of reality, a young man he no longer knew.

He took a seat at the counter, watching Vincent. When things settled, he finally spoke up. "What about my order? You got any more of that corned beef that this fellow's having?"

Vincent turned, and a luminous smile broke across his face. "You bet your ass I do," he said, and rushed from behind the counter to Morris. They embraced, a peculiar moment passing between them. Vincent could feel that something was different about his friend. "Why haven't you come before now? Did Agnes tell you I called and stopped by?"

Morris nodded, but said nothing. He had no excuse for why he hadn't shown up until now. "Sorry."

Vincent shook his head. "Don't be. So, how the hell are you?"

"I'm fine. Can't complain," Morris said.

Vincent gestured to an empty table. "Come on over here. Have a seat. You want a Coca-Cola or something?" Vincent snapped his fingers at a heavyset colored girl who was clearing the table next to them. "Betty, get us two colas."

Morris took a seat, his face cleared into a smile. "How are you? How's your dad?"

"I'm good, but Dad's as high-strung as ever. Working all the time to keep this place running. The war really hit us hard."

"I heard," Morris said.

Morris looked around, searching. He hadn't heard from her in months, and his letters had been returned. He had thought long and hard about coming to the sandwich shop today, whether he should instead make his way over to Roxbury. But he couldn't bring himself to show up there again. It wouldn't be right. He felt terrible being home with Agnes and Emma and thinking of her. He knew if he followed his heart that there would be no turning back. At Pearl Harbor he was able to keep the distance, had even convinced himself that they were merely letters, that nothing could come of it. It was all so very innocent. *Innocent.* But since he'd been home, he couldn't stop thinking about her. He knew looking for her might ignite questions, but he needed to see her again, needed to connect her to the letters.

"So, where's Beatrice?" Morris saw Betty's face go blank as she placed the colas before them, as if she hadn't heard Mr. Vincent's friend, a white man, asking about a colored girl.

Vincent took a sip of the cola. "Beatrice left after she graduated from that teacher's college. Betty's been with us ever since."

Morris raked his mind, mulling whether he should ask more questions. He was slow to speak again. "You know if she still stays in Roxbury?"

Vincent eyed Morris suspiciously. "Why you asking so many questions about her?"

Morris's expression tightened for an instant; a flutter crept up his neck. "I just wondered what happened to her, is all."

"I heard she moved back to Mississippi," Vincent said, showing no concern.

Hearing Vincent's words was like a fist to the stomach. He hadn't allowed himself to consider the possibility of never seeing her again. A long moment hung as he tried to find the words—any words—that would change things, close the hole that was opening in his heart. He closed his eyes, tried to etch things out in his mind.

"You need to pull yourself together before you go home to Agnes," Vincent said, sizing him up.

Morris looked despairingly at Vincent, then with his head and shoulders drawn low, he slowly made his way out of the diner, and finally toward home.

Part Two

Spring 1960

20

Beatrice

After three full days of grief-stricken tears, Beatrice's days had blurred into an incessant stream of random thoughts: her final days with her mother, her mother's last words; the funeral, overflowing with people in the pews, lining the walls, crowding the vestibule. "Esther was a good woman. Better than most folk we know," the pastor had belted. Muffled sounds of *Ummm-hmmmm* and *Amen* filtered through the church. Beatrice had gazed at the three oversized photos that sat atop makeshift easels perfectly centered around the coffin: one of Esther, her face full and round and smiling; another of Esther and her family taken more than two decades ago; and one of Esther and Beatrice taken on a recent Saturday afternoon, a few days after Esther first learned of her sickness. She had rushed home from town with several yards of white fabric. "I'm gon' make us some dresses so we can take a photograph together. We haven't taken one in a long while." Then she called Mr. Henry, a short, stout brown-skinned man who took all the photos of the colored families that side of the Mississippi. It took Esther only a week to make the dresses and no time for Mr. Henry to show up shortly after. He took his time, taking shots from every angle while Beatrice and her mother, in their white dresses with matching gloves and shawls, stared into the camera, smiling.

Beatrice lay in her mother's bed, thinking of her mother's last words. "You all the family we got left now," Esther had said. She looked so small and frail, taking slow, labored breaths, hanging on to what little was left. Esther had died at home, and Beatrice had taken care of her until the end, never leaving her mother's side, comforting her when she called out in pain, bathing her, giving her the medicines that Esther frequently turned away. Oftentimes, Beatrice would sit studying her mother's face as she slept, drawn tight by the sickness that had quickly spread through Esther's body.

Beatrice's mind drifted, sorted through the past sixteen years: the day she returned home, not long after her graduation from the teachers college; the teaching job she took at Greenville Elementary, a small colored school in a dilapidated building with hand-me-downs from the better-funded white schools; the small bedroom off the kitchen where she spent most of her time, the same one she and Robert shared all those years before; the old habits she and Esther had wrapped themselves in—working six days a week, supper in the early evenings, church on Sunday, Sunday dinner and porch sitting.

With each passing year, Beatrice had learned to suppress thoughts of Boston, had put that life behind her. She had even managed to push Morris from her mind. He was a distant memory, except during those rare occasions when thoughts of him suddenly rose up so strong, so brisk, at such odd moments. She might be alone in the kitchen washing the dishes, the soapy suds lathering in her hand, crystal white bubbles that took her mind back to him; or she'd be hanging clothes on the line in the yard, and she'd look up at the sky, the exact shade of blue as his eyes; or she might be sitting alone on the porch in the evening, wrapped in a blanket against the chilly night, and suddenly she'd wonder how it would have felt to have his arms wrapped around her. Those were the times that she'd think of him, wonder if he ever thought of her. She had never tried to contact him. Not once.

And then there was Charles.

Not much taller than Beatrice, Charles was a simple man, with honest ways, soft brown eyes, and a lazy smile. He had met Beatrice at church, and it took months of teasing and coaxing from her mother to convince Beatrice to give in to him. "He a good man," Esther would chide. "Good and decent. Remind me of my Wilbert."

Beatrice was fond of Charles, but she didn't think of him in the way she thought of Morris. Charles was kind and caring, but there was no spark. Through the years, she and Charles had what she called an on-and-off "thing"—nothing really serious, at least not for her. Charles loved her, had tried desperately to convince her to braid a life together—intertwine strands of likeness, trust, and hope against the long and narrow love they had for each other. But Beatrice couldn't see her way through to it. Charles only helped her to keep those lonely nights at bay, force thoughts of a life beyond the South to fade from her mind.

Now, Beatrice wiped the tears from her face, looked over at Nellie. "I can't believe Mama saved every drawing, every letter, almost everything Robert and I ever did," Beatrice said. Nellie sat beside her, rummaging through the boxes they found beneath Esther's bed. "I miss her so much, Nellie. I just don't know what I'm gonna do without her."

"You're going to be just fine, the way you've always been. You're strong like your mama. You'll get through it. She may be gone, Beatrice, but she's always with you right here." Nellie picked up Beatrice's hand and placed it on her heart.

After Beatrice left Boston, Nellie would write and come for a visit at least twice a year, bringing along subtle reminders of the life that Beatrice still craved. Nellie still looked the same, but with a roundness from carrying three hefty babies to term after Clifford came along. Clifford had moved to Roxbury from South Carolina and took a job as a janitor at the school where Nellie taught. For months, he would walk by Nellie's classroom, rolling the bucket and mop, trying to get her attention, until one day he mustered up enough nerve to ask Nellie to go to church with him. Just church, he'd promised. The following Sunday when Clifford knocked on Nellie's door with an armful of white roses, she knew in that moment that he would be her husband, the father of her children.

Beatrice walked over to the open window, stared out at the oak tree by the edge of the woods, the makeshift swing that hung from it. She closed her eyes and thought back on a time when she was six years old, and her mother stood behind her, pushing her on the swing, her small legs carefree and drifting. She smiled at the thought. Then suddenly, a load of guilt and shame came over her as she recalled all the times she had regretted coming back to Jackson, the times her mother would see the painful truth on her face. She cried, hardly aware of herself mumbling, "She's gone, Nellie. I can't believe she's gone."

Beatrice gestured at the blanket on the bed. "Even this reminds me of her. She made it for my sixth birthday. What made you cover me with it last night?"

Nellie looked at her, puzzled. "What do you mean?"

Beatrice thought back. "I remember crying and dozing off at some point. When I awoke, I was covered with the blanket."

"That wasn't me, Beatrice."

"Then who covered me?" Beatrice asked, sniffling.

Nellie gave her a consoling look. "That's your mama, Beatrice. She's always gon' be watching over you."

Beatrice brought the blanket to her face, sniffed it. She could still smell her mother on it. Nellie was right, she felt her presence everywhere—in the kitchen when she and Nellie prepared their meals; in her mother's bedroom, where she now slept; on the porch, where she often sat alone staring out at the same oak tree.

Beatrice suddenly stood, then walked from room to room. It seemed vitally important that she straighten every chair, every pillow, making sure everything was in its proper place, just as her mother would have expected. She wandered for a long while until she heard a knock at the door.

"I'll get it." Beatrice made her way to the front door, and when she opened it, she suddenly changed her face, smiled at the old woman.

"I'm Sadie Mae, a good friend of your mama's. May I come in?" Beatrice stared at her round face and green eyes that told a story; her dark hair, brilliantly pin-striped with hints of gray, was pulled back into a fine bun. She was petite, but her stature and voice made her appear twofold her size, a graceful woman who commanded respect just by her appearance.

Beatrice moved aside, and Sadie Mae stepped in and stopped partway into the living room, taking notice of the framed photographs of Esther and her family, the old plaid sofa and matching chair, an aged piano in the corner, the curtains that hung perfectly at the two small windows. She took her time before she turned her eyes on Beatrice. "You a spittin' image of your mama."

"Ma'am, may I offer you a seat?" Nellie made a comfortable space on the sofa.

"I'se reckon I better take a seat fo' I done wore out these old legs." She made her way to the sofa, sat next to Nellie.

"Sweet Jesus. If'n eva' you don't look just like your mama. Praise be. How you holdin' up, babe?"

"Just fine, ma'am," Beatrice answered, noticing the way the old woman clutched the brown paper bag in her hand.

"Well, you jus' keep holdin' it togetha' and don't you

worry ya'self, the Lord'a see right by you. 'Sides, your mama wouldn't want you wallowin' in no grief."

"Yes, ma'am," Beatrice said, not sure what to make of the old woman.

"I'se reckon' you wonderin' how I know your mama?"

Beatrice looked at her, said nothing.

"Well, no need in all that wonderin.' I'se been friends with your mama a long time. When I got sick, Esther would come nearly every day to check on me, fix my supper, clean my house. She was a good woman. She like a daughter to me— like my own flesh and blood. Ain't nary a day go by that I didn't pray for her."

Beatrice looked closely at Ms. Sadie Mae. She remembered now seeing her mother talking to the old woman at church; or the times her mother mentioned that she was late coming home because she had to stop by to see Ms. Sadie Mae; and the times she called Ms. Sadie Mae on the phone to check on her.

Sadie Mae reached inside the brown bag, pulled a Bible from it. "When your mama would come sit with me, she would read me this hea' Bible. Say it been with her eva' since she was a small chile. Last time she come she asked me to keep it for you, and she wanted me to give you this hea', too." Sadie Mae opened the Bible and pulled a letter from it.

"I made my boy Tomas bring me all this way so I can give it to you." Sadie Mae handed the Bible and letter to Beatrice.

Beatrice gripped the Bible, and took her time opening the letter, watched an old leaf fall from it. She picked up the leaf, brought it to her face, took a deep whiff, and then read the letter.

Dear Beatrice,

From the moment I lay eyes on you, I knew you were gon' be special. Me and your daddy loved you from

the day we came to lern of you. You always be special to
me. I know thangs ain't been so easey for you, but I want
you to know I'm so proud of you. Just cause I'm gon',
don't mean me and your daddy and Robert won't always
be with you.

Love Mama

Beatrice gently folded the letter, brought the leaf to her
nose again, took in the smell of her mother.

"Oh, chile," Sadie Mae said, reaching for Beatrice. "Hush on
up, now. Ain't no sense in all this cryin'. Your mama in a betta'
place now. You hush on up all this cryin' and carryin' on."

Beatrice sank into the old woman's arms, hardly aware of
the Bible clutched at her heart, or Nellie, who sat beside her,
rubbing her back.

The old woman lifted Beatrice's face to hers. "Wheneva'
you missin' your mama, you turn to this Bible," she said,
looking Beatrice straight in the eyes. "This hea' is a special
part of your mama and you keep it with you. God don't do
nothin' that ain't meant for our good. Your mama jus' fine and
you gon' be jus' fine. Jus' fine," she said.

Beatrice let the old woman's words sink into her as Sadie
Mae rocked her like her mother used to. They stayed that way
for a long while.

"I best be on my way fo' my boy come knockin' at that
doo'," Sadie Mae finally said.

Beatrice slowly let her go, and wiped her face.

"You memba' what I say. You turn to that Bible wheneva'
you missin' your mama." She folded Beatrice in her arms one
last time.

Beatrice held on to her for a long while, and when Sadie
Mae finally released her, Beatrice helped her with her cane,
walked her to the door, and opened it.

"I thought you were my Tomas," Sadie Mae said to the man who surprised them at the door.

He quickly removed his hat, gestured his respect. "No, ma'am, I'm Charles, a friend of Beatrice's."

Beatrice gave Charles an awkward smile, surprised to see him.

Sadie Mae turned back to Beatrice, touched her face again. "You hold on to your mama. Don't you neva' let her go," she said just before Tomas appeared, reached for his mother, and helped her down the porch and into the car.

Beatrice and Charles watched the car disappear slowly down the driveway.

"May I come in?" Charles said, after the car was out of sight.

Beatrice moved to let him inside.

"Hello, Ms. Nellie," Charles said, smiling.

"How do you do, Charles?" Nellie smiled, then gave Beatrice a fleeting look. "Well, I've got things to do. I'll be in the kitchen," she said, then rushed off, leaving them alone.

Beatrice gestured to the sofa. "Would you like to sit?"

Charles took a seat. "It was a beautiful service. Your mama looked like she at peace."

Beatrice nodded, forced back tears.

Charles reached for her hand, held it. "You need anything?"

"No, I'm fine. Nellie's here and she's been helping me get through."

"Well, I went to visit your mama's grave again this mornin'. Took some fresh flowers to her."

"Thank you, Charles. That was very thoughtful of you."

"And I done made arrangements with Old Man Jessup to keep an extra watch on your mama's grave. He done assured me that he gon' see to it."

Beatrice nodded, smiled politely. She could hear Nellie

moving around the kitchen. There was a long silence, and they both stared absently around the room.

"Look, Beatrice," Charles finally said. "I know things been hard on you, takin' care of your mama and all. And I know things ain't been what you want between us." Charles twisted his hat in his hands. "But I don't want you to be by ya'self. . . . I mean, what I'm try'na say is that I want to take care of you, for us to make a life together. Now, we ain't got to stay here in your mama's house, or in Jackson if you don't want. Fact is, I heard Montgomery is nice, much more pro-gressin'. It ain't but 'bout three hours from here. And you be close enough to come back and check on your mama. The schools are better for colored teachers, and I can sharecrop anywhere. Crops much more plentiful there. I can make a good livin' for us. We can get married and move there, start a life together."

Beatrice stared at Charles, noticed his coveralls, his plaid checkered shirt, his simple hat. She sat quiet, her face barren. She didn't know where to start, or how to say it, or if now was the right time. She didn't love Charles, not in that way. With Morris, the connection and the attraction had been instan-taneous. With Charles, it never came. "Charles, I . . . I can't marry you. I can't marry anyone right now," she said, staring straight at him.

Beatrice watched Charles's face go slack, the same way it always did when she refused his proposals. He gave her a half smile, trying to cover the hurt that Beatrice could clearly see on his face.

"It was just a thought, is all." Charles looked embarrassed. "Well, I guess I best be on my way. I reckon you know how to find me if you need anything."

Beatrice walked him to the door.

"Please tell Ms. Nellie I say good-bye."

Beatrice watched him walk down the driveway, make his way into an old sharecropping truck, and slowly drive away.

"You gonna be okay?" Nellie asked, joining Beatrice at the window.

"I don't know," Beatrice mumbled. "I know Mama would want me to stay here and marry him and raise a family. But it's not in me to do that. It's never been in me. I only stayed because of Mama. Because I just couldn't let Mama sit in this house alone and mourn the rest of her life. But now that she's gone . . ."

"You gonna be just fine. Your mama just want you to be happy. That's why she wrote you that letter," Nellie said.

Beatrice started to sob again, stared blankly out at the yard. "I remember one day when Mama came home crying about that fourteen-year-old colored boy, Emmett Till, the one who was beaten and shot in the head and thrown in the Tallahatchie River for whistling at a white woman." She looked up at Nellie, pulled her sweater close to her. "It happened less than a hundred miles from here. I knew right then that I wouldn't stay a day longer than I had to. But that was over five years ago, Nellie, and I stayed—for Mama. Not a day went by that I didn't think about leaving. I wanted so much to just get away from here and start a new life. And now I ain't never been married or had no children. I ain't got no more family."

"You got me and Clifford and the girls. We your family. And it ain't too late to marry or have children. Charles is a good man, and he loves you. Maybe you should think about it, Beatrice."

"That's your family, Nellie. And I don't love Charles. I never loved Charles."

A thoughtful moment passed over Nellie. "Then if there ain't no future for you here, why don't you come back to Boston with me and Clifford and the girls? Roxbury's got its share of problems, but at least you'll have a better life. And who knows, maybe you'll meet a nice man, settle down and marry."

"I can't do that . . . . I can't just impose on you and your family. You done enough as it is."

"You hush up with all that silly talk. You like a sister to me. I ain't gonna leave you here feeling sorry for yourself. Doing what you didn't want your mama to do."

"There were days I would just sit here on that porch and dream of the day that I could go back to Roxbury. I just don't know who I am anymore."

"Don't be so hard on yourself. You did what you had to do. Your mama would want what's best for you now, and if leaving Jackson is what's best, then you need to do it."

Beatrice thought of everything her mother had told her that she needed to know—about the house, the life insurance she'd managed to keep up, and the small savings she'd stashed away beneath her mattress. *It ain't much, but it's plenty to hold you over. You do right by things, Beatrice,* Esther had said.

"I don't know," Beatrice said.

Nellie took her hand, and they sat quietly. Nellie's hand was warm and soft against her own.

"You know, you can still keep the house if that's what's worrying you. My mama will keep an eye on it for you."

Beatrice wiped away tears.

"Beatrice, don't let this eat you up. Come on now. You know you can't stay here and live like this. Come back with us. Please."

A quiet peace settled over Beatrice. Over the past years, she had ignored the insatiable craving for something more; had put her life on hold, had become invisible, doing just enough to get by. After her mother had become sick, she'd prayed for her healing, had made a promise to never leave her again. And when Esther's sickness had taken a turn for the worse, Beatrice had absorbed herself into saving her. Now, the thought of another life had begun to take shape, becoming more fervent with each passing day. Nellie watched the strife on Beatrice's face and was relieved when she saw her face change.

"Okay," Beatrice said at last. "Okay," she whispered again to herself, as she felt her heart lift with thoughts of going back to Boston.

21

Agnes

Agnes dragged through the morning like a robot, her body and mind stiff. She slowly took a hot shower; the steam flecked and hovered over her. She had been feeling foggy for the past few days, similar to the way she always felt this time of year, especially on this day. She stepped from the shower, cleared the mist from the mirror, and stared at herself. All night, she had lain there in the darkness, thinking of him. He would have been ten today.

Ten.

Their son, born premature, who they had given Morris's name but who had died six days later. For 137 hours and 13 minutes, he had lived, tiny tubes attached to his body, pulsating air to his little lungs, surrounded by a plastic crib. He had been two pounds and one ounce, not much bigger than the palm of her hand. It broke Agnes's heart to lose the child, so delicate, so pure. She had cried for days, though Morris had not. And she had wanted to baptize him and give him a Catholic funeral. "Agnes, no, please, let's not do this," Morris had said, his face contorted with grief.

Their eyes met, and the pain in hers made his fill, too. "But he's our son," Agnes cried. *Our son.* Morris understood that more than Agnes could ever know. Not a day went by that he didn't think of him. Before he was even born, Morris had already imagined the baseball games he would take him to see, the model ships they would build together. But when he was born, Morris held the puny child in his arms, afflicted beyond any pain he had ever known. He had pleaded with God, promised that if the child lived he was going to be to his son all the things that his own father was not to him. And when he died, a piece of Morris died, too.

At the funeral, everyone tried to be amiable, pretending to be unfazed by the eighteen-inch casket, made to suit the tiny child. They had all walked around, unsure of what to say and how to say it. There was no photo, no eulogy. Just their bare grief. The next day, Agnes took to her bed, her spirit buried along with the child in the hard earth.

Losing their son had made them drift, a drifting that had shaped their lives. Agnes needed her husband, the man she'd fallen in love with and still deeply loved. It had brought her a measure of comfort, the way Morris had taken care of everything, of her and Emma. And through the years, she had taken care of him, too—keeping an immaculate home, cooking his meals, laundering his clothes and his secrets.

She felt so alone, especially since she'd lost her mother five years earlier to pneumonia, a sickness that suddenly snaked into their lives and took Alice away, and Oscar hadn't been the same since. Oftentimes, Agnes would go and sit with her father, cook for him, try to talk to him. But there was no use; Oscar had folded in on himself beyond the callous man he once was. And her best friend, Claudia, had moved away less than a year after the war had taken Jim. Even Gilda, Morris's mother, had gone to live with her daughters in Seattle.

Agnes wrapped herself in her robe and walked back to her room. The rustic hardwood floors glistened from the natural light. Outside, the sun had just risen, and the cold air frosted the windows. She quickly dressed and went downstairs to find Morris at the table. Instinctively she moved around the kitchen, doing as she had done every morning for the past twenty years.

"Do you want some eggs?"

Morris didn't look up from his paper. "Yes, that's fine."

Agnes pulled the pan from the cupboard and cracked the eggs, stirred them in a bowl, each motion stilling her. It was only 7 A.M. and already the day felt so barren, so hopeless. The house was quiet, the creaking of heated pipes the only sound. Agnes unconsciously tossed the eggs in the pan, looked out the window. She watched a little boy at the bus stop, holding his mother's hand. He was about the right age, size, and height, his knitted wool hat pulled over his ears, his small body tucked perfectly in a ski jacket. Agnes stared at him.

I should be out there too. . . .

The smell of the cooked eggs pulled her out of her reverie, and she quickly turned her gaze from the window and scraped the curled, lifeless shape onto a plate. "Would you like more coffee?" she said, placing the dish before Morris.

"Yes, please," Morris said, still looking at his paper.

Agnes had promised herself that this time would be different, that she would not give in to the anguish that suddenly emerged, inexplicably.

He would have been ten.

She imagined him riding his bike and throwing a baseball. Adventurous, so full of energy, and smart, a spitting image of his father.

She poured the coffee and turned to look at Morris sitting there, so strangely calm. She forced back tears, leaned against the counter to steady herself, bare in her own grief.

Ten.

The memories converged, coming together at odd angles. She thought of the day of his funeral, the way they all stood

there, beneath the trees, watching the tiny casket being lowered into the ground; the way Morris looked on, motionless;
the way she wept silently; and then the years that followed, the
times she would turn and imagine him standing there in the
kitchen waiting for a snack, or in the yard throwing the ball
or sitting at the table across from them.

She glared at Morris, studied his eyes, now laden with
wisdom, the way his jaw lined his face, and she felt the anger
lurking. "Do you realize what today is?!" she blurted, not
knowing where the words came from.

Morris looked up. "What . . . ?"

"Today! Do you know that today's *his* birthday? Have you
even thought about it?!"

Morris put down the paper, fixed her with a pained expression, sighed. "Agnes, let's not do this again. Why do we
have to do this every year? The same thing?"

"Thing?! How dare you speak of him as though he means
nothing to you!" Tears blurred her vision.

"Look! I'm not going to stand for this again. This has to
stop, Agnes!" Morris folded the paper, pushed from the table
and past her. "I have to go."

Agnes flinched at the sound of the door shutting. She
hated what that war had done to him, to *them*. That awful
day at Pearl Harbor had changed Morris, had marked a turning point in their marriage, she was sure of it. She sat at
the table, tears sliding down her face. Memories of the past
years burned in her, fueled her quiet rage. For years, she had
learned to live with it, reminded every day of the time that
had transformed their lives. Every time she walked past the
mantel and saw his old navy pictures—the ones he was so
damned proud of.

Without a second thought, she rushed back into the
kitchen, opened the cupboard beneath the sink, and pulled

out an oversized bag. She went to the mantel and yanked a
photograph from it and shoved it into the bag. She snatched
another photo, one of Morris standing on the USS *Oklahoma*.
She studied the photo, as she had done so many times before.
Morris stared back at her, his square face slightly tilted, his
lean and fit body standing at ease in his blue navy jumper. His
handsome face and confident aura disarmed her, made her feel
both proud and sad. She ran her fingers over the photo, tears
streaming down her face—she heard the photo tear before she
had time to think about it. She rushed to the hall closet, retrieved a large box that contained Morris's old military me-
mentoes. She rummaged through articles and more photos.
She dumped them into the bag, hastily retrieving and tossing
anything that fell to the floor. She could not stop herself until
she noticed an envelope with no return address. She picked it
up and pulled the neatly creased letter from it. She scanned the
letter, read it again.

Tears rose in her eyes and throat.

I think of you often. I've never met a man like you before.

I look toward the day that I will see you again.

Agnes gasped.

The letter had been there all these years, tucked away in
the corner of their lives, hidden, and she had never found it.
Never. She sat crumpled on the floor, thinking back on the
years, how Morris had returned from the war a complete
stranger. What he did with his time then was a mystery to
her. She was certain that Morris was no longer unfaithful.
She would have known. There would have been clues—times
when he disappeared, quiet phones calls in the middle of the
night, secret notes, lipstick on his collar. There were none, she
was sure of it.

She closed her eyes. She remembered all the times she had
questioned if he still loved her, if it was *she* that had created

the wedge between them. He had told her she had not. *It has nothing to do with you,* he had said. She had spent her life puzzling over it, looking for answers where there were none. As a little girl, she had watched how her mother had tended to her father, nurturing him, giving of herself unselfishly, fulfilling his every need; and Agnes had mimicked her, doing what was expected of her, giving of herself when she had nothing left to give. And now she understood. For the first time she really understood that Morris did not love her as she had loved him, and she cried, quiet, controlled sobs that grew into an emotional outburst.

"Mom, are you okay?" Emma stared at her mother, at the mess on the floor.

Agnes looked up at Emma, standing just a few feet away, home from college for spring break. She quickly straightened up, wiped the tears from her face, forced a smile. "I'm fine, honey. I was just cleaning out the closet." She quickly stuffed the letter in her pocket. "Are you hungry? Do you want some breakfast?"

Emma could tell that something was wrong. She had known for a long time that things were not right between her parents. Ever since she was old enough to understand, she knew.

"No, Mom. I have to go. I'm already late," she finally said. "Are you sure you're okay?"

"Yes, honey. I'm fine. Just go."

After Agnes heard the door close for a second time, a deep feeling of loss rose up in her. She had to keep reminding herself that Morris was there with her and Emma, every day, barely gone beyond his time away at work. He had taken care of them, worked tirelessly to give them the life, the home, they shared, no matter how modest. Morris loved her, this much she knew. She recalled the times when they'd lie in the dark room, listening to the faint sounds of the night, and then Morris would make love to her, and he would hold her, their hearts beating together.

They'd been married for twenty years now, and that counted for something.

She wiped the tears from her face, and found herself walking back to the kitchen and opening a drawer. She shuffled through it until she found a matchbox. And when she returned to the living room she struck the matchstick until it lit and absentmindedly tossed it into the fireplace, watched the flame catch, spread wildly through the load of wood. Then she pulled the letter from her pocket, tossed it into the flames, and watched it evaporate, determined, more than ever, to make her marriage fit into place like the pieces in a puzzle.

22

Beatrice

Roxbury had changed. The city seemed larger, faster, had grown at a pace uncommon to the South. The first night, Beatrice had lain awake listening to the strange sounds that breezed into her bedroom window. The next morning, she stirred awake, momentarily confused, forgetting that she was no longer in the small bedroom off the kitchen, no longer down the hall from her mother.

Most mornings, she'd lie there, just waiting for the day to come alive, and on Sunday, she'd phone Nellie's mother back home. "Everything okay?" she'd ask, anxious to hear any news of the life she'd left behind. Nellie's mother told her the same as she told her every Sunday: the house was fine, she'd checked the mail and kept the garden, the flowers were blooming. A deep flutter would cross Beatrice's heart, and she'd close her eyes, imagining her own mother in the garden—shucking weeds, tending to her flowers, humming her favorite Sunday hymns. On Monday morning, Beatrice would walk the six blocks to the school where she now taught, throw her energy into the children and her lessons, and at 3 P.M. she'd make her way to New Hope Baptist Church, where she found solace, volunteering her time with the League, protesting against school segregation, advocating for civil rights, and registering the people of Roxbury to vote.

She missed her mother, but she was content to be back in

Roxbury, surrounded by the life that she had long craved. Charles called every week, begging her to come back. *Marry me, Beatrice,* he pleaded. But she just couldn't go back to that life.

Now, Beatrice anxiously opened the door to Mrs. Baker. Though sixty-two, Mrs. Baker moved at an untiring pace, as she had for the last twenty years, dedicating her considerable energies to the League and the Teachers Alliance. "You 'bout ready?" Mrs. Baker said, stepping inside from the brisk, damp morning air. "We got a busload that's already on their way, and the car packed, too, just enough room for one more."

It was just past dawn, and the Boston streets were already alive, bursting with pride at the news of their hero, their senator's victory in his bid for the presidency.

Beatrice was anxious to see *him.* It seemed a fragmented illusion that it was really true—the young candidate who'd been given a faint possibility to win, the one who earned the hope and hearts of nearly every colored man, woman, and child in Roxbury, and cultivated black leaders from Boston to Birmingham, had been elected and was, that very day, about to give his victory speech. For months, Beatrice and the other women from the League had gone door to door, encouraging everyone of legal age to vote. Now, they couldn't wait to see President-Elect John F. Kennedy.

꙳

The motorcade escorted the white Lincoln down South Street in Hyannis Port. Beatrice's heart stirred, a quiet current of tears welling up in her as she stood between Mrs. Baker and Nellie, and they caught sight of him. The crowd screamed and cheered. *Jack!* someone shouted. *We love you.* Beatrice had heard about the young Jack Kennedy back home in Jackson. Oftentimes, she would read to her mother an article from the local paper about him. *See, Mama, he's gonna be the one that will make a difference for our kind,* she'd say. Esther would just nod at the hope in her daughter's voice. And now, as Beatrice stood in the brisk, cool November air, clothed in her warm coat and hope, she couldn't help but feel overjoyed.

The white Lincoln came to a sudden stop. President-Elect Kennedy emerged, smiling and waving, captivating the adoring crowd. Photographers yelled, cameras snapped. *Jack, over here. Over here, Jack!*

"Praise be!" a heavyset, caramel-colored woman standing next to Mrs. Baker said.

"Wow." Nellie leaned over to Beatrice. "Can you believe it? It's really him."

Beatrice had seen the photos, heard his voice on the radio, watched him on the television, but he looked taller, leaner than she'd imagined, more full of life.

"I wish Mama was here to see this," Beatrice said, catching glimpses of him, his cool, greenish-gray eyes, light brown hair, and his smile, the way it curved his young, charismatic face.

There was something special about the young president-elect. Since Beatrice had returned to Roxbury six months ago, she had heard the senator speak about civil rights and the discrimination that stained America, and she remembered reading about the time he had called Coretta Scott King to offer his sympathy when Dr. King was in prison. Yesterday, Beatrice had gone to church and joined the others, waiting for the news of his victory. And as he disappeared into the crowd, she couldn't wait to hear his words, which moved her far beyond the sound of his voice.

"Ladies and gentlemen . . . ladies and gentlemen." The president-elect adjusted the microphone. Jackie, his wife, stood next to him. The crowd hushed. "I have received the following wire from Vice President Nixon. In that wire he says, 'Senator John F. Kennedy, Hyannis Port, Massachusetts. I want to repeat through this wire the congratulations and best wishes I extended to you on television last night. I know that you will have the united support of all Americans as you lead the nation in the cause of peace and freedom during the next four years.' In reply to the vice president, I sent the following wire: 'Vice President Nixon, Los Angeles, California. Your sincere good wishes are gratefully accepted. You are to be congratulated on a fine race. I know the nation can continue to count on your unswerving loyalty in whatever effort you undertake, and that you and I can maintain our long-lasting cordial relations in the years ahead.' "

The new young president looked straight into the camera and addressed the American people.

"May I say, in addition to all citizens of this country, Democrats, Independents, Republicans, regardless of how they may have voted, that it is a satisfying moment to me and I want to express my appreciation to all of them. . . . To all Americans, I say that the next four years are going to be difficult and challenging years for all of us. . . . I ask your help in this effort, and I can assure you that every degree of mind and spirit that I possess will be devoted to the long-range interests of the United States and to the cause of freedom around the world. So now my wife and I prepare for a new administration and for a new baby."

The crowd burst into applause as he stepped from behind the podium, and Secret Service agents escorted him back to the Lincoln. Beatrice's heart raced at the ear-piercing screams.

"His wife is so beautiful," Nellie said, staring at the elegant young Jackie.

Beatrice smiled at Jackie, noticed how bashful she seemed, and turned back to the young president-elect as he waved one last time before he disappeared into the Lincoln. The air had a silvery, magical sheen in the afternoon seaport light, against the calm waters of the nearby Nantucket Sound. As the cheering rose, then tapered off, and people waved their flags, Beatrice watched the motorcade descend down South Street and fade into the distance.

"We best be on our way. Got a long drive ahead," Mrs. Baker announced.

Beatrice followed behind Nellie and Mrs. Baker, mesmerized by the people—white and colored, unkind mixing with unkind, color-blind. For a moment, she had forgotten all about their differences, the emptiness she often felt inside, the staggering loss of her family, and the bouts of grief. There was something about this day, this place, and the young president-elect that made her forget about her troubles. She studied the oversized white clapboard houses and wraparound porches, the white picket fences. She watched two little white girls chasing each other, a colored woman and man strolling alongside her, and a white man and two women walking ahead of her.

Nellie looked back at Beatrice. "Beatrice, you want to ride back with me and Mrs. Baker?"

When Beatrice turned to answer her, she froze.

There he was. . . . Their eyes locked, and they stared at each other as if the world had stopped and everyone around them had slipped away. Time slowed as they became engrossed in a knowing that only they understood. She searched his eyes, his face, felt something stir, something tender and warm. She had thought of him so often, and now there he was, standing inches from her. She watched him, watching her, and she saw something in his eyes, something almost imperceptible.

They stared at each other for what seemed like hours, though it had been only seconds. And then she did it—she couldn't help herself—she smiled. And as suddenly as the moment had come, it disappeared, muted by the sound of her hurried steps as she rushed to follow Nellie to the car.

23

Morris

M orris ignored the sidelong glances, the stares, and walked straight up to the house that he had visited more than eighteen years ago.

The woman who finally opened the door looked the same as he recalled, just more mature, wiser. The scent of home-made stew seeped into Morris's nostrils. Mrs. Baker dried her hands on her apron, eyed Morris suspiciously.

"Hello, ma'am. I'm Morris Sullivan. Do you remember me?" A rush of anxiety snaked up Morris's neck, bolstering his courage.

Mrs. Baker looked carefully at the white stranger, took her time trying to place his face. A long while passed before she seemed to remember him. "You that fellow that came to see my Beatrice round the time of the war?" she said, still not quite sure.

Morris nodded. "Yes, ma'am. It's been a long time."

Mrs. Baker's tone changed, became as expressionless as her face. "What do you want?"

"Ma'am, does Beatrice stay here? I know she's back in Roxbury now." He reminded her about Robert and the time he came to meet Beatrice at her home, and how they began to write to each other.

"Just before the war ended, she stopped writing. She never answered my last letter, and when I came home, I learned that she'd moved back to Mississippi, and I never heard from her again," Morris held Mrs. Baker's gaze. "Not until the other day, when I saw her at Hyannis Port."

Mrs. Baker looked into Morris's pinched face. "You ain't got no business in this part of town looking for my Beatrice. Beatrice don't need no trouble right now. She just lost her mother. She don't need to get strung along by some white man who don't mean her no good. Now, I suggest you go on back across town and let her alone."

"I can't leave her alone!" Morris said, his tone surprising them both. He lowered his voice. "I know what this must look like to you, and you're right. I got no business here. But I need to see her again. Please try to understand. I would never do anything to hurt Beatrice."

Mrs. Baker sized him up, softened by the genuine sadness on Morris's face. Suddenly, she turned and walked over to a secretary that fit perfectly in the modest vestibule. She opened the desk drawer, pulled a notepad from it, and scribbled something down. She ripped the page and held it out toward Morris.

"I reckon Beatrice is a grown woman now, and can make her own decisions about you."

Morris took the paper from her. "Thank you, ma'am," he said before he smiled and walked away.

The mere idea of seeing Beatrice again filled him with the same longing he'd felt during those quiet nights when he would lie awake thinking about her. He found himself growing uneasy, anxious, as he neared Beatrice's home. He had thought about Agnes and Emma every moment he thought of Beatrice, weaving an endless web of guilt. He loved his wife. But he had known for a long time that their love had grown into something more practical. His heart ached for Agnes, the way she often looked at him, a longing in her eyes. From the moment he returned home from the war, he had tried to pick up where he'd left off, being the attentive father to Emma, a loving husband to Agnes, making up for all the lost time. He couldn't help but love Agnes in his own way, and Agnes loved him, too, that he always knew. Their love had morphed into a comfortable fondness. But with each passing year, he found himself burrowing deeper and deeper into the past. He had tried so desperately to put the war behind him, to mend the brokenness between them. He'd often awake in the middle of the night, his body pulsing with the memories. And Agnes was there, always a grasp away, holding him, rocking him, helping him to free his mind of the bitter anguish, remnants of a time that left a scar on his consciousness.

But for all the pain war had brought him, it also led him to cross paths with Beatrice. As the years passed, he often thought of her, wondered where she was and what she was doing. Many times he found himself staring at young black women who stood across the aisle from him at the grocer's, or on the corner at the bus stop, or waiting a table at a local restaurant. Beatrice, her caramel-colored skin, her big, beautiful brown eyes, her smile, the way it brightened her face. He didn't quite understand his unmoving desire for her. Over the years, he had tried to put her out of his mind, but he could not. He just could not. He had often considered writing to her, had even searched for her home address. But he couldn't fetch the proper words, couldn't bring himself to do it. It just wouldn't be right, he had told himself every time the urge took hold of him, year after year after year.

Now, he made his way through the Roxbury neighborhood, eyeing the immaculate three-story brick duplexes, all similar in size and style. He drove slowly down the wide, tree-lined streets, squinting to read the numbers aligned perfectly against the brick exteriors. He slowed his car and parked it once he recognized the address that Mrs. Baker had given him. He stepped from the car and nodded at two colored women who sat on the front porch of an adjacent duplex opposite an alleyway. One, a round-faced, middle-aged woman with large, dark eyes, her hair wrapped in a scarf, stopped talking to the other, a stocky woman of equal size and shape. They both stared at him.

Morris recognized the name neatly displayed next to a bell: *Beatrice Dobbins*. He glanced coyly at the two women again, then rang the bell.

It took a minute before she answered the door. Then there she was.

Morris took in Beatrice's face, plain with no makeup. She looked the same, just a bit older, but still as beautiful as he remembered.

"Hello," Morris said, staring at her.

Beatrice stared at his blue eyes, his hair, shades lighter than she remembered. "Hello," she finally said.

"May I come in?"

Beatrice moved aside and silently led him up two flights of stairs and into her apartment—a large, charming living room nicely decorated with quaint furniture and beautiful curtains and coverings, everything in its proper place. Beatrice peered out the door and then shut it. "Oh, Lord. Gladys will have told the whole neighborhood a white man is in here. Should be a pair of eyes watching you from every window on the block when you leave." She let out a nervous laugh. "Please have a seat," she said, pointing to the sofa.

Morris took a seat and Beatrice sat on the opposite end, facing him.

"How have you been?" Morris said, nervous.

"I've been good. Things are so different since I came back here."

"When did you get back? I looked for you."

Beatrice seemed surprised. "A few months ago. I'm sorry I left without writing."

"Mrs. Baker told me where to find you. I hope you don't mind me showing up like this." Beatrice said nothing. "She told me about your mother. I'm sorry for your loss."

A fan whirred nearby, rattling his nerves. The moment seemed so probable and yet so impossible. Something about her still clutched him, made him feel things that he'd never felt before. He had always wondered if that was what being in love felt like. He looked fixedly at Beatrice, and he admired how beautiful she looked in the flickering light that shone from the window. Still so very beautiful, yet there was something strong and determined about her, too, something resolute. He reached out to take her hand, and this time she allowed her hand to fold into his, and when he squeezed it, he saw a soft smile cross her face, and he smiled, too.

"You got a nice place here. Really nice," he said, finally letting go of her hand.

"Thank you. It ain't much, but it's mine." Beatrice glanced shyly at him. "Was that your wife with you? At the rally?"

Morris held her eyes, nodded.

"She's very lovely."

Morris said nothing, just admired her home—the cozy sofa, the homemade pillows and floral curtains, a wall full of family photos. "You have a beautiful family. Is that Robert?" He pointed to a framed photo of a young Robert in his navy whites.

"Yes," Beatrice said.

Morris approached the photo and looked closely at the man who had saved his life. "He was even younger than I remembered." He looked down the row, taking in every detail of the other photos: one of Beatrice and Robert playing in front of a modest home, Robert no more than ten years old; one of Robert and Beatrice with an older couple, a family portrait; and finally one of Beatrice and her mother, from the looks of it a recent picture. "It's been so long, and there's not much I remember from that day. You know, the day he saved my life."

Beatrice took a step back, started to say something, but stopped herself. She glanced at him, watched how he had become so enamored with her family, the way he seemed to genuinely care. She noticed the gray strands of hair at his temples, the lines that etched his face.

"Why did you come here?" Beatrice said abruptly. "Why after all these years?"

Morris looked at her. "Because I've waited a long time for this day. I never stopped thinking about you. Because your letters meant so much to me. Had it not been for your letters, I don't think I would have gotten through it. When I came home, I searched for you but you had already left. I've lived with the pain of never seeing you again." He watched her shift in her seat, saw her eyes fill with anguish. "I know it's not right. I know that. But I can't put you out of my mind. I've never forgotten about you, Beatrice."

He drew her instantly into him, reminding her of the young woman she once was. He didn't know what he was doing, it was instinctive, just like the pull he had on her all those years ago.

They were silent for a time and Beatrice thought about the last letter she had received from him, and it made her feel sad that she had never written back to him. It haunted her all those years, wondering what would have been if she had stayed in Boston. But she understood then, as she did now, that nothing could ever come of it. She walked toward the door. "You need to leave," she said. "I need to get back to work and I got someplace I need to be soon."

Morris reluctantly followed her to the door, then reached inside his shirt pocket and pulled an envelope from it. "I wanted you to have this." He handed the envelope to her. "I wrote it my last night at Pearl Harbor."

"I can't take that."

"Beatrice, please take it. Please." Morris held the envelope out to her, bidding her to take it.

Beatrice studied him for a moment, then turned away. When she saw him at Hyannis Port, all the feelings had rushed back as if it had been only a day, not years, since she'd tried desperately to force him from her heart. She knew this was just as hard for him as it was for her. But she wanted him to just go away, to never show up at her door again, bringing back the past, all that had untangled itself like a wild weed, growing, festering, taking hold of her. But something pulled at her, something that could not be explained. Her expression tightened, and in an instant she found herself reaching to take the envelope from him. Without a second thought, he reached for her and embraced her. He buried his face in her neck and inhaled her sweet scent. She gave in to it instantly, seeming to have the same impulse—to finally hold each other. Morris held her as long as he dared, before the urge to kiss her became too much to resist, and he finally let her go and walked out the door.

Beatrice shut the door behind him, leaned weakly against the wall. When Morris held her, she felt something she had never felt with another man. In a matter of minutes, he had drawn her in. Much to her dismay, those same feelings she felt so long ago flooded her. It was just the way he looked at her, the way he spoke to her, the way he touched her. The fleeting years hadn't dimmed the memories. She stared at him from

her window, watched him turn around and look up at her. She
didn't turn away, or wave. She just stood there watching him,
watch her. Seeing him again made her feel uneven, an intensity that forced her to feel so very vulnerable. Being near him
was like a drug she knew she had to resist. She just had to, she
told herself, feeling like that young girl again.

24

Beatrice

"Ain't nothin' in no white man but trouble," Mrs. Baker said, looking squarely at Beatrice.

"He doesn't mean anything to me. We're just friends." Beatrice looked over at the envelope that lay on the table, the one that Morris gave her during his last visit. The one she never opened. She tried to conceal all the raw confusion that she'd felt since Morris showed up at her door. After he left, she had picked up the envelope at least four times, curious about what was inside. That night, she had lain awake, told herself that she hadn't behaved in a way that was improper, but still she felt guilty, as though she had prompted the chance encounter. In the weeks following, she couldn't stop thinking about him, and she questioned if her moving back to Boston had anything to do with him. Maybe, secretly, she had hoped that she would run into him; maybe she even yearned for it to happen. She kept telling herself that Morris was an illusion, a dream that had no place in reality, a childish fantasy. She had managed to keep her secret from Nellie and Mrs. Baker, convinced if they saw her they would be able to look right through all her guilt and shame.

Beatrice noticed how Mrs. Baker stared at the envelope, wondered what was going through her mind, the inexplicable mix of insight and wisdom. She imagined what Mrs. Baker *suspected*. Did she know about the letters? The number of times she'd thought about packing a suitcase and leaving Jackson with the hopes of seeing him again? Did she know that she loved him?

Mrs. Baker's eyes drifted toward Beatrice. They had that unmistakable serious expression she gave to her girls when she was about to dole out some advice. "You got so much life ahead of you, Beatrice. So much potential. Don't go messin' your life up over somethin' that don't mean you no good. Besides, he got a family, a wife. Why you want to get involved in somethin' like that? Ain't no tellin' what kind of mess that can stir up." Mrs. Baker took Beatrice's hand. "You like a daughter to me. From the moment I met you, I knew you were special. And later when I met your mama, I could tell that she was a fine woman, that she raised a fine daughter. Now, I'm sure this Morris Sullivan is a nice fellow. Ain't much of his kind that would care for you the way he do. But that's no reason to do something you will regret."

"There ain't nothing between us. We're just friends." Beatrice swallowed hard. She knew Mrs. Baker didn't believe her, that she could see the truth in her eyes. It had been prying away at her for some time now, ever since she saw him at Hyannis Port, and she knew the day would come when she'd see him again, and she'd been imagining what he'd say to her, and her own honest words—that she still read his letters; that after seeing him again she couldn't stop thinking about him; that she had never loved anyone the way she loved him. Words that were much different from the fibs she was now telling Mrs. Baker.

She looked over at Mrs. Baker, relieved that she couldn't read her mind.

"Well, I love you no matter what. And I'll always be here

for you. I just don't want you to get hurt," Mrs. Baker said.
She stood, picked up her purse. "I guess I better be gettin' back
home before Herbert come lookin' for me. I done said all that
I know how to say."

After Mrs. Baker left, Beatrice walked over to the table
and picked up the envelope again, looked at it as if she could
see right through it. For weeks, she'd felt pulled unwillingly,
almost forcibly, to it. Touching it made her chest ache. She
took a seat on the sofa, stared absently at the clay pot with a
small gardenia bush on the tabletop catching light from the
window. And after a while she felt a heaviness lull her, force
her to finally open the envelope and read the letter inside.

October 3, 1945

Dear Beatrice,

*It's been some time since I last heard from you. As
you have probably heard, the war is over and I will
finally return home. There's not a day that goes by that I
don't think of you. I've fallen in love with you, Beatrice.
And the strangest thing is that the love I have for you has
never undercut the love I have for my family. From the
day that Robert saved my life, it has been the one thing
that has made my devotion to the military and this war
all the more important to me. Every day, Robert gave
me inspiration, and you gave my life meaning. A kind
of meaning that others could never understand. But it is
not their approval that I seek, it is yours. Every hour is
another hour that brings me closer to someday seeing you
again, and that day will be very soon. Until then, I pray
that you and your family are well.*

Morris

At the close of the letter, there was a freshly written note, the vibrant ink lighting up against the dull words written so long ago.

> *Every Saturday at 2 P.M., I will be at Franklin Park.*
> *Near the zoo entrance off Columbus Road, there is a*
> *park bench that sits behind some trees by the pond. I will*
> *wait for you, hoping that someday you will find it in*
> *your heart to meet me.*

After all those years of wondering how he felt, if the feelings between them were real, there it was scrawled on a page in front of her. She held the letter, reading it time and again, her mind bombarded with a string of endless thoughts: What would have happened if he had sent the letter back then? Would things have been different? Did he still love her? There were way too many questions, and too few answers. Such an impossible situation.

For the next few weeks, she tended to her schoolwork and children, volunteered at New Hope Baptist Church, and spent quiet nights and weekends where she let herself be consumed with frivolous tasks to atone for the yearning that rose up inside her every Saturday at 2 P.M.

One Friday morning, as she sat in her class, she shuffled through the lessons for that day.

"All right, class. It's reading time. Please pull your *Curious George* books out and read the first five pages. We're going to have a quiz after recess." Beatrice watched the children's faces go somber as they pulled the books from their desks. She walked around the room, checking to ensure that every child was reading. She felt relieved after the class had settled down and she sat back at her desk, taking in the quiet. She glanced up at the wall clock: *11:40 A.M.* It had been a long week and she couldn't wait for the day to end so she could go home to a peaceful weekend.

As she tidied up her desk, an endless parade of thoughts crossed her mind—the chores she needed to tend to, what she would wear to church on Sunday, and what she would cook for Sunday dinner, a tradition that had passed down from her mother.

She needed to see Nellie, too. Since Mrs. Baker had come for a visit, she had convinced them that she had much work to catch up on. And she did—work she contrived to keep herself busy, to ignore that letter.

That letter.

Now in her purse. She'd put it there just the other day, telling herself that she just needed it out of her sight.

Her life was content. Since she'd come back to Boston, she'd managed to weave a quiet but satisfying life for herself. With the time she spent at school and at church, she barely had time to spare, or to fess up to the loneliness she sometimes felt. She had days when she questioned whether her decision not to marry Charles was the right one; or if she would ever know how it felt to really be in love, or be a mother. She'd had dates with a few men who Nellie and Mrs. Baker had tried to pair her up with, but they were all fruitless. "You refuse to give anybody a fair shake," Nellie had said to her after the last date fell through. "They're just not my type," she had retorted. Nellie had looked at her, and she knew in that moment the *look* meant something more, a thought she had not allowed herself to have.

"Miss Dobbins—what's—this—word?"

Beatrice looked up absentmindedly from her papers. "Let's see," she said, looking at the word that seven-year-old Cynthia pointed to.

"Oh, this little word? Let's spell it together. *G–O–O–D.*
Now you say it."

"*G–O–O–D,*" Cynthia delicately pronounced, turning
her beaming face up to Beatrice.

"Yes, GOOD." Beatrice smiled. "Now go on back to your
seat and say it with the whole sentence."

The smile on Beatrice's face stayed as she watched Cynthia
take her seat and puzzle her way through it.

"*Good,*" Beatrice whispered to herself.

That's what she'd been all her life. Good to her family.
Good to the church. Good to Nellie. Good to Mrs. Baker.
Good to Charles. Good in school. Good even to people she
didn't much care for. She was tired of being good.

She reached down into her bottom drawer and pulled
her purse from it. The letter was tucked neatly beneath the
pocket-sized Bible she kept with her.

She pulled the letter out, looked at it for a long while before she shoved it back in her purse.

The next morning, she awoke with a feeling of profound
longing. She paced the small apartment, absorbing herself in
mindless tasks and chores—scrubbing the kitchen floor on her
hands and knees until the checkered tile glistened in the early
morning light, washing the windows until her own reflection
became crystal clear, scouring the bathtub as if she were trying to scrub away her relentless thoughts. As the day neared
noon, she was so filled with anxiety that she filled the tub
with water and got in it.

"*I can't do it,*" Beatrice whispered to herself. She looked at
the light that reflected from the window, and she could tell
that it was going to be another warm day. She thought about
how to spend her time. There was nothing going on at church
today, and Nellie and her family were out of town.

I'll just go for a walk, she thought. *That's what I'll do. I'll walk.*

She lifted herself out of the tub and toweled off, and went to the small closet to retrieve a simple dress. She pulled her hair back, her face clean and beautiful. She grabbed her shoes, her coat, and her pocketbook.

Twenty minutes later she found herself walking up Washington Avenue and crossing Columbus, into Franklin Park. She took her time, watching the people—whole families, mothers and fathers, children—strolling the park, bicycling. Before long, she was on the trail that led to the zoo.

I can't do this, she thought again. *But what if he's there? What if in all these weeks, he showed up, waiting for me?*

She followed the trail along Columbus Avenue.

As she neared the zoo, she noticed a herd of people waiting in line. She looked for a park bench near a pond. She followed closely behind a white woman who pushed a child in a stroller, looking ahead, without seeming to look.

Turn around, Beatrice. Don't do this.

And just when she was about to turn, she saw him.

She grew perfectly still, watched him sitting there, waiting.

In an instant, she saw Morris turn and look at her. The park filled with silence, a perfect peace as she stood frozen, her heart pounding against her chest. People moved around her, unaware of the profound confusion, the yearning that washed over her. For an instant, she was tempted to turn around, be carried away by the same pull that beckoned her in the first place. But there he was waiting for her, urging her forward. Her heart was beating incessantly, a slow drum against her chest. For the first time, she could feel the instantaneous transformation in her body, her mind, the tempo of her heart. She knew that if she went to him, there would be no turning back. A breeze was on her face, quelling her fears, a quiet waft urging her. She wondered to herself, who was this man, sitting on the bench, waiting for her? What did she really know about him? His life? His family? Next to nothing, she surmised. But somehow, it didn't matter as she slowly made her way over to him and took a seat on the far end of the bench, a wedge of space between them.

25

The following Saturday, Beatrice arrived at the park fifteen minutes early, and was surprised to see Morris already waiting.

"You look very nice." Morris smiled at Beatrice, her hair pulled back off her face.

"You don't look so bad yourself." Beatrice's eyes swept over him, noticed how handsome he looked in his khaki slacks and white shirt, those blue eyes boring into hers. He was nearly thirty-eight now, and still he was incredibly charming. Already she could feel something come over her. She took the seat next to him on a secluded bench tucked away on a remote walking trail, a more discreet location where they had agreed to meet.

Suddenly, Morris reached for her hand. "You're so beautiful," he said, smiling at her.

Beatrice smiled back, at ease, no longer concerned by all the things that troubled her, as though he exuded some strange scent that made her forget about all that was wrong about being there.

"So do you come here often?" Beatrice said, feeling like a schoolgirl.

"I used to when my daughter was a little girl. She's all grown up now, in college."

"Emma—?"

"Yes, Emma." Morris was surprised that Beatrice still remembered her name. "She's our only daughter." There was a bend to his voice, something that Beatrice picked up on.

"What about you? Did you ever marry or have any children?"

Beatrice looked off toward a nest of ducks, watched three baby ducks following their mama to a nearby stream. She could never say to him what she could barely admit to herself: that she never married or had children or built a life with anyone because of *him*. She felt his eyes on her, felt him pressing into her thoughts. She looked toward the sky, watched the ducks take off, fly above the earth the same way she wanted to flee now. "No, I never married and I don't have any children. I guess marriage was never in the cards for me."

"Well, it's never too late, I guess. You're still young."

"I guess," she said, in the same tempered voice.

"What about your wife? Your family?" Beatrice asked, more a statement than a question.

Morris didn't want to talk about it. It was too complicated, and he didn't think she would understand. He turned and looked at her again. "I understand your concern." He grew quiet, studied her. "I love my wife, but we've grown apart. Ever since I came back from the war, things have been even worse between us. I know this isn't right, Beatrice. I know that." He did know that. It was unusual, he knew, that he could feel this way about a colored woman. Before meeting Beatrice, he had never paid much attention to women who weren't white, at least not in that way. But he found himself intrigued by Beatrice—her beauty, the color of her skin, her moxie. He had tried to put her out of his mind, convince himself that he needed to let her go. But he just could not.

Beatrice looked straight at him. "I have never done anything like this before, not even with someone of my own race. I care about you, I do, but it's not like we can just carry on topsy-turvy, like I ain't black and you ain't white, like you don't have a wife."

Morris held her gaze. "I know—but you have to trust me, Beatrice. I would never do anything to hurt you. Never."

Beatrice looked away. "Look, I need to get back. I have work to do," she said, and rushed off. She wanted to kick herself the whole way home for coming there again. What in the world was she thinking? Here she was a grown, levelheaded woman acting like a schoolgirl again. Morris made her feel out of control. She hadn't wanted this to happen, and still by the next Saturday, she found herself at the park again. They talked about everything—her family, his family, what it was like for her to be a teacher. They could hardly get a word in edgewise between them. So on the fourth Saturday, when Morris showed up and she wasn't there, he waited, wondering what happened to her.

B eatrice had a change of heart.
     She waited awhile before calling Nellie. "Can you come over? I really need to talk to you about something."

"Let me get Clifford to look after the girls. I'll be right there."

Beatrice paced the floor, trying to keep herself busy until she heard Nellie's knock. She let Nellie in and took a seat on the small chair across from her on the sofa. She looked off toward a potted ivy sitting on the windowsill, vibrant and voluminous. She took a deep breath, finally turned back to Nellie. "Morris Sullivan is back," she said.

Nellie looked fixedly at her as Beatrice told her everything—about the letters, the day in Hyannis Port, and finally their recent meetings in the park.

Nellie listened, surprised. She had known about the letters, but Beatrice had never told her about seeing him again.

"I'm just so confused," Beatrice said. "How could I let this happen? Mama would be so disappointed in me."

"Beatrice, you know that you're my best friend, like a sister to me. I would never say anything to you that I wouldn't say to myself." Nellie looked straight at Beatrice. "You know that, right?"

Beatrice looked away.

"You're gonna have to put a stop to this. You just can't let this go on. There's nothing but hurt waiting on the other side of this. And I don't want to see you get hurt. You done had enough hurt, and you certainly don't need Morris Sullivan. He's married! It's a sin to have relations with a man outside of marriage, let alone a white, married man!"

"I know that, Nellie! Don't you think I know that? That I've lost sleep over this, how ashamed I am!"

Nellie calmed her voice. "Look, I know Morris is a good person. I knew that from the very first letter he wrote to you. But you got to put this behind you and get on with your life. Maybe once you get past this, maybe you need to consider marrying Charles. You don't have to move back to Jackson. Charles really loves you, and I know he'd move here. Charles is a good man, Beatrice."

Beatrice looked blankly at Nellie. "I don't love Charles, Nellie. I love Morris. I have always loved him."

Nellie stared at Beatrice, surprised. They sat quiet for a long while.

"I need to be getting back to the girls. You gonna be all right?" Nellie reached for Beatrice's hand, held it.

"Yes, I'll be fine," Beatrice said, embarrassed to look at Nellie; and after Nellie left, she had made up her mind—she was never going back to that park again. She moped around the apartment, doing mindless tasks, scoured over papers she had graded, smiled when she came across the *A* on Cynthia's paper.

Curious George is good, Cynthia had written.

Beatrice touched the page, the words, paused her finger on *good.* Nellie was right, she thought. She needed to stop this, forget about Morris.

She wanted to be *good.*

She turned and looked over at the envelope that still lay on the coffee table, thought about the letter inside. She was going to get rid of it, put it out of her mind. She quickly grabbed the letter and was surprised when she heard a sudden knock at the door. She rushed to open it.

Morris stood at the door, scanned her face. Noticed that she'd been crying. "Are you okay? I worried when you didn't show up today."

"Why did you come here again?!"

Morris stepped inside, drew her close to him, then suddenly lifted her chin and kissed her. Very gently at first, on her cheeks, her eyelids, her nose. And when his lips found hers, Beatrice's body eased, and he kissed her. Softly at first, then passionately, their bodies coming together.

"I've been wanting to do that for a long time," he whispered, his eyes locked onto hers. He touched her face again. Gentle. Soft.

"No," she said, trying to wiggle from his embrace. "No, Morris."

The sky settled into dusk, flooding the room. "There are so many things I want to say to you. So many things I want to share," Morris said. He pulled her closer to him, touched her face again. "I love you, Beatrice." He reached for her, his hands gently caressing hers.

No man had ever touched Beatrice the way that Morris touched her. As if reading her mind, he leaned in slowly and kissed her again, tender and soft, and she kissed him back, found herself wanting to say *it* back to him as he kissed her, passionately on the lips first, then on her face, her neck, her shoulders. At one point, he stopped and kissed both of her eyes, pressed his finger to her lips when she tried to say something. Then he took her by the hand and led her to the bedroom, and when he began to peel away her clothes, she no longer cared about their differences.

Morris stood there for a moment, just taking her all in—her skin, her curves, her face. She felt his body move against hers. She hesitated, then, following his lead, she slowly unbuttoned his shirt, his skin so pale against her own. She moved her hands lovingly across his chest, nearly afraid to touch him, as though she had never touched a man. He grabbed her hand, kissed it, and then guided her to the bed and slowly made love to her with all the longing and passion that had haunted them for years. And afterward, they lay in each other's arms, as they each thought about what they knew to be true—they had crossed a delicate line.

26

Christmas 1962

"For you." Agnes handed the small box to Morris as they sat beneath the Christmas tree, garnished in white bulbs and ornaments. Swags of greenery and fresh white-bowed poinsettias graced the room. A lush wreath hung above the mantel, adorned with a lighted white garland and three stockings embroidered with their names—*Morris. Agnes. Emma.* A fire blazed in the fireplace, warming the room, and Agnes.

Morris looked at the box in total surprise, and opened it. "This is very nice," he said, staring at the ring inside. "What's the occasion?"

Agnes smiled at him with something tender and hopeful in her eyes. "Well, I know you lost your ring all those years ago at Pearl Harbor, and we could never afford to buy you a new one, and the years just went by so quickly that we just forgot about it," she said, a bit nervous and heady. "So, I found this ring in an antique shop and it looked almost identical to the one I gave you on our wedding day. And I know things haven't always been the best between us, and we've had some tough times through the years, but . . . I . . . I never stopped loving you. Never." Her eyes filled with tears; she wished for a moment that he understood what she was trying to say. "I love you, honey, and I want us to start over. I know that sounds silly, since we've been married for twenty-two years, but maybe we can try to make things better."

Morris stared at her, feeling numb, almost beyond bearing. Looking at her now reminded him of how very difficult it had been for her. He reached for Agnes, held her close to him, wishing he had the nerve to say more. "This is very thought-ful of you . . . thank you," he said, and gave her a chaste kiss on the cheek.

Agnes took the box from him, pulled the ring from it, and took his hand and placed it on his finger. "It fits perfectly. It looks like it was always meant to be there." She said it as though she was speaking about something else, and he smiled softly at her and gently put his hands over hers.

He took her in his arms then and cautiously kissed her. Suddenly, his mind faded to Beatrice, and he had to hold back his guilt. Beatrice was the first woman he had ever loved be-sides his wife, and the shame overwhelmed him as he held Agnes, but she understood none of it.

"Merry Christmas." Emma walked into the living room and smiled, pleased to see her parents embracing, something she hadn't seen in a long time. She joined them on the floor in the pajamas that her mother had given her as a gift the night before.

Agnes bashfully looked at Morris. "Honey, look what I got your father." She reached to hold out Morris's hand. "It's like the one I gave to him when we first got married."

"Oh, wow. That's so nice, Mom." Emma admired the ring on her father's hand, smiled at a thought. "You know what? Maybe you should get married again—you know, renew your vows? That would be so cool."

"Oh no, honey. We're already married. No need to go through all of that. I'm very happy that your mom even thought of the ring. That's good enough for me," Morris said.

"But, Dad, think about it. What if you and Mom renewed your vows? It could be something very small and Mom could just wear a nice dress. We can do it here, maybe on New Year's Eve. That would be different."

"It's actually not a bad idea," Agnes said, perking up. "I hadn't thought of it that way, and it would be nice to do something different to celebrate our anniversary. New Year's Eve would be a bit early for it, but that's okay."

"How about it, Dad? It would be nice to see you and Mom get married again, and I'll get to be there this time." Emma looked hopefully at her father.

"I don't know, honey. It just seems like an awful lot to take on in such a short amount of time. I know it would be special, but I like our vows the way they are now." He glanced over at Agnes, saw the disappointed look on her face.

Agnes tried to ignore the hesitation in his voice, her sense that something was wrong. "Well, I think it would be nice," she said, staring straight at Morris. "We can just do it at the New Year's Eve dinner that I've already planned with our family, so it won't be much work at all." She kept her eyes on Morris, oblivious to the strange look he now gave her.

"Now, honey, open the gift your father and I got for you." Agnes reached to grab a large box from beneath the tree and handed it to Emma.

The next morning, Agnes rose before dawn, and made her way slowly around the dark room, trying not to wake Morris. She quickly showered and dressed and went downstairs. She started a pot of coffee, sliced a grapefruit and some toast, and sat at the table, listening to the coffee percolate. She had tossed and turned most of the night, thinking of renewing their vows. At first, the thought seemed farfetched, but now she realized that this was just what she and Morris needed.

She thought about the way Morris's face had changed in some way she could not define. Something in his eyes seemed to shift as Emma spoke about it. For a moment she thought he wanted to bolt from the room, and she felt utterly weightless, as though the floor had dropped from beneath her. But she did not let Emma see that—just as she had never let her see any of it through the years. They had spent the morning together, the three of them, opening gifts and listening to Emma's college stories. At one point, she had looked over at Morris and watched the way his face lit up at the gift that Emma had given him, and in that very moment, she had made up her mind with a sudden determination. She was still very much in love with her husband.

She finished her breakfast and sauntered around the house, aimlessly putting things back in their proper place. The living room had brightened with the morning light, and as she entered it again, she looked over and saw the ring box that she had given to Morris, still under the tree.

She sat on the sofa and opened the empty box, enamored with it. She had never imagined that they could start over again, but now she could see that things could be different. She thought back to when they first met, how young and naïve they were then. It had not been the marriage that she had fantasized about as a young girl—such happy and sad times, in and out of love, the devotion they shared for Emma.

And now their lives were at a crossroads.

As if to echo her thoughts, Morris suddenly appeared. "You're up early. Did you sleep all right?"

Agnes looked up at him. Her face did not reveal what her impulsive voice said of its own volition. "Do you *want* a new beginning? I mean to renew our vows?" she asked, almost on the brink of breaking.

Morris seemed less shaken by the idea than he had been the day before. "Honey, what difference is it going to make? Why not just let things stay the way they are?"

Since the day Emma had left for college, Agnes had been unable to control the tears. She felt so very vulnerable, a loneliness that often overtook her. "I just want things to work out better between us. I know it's not always been easy, but I never stopped loving you."

"Oh, honey." Morris reached for her, held her against him, her head just beneath his chin. "Honey, I know it's been tough, but things will get better. Now, you got to stop all this crying and talk about renewing vows. Things are just fine." He spoke softly, as though it might calm her mood. Agnes settled into his arms as he rubbed her back, felt her nod into his shoulder. "I tell you what." He pulled back away from her. "Let's do something fun today. Remember how we used to go ice-skating at Frog Pond? Let's go ice-skating today. Just you and me. How about it?"

Agnes wiped her tears. "Okay," she said, a little embarrassed.

"Good. I'm going to make you my famous pancakes, and then we're going to go ice-skating. All right?"

Agnes's whole face smiled softly, still wet with tears. "Okay."

Morris held out his hand for her to take, and for a moment, a feeling passed through her, a familiarity of something she had known long ago. He led her into the kitchen, and she sat watching him with a deep sense of longing and love, and promised herself that things would get better between them, that she would never doubt him again, that she trusted him.

27

Beatrice

"You stinkin' niggah!"

Beatrice kept her face down, her eyes glued to a speck of nothingness on the bare ground, momentarily detached from the words, angry words, hateful words. The boys, she guessed, could be no more than thirteen. Three of them. Two much taller than her and one the size of Nellie's youngest girl, only eleven years old. They surrounded her, their pale faces twisted and ugly.

"Say it, niggah! He did it! Didn't he? Didn't he?!" the tallest boy yelled.

"My father told me that niggahs deserve to be strung up in a tree and tortured," the other boy said.

"What if we did to you what he did to her? Would you like that? Ha? Would you, niggah?" said the smallest one.

Beatrice willed herself not to move, not to lash out at them the way they were lashing out at her. There was nothing to gain by getting herself in trouble. It seemed the entire colored race, from the South End to Roxbury, had been in trouble since James Earl Wilkinson, a colored man, decided one rainy evening to attack a white woman and rape her.

"I said say it. You niggah! He did it! Didn't he?"

Beatrice stood still, petrified by the way they gawked at her, their hateful eyes sharpened by the overhead lamp that emitted just enough light to brighten the dark park's path. There seemed to be no one around. Just she and the three boys and their hatred. The same park where, not even ten minutes ago, she had left Morris. They had met in their usual spot, beyond the park's trail, hidden behind a spread of trees—their secluded place—and had been since the first time Morris made love to her. She now regretted letting it happen. But it was what had sealed their love for each other, and they shared it as often as Morris was able to come to her apartment. First, he'd come every Saturday, but that began to stir talk about why a white man was showing up so often at Beatrice's place. Her next-door neighbor Gladys had even questioned her about it one day. But Beatrice had brushed it off, had told Gladys that Morris was a very close friend of her brother, Robert, who'd died in the war. That explanation seemed to quiet the whispers and the stares, but not enough to lighten Beatrice's own fears of anyone ever finding out.

Beatrice had noticed the three boys sitting on a nearby bench, off the trail from where she and Morris met. She knew there would be trouble.

"Hey, niggah!" one of them had shouted, and Beatrice had picked up her pace when she turned and saw that they were following her.

"Hey, niggah!" They kept up behind her.

Beatrice walked quickly, nearly sprinted down the path, watching for anyone who might take notice. But it seemed the park was empty. At first she thought they were men—they seemed huge as they lurked closely behind her. She would not come to know they were only boys until they surrounded her. Boys, no less, who were just as dangerous during these shifting times. Tension between coloreds and whites had steepened, widened, as word spread that the police had arrested

James Earl Wilkinson for raping the young white mother of three. And when her husband appeared on the evening news, crying and promising no mercy for whoever did this to his young wife, the mother of his children, it heightened an already delicate situation. Every colored man, whether he fit the description or not, was stopped, often beaten, and taken into custody.

And now the boys were gawking at her, taunting her. Suddenly, the middle boy picked up a long branch and jabbed it at her arms and legs, the ragged edges poking into her flesh.

"I said say it! Say it, niggah!"

Beatrice panted, her face swaying between agony and anger, the tears now flowing. "I don't know if he did it! I don't know!"

"You do know! Don't you! All you niggahs know when you've done something wrong. You think you can just move to this town and do whatever you want?" the oldest boy said. Then he hocked a swirl of saliva and spit it in her face, the slime mixing with her tears.

"Hey! . . . Hey!" A man suddenly appeared out of nowhere, rushing to Beatrice's rescue.

The boys scattered.

"Are you all right? Are you okay?"

Beatrice shrugged, wiped the slime from her face. "Yes, I'm fine," she said, pulling away from the man's reach.

"Beatrice, it's me. Morris."

Beatrice looked at the man for the first time. It took a while before she recognized him.

Morris took her into his arms.

"I'm so sorry. I'm really sorry. I should have never let you walk alone this late. I thought about it after you left, and I turned around to catch up to you. I would have never forgiven myself if they'd hurt you," Morris held her, rocked her, and let her cry. He glanced around the park, realizing the enormous risk they had been taking.

Beatrice lifted her head from his shoulder. Even in the dimmed light, she saw that he looked as anguished as she. A feeling of profound agony, of shame, suddenly washed over her. She pulled away from Morris, the tears still streaked on her face. "This is not right," she said, backing away. "This is not right! I can't do this!"

Morris stared at her, momentarily confused. "What do you mean? What's not right?"

"This!" Beatrice said. "Us!"

They stood facing each other, the park going still.

"I love you," Morris persisted. "I don't care what's going on. I need you."

"You need me? How can you need me when they hate me so much?"

"I don't care what they hate. They are ignorant!"

Beatrice made her face serious. "What do you see when you see me?" she said.

Morris could hear the anger in her voice, the way it quivered in her throat. "I see you, Beatrice. I see the woman I fell in love with."

"No. You can't see me. Not me. You see what they see."

"No, Beatrice. I will never see you that way. Never!" Morris reached for her.

Beatrice shrank back, broadening the gap between them. "No!" she said, shaking her head. "No, this has gone on for too long already. It's not right! It's just not right!" She held his stare.

"Beatrice, I know how you must feel. What they did to you was wrong, but I love you. You know that. Please give us a chance."

Beatrice's face closed into a grimace. "Give us a chance?! You think I didn't notice that ring on your finger! How dare you treat me like some whore, thinking you can just glide between me and your wife! I tried to ignore it, told myself that it didn't matter. That I know you love me. Hell, what's the point in complaining about it now. You were married when I met you, and you're still married!"

"It's just something Agnes gave me for Christmas. I wanted to tell you!"

"You had plenty of opportunities to tell me. You just thought you were going to come around and flaunt it in my face." Beatrice abruptly stopped talking, and just stood there looking at him. "At least with those boys, I know how they feel . . . I know who they are, and what they think. But you!" She hesitated, tears burning her eyes. "You say one thing and do another. You don't love me. You love the idea of me. You love that I'm something different. How dare you treat me like a rug you can just wipe your feet off on? I want you out of my life! Just leave me the hell alone!"

She backed away from him then.

Morris started to go after her, but then stopped himself. He never intended to hurt her, but deep inside he'd known that it would come to this—how could it not? But most of all, he was sorry for how those boys treated her, and he despised them for it. But Beatrice was wrong about one thing. He *did* love her. He loved her more than words could define. At times, he wanted to tell her that yes, he was still with Agnes, that it was complicated and their marriage had morphed into a union of convenience and contentment, nothing more or less; and no matter how wrong their relationship seemed, he was deeply in love with *her*. He wanted so much to tell her those things, but he knew she would never understand. He had caused her so much pain, and had expected her to make such huge sacrifices. He had wanted her more than anything, loved her more than he had ever dared. It was a secret he'd been carrying for a long time, and now he stood there watching her walk away, unable to bear the thought of ever losing her again.

28

Agnes

Agnes drove through the city, past the tree-lined streets, and straight to Boston Children's Hospital. Just yesterday, she had seen an ad in the paper for a nursing assistant while she was having her morning coffee; then, impulsively, she had called, and the nice lady who answered told her to come in right away. She had combed her closet for the perfect dress and she had gone, not thinking twice about it. She had been contemplating going back to work ever since Emma left for college. She had not worked since the time she'd volunteered at Children's Hospital when Emma was in middle school. Sitting there, in a gray-and-white scoop-neck dress with a pleated skirt, clutching her white purse in her lap, she realized just how much she wanted the job, needed it. Especially after the nice lady complimented her on how well put together she seemed. "I can tell you take great care in everything you do," she had said to Agnes. Agnes liked her, and she could tell that the lady had liked her, too.

"The job doesn't pay much, and it's entry level—you'll have to work your way up—but the job is yours if you want it." Agnes refrained from jumping from her seat. She shook the lady's hand and walked out of the hospital feeling pleased with herself.

Now she drove slowly around the hospital's campus, remembering the satisfaction she'd felt just yesterday when she sat across from the hiring manager, imagining what it would be like to earn her own living, to have her own *life*. The thought of it made her heady. She felt disconnected, untroubled even, about what Morris and Emma would think. For the past year, that yearning had sprung up inside her like a dandelion, pulled from the soft earth, a brisk breeze sprouting its seeds, flourishing them gently into the air. That nice lady was right, she did take great care in everything she did—the same care that she had taken for more than twenty years being faithful to her husband, fulfilling his every need, raising their daughter. Morris and Emma both had their lives—he had his career and passion for building ships, and Emma was studying to be a teacher. She longed for something more, too.

Agnes sat there for a while, parked in the corner of the lot, just staring at the white building. She watched a young nurse exit from her car and make her way up the walking path, toward the double doors, her pocketbook slung over her shoulder, gliding as though her life had meaning. Agnes closed her eyes and imagined that was her—beyond her shallow life at home, beyond the label that had been stamped on her for as long as she could remember. She craved a new label now. *Me*—it whispered to her soul. *Me*. A life, a meaning, above and beyond the thankless existence of wife and mother.

With her eyes still closed, she could hear the chatter of passersby, an exuberance that she had not been privy to in a long, long time. The doctors in their white coats, nurses in their white uniforms and hats, patients coming and going, everyone scattered; a world, moving swiftly without her.

She drew into herself, not thinking or caring how long she had been sitting there before she pulled slowly out of the parking lot and drove steadily across town. As she entered the campus, the traffic drew to a near crawl with the scurry of students and faculty. She parked in the visitors lot and made her way to Emma's dorm. As she neared the girls' dormitory, she heard a swelling of voices, energetic and enlivened, full of vitality that was akin to a joy bursting inside her. When she entered the redbrick building, scents of perfume and jubilance filled the air, and brought back memories of the time when she was a young girl.

Agnes took the elevator to the third floor, and walked confidently to Emma's room. It wasn't until she knocked that she wondered if Emma would be there, since she had not called. A young girl answered.

"I'm sorry. Did I get Emma's room number wrong? Is she here? Emma Sullivan?"

"Mrs. Sullivan, hi," the young girl said, recognizing Agnes from the photos that Emma kept on her desk. "Emma has class, but she should be back any minute now. I'm her new roommate, Kay. I was just about to leave for class, but you're welcome to wait for her here if you like."

"I see," Agnes said, a little embarrassed that she hadn't called. "Sure. I'd like to wait if you don't mind. Emma's not expecting me."

"I'm sure she wouldn't mind."

Agnes stepped inside and took a seat at Emma's desk. Kay looked at her awkwardly. "I have to go to class. You don't mind waiting alone, do you?"

"Of course not. You go. I'll be fine."

"All right, then. It was nice meeting you."

"You too, honey. Maybe you can come for a visit sometime with Emma. We'd love to have you."

Kay waved good-bye, and after she left, Agnes found herself glancing around, taking notice of Emma's things—the family photos that sat atop a shelf above her desk, the teddy bear she had given Emma when she was six, the watch that she and Morris had given her as a high school graduation gift.

She walked over to the shelf and picked up a framed photo of Emma, Morris, and her at Emma's graduation. She smiled, thought about how very quickly time had passed. Already Emma was a young woman with her own life, her own mind, her own things. How was it possible that she grew up so fast? One day, Agnes was a young mother, catering to Emma's every need, coveting her sacred role. There wasn't a day that went by that she didn't think of Emma first, her days wrapped into a seamless jumble of activities—ballet classes, cheerleading practice, soccer games, homework. Their lives moved at such a pace that she rarely had time to notice that Emma had been growing an inch every six months, her body blossoming into a woman's.

Agnes studied the graduation photo, wondering about her life without Emma.

"Mom? What are you doing here?"

Agnes turned around to a surprised Emma standing in the door. "Hi, honey. I should have called, but I needed to see you."

"It's fine, Mom. I'm just surprised to see you here. Have you been waiting long?"

Agnes smiled at Emma in a pleated skirt and white blouse, the knit sweater that hung loosely around her shoulders. She missed her daughter terribly. "No, honey, I haven't been waiting long. Kay let me in. She's really nice. I like her."

"Me, too." A quiet moment passed between them. "Did you want to grab something to eat, maybe a burger or something?"

"Oh no, honey. I'm not going to be staying long. I just . . ." Agnes paused, suddenly embarrassed about the reason she had come. "Well, I just wanted to talk to you about something."

"What's wrong? Did something happen between you and Dad?"

"No . . . no, honey. Everything's fine. Well, kind of. I

mean. . . . Well . . ." Agnes saw the concerned look on Emma's face. "Well, it's nothing, really. I mean, I've been thinking about going back to the hospital lately, especially since you left for college. And although things are good between me and your father, well, he has his life, and you're gone, and I need something to do with my time. I found a job."

"Mom, that's great! I think that's good news."

"Really, honey? I mean, you don't think your dad would mind?"

"Of course not, Mom. You've been taking care of me and Dad all my life. You need to do something for yourself now. Dad will understand. Why wouldn't he?"

Agnes felt suddenly foolish. Why *would* Morris mind her going back to work? And why had she come to seek Emma's approval, too? "You're right, honey. I don't know what I was thinking. I guess I've spent my life taking care of you and your dad for so long, sometimes I don't know what to do with myself."

"Mom, you deserve to be happy, too. Me and Dad will be fine. You gotta stop worrying about us so much."

"I know, honey." Agnes touched Emma's hair the way she did, since Emma was a little girl.

"You sure you don't want to grab a burger or something? I can skip class."

"No, honey. I need to get going. Your dad will be home soon."

Emma walked her mother back across campus to her car.

"Call soon," Agnes said before she got back in her car and drove home, arriving just shy of the time that Morris was expected. She changed quickly into a red lace-bow dress, let her hair down, and dabbed on red lipstick, then rushed to the kitchen and pulled two sirloin steaks from the fridge. Emma was right, she thought. She deserved to be happy, too. Her news was a cause for celebration. After she put the steaks in the broiler, she went into the living room and pulled Frank Sinatra's "Come Fly with Me" from the stereo console, dusted it off, and placed it on the spinner. She let the music gently move through her in waves, soothe her, in a way that nothing else could. She closed her eyes and danced around the room, letting Frank Sinatra take her to another place. A deep sense of contentment rose up in her, so forceful, woven through all the timeless moments that she felt invisible. She would never feel invisible again. Bright darkness meshed against her closed lids as she danced, and danced, and danced; and when the music stopped, she went to the console and lifted the needle to place it on the vinyl again. This time, she turned up the volume and made her way back into the kitchen and pulled the greens and tomatoes and onions from the refrigerator and chopped a salad. The steaks would be ready soon, medium rare, the way Morris liked them.

She sauntered into the dining room and pulled the linen and china from the china cabinet. Usually, the linen and china were reserved for special occasions. Tonight was an exception.

Moments later, she removed the perfectly cooked steaks from the broiler and laid them enticingly on a platter, and then tossed the salad once more and warmed two rolls. She pulled out a bottle of expensive French red wine, a gift one of their neighbors had given them last Christmas. Then she dressed the table with the food and wine and went back into the living room to start the record again. This time, she sat on the sofa and closed her eyes, let the music move through her again as she waited for Morris.

After the record played for the fifth time, she realized the time—6:30 P.M. Usually Morris would be home by now, and he hadn't called. She stood and went to the console and removed the record from the spinner. She looked out the win-

dow, hoping to see Morris's car. But she did not. And she stood
there, waiting and watching, until finally, she made her way
back into the dining room and poured herself a glass of wine.

Darkness spread throughout the house, so very quiet. She
carried her glass and the wine bottle into the living room, set
the bottle on the table next to her chair, and sipped the wine,
waited. She had always been waiting, she thought, the wine
making her feel warm inside. Waiting to pick Emma up from
school. Waiting to take Emma to her activities. Waiting to
cook dinner every night. Waiting for Morris to come home.
Waiting. Waiting. Waiting.

She was so damn tired of waiting.

An hour later, the bottle was nearly empty, and she made
her way to the dining room, unsteady.

She sat at the dining table and picked at the steak, at the
curled salad. She grabbed a tomato, forced it down. It felt bland
against her tongue, along with the steak, and she reached for
her glass again, a bit pleased with herself for feeling so tipsy,
the wine almost gone.

Suddenly, she pushed the chair back away from the table,
and stacked the dishes, the salad bowl, and wineglasses onto
the platter. She carefully carried the pile into the kitchen,
opened the trash can, and scraped everything into it. Then she
made her way upstairs to their bedroom, undressed, and lay
down.

Where is he? she wondered. Why hadn't he at least called?
She lay in the dark, her back to the window, trying to block
out the car headlights and sounds. The wine now seemed to
course through her, heating every limb in her body. She lay
there stilling herself against her own dangerous thoughts,
watching the clock: 9:30 P.M.

She sat up, struggled to clear her head, and looked over at
the window again; and this time, when she heard a car door

slam, and footsteps against the cobblestone, she knew it was
Morris. She quickly lay back down, turned her back to the
door, and pretended to sleep.

She listened to him moving around in the kitchen, and
then making his way to their bedroom. When he opened the
door, she didn't flinch. She felt him take a seat on the edge of
the bed and remove his shoes and his shirt.

"I made us a special dinner because I wanted to share some
good news with you," she said, her back still to him. She felt
him turn toward her.

"Oh, honey, I'm sorry. I had to stay at work late tonight.
One of our guys didn't show up."

"Why didn't you call? You could have called."

She heard him take a deep breath. "I know. I just forgot.
Things have been really hectic there lately. I know I should
have called. I'm sorry." He reached over to touch her, and he
felt her grow still with hurt. "What's the news you wanted to
share? I'd like to still hear about it."

Agnes started to sob. "I found a job at the hospital. Emma
has her own life now. You have your work, and now I want
to do something for myself." The tears came out of nowhere.

"That's great, honey. I think that's a good idea. I'm really
proud of you." He reached over, touched her, then made his
way into the bathroom. And when he returned, they lay opposite each other, an island of silence in the dark, quiet room, the
streetlight beaming within.

29

Emma

Emma had been home visiting for two weeks since she had graduated from college.

She had noticed how distant her parents had become, one minute appearing to be very content and the next as different as night and day. It was not the lack of affection between them that bothered her. They'd never been openly affectionate for as long as she could remember. It was the way her mother catered to her father, like a child peddling for attention. Then, just last week she overheard her parents in their bedroom arguing, and when she watched her father storm from the room, she had knocked on her mother's door and had found Agnes lying in bed, sobbing. She sat on the bed next her and touched her back lightly. "Mom, are you okay?"

Agnes didn't respond.

"Mom, please tell me what's wrong," she pressed.

Agnes lay there, her back to Emma, saying nothing, and Emma thought about a similar time not so long ago when she'd found her mother on the living room floor, her father's personal things discarded around her. They had never talked about it, and her mother had pretended nothing happened.

Now Emma quickly showered and dressed, and went downstairs. Her father was sitting in the living room reading the morning paper. The kitchen had already been cleaned and a plate lay wrapped on the counter. She grabbed a glass of milk and took it with her into the living room.

"Your mother made you breakfast," Morris said.

"I know. Where is she?" Emma took a seat on the sofa across from him.

"She went to the store to pick up dinner." Morris looked at his daughter. Emma's hair was pulled up, strands of it falling to her face. He could not believe that his daughter had graduated, sitting across from him with such poise. He had observed this about her ever since she was a little girl. She was so young, yet there was something settled about her, an uncanny wisdom. Morris had noticed it when Emma was just six years old, the way she wove together her thoughts, so observant. Though Emma favored her mother, in ways she was so much like him. So acute, paying attention to the slightest details, the way things came together.

"You're becoming more and more beautiful every time I see you," Morris said, his heart warming.

Emma smiled. The room seemed to dim, framed picture-perfect with just the two of them, time they rarely spent alone.

"So, tell me about this new fellow of yours? Is he good to you?" Morris closed the paper.

Emma blushed, thought about the day she'd first met Johnny, in their history class. He had raised his hand when the professor asked the class to share their thoughts about World War II and the Pearl Harbor attack. It was Johnny who had spoken up first, sharing how his father had served on the USS *Arizona,* had been one of the many who had perished. She sat three rows away from him, a sadness filling her as she thought of her own father. Later, she would work up the nerve to approach him, and they would spend the next four hours talking, sitting alone, oblivious to everyone around them.

Johnny worshipped her, and he would do anything to

make her happy. And she was, and everyone knew it, including her parents. She had told them about Johnny the last time she'd come home. Her mother beamed and reminisced about the time she'd met her father, and how very much in love they were. Emma had smiled at her, listening as she watched her mother's eyes fill with tears.

"Johnny's very special, Dad. I really like him. You'll like him, too," Emma said now.

Morris met his daughter's eyes, ashamed that he could not share the same fondness about him and her mother.

"I'm sure he's a fine fellow. I can't wait to meet him."

Emma knew her father was longing to say more, but could not.

"Dad . . ." Emma hesitated for a moment. "You never really shared much about your past life, you know, about your life at Pearl Harbor. Johnny's dad was there the same time that you were. Johnny said he served on the USS *Arizona,* and he was one of the men who didn't make it off the ship. It's still very hard for Johnny to talk about it. He was just a baby when it happened so he never really got to know his father, and I know if it was hard for him, it had to be hard for you, too. Why don't you ever talk about it?"

Emma's words darted through Morris like an electric current, reigniting memories. He was at the point of saying something, but then stopped. He wanted to tell her everything, the things that he had seen, how terrible it all was, but he could not.

Emma sensed her father clamming up, as if she had pricked open a course shell. The discomfort was as visible on his face as the way his eyes lit up when she first walked into the room.

"Dad, I know it may be hard to talk about it, but I just want to know. You've never really opened up about it, and I can sense that it still bothers you. Please, Daddy, talk to me."

Morris looked at her, frowned. "Honey, I don't want you to worry about the past. It's behind me now. There's no need in talking about it. I'm fine. Your mother's fine. We're doing fine."

"No, Dad! You're not fine, and Mom's not happy! That's why she took that job, because she was feeling so unhappy. All she's ever done was cater to us, Dad. She's never had her own life, and now she's so sad. And you, Dad! You won't talk about what happened to you at Pearl Harbor, how it changed you. You think I don't hear you at night sometimes? Mom trying to calm you down? You think I don't know, Dad? I know. I've always known. So why won't you admit it and stop pretending like everything's okay with you and Mom?" Emma looked fixedly at her father.

She understood well enough why he did not want to talk about it, and she didn't want to stir the memories. But she had no choice. When she was a little girl, she thought her father could fix anything—the chain on her bicycle, the hinge that fell off her dollhouse, or the piece that broke on her baby doll crib. Now she wanted him to fix *them*.

"Honey, why are you upsetting yourself like this?" Morris still saw his little girl in Emma's sad eyes, so he could never tell her the truth, that he and her mother had not been happy for a long time, a very long time; that he loved another woman. The truth would crush the very soul of Agnes. Instead, it was his soul that had been crushed—especially since the last time he'd seen Beatrice, months ago at the park, when he rescued her from those terrible, terrible boys, and he had tried to convince her that he loved her, that he would always love her, no matter what others thought. But that wasn't enough. Not enough to ward off a senseless world that made their love a burden. He had gone to the park every Saturday at the same time, hoping that she would show. But she did not. And after several more weeks passed, and he could bear it no longer, he had gone to her apartment, and when she opened the door to let him in, he had reached for her, and held her, and he had told her that he would never let anyone *ever* hurt her again. *I love you more than you could ever know,* he had said to her. And he could tell by the way she looked at him, the way she settled into his arms, that she believed him.

At some point, he stood and walked over to the mantel, thought about how he had woken up every day for the last twenty-plus years ready to walk away, about the secret that had worked its way through their marriage like an old vine, growing and twisting and tangling the truth.

Morris's eyes met Emma's. "Your mother has been troubled for a long time," he finally said. The tension in his voice relaxed, and he tried to balance his words. "Things have been difficult for her."

Yes, Emma knew. She had known for a long time. Ever since she was a small child. Often, she wondered if something had happened between her parents, something that they never told. Curious, Emma had asked her mother one day, and her mother had reminded her about her brother, born and gone in six days' time. "He was beautiful." Agnes had smiled through tears, then she kissed Emma on the cheek and walked unsteadily back to the kitchen.

Emma looked at her father again and a revelation materialized in her mind, something she had always wanted to know.

"Dad, when you married Mom, did you do it because you really loved her, or because she was pregnant with me?"

Morris stopped and looked at her, surprised. "I did it because I loved her. For us both."

Emma looked off toward the fireplace; a small flux whirled in the pit of her stomach. Something in the way he said it made her uneasy. They sat there for a time not saying anything until they heard the front door open, and Agnes making her way into the living room.

"The market was so crowded today. It took nearly an hour just to get through the checkout line. I almost forgot where I parked the car I was in there so long. And with all that time that I spent there, I forgot to grab the brown sugar to make the chocolate chip cookies you like, Emma, and . . ." Agnes stopped suddenly and noticed Morris and Emma just sitting there, saying nothing. "Are you two okay? You look like you just saw a ghost."

Morris rushed to help her. "Let me take those bags."

Agnes noticed Emma's face. "Honey, what's wrong? Are you okay? Is it Johnny?"

Emma straightened up. "I'm fine, Mom," she said, breaking into a soft smile.

"Good. I'm going to get dinner started. I'm making your dad's favorite, pot roast. Why don't you help me?" she said, rushing off into the kitchen.

"Okay, Mom," Emma said, and then followed her mother into the kitchen.

30

February 1963

Beatrice slumped at the toilet, her stomach knotted with the same nausea that crept up every morning. She lay on the floor, allowed the cool tiles to steady her before she made her way back to the kitchen and forced down some tea and turpentine, a tasteless concoction her mother had given her as a child. But no tea, no turpentine, none of her mama's old remedies could ease the sickness that consumed her.

After a time, she took a warm shower and quickly dressed. She was late for Sunday brunch at Mrs. Baker's house with Nellie's family. It had been weeks since she'd seen them. Her life had turned into something she could no longer recognize. The thought of carrying a white man's baby frightened her beyond anything she had ever known.

Before long, the days had drifted into weeks and then months, and now she wore loose-fitting clothes to conceal the small bulge. Even today, she had put on a baggy dress to draw attention away from it. But no sooner had she arrived at Mrs. Baker's house and took off her coat than Nellie cornered her.

"After carrying three babies, don't much get by me," Nellie whispered.

Beatrice turned away, and pulled the china from the cabinet, ignoring Nellie.

"I noticed you ain't been comin' round much lately and

every time I see you in church, you quick to avoid me. I'm your best friend, Beatrice. Talk to me."

Beatrice eyed Nellie cautiously. "Wh-What are you talking about?"

"Beatrice, you can't hide it much longer."

"Hide what, Nellie? I don't know what you're talking about." Beatrice brushed past Nellie to set the table.

Nellie followed her and glanced in the living room at the others, careful to keep her voice low. "I know, Beatrice! So you might as well tell me."

Beatrice felt the tears, fear welled up inside her. "Oh God, Nellie. What am I gonna do?"

Nellie looked at her. "I'm gonna stop by your place tomorrow after school so we can talk," she whispered, then went to tend to their supper before anyone else noticed them.

The moment Nellie stepped inside Beatrice's apartment the next day, Beatrice broke down, flooded with shame—humiliating, inescapable shame.

"You should have come to me, Beatrice. I'm your best friend, your sister."

Beatrice tried to speak, but she could not. She had even gone to see Pastor Gilbert, ready to confess it all, but as soon as she set eyes on him, she felt disgraced. "I just wanted to tell you that I ain't been feeling so well, that's why I ain't been coming to church much, Pastor," she had said. And the moment she left, she felt terrible about fibbing to the pastor, and in church of all places. Even Mrs. Baker had come to her apartment eager to figure out why she hadn't shown up for Sunday dinner for a while. "It's that Morris Sullivan, ain't it?" Mrs. Baker had said when Beatrice opened the door, wasting no time. Beatrice denied it, told her the same tall tale she'd told Pastor Gilbert. She was relieved she didn't have to plant another tale with Nellie.

She told Nellie everything, and when she was done, she felt a boulder lift from her spirit.

"Does Morris know?" Nellie asked.

Beatrice shook her head. "No. Nobody knows but you."

They sat quietly for a moment, Nellie taking it all in.

"You know you're gonna have to tell him, Beatrice. You can't face this alone. He needs to know."

The thought of telling him sickened Beatrice. She thought about the last time she'd seen Morris. "I can't, Nellie."

"But you have to, Beatrice! You can't do this on your own."

"What's it going to change?! He's got a family! And he's a white man, Nellie! A white man!" she cried at the shame of it.

Nellie took Beatrice's hand. "I know how you must feel. But you can't do this alone. Morris needs to know. He would want to know."

"The last time when I saw Morris in the park, there were these white boys, three of them," she said, her face drawn into the memory. "They . . . they said some awful things to me, and when I saw Morris afterward, for the first time, I looked at him. I mean really looked at him, Nellie, and I saw those boys. How could I have allowed this to happen? How could I?"

"Beatrice, don't do this to yourself! Morris is not like them. You know that."

"Then how come every time I think of him I feel so bad, Nellie? Why every time I look in the mirror all I see is Mama's disgraced face staring back at me?"

"Your mama is not ashamed of you, Beatrice. She's proud of you. You are a beautiful, caring woman. And you're going to have a beautiful child. Don't beat yourself up over this."

Nellie suddenly reached for Beatrice's hand, and when Nellie squeezed it, Beatrice just leaned into Nellie and cried.

🙙

Beatrice had been at the park since noon, and had wanted to leave at least three times, but she knew she had to stay. She had no choice. It was nearing 2 P.M. She glanced in one direction, then the other. Nellie had told her that she had given Morris the note. "It's from Beatrice," Nellie had said to him when she surprised him outside the Charles Street Sandwich Shop.

Beatrice had spent the last few days puzzling over whether to write the note, changing it at least ten times. *I need to see you. I'll be at the park, same place, same time, this Saturday.* She checked her watch. It was five minutes past the hour. *What if he don't come? Maybe this is not a good idea. I shouldn't have come,* she thought. She grabbed her purse, ready to walk away.

"Beatrice . . . Beatrice . . ."

She turned to an apologetic Morris. "I'm sorry. There was traffic," he said, rushing to catch up to her.

For a second she felt her stomach turn.

"How are you?" Morris stared at her. She seemed a bit different than the last time he'd seen her.

"I'm doing okay." Beatrice looked him in the eyes. "Morris, I need to talk to you about something."

Morris led her back to the bench, and when they were seated, Beatrice turned to him, and the words tumbled out impulsively. "Morris, I'm . . . I'm pregnant."

Morris looked at her, unsure if he had heard her. "What? . . ."

She looked straight at him again, lowered her voice. "I said I'm pregnant."

Morris sat there, not saying anything. It took awhile before it sank in. He could feel Beatrice looking at him. He finally turned to her. "We'll work it out," was all he could say. Then he pulled her close to him.

Beatrice leaned into him, felt Morris's knee touching hers, his hand rubbing her back, and she closed her eyes. After a while she pulled back from him and searched his eyes. And in that moment, she knew he really loved her, and they now had a bond that would tie them together for life.

⁓

Morris did not go straight home. He did not go anywhere. He just stayed there, sitting on the park bench, the day fading into night, darkness growing around him.

He had not expected it. Never thought about the consequences beyond the obvious—their differences, and the way it would unnerve others. He often thought that Agnes somehow knew, that she sensed there was someone else. But she never said anything, as though she had come to accept those times when he would disappear for hours, sometimes a full day, and he'd return home to a tidy house and a content Agnes.

He knew from the moment Nellie approached him and handed him the note that something was wrong. Now he walked slowly down the dark trail. The park—its sounds, the way it comforted him—had always been a place where he could lay his worries on the earth. He wished he could lay this worry on the earth and leave it there, bury it deep within the malleable soil. But he could not. He could never hurt Beatrice.

He found his way back to his car, and drove home in silence. At the first light, he took the note from his shirt pocket and read it again. He closed his eyes and tried to remember Beatrice's face as she said those words. Those heavy, heavy words.

I'm pregnant.

A horn honked, and he instinctively pressed his foot on the gas, gliding through the streets with thoughts of his life, the way it had unfolded, the unexpected pregnancies—first his mother's, his very birth, which had turned his own father against him; then he and Agnes, so young, so unprepared for a child; and now Beatrice, an unusual love that led to the unthinkable, unimaginable.

When he reached their street, he stopped the car, stared at his house, their home—his with Agnes—the bright lights illuminating the bay window, and he imagined Agnes inside, pulling a roast from the oven, her apron wrapped so tightly around her, sealing off her emotions. Emotions that she kept hidden, forcing herself to ignore her pain, *their* pain. Usually, he would go inside, kiss her cheek, and they'd sit at the dining table, Agnes at one end and he at the other, making small talk, mishmashing the truth.

But tonight he couldn't do it. Couldn't face that roast. Couldn't face Agnes.

He sat for a long while, an hour, watching the light, Agnes's shadow moving about, and then no movement at all. He knew where she now sat, at the dining room table, waiting for him, willing him to walk through the door. And after another hour, he watched the first light go out and then another and another, just as his light, his exuberance, had gone out all those many, many years ago.

⁂

Had it not been for Nellie, she would have never written that note. She couldn't sleep since she had last seen Morris, almost a week ago. She had rushed home and stood next to the window, watching the darkness unfold into night, drumming up all kinds of reasons why she wished she'd never given that note to Nellie. But it was too late now. Morris knew she was carrying his child. A child with no racial identity. A half-breed.

It troubled her that she was going to have a baby out of wedlock, a baby no less that would shame her family.

Nellie called the next morning. "I must've called you twenty times yesterday. Did you go? Did Morris show? What happened?"

Beatrice held the phone to her ear, overcome with emotion.

"Beatrice, are you okay? Do you need me to come over there?"

Beatrice shook her head into the phone. "No. No. I'm fine."

"It's going to be okay. You did the right thing. No matter what happens, you did what's right."

"I know," Beatrice said, barely above a whisper. "It's just that I feel so bad about it. About everything."

"There's nothing to feel bad about. You are going to have this baby, and love it, no matter what. And if Morris wants to be part of that, that's okay; and if he doesn't, then that's okay, too. You have to start thinking about yourself and your child. You're going to be a mother soon."

Beatrice became quiet.

"Maybe you should talk to Pastor Gilbert about it," Nellie said suddenly.

"No, I can't do that. I can't talk to nobody about this."

"But, Beatrice, when the baby is born, people will know. You can't hide it."

"I'm not hiding anything. I just don't want people judging me."

"You're gonna have to stop worrying about what other people think. You have to raise this baby and teach it to be strong."

Beatrice knew that Nellie was right, but she just didn't know how to put the pieces together. So many pieces tossed recklessly, like metal jacks. There was a knock at the door. She felt a flutter in her belly, felt the baby move.

"I got to go," Beatrice said. "Someone's at the door."

"Okay, call me if you need anything."

Beatrice hung up the phone and rushed to open the door, and was shocked to see Charles, in a new suit and tie, his arms full of flowers, smiling.

"Can I come in?"

Beatrice led him inside. "Please have a seat," she said, directing him to the sofa.

Charles removed his hat, looked around. "Woowee! You got a nice place here, gal! I knew you was gon' make somethin' of yourself. I told my mama that you be all right on your own. I knew you would."

"Charles, what are you doing here?!" Beatrice said at once.

Charles remembered the flowers, handed them to her. His face got serious. "Well, I got to thinkin' after you left Jackson that I needed to make myself a better man, to take care of you," he started, searching for the right words. "So, I done spent the last year sharecropping, saving enough till I can afford to move up North. I know I ain't got much right now, but with hard work and time, things gon' get better. I'ma be able to fend for us both. You know, find a job, get us a place, start a family." Charles looked at Beatrice's pinched face. "Now, I know you got your own life here. I understand that. But I figure that since you ain't wanna live in Jackson, then I can come this way."

"Charles you got to get back on that bus and gon' on back home!"

"Beatrice, please just hear me out! Now, I done come all this way. You can at least listen for a change!"

"Charles, please! You need to go back home!"

Charles's face became serious again. "Why you not willin' to give us a chance, ha? Ain't I always been good to you? Wasn't I always there for you and your mama? You know I come from a good family, Beatrice. You know what kind of man I am. Why you won't accept me?"

Beatrice hated to see Charles like this; hated to hurt him. She drew in her voice, making it gentle, conciliatory. "Charles, you are a good man, and I appreciate what you did for me and my mama. You're kind, and loving, and thoughtful." She took a deep breath, slowed her words. "But I can't marry you. I can't marry nobody now."

"Is that how you see it?" Charles said, his voice trembling, forcing back tears.

Beatrice thought about her life, the baby that was now growing inside. She didn't want to hurt Charles, hadn't meant to sound so harsh. But she didn't want Charles caught in the web she and Morris had weaved. There was a long silence before she spoke again. "Yes, Charles, that's how I see it," she said, pushing back tears.

Charles twisted his hat in his hand, then stood. "All right. If that's how you 'spect it to be." He put his hat back on and walked dejectedly out the door, never looked back to see the tears now on Beatrice's face.

31

Beatrice stooped down, eye level to the child.
"We already talked about this, didn't we? You're gonna have to learn to share. You can't throw a temper tantrum every time things don't go your way."

The boy lowered his eyes.

"Look at me, Jimmy, when I'm speaking to you."

Jimmy slowly looked up, bashful.

"You stop all this nonsense. You're a big boy now. Third graders don't throw temper tantrums, and they don't force their teacher to keep them after school every day. This is the second time this week you had to stay. I don't want to have to keep you again or I'm going to call your parents. You understand?"

Jimmy looked at Beatrice, his small face contrite. "Yeeeesss," he said.

"Good. Now give me some sugar." Beatrice tapped at her cheek.

A feeble smile broke across the boy's face. He gave Beatrice a shy kiss on the cheek.

"Now you go straight home." Beatrice watched Jimmy make his way down the street. The June sun beamed on her face, reminding her that summer vacation was only two weeks away. The heat and the extra weight slowed her, the baby uncommonly large, considering she was only five months pregnant.

Beatrice watched little Jimmy fade into the distance. She loved her children. Often she'd sit at her desk and watch them as they worked on their assignments, taking in every child's face. Her precious little ones, so innocent.

Every day, she felt herself getting stronger, readying herself to take on the greatest role of her life, to be a mother, to raise her child with all the values that her mother had instilled in her. Values that, even still, she passed on to her *little ones*. She had served as a surrogate mother to them—going above and beyond the call of duty, caring for them, loving them, giving them the best education she knew how to give. And now, with Jimmy no longer in sight, Beatrice smiled to herself and looked around the school yard to make sure all the children were gone. Before she turned to walk inside, she caught sight of a man across the street, staring at her.

Morris.

Neither one moved until Morris finally made his way toward her.

"Hello, Beatrice," Morris said, his voice conciliatory, with no mention that he'd already been there to see her many, many times, watching her from a distance. "You look beautiful."

Long moments passed before she could speak. "What are you doing here?"

"I wanted to see you," he said, a look of pity on his face.

"How dare you think you can just show up after not coming around for months?"

"I'm sorry. I just needed time to think things through. Please, Beatrice. Please try to understand."

Beatrice looked at him as if she had the mind to walk away. After he didn't show up for two months, she had told herself that she didn't want anything more to do with him, that she was going to raise this baby on her own. At one point, she even thought about finding out where he lived, but she could never bring herself to do that. It just wouldn't be right. She blamed herself often for allowing this to happen, told herself that it was *her* fault.

"I miss you, Beatrice. I still love you." Morris reached out and touched her arm. "Please, Beatrice, there's so much . . ." His voice sounded on the edge of breaking.

She thought about the nights she lay alone in her bed, wondering if she'd ever see him again; about the times she had wanted to go to the park, hoping he'd be there; and those mornings when she was too sick to get out of bed. Now, she felt something come over her. Relief. Forgiveness. She looked away, and for a long moment she just stood there, the sun beating down on her, and she felt light-headed, found herself being drawn in again.

"Can I walk with you?" Morris watched her think about it, and when she turned and starting walking, he followed her. They walked the six blocks in silence. He knew that he stood the chance of losing her, and he had already thought about what he planned to say, to tell her everything—about how much he missed her. About how he couldn't live his life without her, and now the baby. When they reached Beatrice's apartment, two women sat on the porch and watched them. Beatrice could almost feel what they were thinking. She gave them a cursory nod, smiled as Morris followed her inside.

"Would you like something to drink?"

"Yes, a glass of water." Morris took a seat on the sofa. He watched Beatrice walk away, appreciating how very pregnant she was, her plump belly slowing her—the weight, the glow on her face, made her beautiful. In spite of everything, the sight of her in this state made him smile. He took a deep breath, feeling the tension in his shoulders relax. He had been weary for weeks, anticipating the day he'd finally get to see her again; now that he was there, he felt a calm come over him. From where he sat, he could see Beatrice moving around the kitchen, the door that opened to her bedroom, a white crib angled in the corner.

"God, you look so beautiful," Morris said, looking at her.

Beatrice felt a rush of emotions. She handed him the glass and took a seat next to him. For a time, she didn't say anything, wondering if he really meant the things he had said, if he would disappear again. She had missed him, too, though she could never bring herself to say it.

"Is everything all right?" Morris glanced at her belly.

"Yes, I'm fine. We're fine," she said.

Morris smiled at the bulge, then looked back up at her. "And what about you? I mean . . . are you okay?" he asked, concern on his face.

Beatrice gave it some thought. "Yes, I'm okay. I've had some time to sort through things. We're going to be fine," she said, instinctively touching her belly.

Morris noticed a subtle change in her. There was something more resolute. "Beatrice, I'm really sorry. I didn't mean to hurt you." He didn't take his eyes from hers.

Beatrice looked away. It had been difficult for her the past few months, not knowing if he'd ever show up again. It was all she had thought about over the past few months.

He pulled her over to face him. "I want to be a part of your life again, and the baby's. Please, Beatrice." He looked down at her belly. A pensive look came over his face. "Can I touch it?"

Beatrice reached over and grabbed his hand, placed it on her belly.

Morris let his hand rest there.

"You feel that?"

"Yes, I feel it." The room fell quiet, a calm shadowing

them. Morris drawn into the moment, so many feelings disarming him. He looked up at Beatrice. "Beatrice, I want to be a part of this baby's life. Please let me help you."

"Why? Why do you think you can just show up here like this, and I'm supposed to just let you back in?"

"Because I love you, and I want to help with your baby. Our baby. I know I was wrong for not coming around, but I panicked. I didn't know what to do. The baby's stuff, all the things you'll have to buy . . . I want to help."

Morris held out an envelope, one week's pay inside—all he could put together at the last minute.

Beatrice ignored his outstretched hand.

"I can't have you coming in and out of this baby's life. I won't allow it."

"I would never do that, Beatrice. I want to be there, for you and the baby. I'll never leave you again. I promise. Please, Beatrice. Please let me do this." His voice was very gentle and when he looked her in the eyes, something inside made her want to tell him to go back to his wife, to leave her alone, but instead, she said in a quiet voice, "All right. Okay."

She took the envelope and tucked it into her pocket, wondering what would become of them.

The next day after school, Beatrice made her way straight to the church, anxious to talk to Pastor Gilbert. After Morris had left, she had called Nellie and told her about Morris's visit, the things he'd said. "That's good, Beatrice, but you need to go and talk to Pastor Gilbert. It's time you told him. He can pray for you and the baby, help you figure things out."

And Nellie was right. She was tired of hiding the truth. People had long since suspected that she was pregnant. Ever since Nellie cornered her at Mrs. Baker's house, it seemed that her belly blossomed, sprouted overnight. At first, she thought the loose dresses would conceal it long enough until she had time to weave a story around it. She had even thought to go back home to Jackson for some time, just long enough to allow her story to twist itself into place. But that was senseless, too. She was tired of hiding in the dark something that was bound to come to light. And already that light had peeked through one afternoon when she was surprised by her neighbor, the heavyset older woman who always sat on her porch, nothing getting by her. "Miss Beatrice, I was curious to know about that white man I sees comin' round sometimes. Do you work for him or somethin?" she said, eyeing Beatrice suspiciously. "No, ma'am, I don't," Beatrice answered matter-of-factly, and grinned to herself as she walked away, leaving the old woman stunned.

Though that gave her some small satisfaction, she needed to find another way. If not for herself, then for her baby.

She quickly made her way to the church, and the moment she walked into Pastor Gilbert's office, she felt a calm come over her, a peace she had not felt in months. It was the way Pastor Gilbert greeted her with a warm hug, then guided her to two chairs that faced each other.

"Miss Beatrice, to what do I owe for this surprise visit?" Pastor Gilbert said, flashing a genuine smile.

At first, Beatrice made small talk, fumbling her words, and then suddenly she poured out everything to Pastor Gilbert— about her brother and Pearl Harbor, and the first time Morris had come to see her and about the letters and then how they had lost touch after she moved back to Jackson, and years later when she ran into him again at Hyannis Port, and how he came looking for her. She couldn't bring herself to tell him that Morris was married, and when she was done, she lowered her head and waited for Pastor Gilbert to say something, anything.

"God loves you no matter what," Pastor Gilbert said. "He already has forgiven you. So go on and have this baby, and love it the same way God loves you."

Beatrice started to cry. There was still something unfinished, something that she knew had to be faced. Even after talking to Nellie and now to Pastor Gilbert, still she felt something nagging at her. It took long minutes before she said: "But what are others going to think? They ain't gonna take it so easy like you, Pastor Gilbert."

"Beatrice, you can't go around worrying 'bout other folks' business, just as they can't go around worrying 'bout yours. Now, you're gonna have to take all that worrying you got goin' on and invest it in your child. Yes, folks are gonna talk, especially after that baby is born and it look different from them. But that's for them to worry about, not you. You got to turn that hatred into love for your child."

Pastor Gilbert took Beatrice's hand. "Bow your head now, and let's pray for this child."

Beatrice closed her eyes, and prayed. Prayed like she had never before prayed in her life.

It took two days after talking to Pastor Gilbert for Beatrice to find the courage to face Mrs. Baker. She approached her in church and told her that she wanted to stop by to talk to her.

"Of course, babe." Mrs. Baker smiled. "Why don't you come for dinner today? Herbert will be away, and you and I can have a nice supper and talk."

"Yes, ma'am," Beatrice said. She had wondered how Mrs. Baker would take the news, had thought all day about what she intended to say.

Two hours later, Mrs. Baker patted a seat next to her on the settee. "Sit here, chile. I'm gon' get us some tea and biscuits."

Beatrice listened to Mrs. Baker moving around the kitchen,

the hot tea pouring into the chinaware. She had waited a long time for this moment.

"Here we are. A nice cup of tea and biscuits. Always good to settle your stomach and your thoughts," Mrs. Baker said, bemused by her own words.

Beatrice felt perplexed by Mrs. Baker's tone, thought that maybe Nellie or Pastor Gilbert had told her.

Mrs. Baker handed Beatrice the cup, and lifted her own cup for a sip. "Hmmmm. That's really nice. An old recipe my mama taught me long ago—black tea, a teaspoon of honey, and one cinnamon stick. It's the honey that flavors it, but the cinnamon that calms your belly. You ever have it before?"

Beatrice shook her head. "No, ma'am. Mama only fixed tea and turpentine for me and Robert. We didn't drink tea for leisure."

"Well, I guess your mama knew best. My mama always said tea good for the soul, keeps the spirit intact."

Beatrice tried to smile.

"So. What you been wanting to talk about, babe? Everything okay at home?"

Beatrice put down the teacup, gave Mrs. Baker a sidelong glance. "Yes, ma'am. All is well at home, and the children are wonderful at school. Things been going very good. And I can't wait for summer break."

"I reckon we all can't. Be nice to have a little time off, get things prepared for what's to come."

Beatrice shifted in her seat. "I been wanting to tell you something. Just didn't quite know how to say it. Well, I . . . you see, I'm . . ."

"When are you due, babe? Should be 'bout September or October, right?" Mrs. Baker blurted.

Beatrice gave Mrs. Baker an astonished look.

"Chile, I may not have no babies of my own, but I done witnessed enough of them to know better. I've known for some time that you were expectin'. Just wanted you to come to me in your own time. Now, the only thing I don't quite know is how you gon' raise this child on your own."

"I used to have these ridiculous thoughts that maybe there might be a life for Morris and me." She saw the way Mrs. Baker looked at her. "I know . . . that's a silly way to think, especially since he's married," she said, feeling embarrassed. "Now I realize that I'm gonna have to raise this baby on my own."

"I know these are some changin' times, but you carryin' a white man's baby, and one that's married, no less? Things gonna be hard enough for you as it is, especially when others get wind of this. You got to figure out a way to do right by you and that child. I don't expect that he'll want much to do with this baby, but you need to put aside your stubbornness and accept whatever help he willing to give. You and that child gonna have it hard enough."

"He said he want to help," Beatrice said. "But I feel bad already about the circumstances. I don't want to keep going on with it." Beatrice paused, looked away from Mrs. Baker to find the courage to say what she had wanted to say for a long time. "I think about his wife sometimes. You know, what kind of person she is. Whether she know anything." Beatrice turned back to Mrs. Baker. "I feel sorry for her. I mean . . . I know that sounds silly. But I feel sorry that she may someday find out, and I wonder how she's going to take it. I feel so bad that I allowed this to happen."

"Babe, you can't go beatin' yourself up for somethin' that done happened. And it's that white man's job to worry about his wife. What's done is done. Now you need to concern yourself with how you're gon' raise that child."

Beatrice closed her eyes, saw the intricate picture of herself and her child and Morris.

"You a strong woman, and you're gon' be a good mother. Me and Herbert gon' help you in any way we can." Mrs. Baker patted Beatrice on the knee. "Now you pull yourself together and stop worrying. You're gonna be just fine. Just fine, babe."

32

September 1963

P astor Gilbert stood at the podium, gazing out at hundreds of men, women, and children, some seated, some standing. Faint light streamed through the stained glass windows, accentuating the sanctuary's solemn mood.

"Church," Pastor Gilbert began, his voice sullen. "Just eighteen days ago, many of us stood on the pillars of hope when we filled the mall from the Lincoln Memorial to the Washington Monument—a day of reckoning, a day that will go down in history, a day we shall never forget. For on that day," Pastor Gilbert exclaimed, his voice rising, "with cherished hope, we all watched and listened as Dr. Martin Luther King told us about his *dream*." Pastor Gilbert paused, scanned the congregation.

"Then . . . that very hope was stripped from us as we watched the lifeless bodies of four little girls, our babies, being carried away from the Sixteenth Street Baptist Church in Birmingham, Alabama, this morning.

"Away from God's house! God's house!" Pastor Gilbert shouted. "How could anyone be so evil, so blasphemous, as to go into the house of the Lord and kill innocent children?!"

Pastor Gilbert gazed out at the congregation, became misty-eyed. "Church, I don't know about you. But tonight, I am a broken man. Tonight, I am a humbled man. Tonight, I am a hopeless man.

"I am a man, no less, who knows the power of God. I've seen the dogs turned loose on us. I've seen children, women, and men being hosed. I've seen the lynchings. But on this day, I ask God to have mercy. No matter how broken, or humbled or hopeless. I ask God for forgiveness." Pastor Gilbert stopped, looked up from his notes, his gaze skimming their sad faces.

"The love that forgives," Pastor Gilbert lamented. "That was this morning's Sunday school lesson. The lesson those four little girls learned, a lesson that only God, in His wisdom, could have bestowed upon that church before a moment of evil.

"The love that forgives, I say again.

"The . . . love . . . that . . . forgives . . ."

Pastor Gilbert slowly backed away from the podium, pulled a white handkerchief from his vest pocket, wiped his face and eyes.

Nellie reached over and touched Beatrice's hand. "Are you okay?"

Beatrice nodded, sobbing.

"It's so awful. I can't imagine what the parents of those girls are feeling right now. I couldn't imagine the pain if that was one of my girls." Beatrice looked at Nellie, her eyes sad.

"There's talk of a group of us going to Birmingham to attend the funeral."

"When?" Beatrice said. "I'd like to go."

Nellie gave Beatrice an unsettled look. "Beatrice, you can't go. You're eight months pregnant. That wouldn't be good for you. Birmingham is in an uproar now. Two other boys done been killed. It wouldn't be safe."

"I have to go, Nellie. I already missed the March on Washington. I need to be there."

Nellie looked concerned. "Are you sure, Beatrice?"

Beatrice looked up at the pulpit, thought about those little

girls. "I would regret it for the rest of my life if I didn't go,"
she said quietly, more to herself than to Nellie.

The next day, Beatrice paced the floor of her apartment,
her belly jutting out big and round, sharp pains stabbing
at her. She had thought about the pastor's sermon all night,
those four little girls, and she hadn't been able to sleep, could
barely eat all morning. She finally leaned back on the sofa to
soothe the aches she'd been feeling for the past few weeks. "It's
nothing to concern yourself with," her doctor had told her.
"This is normal. The baby is just moving into position."

"You're due in less than four weeks!" Morris reminded
her when he surprised her later with a visit after he had heard
about the Birmingham bombing. Since he had shown up at
her school a few months ago, he had kept his promise, had
come nearly every weekend, even sometimes during the week
to spend time with her. He had brought gifts, everything he
thought the baby needed. They no longer went to the park,
and had become even more careful with his visits, avoiding
the slightest chance that her neighbors, or anyone in Roxbury,
would ever find out that he was the father.

"I know, but I can't stay here and do nothing." Beatrice
clumsily made her way to the window and opened it, letting
in a blast of cool air, the antidote to the overheating that often
hijacked her body.

"What do you mean, do nothing? Look, I know it's awful
what happened to those little girls. But there's nothing you
can do by going there!"

"You don't understand! You could never understand!"

Their eyes met, and he was startled to see the way she
looked at him. "What do you mean by that? What are you
trying to say?"

Beatrice held his eyes. "I didn't mean anything by it," she

finally said. "It's just something I need to do, and I don't want you to try to talk me out of it."

"I just don't think this is a good idea." Morris stared at her. "The long drive, then the funeral, and no telling what other kinds of stuff may be going on there. The news said there's all kinds of violence. I just don't want you to get hurt—you or the baby." Morris touched her on the shoulder. She shrugged off his hand.

"What do you care about me getting hurt? Why should it matter to you anyway? You have a family to worry about!"

"What does *my* family have to do with you?!"

Beatrice frowned, hurt bare on her face. They hardly talked about his family. It was just an unspoken rule, something they both knew better than to bring up. "How dare you?! How dare you come over here and throw your family in my face!"

"Beatrice, I didn't mean it like that! You know what I meant."

"I know what *you* meant? You think because you come over here and eat my food, share my bed, and knock me up, that you have a right to stand in judgment of me? You don't know what I'm thinking or how this is affecting me. You think because you sneak your ass over here once or twice a week, that's enough! That because you say you love me, I'm supposed to bow down and act like I don't need more? You don't know the first thing about *me,* so how could you even begin to know what I'm feeling right now?! Get out!"

Morris's eyes stayed on her face. He seemed to consider what she said. Something in the way she said it made him think twice about leaving. He took a deep breath, waited until she calmed down.

"Beatrice, don't do this, please. You know I didn't mean it like that. I'm just worried about you. You're due soon and I just don't think it's a good idea for you to be traveling all that way. You know how I feel about you, so why do you keep trying to throw me out every time we have a disagreement?" He tried to reason as gently as he could. He didn't like when they had disagreements, and he couldn't stand the anger, the accusations, or the guilt anymore. "Look, I know things are not ideal. I know that, Beatrice . . . but please let's just try to be sensible."

"Sensible? I think it's a little too late for that!" Her scathing tone snaked across at him, made him feel uneasy. He didn't want to push her anymore, didn't want to make more trouble. It would be foolish and insensitive, especially given her condition. He could tell that she was beginning to feel miserable. It seemed that within the past few weeks, as her belly doubled in size, so did her mood. But he couldn't help but notice that there was something much deeper lurking. He stared at her, trying to find the right words, but there were none. Anything he thought to say would only make it worse.

"So when are you leaving?" he finally asked.

Beatrice didn't tell him that her bags were already packed, that she'd planned to leave early the next morning. She just held the door open for him while he grabbed his things and left.

*

Men, women, children—family and strangers, black and white—sat in the pews, their hearts swollen with grief. Beatrice held Nellie's hand as she sat close to her, her eyes glued to the pulpit.

"This afternoon we gather in the quiet of this sanctuary to pay our last tribute of respect to these beautiful children of God," Dr. Martin Luther King Jr. said, his melodic voice striking emotion in the masses, the hundreds who packed the church, mourning the little girls in the caskets covered in flowers.

"These children—unoffending, innocent, and beautiful—were the victims of one of the most vicious and tragic crimes ever perpetrated against humanity." Dr. King peered out at the congregation, his face a mask of thoughtfulness and contrition.

Beatrice stared straight ahead at Dr. King, too afraid to look at the caskets. She had seen him on the television, had heard his voice on the radio, listened to Pastor Gilbert speak about him. She had cried as she listened to his "I Have a Dream" speech—at the beauty of his words—and she had thought about what it would be like to meet him. And now there he was only six pews away as she sat between Nellie and Mrs. Baker, among wails and moans and caskets.

Beatrice listened to Dr. King, tried to take strength from him, and when he said his final words about life being hard as crucible steel, and encouraged them to *hold on,* Beatrice thought his words were meant for her.

As she stared ahead at the caskets, she felt ashamed and she cried, harder than she'd ever cried before; and when the service drew to a close, Nellie leaned over to her. "I really don't think you should go to the burial. Clifford can drive you back to my aunt's house."

Beatrice nodded, still sobbing.

"Here, take this." Nellie handed Beatrice her Bible.

"Everything's gonna be just fine. They're in a better place now, and I know it's hard, but maybe something good will come of this. God has a purpose for everything."

Beatrice took the Bible, felt nauseous as she thought about what Dr. King had said about the children, how innocent and beautiful they were, and what he had said to their families, as though he was speaking to her, knew about the disappointment floating within her, too: *It is almost impossible to say anything that can console you at this difficult hour and remove the deep clouds of disappointment which are floating in your mental skies.* She felt so very ashamed sitting there, carrying a white man's baby, tears flowing down her face. She thought about the horrible things that were going on in Birmingham, and all across the South. She had not been back to Jackson since she moved to Roxbury. Living in the North had shielded her from the sacrilege of the South, gave her a false sense of freedom. Now, as she watched hundreds of men, women, and children slowly follow the procession out of the church, she was too grief-stricken to move.

"Beatrice, Clifford's gonna take you back to the house now. Come on. You need your rest." Nellie held out her hand for Beatrice to take.

Beatrice took Nellie's hand, rose stiffly with the weight of the baby. Nellie slipped her arm through Beatrice's and Beatrice leaned on her the whole way to the car. When they reached the car, Nellie hugged Beatrice for a long while before she helped her into the car, and then she whispered to Clifford to stay with her until she was okay.

Beatrice stared out the window at the streets and the homes and the people they passed, a sense of gloom suspended in the air. She sobbed quietly, nodded at Clifford's futile attempts to talk about anything to keep her from crying.

"Dr. King sho' preached a good sermon," Clifford said at one point, glancing over at her. Beatrice nodded, watched a little boy who stared back at her as they waited at a stoplight, his face as dejected and dismal as all the faces they had passed on the streets. When they arrived at the house, Clifford helped her to her room.

Beatrice lay there thinking of the little girls, of her own

child. Ever since she first learned that she was pregnant, she had tried to tell herself that everything was going to be okay, each new day revealing a glimpse into a future that held small promise. Her life seemed flat and foreign to her, absent of all the things that had shaped her into the woman that she once knew. The thought of the new life growing inside her thrilled and terrified her all the same, she thought, as the sun melted into the clouded sky, and she slipped into a fitful sleep.

Hours later, Beatrice awoke to piercing cramps that struck through her whole body. She lay there, taking slow, measured breaths. When another cramp hit her, she sat up, trying to ease the pain. She thought about what the doctor had told her to do—breathe, and count the minutes between each contraction. The contractions were ten minutes apart, and for the next two hours, she paced the floor until she heard Nellie knock.

"Beatrice, are you okay?"

"I think I'm in labor," Beatrice answered.

Nellie stepped inside the room and closed the door behind her. "How long you been having pain?"

"All night."

"That sounds like labor, but you're not due for a few more weeks."

"I know. But the pain is coming about every seven or eight minutes now. Just like the doctor told me. I've been timing them. I'm scared, Nellie."

"No need to be scared. Let's just wait and see what happens." Nellie helped Beatrice lie on her side, and she lay next to her.

"I just can't get those little girls out of my mind," Beatrice said as Nellie rubbed her back.

"Don't you think about that right now. You just focus on

your breathing. That baby's gonna come soon, and you got to have good thoughts so you can bring that child into the world without all that heaviness on your heart."

Beatrice let that thought trail away, borrowed by another thought. "You reckon it's gonna be a boy?"

"You carrying high, and don't no boy fuss as much as that baby done fussed in you. That looks like a girl to me. Carried on the same way my girls carried on. And she gonna be a big one, too. You 'bout twice as big as I was with all three of my girls."

"Well, I hope it's a girl. I haven't given thought to no boy names. Just wouldn't know what to name it if it's a boy. I sho' can't name it after the father."

"How about that? I reckon you can't," Nellie chuckled.

Beatrice smiled, too, then became serious again. "I felt so bad sitting in that church today, watching those parents grieving over their children. It's so sad. I just can't get them out of my mind."

"I know. It made me think of my girls. I can't imagine what those parents are going through."

"I don't ever want to move back to the South, and I don't want to raise my child here, either."

Nellie pondered. "Yeah, I guess the South done got worse. No telling what liable to happen when they decide to start bombing churches and children."

Beatrice's mind trailed. "I can't believe I'm in Birmingham about to have my baby."

"I know, but try not to think about that right now. You got to think about bringing that beautiful child into the world."

Beatrice tried to lay still and think only of the baby. It was hard not to think of the funeral, and Dr. King, and even Morris. She could feel the force of the baby pushing at her, and the contractions that now seemed to come more quickly. There were so many things on her mind, and thinking about them all troubled her in a way that nothing had for years. She was too worried, too nervous, to lay still. She stood finally, started pacing the floor.

Nellie got up and walked slowly back and forth across the room with her. They stopped whenever another contraction came. Nellie held Beatrice, looking miserable for her. "I think we're gonna need to leave for the hospital soon."

Beatrice looked at her, then bent in pain when another contraction hit her. "Oooohhh."

"What's wrong?"

"I think my water just broke!"

Nellie looked at the puddle on the floor, and eased Beatrice back onto the bed. "Let me get Clifford." She rushed from the room.

Beatrice breathed through the contractions, and when Nellie returned, Clifford and Mrs. Baker were behind her.

"That baby ain't waitin' till we get back home, huh?" Mrs. Baker smiled, trying to make light of the situation.

Beatrice took Mrs. Baker's and Nellie's hands as they helped her from the bed. When the next contraction came, Beatrice squeezed Nellie's hand so hard, she winced.

"Clifford, go on and pull the car up to the front door."

Beatrice felt a sudden spate of fear rush through her, all the preparation for this moment suddenly forgotten. It wasn't supposed to be this way. She had made plans back home, had even packed a bag with all the things she would take to the hospital. Everything was ready, back at home. Not here in Birmingham. Not like this.

Nellie grabbed a bag and stuffed it with a flannel housedress her aunt had given her, and anything else she thought Beatrice would need. She helped Beatrice into her jacket, which strained against her extra girth.

"Let's get you in the car." Nellie helped Beatrice down the porch steps and into the backseat.

"You never told me it would hurt like this." Beatrice forced a smile.

"You never asked."

Nellie and Mrs. Baker sat in the backseat with Beatrice while Clifford drove as fast as he could, thinking how quiet and beautiful Birmingham was under the peaceful sky. Once he turned into the main entrance of the hospital, Nellie rushed inside.

Beatrice breathed through the contractions until Nellie and a colored nurse emerged with a wheelchair and helped Beatrice into it.

"Since your water has already broken, we're going to take you straight into the delivery room."

The nurse wheeled Beatrice inside and took her to the maternity ward, full of colored women in skinny beds, some moaning, others lying with wet towels on their heads. The nurse helped Beatrice undress, and then a colored doctor came in and examined her.

"You are fully dilated. Seems like this baby's ready to come." The doctor read the notes that the nurse had given him, and he motioned for the nurse to join him. "It's time for you to start pushing. Now, I want you to push and take three deep breaths, then push again."

The nurse helped Beatrice sit up.

"Are you ready?" the doctor asked, sitting on a stool at the end of the bed.

"Yes." Beatrice strained.

"Okay, go ahead and push."

Beatrice pushed and pushed and pushed until, at last, a silvery, pinkish-blue baby slid into the doctor's waiting hands.

Quickly the doctor cut the cord and spanked the baby. "It's a girl!" he announced after a small wail rang out in the delivery room.

Beatrice lay back, exhausted. "Can I hold my baby?" Beatrice reached for the child. Suddenly, her belly tightened with another contraction.

"Nurse!" the doctor called.

The nurse left the baby on the weigh table and came to the doctor's aid. She handed the doctor another instrument.

"I need you to push again, Beatrice."

Beatrice pushed again, confused, as another baby slid its way into the world.

The baby cried out after one swift spank.

"You have another baby girl," the doctor said, surprised. "Twin girls."

Beatrice lay back, stunned. She thought of the single crib, the perfect little home she had created—for *one* baby. She couldn't help but smile, instead of cry, about Morris's surprise at the news. Two biracial babies. Well, at least they'd know there was someone else just like them in the world. At least they'd have each other, Beatrice thought as her twins were gently placed in her arms.

She didn't have to choose between her two favorite names after all.

33

Agnes

Dr. John moved carefully around Agnes's desk, review-ing the files that she had pulled for him. The expression on Agnes's face was the same since he had cornered her two days ago in the storeroom—a simple, girlish look of bewilder-ment, fascination, and then of surprise. Every time he came to her desk, Agnes would smile slyly as though they had a little secret, not his, but her very own. She had no interest in him whatsoever, but there was something about the way he spoke to her, made her feel alive.

Dr. Howard John wasn't the most handsome man Agnes had ever seen, but his confidence, and the way he looked at her—it was flattering. He was one of six doctors to whom Agnes was assigned, managing their files and handling ad-ministrative work. She was fascinated by the pace of it all: by the doctors and the nurses, by the care they gave to their pa-tients. Her restlessness and yearning had faded as she absorbed herself into her new life. At home, she felt stiff and astute, like a piece of the furniture, laden with the wallpaper and curtains. But at the hospital, she had learned everything there was to know about her job, had even organized the office, and in a short time, she'd become an expert at practically running the whole unit. Last month, when she was called to her super-visor's office and told how very pleased they were with her work, Agnes gloated the whole day.

At home she had been a wife and a mother, roles that she had handled with great precision and care. But now, she was a doctor's assistant, a nurse's confidante, and she had discovered that those things meant something to her. And she was even enchanted by the way Dr. John had begun to depend on her.

At first, she had paid no attention to it, told herself that he just appreciated how hard she worked, the way she especially took care of him. Then just the other day, he had followed her into the storeroom, and when she turned to see him standing there, he just looked at her. At first with an inquisitiveness on his face, like he had remembered something he needed from her, then his eyes softened.

"May I help you, Dr. John?" she asked.

He hesitated, uncertain about what to say, and then a look of intrigue came onto his face. "Agnes, you are a very beautiful woman. You do know that, don't you?" There was intensity in his voice.

Agnes felt herself blush, then quickly straightened up and rushed from the storeroom, leaving him standing there. A few minutes later, she watched Dr. John leave the storeroom and walk past her desk as though nothing had happened. Now, Dr. John stood at the corner of her desk, absorbed in the file until he handed it back to her. Then she got up from her desk and took the file to the storeroom.

A moment later, Agnes heard Dr. John step inside the storeroom. She turned to face him.

"I have to apologize. I'm very sorry about the other day. I've never done that before."

Agnes did not speak.

"I've been thinking about it since the other day. I've behaved terribly, and I know I've violated your trust, and I'm very sorry." He looked at her, embarrassed. "I guess I've been a bit taken with you since you started. You are so striking. I got carried away."

Agnes looked at him shyly. "It's okay. Don't worry about it. I accept your apology."

Dr. John nodded, thought to say something more. "Maybe you'll let me make it up to you by taking you to lunch sometime? Nothing more. Just lunch."

Well, why not? Agnes heard the words in her head, but she didn't say them. Instead, she said: "No, that wouldn't be a good idea."

"I understand." Dr. John smiled at her again. "I'm sincere about my apology and it will never happen again," he said, then turned and walked out of the storeroom.

For an instant, before she gave him a chaste smile, their eyes met. It was a moment that was real only to her, something that she would not admit to later, a faint instant of gratification. She stood there, remembering times when Morris used to tell her how beautiful she was, how much she meant to him. It made her sad because he no longer spoke to her like that. *Are you and your husband still in love after more than twenty years?* Janet, one of the nurses, had asked her one day while they ate lunch in the cafeteria. Agnes was surprised to hear herself say yes, although she knew she was speaking only of her, not of her husband.

When she finally left the storeroom, Agnes went back to her desk, busied herself until it was time for her to leave. All the way home she thought about what Dr. John had said to her, and she smiled at the thought of how bashful he seemed around her, the same way Morris used to be when they had first dated.

That evening when she arrived home, the house was completely dark, and Morris was asleep on the sofa. Agnes put down her things and took off her coat, then went into the living room and turned on the lamp. She stood there watching him snore softly. His face was peaceful, far removed from the tense face she'd noticed over the past several months. So strange, she thought when she saw how very roused he seemed, like something worried him. She had tried to talk to him about it, but he would only tell her that it was nothing, that things were just very busy at work. She imagined the times, long ago, when he couldn't wait to come home to her and Emma, just the three of them, so immersed in the soft, quiet world. He tried so hard in the beginning to measure up to the promise he'd made when they were jubilant, unprepared for the jagged world, time passing as fast and wide as the gap that had grown between them.

How was it that he grew more puzzling to her over the years, and so very distant? In that moment she realized that he had not looked at her the way Dr. John had in a very long time. *A long time.* Untamed thoughts rose and melted away and then rose again, and she stood there, just watching him. "*Morris,*" she whispered, but he did not budge. She leaned in a little closer. "Morris," she said again, and still nothing.

She quietly made her way to the kitchen and reached up in the cupboard, far in the corner, and pulled out the bottle of gin. She poured herself a gin with lime juice and then opened the window and just stood there, looking out into the cold night, letting the breeze and the gin still her. Moments later, she put on her apron and moved dreamily around the kitchen, pulling pots and pans from the cupboard. Then she pulled the vegetables and meat from the refrigerator and began chopping them. Warmth radiated from her toes to her fingertips, filling her with a calm that eased her mind. She sipped the gin, felt every cell in her body slow into a fluency, as if she had devoured a small piece of heaven.

34

Morris

This time when Nellie went to the sandwich shop and waited for Morris to come out, she walked straight up to him and said: "Beatrice had the babies."

Morris looked at her, a question mark on his face. "Babies?"

"Yes. Babies! Twin girls," she said, and walked away.

Three months later, Morris sat in his car a block away from Beatrice's apartment, two teddy bears in the backseat. He'd kept them in his locker at work, intending to take them to her. But when he'd open his locker and look at the teddy bears sitting upright, their arms outstretched, their beady little eyes gawking back at him, he couldn't do it.

How was he ever going to break the news to Agnes? He had tried many times, but he just couldn't find the right words, the right time. One day, while he and Agnes sat at the dining table, she told him about a new position that she was going to apply for at the hospital. "I want to work in the maternity ward, with the babies. I love babies," Agnes added. And it was in that tender moment when he and Agnes were connected in a way that she didn't understand that the words almost passed his lips. A pan of lasagna and a salad and homemade rolls lay on the table between them. Agnes could sense that something was wrong. "What is it?" Morris looked away. "Nothing," he managed to say.

And now there he was sitting a block away from Beatrice's

apartment. He pulled the key from the ignition. Sweat beaded his forehead, though freezing snow iced the cold December ground. He opened the car door and stepped out carefully, the slippery ice sloshing beneath his steps, the teddy bears held tightly against his coat. The walk felt long, void of the anticipation that he once had when he visited Beatrice.

When he reached the door, he took a deep breath before he pushed the number next to Beatrice's name. He stepped back and waited until he heard the lock turn from the inside, and then she was standing there.

"What are you doing here?" Beatrice whispered through the cracked door.

Morris scanned her face, watched her take notice of the two teddy bears, the way his eyes pleaded with hers. "May I come in?"

Beatrice arranged her face in a serious expression. "Why? So you can disappear again? It's been three months and you're just finding your way over here?!"

They both turned toward a door that suddenly opened, looked at an older woman, who gave them a sly look and then quickly closed her door.

Beatrice stepped back then and let Morris inside. She wiped her hands on her apron, walked over to the television, and turned it down. "Why did you come here after all this time?!"

"I . . . Beatrice, I'm sorry. I just needed some time."

"You needed time! What about me? What about your daughters? Did you forget about us? Did you forget about the promise you made to me?"

"It's just that the last time I was here . . . well, you made it clear that you'd been having second thoughts about us. You almost made me feel like I was responsible for what happened in Birmingham. . . . Look, I know we have our differences, and I know this is hard for you, especially given the circumstances.

But I never stopped loving you. I'll never stop loving you! And now that the babies are here, I've decided that I'm never going to leave again. I promise. Please, Beatrice. Please just give me a chance."

Beatrice kept her stance. When he did not come to see the babies after Nellie delivered the news, she began to wonder if he was going to make good on the promise he'd made to her. She had not seen him since she left for Birmingham, and she had wanted so desperately to call him, to tell him about the twins, but she knew she could not. And when he did not come within the first week, and another week passed, and yet another, she began to resent him. But no matter how she felt, her daughters needed their father. It would be hard enough to raise them on her own, but harder still for them to be without a father. "Fine!" she said, keeping her voice even. "But I'm not going to let you come in and out of their life. You're either going to be their father, or you're not!"

Morris looked at Beatrice's serious face. He had told himself that if she let him back in this time, he would never break his promise again. He needed Beatrice, and he wanted to be a father to their daughters. When Nellie had told him about the twins, he had panicked. His secret had morphed into something that was beyond his own comprehension and he had tried to stay away. But he could no longer bear the thought of living without her. "I'm so sorry," he said. "I will never leave them . . . or you . . . again."

Beatrice didn't quite trust him. "Do you want to take a seat?" she said, skeptical.

Morris took a seat and looked around. The apartment looked different, full of new smells and new things. Two bassinets sat near the mantel, baby blankets hung over the kitchen chairs, sterilized bottles and a bag of diapers sat near the sofa. Morris took it all in. He remembered similar things when

Emma was born—the small clothes, the bottles, the bibs—
and he remembered how very proud he was whenever he held
Emma in his arms, the way her tiny face looked up at him. He
loved Emma. And he would love these girls, too.

"So, how have you been?" Morris's voice was gentle, passive.

"I'm managing."

"I brought these." Morris remembered the teddy bears.

Beatrice took the bears from him and walked over to the
bassinets and placed a teddy bear in each one. They sat for a
while, both confined to their own thoughts. Beatrice thought
about the times she would stand by her window, imagining
she saw Morris approaching in the distance, or peering into
the face of every white man, hoping it would be his face.

"Would you like to see them?" Beatrice asked after a while.

It took Morris a moment to find his voice. "Yes."

Morris watched Beatrice disappear into the bedroom. He
could see her moving around. He sat quietly, his stomach
squirming. He had tried to prepare himself for this moment,
but when Beatrice walked back into the room with the bun-
dle, he felt his heart drop.

"This is Samantha. I call her Sam for short." Beatrice delicately placed the baby in his arms.

Morris looked down at her face, her brows and blue eyes,
the shape of her small nose and lips. Her cheeks were flushed
pink, stark against her olive skin. He pushed his forefinger
into her small hand. He smiled when she grasped his finger
and looked up at him. "She's so beautiful," he said.

"Sam's the youngest. She was born six minutes after her
sister, but she's already trying to boss her big sister around, taking up most of the crib." Beatrice smiled at him holding Sam.

"She's so small." Morris noticed how light she felt in his
arms.

"Yes, they both are. They were born premature, almost

four weeks early. Sam weighed three pounds fifteen ounces, and Sadie Mae weighed four pounds eight ounces, but they are both very healthy and strong.

"Let me get Sadie Mae for you."

Beatrice disappeared into the room again, and returned soon after with a more alert and fussy Sadie Mae. She placed the squirming child in Morris's other arm.

Morris stared down into Sadie Mae's small face, the same size and shape as Sam's. Her eyes, he noticed, were hazel, her skin tinted brown. Even so, the resemblance was still visible and he could see himself in them.

"They are really special. Already their personalities are beginning to show, and they are getting bigger and stronger every day," Beatrice said. "They're four months, and Sam now weighs eight pounds thirteen ounces, and Sadie Mae weighs ten pounds three ounces."

"How did you decide on the names?"

"They are both named after their great-grandmothers. Sam is named after my father's mother, and Sadie Mae, she's named after a woman who was like a mother to my mother."

The babies settled into their father's arms, even Sadie Mae, who now lay still. Morris looked from one to the other. For a moment he seemed to forget about his other family.

Beatrice could tell by the way he held them, the fondness in his eyes, that he loved them. He had loved them from the moment he'd first touched her belly. There was bittersweet pleasure at the sight of Morris holding the girls. For months she had not allowed herself to think too long or too hard about what life would be like after the babies were born, but now it rose up with such intensity—how would she explain to her little girls why their daddy couldn't tuck them in at night or come see them take piano lessons or teach them how to ride a bike?

"I used to wait for the phone to ring, hear your knock at the door, look for you at the grocery store," Beatrice said suddenly. She looked away from Morris, her eyes lost. "Then I'd tell myself that you just needed time, and you never came. You never came, and I'd cry myself to sleep, and still I never stopped thinking about you. Never. I even wondered what it would be like for us to be together. You know, like a family." She stopped, looked over at him. "Did you ever think about it? I mean, has it ever crossed your mind?"

Morris looked straight at her. "Yes, I thought about it a lot. I still do."

They looked at each other. When he spoke again his tone was tender. He had caused her so much pain. His deception had made her suffer in ways he never intended. "I wanted so much to be here with you. I thought about you as often as you thought of me. I even called a few times, but would lose my nerve every time you answered. I never stopped loving you."

The admission made Beatrice feel light-headed.

"I spent so much time imagining a life with you."

Beatrice felt the tears in her eyes; that wiser and stronger woman gone, replaced by the younger version of herself that still loved him. It made her uncomfortable even now that he still had that kind of power over her.

Part Three

Fall 1971

35

Two days after her eighth birthday, the morning her assignment was due, Sam studied her lesson again. While her sister, Sadie Mae, slept in the twin bed across from hers, Sam slipped from the warmth of her blanket, quietly tiptoed across the room to her tote, and pulled her lesson from it. Ever since Mrs. Lanaham gave them their assignment—to read the story about Dr. Martin Luther King Jr.—Sam knew that he was her hero. She had been enthralled with him from the moment her mother had told Sadie Mae and her about him: the time she had met him the day before they were born in Birmingham, and then later, the things he'd done. Sam cried when she read about April 4, 1968, the day he was assassinated. And when Mrs. Lanaham chose her to recite his "I Have a Dream" speech, such an honor for a third grader, Sam had already claimed her A.

The day was unseasonably warm, felt more like summer than fall. It was an unpredictable time for weather in Roxbury, shifting from day to day. Today proved to be temperate enough for Sam to wear her light-blue-and-white princess-seamed dress, a pretty dress for a special day. The warm temperature and Sam's excitement eased Beatrice's worries about Sam wearing one of her best dresses, which was usually reserved for church on Sunday.

Sam wasted no time dressing. Although the girls were

twins, Sadie Mae was inches taller than Sam, and they shared
very few habits and looks, such an odd pair. Sam's olive skin
and blue eyes against sandy hair, features that matched her
father's, were a stark contrast to her sister, Sadie Mae, with
her cocoa-colored skin, dark coarse hair, and hazel eyes that
favored her mother. The girls behaved as different as they
looked. Sam was the more adventurous and outlandish one, as
opposed to Sadie Mae's more subtle, subdued personality. And
though Sadie Mae, ever the more cautious and responsible one,
was often expected to keep an eye on her sister, it was Sam who
excelled in school and was handpicked to be in an advanced
reading and math class, already skipping ahead of her sister.

Beatrice rushed to grab the last of their things before they
walked out into the warm air and headed toward Sadie Mae
and Sam's school. She kissed them after she walked her girls to
school, something she did every morning. "Y'all have a good
day, and you mind your sister, Sadie Mae. And, Sam, remember what I told you. Just take your time and you'll do just fine."

"Yes, ma'am," Sam answered, and Sadie Mae followed, before Beatrice made her way to where she taught.

Later that afternoon, Sam stood in front of the class, her
dress and hair picturesque, complementing her voice. She
looked straight ahead.

" 'I say to you today, my friends, that in spite of the diffi-
culties and frustrations of the moment, I still have a dream. It
is a dream deeply rooted in the American dream,' " Sam said,
careful to pronounce every word.

" 'I have a dream that one day this nation will rise up and
live out the true meaning of its creed: We hold these truths
to be self-evident, that all men are created equal . . .' " Sam
paused, her blue eyes taking in every face that peered at her,
glued to her every word. " 'I have a dream that my four little

children will one day live in a nation where they will not be judged by the color of their skin but by the content of their character. I have a dream today,'" she belted, her voice rising.

Mrs. Lanaham's face lit up. "That was wonderful, Sam! Class, let's give Sam a hand."

The class gave Sam a resounding ovation. Sam smiled bashfully and walked back to her desk, just as the bell rang.

"Now, class, tomorrow we will learn about the Civil Rights Act of 1964," Mrs. Lanaham shouted above the children's rustling. "Get your homework done this afternoon, and a good night's rest. We got a busy day tomorrow."

The children lined up at the door and waited for Mrs. Lanaham to escort them to the yard. Once outside, Sam could see Sadie Mae waiting for her in their usual spot, and the minute Mrs. Lanaham announced, "Class dismissed!" Sam broke from the line and ran toward her sister.

"I got an A. I got an A!" Sam held up her report.

"So?" Sadie Mae gave her sister a callous look.

The girls started walking down the path they took every day.

"You should have seen me," Sam said, ignoring her sister's mood. "Mrs. Lanaham said I didn't miss a word! I did very good!"

Sadie Mae walked alongside her sister, not saying anything, careful to stop at every light.

"*I—have—a—dream,*" Sam said in her speech voice. She could still feel the wonder of the day, the way she stood in front of the class, the words so even, so perfect. Even her dress and hair, neatly divided in two pigtails and tied with white ribbons, were still perfect.

"What did you do today?" Sam finally asked.

"Nothing! Just leave me alone!" It was Sam who always did so well at her lessons, and Sadie Mae who struggled with

the slightest assignment. Her mother would spend extra time
with her, prodding her to do better. But no matter how hard
she tried, she just couldn't do as well as Sam. She would spend
her playtime studying, would even stay sometimes after school
with Mrs. Clark, for tutoring. She was eight years old now,
and she was meant to do better. Everyone—her mother, Aunt
Nellie, Pastor Gilbert, Mrs. Clark, and even her daddy—told
her how smart she was.

On most days, she could understand the lessons. She would
memorize every word, the numbers. Then somehow when
Mrs. Clark would put that paper in front of her, the one with
the word *Quiz* written in big letters, her mind would freeze,
and all the preparation, tutoring, and studying would fade. It
did not come as naturally for her as it did for her sister. Sam
did everything with ease. Even the way Sam looked made
things easier for her.

When they reached the park, Sam dropped her tote and
darted for the swings.

"Where are you going? We need to get home. Come now,
Sam!"

Sam turned to Sadie Mae, gave her a puzzled look. Sadie
Mae had never stopped her from playing before. They always
took time in the park.

"If you don't come now, Sam, I'm going to leave you!"

Sam stretched her legs, catching the wind, the swing pro-
pelling her. She held her head back, her face tilted to the sky.

"I said come now, Sam!" Sadie Mae said, and gave Sam one
last look before she stomped off.

Sam felt the breeze on her face, the cotton from her dress
tingling against her skin. She moved her legs back and forth,
rising higher. She loved the park, the swing, the way it made
her come alive. Every weekend, her mother would bring her
and her sister to the park, and she'd let them play for hours

while she sat nearby, watching them. Sometimes, her daddy would come, too. But he wouldn't always sit with them. Most times, he'd stand in the distance, his eyes glued to them. For as long as she could remember, Sam knew why, too. Sometimes she thought she understood their differences and why they had kept her parents apart. Sadie Mae had always struggled more with it.

After a while, Sam jumped off and ran to the slide, and then to the monkey bars, going from one thing to the other, the warm breeze filling her. She was tempted to stay longer, but already she'd lost track of time. She jumped down from the bars and wrestled up her things.

"I have a dream that someday my four little children will not be judged by the color of their skin but by the content of their character. I—have—a—dream—today." The words rolled from Sam's tongue freely as she pulled her white sweater tighter against the evening chill, and skipped down the same path she and her sister took every day. The park lights came on, lighting up the darkening path. She walked dreamily, traces of the speech still on her mind.

"I—have—a—dream. I—have—a—dream."

It was such a relief not to be under the watchful eye of Sadie Mae, always having to mind her. She was glad Sadie Mae had left. She felt more free than she'd felt since they were little girls. They were both eight now but Sadie Mae was always acting like she was so much older than her, as if they were not only minutes apart.

Sam walked briskly toward a remote trail, the same one her mother often used to take her and her sister to see their father. She quickened her pace, anxious to make her way to the other side. Suddenly, she heard the squeak of footsteps against the grass, signaling a man's approach.

"Hello, little girl. Where are you goin'?"

Sam came to an abrupt halt.

"Home. My mommy's probably worried," Sam said, realizing that already she had overspoken.

"Where do you live?"

Sam thought about it, wondered if she should tell. Her mother had always warned her and her sister never to talk to strangers. *Y'all come straight home, and don't you ever break apart. Ever! You hear me, Sam?* Sam heard her. Had heard her every time she said those words. Only to her. Never to Sadie Mae, as though she knew that Sadie Mae would never leave her. But she did.

"I better be getting home," Sam said, pulling her tote close to her. She stood only a few feet from him, her eyes fixed on his face—big, dark eyes set inside a long, dark face with a prominent nose, a wide mouth, and coarse dark hair. He was slightly taller than her daddy, his body thin but muscular.

"Ain't no need in rushin.' I'm not goin' to hurt you." The man stepped in closer, the vile smell of liquor seeping from him. "That's a pretty dress you got on."

"I better be getting home," Sam said again, her voice dwarfed, tiny against her own ears.

"Just let me see your dress. It look so pretty on you."

Sam felt her heart beating fast. She closely pressed her tote against her and quickly turned to leave.

In an instant he grabbed her, one swift, vicious move, forcing Sam's tote to drop to the ground.

❧

"Sam didn't come home. I've looked everywhere for her. Everywhere!" Beatrice cried. Nellie had rushed over to Beatrice's apartment after receiving her panicked call minutes earlier.

"Sadie Mae left her in the park. I went to the park, but I can't find her. I can't find her, Nellie!"

"We'll find her." Nellie walked over to Sadie Mae.

Sadie Mae sat on the sofa, her head down, too ashamed to look at her mother.

"Sadie Mae, baby. Tell your auntie what happened again. Where were you and Sam when you left her?"

Sadie Mae kept her head down, sullen.

"It's okay, baby. Just tell me."

Sadie Mae wiped her tears with the back of her sleeve. "Weee . . . Weee . . . was in the park walking home like we always do. I wanted to get home to tell Mommy about my spelling test. I got a D, and Sam got an A, and Sam wanted to play, but I didn't. I told her to come, but she wouldn't listen. I tried to do what Mommy told me, but Sam wouldn't listen. She wouldn't listen," she cried.

"Okay, baby." Nellie moved closer to Sadie Mae, embraced her. "Now when you left, where was Sam?"

Sadie Mae laid her head against her aunt's chest. "She was on the swing."

"I went to the park, I looked by the swings, searched the entire play area. That whole side of the park. She ain't there, Nellie! She's gone!"

Nellie looked up at Beatrice. "Have you called the police?"

"Yes, they're on their way now."

"Have you called Morris?"

"Why would I call him?"

"Because he's their father. He needs to know, Beatrice!"

"You're right. He *should* be here!" Beatrice made her way to the kitchen, scuffled through the cupboard drawer, looking for her telephone book, and when she found it, she hastily turned to the first page. She didn't really need to look at the two letters and five digits that made up Morris's home number. She knew them by heart from all the times she had thought to call him: when the girls were sick with 102-degree fevers; when he didn't show for their fifth birthday party and Sam cried for two days; when the irresistible urge overtook her in the middle of the night while she lay sobbing into her pillow.

She grabbed the phone and dialed Morris's number. This time there was no Nellie. No note. No code. Just her and her sheer will. She did not think about his wife or his daughter, not until she heard his voice on the other end. "Sam's missing!" she blurted.

"What?" Morris said, confused.

Beatrice closed her eyes, pressed the phone closer to her ear, calmed herself. "It's me. I said *Sam's missing!*"

She heard Morris take in his breath.

"Sadie Mae left her in the park on their way home from school, and she never came home!"

"What park? Highland?"

"Yes," Beatrice said, a little calmer now.

"I'm on my way."

Beatrice heard the dial tone, and turned back to Nellie.

"What did he say?" Nellie asked, waiting.

"He's on his way. He's coming."

A few minutes later two uniformed officers showed up. One short with a youthful face and sandy hair; the other much taller with dark hair and unfriendly eyes. They took a seat on the sofa, the dark-haired officer doing all the talking.

"So, you said the last place you checked for her was in Highland Park, near the east-side play area? Is that correct?"

Beatrice nodded.

"And you say that her sister, let's see, what's her name?" The officer flipped through the small notepad. "Oh, here we are. Sadie Mae, I guess this little girl here, was the last one to see her in the park? Is that correct?"

"Look, we already went over all of this twice. Shouldn't you be out looking for her?" Nellie interrupted.

The officer shot a look at Nellie. "Who did you say you were again? What relation are you to the missing girl?"

"I'm her aunt! What difference does that make? We need to be out searching for her, not sitting here answering questions that you already asked twice."

"I suggest you change your tone, mizz! Now, I told you there's nothing we can do until she's been missing for twenty-four hours."

"Twenty-four hours!" Beatrice blurted. "My baby got to be missing for twenty-four hours before y'all gonna do somethin'?!"

The other officer butted in. "Look, miss. This is standard procedure. We've taken a report. Next we'll file it, and in twenty-four hours, you give us a call back and we'll begin a search for her. In the meantime, if she comes home or you find her, just call us and let us know," he said, just as a frantic pounding came from the front door.

Nellie opened the door to Morris, and they all turned to him. Pastor Gilbert nodded kindly. He had come the moment Beatrice called him.

Morris returned the nod and quickly went to Beatrice. "I went to the park, looked everywhere. Did they find her yet?"

"Who are you?!" the dark-haired one snarled.

Beatrice watched Morris's face tighten. "I'm her *father*," Morris said without hesitation. "What are you doing to find her?!"

Beatrice couldn't help but look at him. Morris had never admitted this to anyone, as far as she knew. And here he was stating it in front of a roomful of people. The officers scrutinized Morris.

"Like I told *her*"—the unfriendly officer gestured his head toward Beatrice—"we can't begin a search until she's been missing for twenty-four hours."

"That's ludicrous! Why does she have to be missing a whole damn day before you do something?"

The officer sized up Morris, reached his hand to touch his weapon. "Let's go," he said to his partner. "I think we're done here."

Everything moved slowly—the air, Pastor Gilbert's words, the time. It had been hours since the officers left. Morris put Sadie Mae to bed, telling her that it wasn't her fault, that Sam was going to be okay.

"But Mommy told me not to leave her, and I did," Sadie Mae said, crying herself to sleep.

Beatrice wrapped her sweater tightly around her, sealing off her emotions. She felt numb, oblivious to Morris, who sat next to her on the sofa. Any minute she expected to see Sam walk through the door, her dress and hair disheveled from play. That's all, just harmless, mischievous play. And when she heard a knock on the door, she jumped up and rushed to open it to the same two officers who had been there earlier.

"Ms. Dobbins," the friendly one said. "We found a little girl in the park fitting the description of your daughter." He paused, looked solemnly at Beatrice. "She's in intensive care at Boston City Hospital."

Beatrice dropped to her knees.

Had it not been for Morris, Beatrice would have stayed on that floor. But it was Morris who went to her and held her in his arms. It was Morris who told her she had to be strong. It was Morris who pulled her from the floor, put a coat over her, and gave her legs the strength to walk out into the night.

Beatrice sat in the backseat of the patrol car staring out

the window. Nellie sat next to her holding her hand. Morris drove alone in his car.

There were no words. No sound. No movement. Just the car gliding through the dull moonlight. The cold stung Beatrice's face as she stepped from the patrol car and forced herself to follow the officers through the emergency corridor and over to intensive care. There were hushed voices in the distance as they neared the nurses' station. Two nurses turned to look at them.

"Miss Dobbins," one of the nurses said. "Officer Cartelli told us that he would be bringing you here to identify the little girl in our care."

Beatrice's eyes dulled; she didn't say anything. Morris became her voice.

"Yes, they've explained everything to us. Can we see her?"

The nurse eyed Morris. "Yes, of course," she said. "But there's something we must tell you first." She looked at the officer, waited for him to nod.

"She's been badly beaten." The nurse took her time, her voice calm. "And raped. . . . The swelling to her face is very severe. It may be hard to recognize her. She's in a coma."

Beatrice's hand went to her mouth, a wretched cry escaping her. Nellie cried, too. Morris turned away, his eyes clouded with tears.

"Would you like to go in now?" the nurse said after a while.

Morris became Beatrice's voice again, nodded his head yes, and led Beatrice down the corridor, following the nurse.

The moment the nurse opened the door, Beatrice let out a slow, hurling howl that made the earth go still. No words, no injury, no swelling could keep her from knowing her child. It was Sam—her tiny frame swallowed in the white sheets, a trail of tubes and tanks surrounding her.

36

Morris

Morris had seen the girls just the week before, had taken them dolls for their eighth birthday, carefully selected each one. One for Sam, her hair curly blond, her face perky and pink with blue eyes, and one for Sadie Mae, sandy brown hair and brown eyes, inside a demure round face.

"You got this for us, Daddy?" Sam had beamed, her eyes lighting up.

Morris had picked her up and kissed her. "Just for you, honey," he said, and reached for Sadie Mae to hug her, too. His little girls, so different, but so much the same. He recognized himself in each of them. Sam's blue eyes and sandy hair, and the way Sadie Mae smiled, her face curving to form the shape of his.

He thought about the countless times he had taken them to Highland Park and watched them play. And he remembered the way Sam's eyes lit up. "You wanna get on the slide with me, Daddy?" she had said one afternoon, oblivious to the stares of passersby. Morris had ignored the stares, too, savoring the limited time he had with them. "No, honey, you enjoy it. Daddy's gonna watch you," he said, unable to fathom what his life had been like without them. Often, he'd leave work early and go to their school and wait for them. And when they would see him, they'd both run up to him. "What are you doin' here, Daddy? You came to walk us home again?" He'd smile, grab both their hands, and walk with them. "Daddy, can we get on the monkey bars and the slide? Can you push me on the swing, Daddy?" Sam would ask, skipping alongside him. It was during those times, in those rare moments, that he knew he had to tell Agnes. But the words never came. His secret began to fade the moment Beatrice surprised him with that call, and he had quickly rushed to grab his things and gone into the kitchen to find Agnes. "I need to go back to work. One of the guys didn't show up for his shift."

"Okay," Agnes said. She noticed he looked bothered, skittish.

Morris frantically drove to Highland Park. He had looked everywhere—near the play areas, down every path. "Sam? Sam?" he had shouted. He had stopped strangers, describing her, asking if they'd seen her. Many just shuffled by, shaking their heads *no*. Some stopped to talk to him with a hint of apprehension on their faces. No one had seen her.

Then he had rushed to Beatrice's apartment. He'd never felt pain like when those horrible words passed through the nurse's lips and shattered on the air like stone hitting glass. And again when those same two officers took a report, outside of Sam's room. The nicer of the two had asked Beatrice to share anything she could remember about that day, and Beatrice had closed her eyes, forcing herself to remember. The day seemed no different from another, she remembered. A usual day. Until she had come home and found Sadie Mae, and no Sam. "Sam was fine. We were fine," she had said, sobbing. "How could somebody do this to her? How could he . . ." The words stopped abruptly, midsentence.

It was not until Morris went home the following night and lay next to Agnes, unable to sleep, that memories of the first time he held his daughters flooded him—a day filled with so much joy and sorrow. Afterward, he and Beatrice had come to an understanding. Though he could not spend much time with them, it didn't take away from how much he adored his girls, a fondness that he had to conceal, a separate life. Over the years, he had tried to bring himself to tell his other family, but every time he thought of broaching the subject, he just couldn't do it. And now, here he was again, stepping tentatively through the hospital corridors. He hated hospitals. He had managed to stay away from them, except on occasions like the time Emma had broken her arm, or they had lost their son, or his mother had suddenly become ill. And now Sam.

His sweet little blue-eyed angel.

Morris walked up to the nurses' station, his face filled with grief. "I'm here to see Samantha Sullivan."

The nurse looked up. "What's the patient's name again, sir?" she asked.

"Sam. Samantha Sullivan."

She thumbed through a list, and found Sam's name. "Down the hall. The last door on the right."

"I know," Morris said pensively, and followed the bright lights. Lights not much different from the ones that hung at the *Solace,* illuminating the same ill feelings. He took his time, each step labored. He paused when he reached the door, slowed to open it.

Beatrice sat at the bedside, watching Sam, her chest rising and falling with each breath. Her small, battered body shrouded in white sheets. Sunlight passed through the picture windows, glaring on Sam's bruised face. Another bed sat empty on the other side of the room. An IV hung above Sam's bed, dripping fluid into her.

Morris stared at his little girl. Then he went to her and rested his head lightly on her small chest. He closed his eyes and the tears came. First slow and steady, then in streams.

He cried.

He cried for all the time he had missed with her, for the words he never said to her. He cried for her pain, their pain. And, most of all, he cried for *his* secret. "I'm so very sorry," he said. "I should have been there!"

Beatrice looked at him, pity on her face.

It had been two days since Sam had been found, and he had stayed at the hospital with Beatrice the first night, never leaving Sam's side; and the next morning, he had gone home only long enough to rest for a few hours. He was relieved that Agnes was not there, and he had taken a long shower, then lay down, barely able to close his eyes before images of Sam rose up so powerfully—Sam, so small and so frail, so very vulnerable lying there in the hospital bed, unmoving—and he had cried, drumming up a force of sheer guilt and shame for having not been there to protect her. The years had passed so quickly. Yet he had wanted so desperately to reach back in time, to right all the people he had wronged—Agnes, Emma, Beatrice, Sadie Mae, and Sam.

He had closed his eyes; his head throbbed and he had dozed off for only an hour before he woke again with thoughts of the shame, the guilt. Time stolen from one to make up for another. He thought again about Sam, the last time he had seen her, the way her face lit up when he gave her the new doll. How could he have betrayed them all for so long? This was the shame he had carried with him, a heaviness in his heart, the grief he had tried to spare them all. Now, he looked over again at Beatrice. Her eyes were red from lack of sleep, and she had not eaten in days. It pained him to see her this way.

"I . . . I wish things were different. You know, between us," he suddenly said. "I never intended for things to turn out like this."

Beatrice looked over at Sam, and turned back to him. She didn't feel anything. She wasn't crying anymore. She just sat there. Thinking only of Sam. She had barely left Sam's bedside, only long enough to talk to the doctors and nurses, or to go to the restroom, or to call Nellie. She couldn't stop thinking about all the choices she had made that could have steered the course of their lives in another direction. She blamed herself now. She thought back on the countless times she had wanted to leave Roxbury to move to Philadelphia, New York, Chicago. But when she told Morris, he had pleaded with her to stay. Things would be better, he had promised, and each time, she believed him. And now, she couldn't help but blame herself for not leaving, for not protecting Sam. She couldn't bear the thought of losing her baby. Maybe losing Sam was the price she would have to pay. Until now, she had never once thought about how terrible things could get. Yes, she had often thought of his other family, and of someday leaving him. But never had she imagined that it would come to this. She looked at him in disbelief. Suddenly, she felt tears fill her eyes, and stubbornly wiped them from her face. How many tears had she wiped over the years? She let the thought fade away, taken with another thought. "Do you know Sam's favorite color?"

Morris looked at her perplexed. He tried to identify the tone of her voice, the listless and leaden slope of it.

"Do you know the name of Sam's favorite doll? Or her favorite teacher's name? Or her favorite game? Or that she doesn't like to sleep in the dark? Or that she's allergic to string beans? Or that she likes to eat ice cream with a fork? Or that she wakes up sometimes crying for you? Do you?!"

Morris held her eyes, watched the tears fall slowly down her face.

"You have no idea how painful it's been, do you?! How painful it's been all these years to lie to them, to tell them why you can't be there every Christmas, or Easter, or for their birthdays?"

Morris remained silent, his wariness palpable.

Beatrice observed the almost imperceptible sadness that showed on his face. She had not said much of anything to him in the past few days, until now. "Things have got to change. I can't continue to live like this. Not like this. No more," she said, glancing over at Sam. "They deserve better. Sam deserves better."

Morris began to sob, then turned to Sam, touched her hand. "I love you and the girls," he said. "I never meant to hurt you or them. I . . . I want to do things right. I want to be in their lives more."

Looking at him, Beatrice instinctively knew that this time things would be different. She could tell by the way he looked at Sam, by the way he cried every time he left her hospital room. When he reached for Beatrice's hand, she let him have it, and then he took Sam's small hand in his other, and held on to it tightly. They sat there for a long time, almost without moving.

Suddenly Morris felt Sam stir. Beatrice saw her move, too. He leaned closer to her, squeezed her hand again. "Sam, honey, it's Daddy. I'm here, baby. Me and Mommy. We're here," he said. Beatrice got close to her, too, touched her face, her arm.

Gently, Sam's eyelids fluttered, the pain throbbing in her face. She pushed against gravity, forcing one eye to open, then the other.

"*Hi, Daaaddy. I—I—I got an A,*" she said, above a whisper, then closed her eyes again.

37

Morris stopped the car in front of the house long enough to gather his thoughts. He had stayed at the hospital all day again, occupying the same seat where Beatrice often sat, as he watched his little girl and her incredible will to survive. Since Sam first opened her eyes six weeks ago, she had drifted in and out of consciousness, showing slow signs of improvement. First, she tried to form her lips to say the words that floated just out of reach. "Not yet, Sam," Beatrice had said. Sam would look at her mother, full of confusion. In time, the pain subsided, and Sam grew strong enough to push through sounds and sentences that gave voice to her thoughts. Soon, she was up and amusing the doctors and nurses. Everyone grew fond of the little colored girl with the infectious laugh and blue eyes. But there was a different mood about the white man who did not miss a day's visit. At first, they thought he was merely someone who had ties to the colored woman and her twin daughters—maybe she was his maid, a housekeeper, the hired help. But what at first seemed explicable had soon turned suspicious. There he was, day after day—his closeness with the little girl, his kindness toward their mother. Little time had passed before the sidelong glances, the whispers, the blatant speculation. Yes, they were fond of Sam, but only until they connected the dots.

Morris was making his own connections. Every day that

he spent with Sam made him more aware of his reality. Now, six weeks had come and gone, and there was one last connection to be made. He could not continue to deny them. He had made a promise to Beatrice and, in his own silent way, to Sam, and this time he planned to keep it. He stepped from the car, taking his time walking down the cobblestone path that led to his front door.

Once inside, the familiar smells hit his nose and he heard Agnes moving around in the kitchen. He walked in, and Agnes turned to face him. "Emma's home," she said, her face lighting up with a smile.

Emma suddenly appeared. "Hi, Dad. Where you been? We've been waiting for you."

Morris forced a smile. "Hi, honey. I didn't know you were coming."

Emma kissed him on the cheek.

"Dinner's ready," Agnes announced, pulling the roast from the oven. She carried it into the dining room and set it in the center of the table. Emma grabbed the potatoes and the peas.

"Dad, can you bring the iced tea and some glasses?"

Morris stood there, momentarily frozen.

"Dad. You okay?"

Morris turned to Emma. "Yes, I'm fine, honey. I'll grab the glasses."

After they said the grace, Agnes smiled at Morris. "Emma and Johnny have set the date for their wedding."

"That's good, honey," Morris said.

Emma grinned at her mother, beaming. "We've decided to get married. It's going to be beautiful. Don't you think, Dad?"

Morris arranged his face into a smile. He had known about the engagement. In fact, Johnny had come to seek his blessing. "I love Emma. I've loved her since we met, and now I would like to take care of her. I would like to marry her, sir," Johnny had said, his words carefully rehearsed.

Morris eyed him inquisitively. "Are you sure, son? Maybe you and Emma should wait a little longer, you know, before you rush into marriage."

"I'm sure, sir. I love Emma and she loves me. I want to spend the rest of my life with her, sir."

"The rest of your life? That's a long time, son. To spend the rest of your life with someone. So many things can happen. Things change. People change."

Johnny gave him a peculiar look. He'd spent many Sundays with Emma's parents, and they had always welcomed him, treated him practically like a son. Now, here was Morris asking questions and saying things that didn't add up.

"Sir, I love Emma, and I plan to marry her," Johnny said, surprising himself.

Morris looked at him, befuddled, the same look he now gave Emma. "That's wonderful, honey. I'm very happy for you." Morris reached out and gave Emma's hand a reassuring squeeze.

The room fell silent. The forks hitting plates and the creaking and sighing of the house were the only sounds.

Emma finally spoke up. "Is everything okay, Dad?"

Morris glanced at Emma, then Agnes. The words, unfamiliar words, so long unspoken, escaped him before he had time to think them through. "No, honey. Everything's not okay. I have something I need to tell you and your mother." He sat there, unsure of what to say, or how to say it.

Agnes gave him a peculiar look. The gin always made her feel warm, numb. She gazed at her husband. It had been an hour since she had snuck a glass from the bottle she kept tucked in the cupboard.

Morris made a little nervous movement with his hands,

and finally, like jumping from a cliff, he plunged into his confession. "There's someone else. Someone I've known for a long
time," he finally said. He turned to face Agnes, then looked
over briefly at Emma. "There's a child. Two. Twin girls."

Agnes stared at her husband, trying to understand.

Morris looked fixedly at her. "We met a long time ago. We
became friends, and years later, well . . . I made a mistake . . .
and . . . the girls, they're mine."

Emma let out a gasp. Agnes didn't flinch, tried to figure
out what tricks of the mind the gin was playing on her.

The room went still. No one moved.

"How could you?! How could you?!" Emma finally said, a
look of repugnance on her face. "I hate you! . . . I hate you!"
she screamed, and ran from the room.

Agnes stared at her plate, the food and gin sickening her.
When she spoke again her tone was calm, though her face
showed a different mood. "Do you love her?"

Morris looked at Agnes, not taking his eyes from her.
"Yes," he said.

The *yes* disarmed her. She thought of the countless times
that he'd come home after being gone all day, the way he
looked at her, a knowing in his eyes and hers. She knew. She
always knew.

"I never meant to hurt you."

Agnes turned away from Morris and stared out the window, watching the trees.

"There's something else you must know." When he spoke
again his tone was soft, conciliatory. "She's . . ." Morris paused.
"She's a colored woman. Someone I met during the war." He
added the last words as if they would soften the blow.

Agnes went still, felt something fill up inside her. She
closed her eyes to suppress the tears.

Morris waited for her to say something. But Agnes didn't

trust herself to speak. An eternity of silence passed before she finally turned and faced him. "Are you still seeing her?"

Morris looked at his wife, then away from her. "No. We are just taking care of the girls together, that's all. Nothing more."

Agnes took in her breath, sobbed.

"Agnes, I'm so sorry. So very sorry."

"Sorry?! You're sorry! You go out and fuck a nigger and father bastard children and you think you can just say you're sorry?!"

Her words shocked Morris. Never had she uttered such foul language.

Agnes pushed her chair from the table and stormed into the living room. Morris could hear her moving around before she returned with a framed family photo and, in one swift move, flung it at the window, shards of glass flew everywhere.

"I hate you! I hate you!" Agnes said, sinking to the floor.

Morris jumped from his seat and went to her, pulled her close to him and rocked her in his arms, as Agnes allowed herself to cry.

38

Agnes

"I want to see them," Agnes said, her face fixed into a grimace. Morris looked at her, standing there in the same dress she'd worn to mass that morning. They had returned from church hours ago, and Agnes had walked straight up the stairs and into their bedroom, without saying a word. She lay across the bed in her dress and slept. Sleeping had become a necessary part of her day, the only thing that consoled her pain. After that awful day, Emma had come to stay with her, hardly leaving her mother's side for a full week while Agnes moved around in a daze, tracing back over the times he'd disappeared. Of all the horrible things she'd imagined, it was nothing compared to this. Yes, he was kind to colored people. There were a few women who had come to work for them—a housekeeper here, a gardener there, even a lady who had helped her care for Emma after they had lost their son. But there were never any signs that Morris could be *attracted* to them.

The thoughts consumed Agnes, and she'd kept busy—tidying the house, fixing meals, laundering clothes, anything to keep her mind off her pain. When the chores weren't enough, she'd take long walks to get as far away as she could get. One day, she undid her apron and walked out the door, and found herself at the Parker House Hotel, standing at the concierge desk, asking for a room.

"Right away," the concierge answered, intrigued by the beautiful woman with the food stains on her dress. Agnes took the key from the clerk and went straight to her room.

The room reminded Agnes of a Victorian painting, with its luscious bedding and elegance. She stood there looking around, the key still in her hand, before she closed the drapes and watched the room fade into darkness. The dark room was tranquil, forcing Agnes to close her eyes and think about *them* again. She didn't want to know their names, convinced that a name would make them more real. She walked over to the bed and looked down at the bedspread, so beautiful and tidy, and she lay on top of it, huddled into a ball, and cried. She had not cried since that awful day.

For four days, she stayed in the dark room, unconcerned about anyone.

Now, Morris looked up at her from his Sunday paper. "What?" he said, not sure if he'd heard her.

"I want to see them. Not *her!* Them . . . the girls," Agnes said again.

Morris closed the paper, studied her. "Are you sure you want to do this?"

"I can't pretend like this is going to go away. I will not pretend like this isn't real."

"Maybe we should wait. Give it more time."

"I want to see them. I need to see them," Agnes said, her voice cracking.

"I don't know, Agnes." His face showed the strain of conflicting emotions. When he spoke again, the words, understanding and soft, seemed addressed more to him than to Agnes, some kind of end to his own personal beginning. "Honey, look, I just don't think it's a good idea. I mean, you need more time. I know this is really hard for you, and I don't want to upset you anymore. Maybe we should wait a little longer." He reached out and touched her hand, but she pulled away.

"No! I want to see them! I need to see them!"

"I am sorry. Believe me. I am so very sorry. I never meant to hurt you or Emma. I know how you must feel. But what good is it going to do to have you meet them so soon?"

Agnes was silent for a moment, and Morris was grateful for that, hoping that he'd gotten through to her. He paused, considering what to say next, and then with a delicate voice he said: "All right, then. Maybe you're right. Maybe it would be best for everyone."

The next day, Morris made his way to Beatrice's apartment. When she opened the door to let him in, she could tell that something was bothering him. Sadie Mae and Sam were sitting at the table, doing their homework. "Daddy!" Sam jumped from her seat and ran to embrace him. Sadie Mae followed. "What are you doing here, Daddy?" Sam asked.

"You came to take us to the park, Daddy? For some ice cream?" Sadie Mae said.

Morris smiled at them. "No, honey. I came to talk to your mother."

"Can you stay and eat dinner with us? Mommy's making spaghetti," Sadie Mae said.

"We'll see, honey. But first, why don't you let me and your mother talk."

Beatrice gave him a look, then turned to the girls. "Y'all take your homework in the bedroom and finish it up. Your daddy will see you when you're done."

Sam was the first to kiss her father on the cheek. Then Morris turned his other cheek up to Sadie Mae before they shuffled off into the bedroom and closed the door.

Morris took a seat on the sofa. Beatrice sat on the chair opposite him. At first, Morris hesitated, then finally turned to her and said: "I told Agnes about us. And about the girls. Everything."

"Agnes wants to meet the girls," Morris continued. He looked deeply uncomfortable now, trying to read the expression on Beatrice's face.

Beatrice stared at him. "Why?"

"She just wants to get to know them." He met Beatrice's eyes. "Maybe this is best for everybody."

"Everybody? I don't think I'm concerned about everybody! I only care about my girls."

"Beatrice, you know I would never let anything happen to them. I love them as much as you do." Morris stared at Beatrice. "I think this is a good thing. It's time for them to know about the other side of their family."

"But you never wanted them to meet before now! Why now? Because of Agnes?!"

"I've always wanted it. I've just been waiting for the right time. For them to get a little older."

"Don't you give me that bull! If Sam hadn't been hurt, you would have been content to keep things the way they were!"

"That's not true, and you know it!" Morris relaxed the muscles in his face, seemed to consider something very carefully. "Beatrice, you know how I feel about you and the girls. That's never changed. And yes, I'm sorry that it took this long for me to tell Agnes. That should have never happened. But now I want to do what's right for the girls. I would never let anyone hurt them."

Beatrice struggled to sort out her feelings. She knew Morris would never intentionally let anything happen to them. After Sam was raped, she had seen how he'd changed, spending more time with the girls. But she never thought that he would want to take them to meet his other family. It was something they had never discussed. At times, he'd come to her, and he wouldn't say much at all, as though being close to them was enough. It was during those times that Beatrice thought about what it would be like for them—for her, Morris, and the girls—if there was no Agnes.

Once, in the grocery store, she saw a couple, a white man and black woman, and she had followed them until she saw how people looked at them, and she told herself then that she never wanted to live like that. It was what prompted her and Morris's love to drift. They had stopped sleeping together, though the desires were still there, especially after Morris started spending more time with the girls, often showing up during the middle of the week, sometimes staying to tuck them in at night. She trusted him.

"All right," Beatrice said at last. "But I'm trusting that you won't let *anything* happen to them, and I mean *anything*!"

For the first time in years, Morris seemed to relax, as though the thought of it calmed him.

The following Sunday, Sadie Mae and Sam looked pretty. Sam wore a sky-blue-and-white floral dress with a wide blue silk bow; and Sadie Mae wore the same dress, in mint green and white. Both wore black patent-leather Mary Janes with ruffled white socks. Their hair was tied with white ribbon. Beatrice knew that neither of them had slept much the night before. And she was pretty sure the fullness of it was lost on the girls.

"Your father should be here soon," Beatrice said, inspecting the girls one last time. "Now y'all remember what I told you. Mind your manners, and, Sadie Mae, you keep an eye on your sister, and make sure you sit up; and, Sam, don't you run that mouth too much."

Sam nodded, already feeling constrained by her mother's words, similar to the way she'd felt when she came home from the hospital. As time wore on, Sam noticed that her mother had changed, barely letting them out of her sight, watching their every move. In fact, the girls now attended the same school where Beatrice taught. They walked to school with their mother, came home with her, did everything with her. Sam hadn't slept a full night without being tormented by flashes of that man's face, or the most chilling moments that stripped her from her sleep in the middle of the night. Beatrice would come running to her room, and she'd rock Sam in her arms until she fell back to sleep.

Things had also changed between the sisters. Sam never asked Sadie Mae why she'd left her in the park, and Sadie Mae never told.

Time unfolded Sam's fears, Sadie Mae's guilt, and their mother's pain.

"Go and get your sweaters," Beatrice said, hearing the knock at the door.

"Are they ready?" Morris stepped inside.

Beatrice turned to look at Sam and Sadie Mae. "Y'all remember what I told you."

"Yes, ma'am," Sadie Mae answered. Sam nodded in agreement.

Beatrice watched Morris load them into the car. Her little girls, growing up so fast, in a world with so many differences, so many things that would change the course of their lives. Today would be one of those changes—learning about another side of their father, his other family. When she'd agreed to let them go, she had sat the girls down and told them the truth. Yes, Morris was their father, but he was also a father to another little girl who was now all grown up, and that little girl had a mommy, too, who was Daddy's wife—his other family. Sadie Mae listened like she had always suspected there was something not right about her father. Sam was another story. She cried. He couldn't be a daddy to someone else. He was their daddy. *Her* daddy. Beatrice held Sam in her arms and let her cry. Then she lifted up Sam's sad face and wiped her tears. "But daddies can have more than two little girls," she had told Sam.

⁂

Emma sat next to her mother in silence, listening to every footstep, every drifting conversation that passed by their window.

What will they look like? Who are they? Agnes thought, the same questions that kept her awake at night. It hurt to even imagine them. For heaven's sake, hadn't he realized how much this would destroy her? And what about Emma? Her identity as his only child, stolen from her. Emma had not said much about it, as if speaking about it would make it more real. "It doesn't matter. I don't care," Emma told her mother one day. But it did matter to her. Agnes could see it in her face.

"Are you okay, Mom?" Emma's voice drew Agnes back.

"I'm okay, honey," Agnes said, and quickly turned away to fight back tears.

This time when they heard a car door open and shut, they knew it was them. Agnes's face sobered the moment they walked into the living room.

Sam and Sadie Mae stood on either side of their father, holding his hands. One taller than the other, their coloring a stark contrast—the smaller one nearly as light as Emma, and the taller one shades darker. Their faces similar, but not the same. And though their dresses were nearly identical, there was something very different about them.

Agnes and Emma looked from one to the other. It hardly

seemed real that they were standing there. For a while, no one spoke or moved.

Suddenly, Sam stepped forward. "Hello. My name is Sam." She held out her hand to Agnes.

Agnes's gaze fastened on Sam's blue eyes.

"We brought these for you." Sadie Mae offered up the basket of cookies to Emma.

Emma looked at her mother, then back to Sadie Mae. She forced a smile and took the basket.

"Girls, why don't you have a seat over here?" Morris cleared a space on the settee.

Sadie Mae and Sam followed their father. Morris took the seat in the armchair across from them. The room became eerily quiet.

"Well, you know Sam," Morris said awkwardly. "And this is Sadie Mae." He looked at Sadie Mae. "Sadie Mae, why don't you tell us about your art, the paintings you did at school?"

Sadie Mae glanced at her father, shy-faced. She took her time, thinking of the right words. "I . . . I like art," she said finally, her voice meek. "I won the art contest at my school. My mommy framed my award. And I like to draw all the time. Sometimes, I can draw anything."

"And I like to write," Sam blurted. "And Daddy said I could win a contest, too. See, I wrote you a letter." Sam anxiously pulled the letter from her sweater, held it out toward Agnes.

Agnes's face went pasty. Emma's heart dropped. Morris felt his breath stop. And Sam's eager blue eyes became confused.

Agnes stared at Sam, at the letter. "I . . . can't . . . do . . . this! I can't do this! Get them out of here! I want them out of my house now!" she said, and stormed from the room.

"Agnes!" Morris started after her, and then stopped. Embarrassed now to turn around and face his children.

Emma looked at her father with disgust, then turned to the

girls. For a second, she imagined what it must be like for them, and her eyes softened. "It's not your fault. He never should have brought you here," she said, then rushed off after her mother.

Morris looked over at Sadie Mae, then at Sam, the letter still in her hand. "I'm really sorry. It's been very hard for her."

Sadie Mae looked up at her father, held his gaze. Sam didn't look at him at all.

"Can I see it, honey?" Morris said gently to Sam.

Sam hesitated, then handed the letter to him.

Morris's heart sank as he read the letter, then handed it back to Sam. "That was nice, honey. Maybe you can give it to her when she's feeling better. Okay?"

Sam turned away, tears flowed down her cheeks.

"I guess I should get you home now," Morris said.

Sadie Mae stood first, and waited for Sam. Sam sat unmoving. Morris reached his hand out for her to take. Slowly, Sam grabbed her father's hand as they followed Sadie Mae out the door.

The moment Beatrice saw the girls, she knew something was wrong.

"Y'all gon' and get out of your pretty dresses, I need to speak to your daddy."

After Sam and Sadie Mae were out of sight, Beatrice turned to Morris. "What happened?!"

"They're fine."

"They are not fine! What happened?!"

"Calm down!" Morris's mind raced to sort through it. "Nothing happened to them, okay? It's just that everybody's got to get used to this."

"Calm down? How dare you!" Hardly a muscle moved in Beatrice's face; her whole demeanor was different now. "They are *never* going back over there. Never!"

"Beatrice, please! It's just going to take some time."

"Time? I think you've had enough *time*! I should have never let them go over there! Dammit! What was I thinking?!" Beatrice brushed past him and made her way to her girls.

Morris closed his eyes to clear his head. Beatrice was right. He should have never taken the girls to see Agnes. He thought about the look on Sam's face when Agnes refused to take the letter, and felt his heart squeeze again.

When Beatrice returned an hour later, Morris was still waiting for her. She seemed calmer now.

"What are you still doing here?"

"I just wanted to apologize. You're right. I should have waited, gave everybody more time, especially the girls."

Beatrice looked away, and when she looked back at him, they eyed each other.

"I think we all could use more time." Hearing Beatrice's tone made him feel more regretful. "We can't continue like this. The girls are older now, and we can't just keep carrying on like this."

"What are you saying, Beatrice?"

Beatrice looked directly at him. "I guess I'm saying that it's time that you get your life together with your other family, and do what's right by us both. The girls need you and I suspect your daughter and your wife need you, too. I can't do this anymore. You either be a father to these girls and do what's right, or I don't want you coming here no more."

"When did you decide this?" Morris looked annoyed. Talking about it made him feel trapped and, worse, guilty for letting this all happen.

"I decided a long time ago." Beatrice looked straight at him. There was an edge to her voice.

"Look, you need to go. I'm tired." She stood and walked to the door, held it open for him.

When she got into bed that night, she lay there for a long time wondering if she had made the right choice. She knew that in spite of what she said, she loved him, and he loved her, maybe enough to leave his wife. But now, she wasn't so sure she wanted him to do that.

39

Beatrice

Beatrice watched a bird flutter in the cast iron birdbath that sat in the middle of Nellie's yard. Lush trees, vines, and flowering shrubs graced the small garden that Nellie had nurtured for more than a decade.

"I just don't know what to do," Beatrice said. Nellie sat beside her, admiring her work. Nellie still looked as vigorous as Beatrice, though her girls were all grown. Two had already graduated from college, and her youngest was due to graduate soon. To look at her, you couldn't tell that just that past fall she had become a widow when Clifford suddenly died in a car accident, only days before they were to celebrate their twenty-fifth anniversary. They had been married for half of her life, nearly a quarter of a century. When Nellie had first learned that Clifford was gone, it had been impossible to imagine life without him. It took months for her to finally accept it, and it would take years before she would ever stop grieving for him. Yet the experience had changed her, too. She laughed more and took more time to enjoy her life, especially her time with Beatrice.

"What does your heart tell you to do, Beatrice? Really?" Nellie looked over at her.

Beatrice stared at the birds, thinking back to that past Sunday when Morris returned with the girls after their visit. Since then, she had not spoken to him, avoiding his calls, giving herself time to think things through. He wanted so desperately to make things work. "I don't know, Nellie," she finally said. "I mean, I want to do what's best for the girls, but I also know that we just can't continue to carry on like this. The girls are older now, and that's not the example I want to set for them."

"I think you're going to have to do what's best for the girls. Morris is their father, and you just can't cut him out of their lives. They will never forgive you if you do that."

"I know, but you should have seen when he brought them back, Nellie. I've never seen Sadie Mae so upset. And Sam." Beatrice turned and looked straight at Nellie. "I'm worried about Sam. She's so fragile. I mean, it's not been that long since her recovery, and then to have this happen. Dammit, Nellie, I should have never let him take them over there."

"Don't beat yourself up about it. You did what you thought was right at the time. Eventually, they were going to find out. You couldn't keep it hidden forever. Besides, kids are very resilient. After we lost Clifford, I thought the girls would never get over it, but every day, I see how strong they are. They are much stronger than we give them credit for."

Beatrice looked at Nellie. "You always know just what to say. You're right. Maybe I'm trying to figure this out too much. Maybe I should just let things be, but still, I don't want to see them hurt again."

"I know the relationship between you and Morris isn't ideal, but given the circumstances, he does try to be a good father to them. You have to just build on that."

"I know," Beatrice said, thinking about the way Morris doted on the girls, adored them. And he had kept his promise to spend more time with them. One day, he even took them for ice cream, the girls and Beatrice. The ice cream diner was full of people, staring at them. Still, it had brought Beatrice some satisfaction to see how much he had grown to love the girls, not caring about the way people looked at them. People must have thought it odd, how he held the girls' hands, the way Sam clung to him.

"I always wondered when he would tell his family about the girls," Beatrice said, gazing at the lilacs absentmindedly. "As strange as it may sound, I can't help but feel sorry for Agnes and Emma."

"Agnes and Emma? Who are they?"

"His wife and daughter," Beatrice said without pause.

Nellie turned to look at her. "All this time, I've never heard you once mention their names."

"No, I've never really said their names out loud, but I do think about them, wonder what his wife must be going through. How hard it is for her."

"Yeah, I reckon you right. I know if I found out that Clifford fathered some children by another woman, it would've torn me apart."

A strange feeling came over Beatrice. She remembered when she and Morris had first started writing to each other, and she had thought of him then as one piece to a puzzle—a complex contour of shapes and sizes and colors, connected to his family. But as the years passed, somehow, she no longer thought of him like that, only as the man she loved, the father to her children.

Beatrice looked at her watch. "It's about time for me to pick up the girls," she said, standing. "And then I have to rush home to pick up their bathing suits to take them to their swim lessons. I forgot to bring them with me."

"I remember running from one activity to the next with my girls. I'm glad they're old enough to do those things on their own." Nellie walked Beatrice to the front door, then gave Beatrice a comforting look. "Are you going to be okay?"

Beatrice took a deep breath. "Yes. I'm going to be just fine. Really, I am."

"Good, I'm glad to hear that." Nellie reached for her hand, squeezed it. "Call me if you want to talk. Anytime, okay?"

"Thank you," Beatrice said, then she grew pensive. "And thank you for never judging me. You've always been there for me, and never once did you ever make me feel bad about anything. I love you for that." She smiled through tears, and embraced Nellie before she turned to leave.

Beatrice quickly walked to the music studio to pick up the girls. When she arrived, Sadie Mae was finished with her lesson, and Sam was just finishing up.

"Mommy, we forgot our bathing suits," Sadie Mae said.

"I know, baby. We're going to stop by the house and pick them up." Sam emerged and rushed up to her mother, a big grin on her face.

"Mommy, I did good on my lesson today. You should have heard me."

"I know, baby. I can't wait to hear you play at the recital."

"You think Daddy gonna come, too, Mommy?"

"We'll see. Maybe."

As they walked, Beatrice ticked off a list of things she had to get done today—laundry, food shopping, helping Sadie Mae with a class project that was due on Monday, preparing for church on Sunday. She was so absorbed in her thoughts that she didn't notice Morris standing in front of her apartment until she felt Sadie Mae pull away from her and run to him, leaving her side. *"Daddy!"* Sam followed suit.

Morris raised his hand and waved, smiled.

Beatrice stared at his clean-shaven face and freshly cut hair. When she got closer, she felt herself softening toward him.

"I came to see the girls. I miss them." Morris held her gaze.

Beatrice saw the way he looked at her.

"Daddy, can you come with us to see us swim? Can you, Daddy?"

Morris looked down at Sam and touched her face, then back up at Beatrice. "Can I?" he said to Beatrice in Sam's voice.

"Please, Mommy! Pleeaaase," Sam said.

"All right," Beatrice said. "I need to grab their bathing suits. I'll be right back."

Beatrice rushed off into the apartment, and when she came back out, Morris was standing there with Sadie Mae and Sam, holding their hands. In that instant, an image flashed in her mind, the same image she'd have when she'd sometimes picture what it would feel like if they were a family. She didn't believe for one moment that it could be possible. Not in this lifetime.

As if to confirm her thoughts, a white man and woman drove by in a car, gawking at the sight of them. Morris pulled both of the girls closer to him.

"We need to hurry before we're late," Beatrice said. They walked quickly, the girls still holding their father's hands. Beatrice could feel the eyes on them. What were they all thinking? she wondered. But as the girls grew older, she no longer cared.

40

Emma

Emma glanced through the rack of dresses, pausing occasionally to put aside the ones she liked. "Let me know what you think, dear," the saleslady pressed. "We have every one of these in your size, and you won't know the right dress until you try it on. With your complexion, I'd suggest you consider ivory."

Try as she might, Emma wasn't in the mood today. It wasn't fair. Brides were supposed to be ecstatic. Since her dad had dropped his bombshell, she could barely muster the interest to plan a wedding. *Let's face it,* she thought, *my faith in marriage isn't what it used to be.* She glanced at her mother. Agnes looked through a rack of dresses at the other end of the room, flushed and happy.

After finding out about her husband's other family, Agnes had thrown propriety aside, sneaking drinks into her morning coffee. Emma had caught her one morning, and both pretended it never happened. Who could blame her mother, really? Emma thought. The problem was, Agnes seemed to hit rock bottom at about noon, and her mood would go downhill from there. By evening, she was likely to make bitter, angry comments about anything, had even started using foul language, as if the liquor unleashed her thoughts and tongue.

Emma was too angry with her father to discuss it, punishing him with her silence—and she was too worried about her mother's state of mind to confront her. It seemed no one in their family wanted to talk about it.

"Oh, honey, look at this one!" Agnes pulled a princess gown off the rack, and twirled around the aisle with it. "Isn't it gorgeous? You have to try it on!"

Emma took the gown from her mother, hung it back on the rack, and waved apologetically as she guided Agnes out the door. "But you didn't try any on! Emma. We have to find your dress."

"I don't feel like looking for a dress today. I'd rather take a walk in the park."

They made their way to a bench. As she sat down, Agnes gestured at a young couple with a curly-haired toddler. "Look at that. Can you imagine anything more perfect? I hope you will have children, Emma. I always wanted you to have a brother or sister . . ."

Emma could almost feel her mother's pain, thinking about the sisters Emma suddenly did have, the ones she would probably never know.

"Marriage is supposed to be sacred. How can I marry knowing that someday Johnny could come home and drop a bombshell? I can't get married. I won't."

Agnes understood more than Emma could ever know. She looked at her daughter with uncompromising eyes. "Honey, don't do this. Don't let your life be ruined by something between me and your father. I've forgiven your father. You have to do the same. And Johnny's a good man. He loves you. He would never hurt you."

"How do you know, Mom? You thought Daddy loved you, that he would never hurt you, but he did!"

Agnes looked at Emma. "Oh, honey, no. Don't. Please don't ruin your life over this."

"How can you forgive him so easily? He's ruined everything."

Agnes suddenly put her arm around Emma. "No, honey. Don't be confused. This has nothing to do with how your father feels about you. You will always be his first daughter. He loves you more than anything. I may not be sure of much, but I know that. Please give Johnny a chance, honey. You two could have a good life together. Don't throw that away over your father's mistakes. Have the wedding. Please, honey."

"Really, Mom?"

"Yes. I could never forgive myself or your father if I thought we robbed you of the perfect wedding. Johnny is a good man. He's been very patient. I'd say he's already proved he'll stick by you."

Emma considered what her mother said. "Poor Johnny. I've really put him through the ringer."

"I'm sure some men have been put through worse." Agnes grabbed Emma's hand with both of hers. "Now what do you say we go back to the shop and try on some gowns?"

"Actually, Mom, I've been meaning to ask you something." A soft smile broke on Emma's face. "Would you mind if I wore your wedding dress?"

Agnes looked surprised.

"Growing up, I loved looking at your wedding pictures. I've always thought you were the most beautiful bride in the world."

Agnes stared blankly at her daughter. A long moment passed before she could speak. "Emma, I think that is a perfect idea," she said, tearing up. "It never occurred to me you'd want to wear that old thing. It would mean the world to me."

"It's settled, then."

"Oh, honey. I can't wait to tell your father," Agnes said, thrilled at the idea.

41

Beatrice stood at the bus stop with Sadie Mae and Sam, unsettled by the school buses that lined the street, surrounded by armed guards. If she hadn't been so nervous about the way people would react, she might have been excited that her girls' school had been one of several in Roxbury chosen to be integrated with the white schools in South Boston.

"It's gonna be okay. Y'all gon' like your new school," Beatrice said.

"But I don't want to go to a new school. I want to stay in the school with you," Sam sobbed. Sadie Mae stood nearby, quiet.

"You got to be brave. You're big girls now. 'Bout to start the sixth grade. You'll only be there for one year, then you'll go to another school, maybe a school back here in Roxbury. Now go on and get in line. They're about to board the buses."

Sam wiped her face, gave her mother a hug, and followed Sadie Mae to the bus.

"You want to sit with me?" Sadie Mae asked.

Sam nodded and took the seat closest to the window, and looked out at the swarms of police and armed guards. The silence revealed just how much they all dreaded going to a new school in an all-white community. She had seen their faces on the television news, heard what they had said: *We don't want those niggers coming to our schools, our neighborhoods*. If it had been up to Sam, her own choice, she would never leave Roxbury. She was content at the school where their mother taught. When their mother had started working at the same school that Sam and Sadie Mae attended—after that awful thing happened to her—she had felt peace knowing that her mother was always nearby, that nothing like that could ever happen to her again. Now, the bus moved slowly down the street, and Sam watched everything that she knew—her mother, her school, Roxbury—fade away.

Sam didn't want to go to a place where they weren't welcome, like when her daddy had taken them to meet his *other* family. She remembered it so vividly. The way she couldn't sleep the night before, and that morning when she had put on her special dress and had helped bake the cookies, she and Sadie Mae. And that house, with its pretty curtains and fancy chairs. And how she had handed Agnes the letter, and her hand was left dangling, as if she had no hand at all.

Yes, she remembered as she stared out at the raging mob.

Go home, niggers! Niggers, go home! . . . Go home, niggers! Niggers, go home!

Sam heard the splatter before she saw it. Eggs. Rocks. Bottles—crashing against the bus. She froze with fear. Sadie Mae reached for her sister's hand, and when they heard a window shatter in the back, Sam could not stop shaking. Sadie Mae was shaking, too.

"Children, stay seated! Do not leave your seats!" The bus attendant moved quickly up the aisles, and closed the windows. "Put your heads down, children! Cover your heads!"

"I want to go home!" Sam cried.

"We can't go home. We have to go to school," Sadie Mae whispered.

"Nooo. I don't want to go to that school. They hate us! Look at them."

Sadie Mae kept her head down, refusing to look out at the frightening sight.

⅍

Morris had barely slept the night before. For weeks, talk about plans to integrate the schools had aggravated an already delicate situation. When Beatrice showed him the letter about Sadie Mae and Sam being selected to transfer to the South Boston school, he knew there would be trouble.

"I hate the thought of them having to be in the middle of this," Beatrice had said.

"But at least they'll get a more decent education now."

"What do you mean by that? They are getting a decent enough education right here in Roxbury!"

"I didn't mean nothing by it, but I've heard you complain about the lack of resources at your school. Don't let this sidetrack what's important here."

"Sidetrack? Ain't nothin' gonna be any more sidetracked than what it already is."

Beatrice was right. Things had been *sidetracked*. Ever since that day he brought the girls back home after taking them to meet Agnes, things had changed. Especially Sam, who had become more subdued. It was difficult enough for Sam, though they never talked again about that horrible thing that happened to her. People would never know the horror Sam had been through in the months that followed the attack, her body healing sooner than her mind. She suffered terrible nightmares. Then the repeated interviews by the police, forcing her to remember. And the many times she saw her mother crying, hoping that they would catch him. *But they never did. They never did.*

Morris had never felt so powerless. Then and now, as he

listened to the reports on the radio about what was happening to his girls.

Police Commissioner Robert DiGrazia has just arrived at South Boston High School. He's conferring with officials, trying to get a handle on the situation. Things have erupted here at South Boston High. Angry crowds fill the sidewalks and streets, trading nasty remarks and hurling things at the buses that have just arrived. And I hear that these crowds aren't even sparing the elementary school children. Word just came in that a bus at Lee Elementary School was attacked.

Morris grabbed his stuff and ran out the door. The drizzling rain was coming down harder now, making already congested traffic come to a near stop. Morris weaved in and out of traffic. As he neared the school, he could see the crowds, hundreds of people lining the streets, signs above their heads. Go Home Niggers, Go Home, the signs read.

"Go home, people. Either you go to school or go home," a plainclothes cop shouted.

"Make them niggers go home! These are our schools. Our children. We don't want them here!"

Morris made his way to the officer. "My daughters are on those buses. I need to get through. Let me through."

The cop gave him a peculiar look, not sure if Morris was referring to the lone busload of white children, those few whose parents stood for integration. Or the three buses packed with black children, waiting for the crowd to settle down.

"Let me through," Morris shouted. "I need to get through!"

"Sir, stay where you are. No one is getting through," another officer said, shoving Morris back against the crowd. "I said *step* back!"

Morris struggled to keep his place. Suddenly, a loud crash startled the crowd. Shards of glass crashed to the ground.

"I need to get my daughters! Please let me through." Morris pushed forward.

"I said step back! You are not getting through!" The officer pulled his nightstick from his holster, threatening to use it.

The crowd kept at it, fueled with a hatred often seen in the South. Morris could see that they were capable of anything.

As the bus slowly pulled away, Morris looked for Sam and Sadie Mae. Eggs splashed against the bus. And then Morris saw her, Sam, looking so small and scared, and when she spotted her daddy, their eyes met and Morris knew he had to do something.

42

Morris

No sooner than Beatrice opened the door, Morris made his way inside and looked around, frantic. "I heard what happened. Are they okay?"

Beatrice had not expected it to be that terrible. There had been talk about the violence, but never had the hostility been so blatant as what she'd witnessed today.

For weeks, she had tried to prepare the girls: *Your daddy went to a school not so far away from the one you'll be going to,* she had told them. It was Sadie Mae who asked if she could teach at their new school the way she taught at the school they now attended. And then Sam, who said, *But Daddy ain't like those mean people. They hate us.*

"I can't believe what happened today. They terrorized those children. How in God's name could they do such a hateful thing? They are never going back to that school again! Never!"

"I'm going to pay for them to go to private school. Even if I have to take them to school every morning myself," Morris said.

Sending them to a different school wouldn't protect them from the fragile world that awaited them. How had she forgotten about what it was like for her? What it would now be like for her daughters? It was something Beatrice had always expected, the dissension always there. But somehow she had

let down her guard, allowed the distance between Mississippi and Roxbury and the unfathomable love that she had for
Morris distort her better judgment.

"That would be nice, but it's not going to change what
happened to them today, and what will probably continue to
happen to them throughout their lives."

"I know, but at least it's a start. Let me do this, Beatrice.
Please."

A deep sense of distress rose up in Beatrice, knotted with
so many emotions: thoughts of those ugly faces she saw today;
the girls, how frightened they looked; and the way she wanted
so desperately to protect them. "Okay. You're right. Let me
get them." She called Sadie Mae and Sam to the living room.

Sadie Mae came first, then Sam. Neither one said a word.

"Your father has something he wants to tell you," Beatrice
said.

"Hi, girls." Morris reached to touch Sadie Mae's arm and
she turned away. And when he reached to touch Sam, she
flinched, too.

"Sweetheart, I know how you must feel, and I'm sorry.
They were bad people. You did nothing wrong. I'm sorry that
I wasn't able to do more. I tried. Believe me. I did."

Sam eyed her father suspiciously. The last time she'd seen
him, he looked like one of *them*. His face. His hair. His eyes.
There he was standing there, not doing anything. It was *his*
fault. Anger rose up in a rush, brought fresh tears.

"Come here, honey," Morris said, reaching for Sam.

Sam didn't trust herself to move, then looked haltingly
at her father. "But you let them be mean to us, Daddy! You
stood there watching them throw those eggs and bottles at us,
and you didn't do anything! Anything! Like when Aknes was
mean to us!"

"No, honey! I will never let anyone hurt you. Never!"

"But why do you have to live over there, Daddy, with those mean people? Why won't you come live here with me and Sadie Mae and Mama? We your family, too!"

Morris looked at Sam, and he clearly saw the pain that was beyond what happened on the bus. He glanced over at Beatrice and Sadie Mae, and then turned back to Sam. Sam's words had surprised him. "Honey, you know I love you no matter where I live," he said gently. "Remember what I told you about me having two families?"

Sam refused to nod, refused to even look at her father.

"Well, I have to live in that neighborhood with my other family, but it doesn't mean I don't love you. I'll always be your father, and I'll never let anyone ever hurt you again. Never again," Morris reached for Sam again.

Slowly, Sam wiped her face with the back of her wrist and finally allowed herself to cry on her father's shoulder.

"Oh, sweetheart, I'm so sorry. So very sorry. You never have to go back to that school again. I'm going to find you a new school. Here in Roxbury, where you'll be safe."

This time Sam nodded as he pulled her close to him, then he reached for Sadie Mae, too, who stubbornly fought back tears.

Two weeks later, Morris stood at the front desk of Mission Catholic School. "I'm Morris Sullivan. I called a week ago. I'm here to enroll my daughters." Morris looked at the woman who sat behind a heavy dark wood desk, her stern face looming from behind the habit—a starched white wimple and black veil over her hair, matching the black dress that hung to the floor.

"I'm sorry, sir, what did you say your name was?"

"Morris Sullivan. I called last week and spoke to Sister Mary Louise. I have an appointment with her today to enroll my daughters."

"Your daughters? Where are they, sir?"

Morris turned to the entry door. Sam and Sadie Mae stood quiet.

The woman eyed the two little girls, and a flash of surprise crossed her face. "Very well, then. Please take a seat. I will summon Sister Mary Louise for you."

Morris waved to Sam and Sadie Mae to join him. Sam sat with her head down, not saying anything. She had not been able to sleep since that awful day, terrorized by all those faces, angry white faces. She was surprised when she woke each morning to find herself in her own bed, and not on that bus. She hated that bus. She didn't like the way those angry people made her feel, so *different*. She felt as sad then as she had when that awful thing happened to her. Often, she would lie awake in her bed across from Sadie Mae's. "Are you asleep?" she'd whispered to her sister. Sadie Mae would shake her head no. "Do you think the new school will be as bad as the old school?" Sadie Mae ignored her. Sam wondered if her sister had thought about that day on the bus at all.

"Mr. Sullivan, I'm glad you could make it today." Sister Mary Louise's smile glowed on her round face, the only thing not covered by the all-white habit draped from head to toe. "And this must be Sadie Mae and Sam?"

"Yes," Morris said, standing quickly.

"This is Sadie Mae." Morris put his arm around Sadie Mae's shoulders. "And this is Sam," he said, reaching for her. The girls stood beside their father, intrigued by Sister Mary Louise.

"What precious sweet angels you both are, so pretty. And look at you with those beautiful blue eyes," she smiled at Sam.

Sam managed a fragile smile, and then Sister Mary Louise stretched out her arms for a hug.

Sam and Sadie Mae walked into her arms. For an instant, before she let them go, before their father had time to say anything, they felt something from Sister Mary Louise. It was a moment that was real only to them, something that could not be missed. *I know what they did to you, and I'll never let that happen to you again. You're safe here,* it whispered.

"So is their mother with you? Should we wait for her?" Sister Mary Louise said, looking past Morris.

"No. It's just me. I came alone." It was gratifying to do this on his own, to publicly claim his daughters, something he had always wanted to do. There was pride in telling her that they were *his,* that he was their father.

Sister Mary Louise led the way to her office, pausing along the way to point out the classrooms encased in mahogany wood, the immaculate grounds, a statue of Our Lord and Savior. They stopped in front of a wide entry door that led into her office. "Have a seat, please." Sister Mary Louise's office was accented in the same dark mahogany; a pale green color dressed the walls. A statue of Our Lady sat prominently behind her desk, near a window that looked out into the gardens. Potted plants encircled the window, and rosary beads laced a rosary vine that scaled the wall, making the room feel warm, inviting.

Morris took a seat on the opposite side of her desk. Sam and Sadie Mae sat on a small sofa in the corner.

"Okay, here we are." Sister Mary Louise pulled a file from her drawer. "Mission Church prides itself on our education model. Learning is just as important to us as worshipping. Every child gets special care. Most of our students score above grade level in reading, math, and science," Sister Mary Louise said, thumbing through Sadie Mae's and Sam's school records.

Morris watched her pull two forms from the file, one with Sadie Mae's name and the other with Sam's.

"Here we are." Sister Mary Louise grabbed a pen from a tin can covered in a knitted sleeve, one crocheted with precision, the same precision she used now to complete the form.

"I have all the information already completed. Just need you to fill out your address and sign here." She pointed to a blank section, and handed the pen to Morris.

Morris scanned the form. *His address,* not far from theirs, but divided. He always knew that things were different, but somehow, he'd managed to put it out of his mind, conceal it. But that day it all became so clear. There was more to the street lines that divided them. He was reminded again of the way his father treated his friend Charlie all those years ago, and now, he had his very own Charlies—Sadie Mae and Sam.

"Okay," Sister Mary Louise said. "Did you bring the enrollment fee?"

Morris pulled a check from his shirt pocket.

"Very well now. I think we have everything we need. Are you ready to take a tour? To see your new school?" Sister Mary Louise smiled at Sadie Mae and Sam.

They both nodded.

"You're going to love it here." Sister Mary Louise stood and walked around her desk, ready to lead the way.

And for the first time in weeks, Sam and Sadie Mae felt safe, a world apart from South Boston.

43

Agnes stepped back to admire Emma's wedding dress—the flowing train, the tiara, and the silk veil complementing it perfectly. "You look so beautiful. There's something I want to give you." Agnes walked over to her purse and pulled a small box from it. "These were given to me by my mother, and now I want you to wear them."

Emma smiled at the diamond-and-pearl earrings. "Oh, Mom, they're beautiful."

"My mother wore them on her wedding day. I wore them on my wedding day. And now you get to wear them."

"Mom, thank you. Will you help me put them on?"

Agnes fastened the delicate earrings in Emma's ears. Everything about Emma reminded Agnes of her special day all those years ago. The dress, Emma's hair, her glowing face. "I know you're going to be so happy," she said. "Johnny loves you, and he's going to make you so happy."

A quiet moment swept over them.

"My God, look at you." Morris stepped inside the room, and for a moment he just took it all in. "You are absolutely beautiful," he said, struggling to maintain his composure. He smiled at Agnes. "The spitting image of your mother on the day I married her."

Morris reached out to embrace Emma, and she quickly pulled away.

Morris fell silent, held her gaze. Since his confession, he had spent the last several years trying to make amends with her. But Emma rarely spoke to him, and when she did, she was short, barely giving him the time of day.

Morris and Agnes locked eyes as he took Emma's hand. Agnes wiped away tears, too, then smiled.

"Are you ready? Everyone's waiting. Poor Johnny's sweating bullets."

Emma broke into a smile. "Yes, Dad. I'm ready."

Agnes took one last look at her daughter, touched her arm. "I'm so proud of you. I'll see you out there."

Emma nodded, her eyes clouding. She took her father's arm. Morris folded her hand into his and squeezed it, a final reassurance as he took his time walking her through the church's vestibule and up to the oversized wooden doors, the same doors that Agnes had come through. Suddenly, the doors opened and the congregation stood and turned. Emma squeezed her father's hand, covering hers. From where she stood, she could see Johnny standing next to the priest, so handsome, so proud and decent. And in that moment, Emma believed everything would be all right, that all that had happened was behind them. Her father's hand gripping hers, her mother's eyes filling, and Johnny, sweet, sweet Johnny, waiting for her, was all she needed to keep her shaky legs from buckling.

*

Sam lay on the cool tiled floor, listening to her mother talking on the phone to her aunt Nellie, and she could hear Sadie Mae in her room, too. The light from the noonday sun glinted off the porcelain sink, the bathroom tiles, the white walls. Everything so bright, except for the red scarlet that spotted her underpants. She had noticed it the day before, but had thought nothing of it. But this morning when she felt the odd moisture that woke her from her sleep, she rushed into the bathroom, removed her underpants, rinsed them, and stuffed them far down into the hamper where no one could see them. But that didn't keep the scarlet from coming. Even when her mother called her for breakfast—grits and pancakes, her favorites—she declined. She didn't feel well, hadn't felt well for months now.

And there were other strange things happening to her— the sudden outbursts at her sister, the need to sleep more, and the voices. It was the voices that worried her the most. Sometimes at night, and occasionally in the middle of the day, she'd hear strange sounds and see things that weren't there. At first, she thought it was because of the new house they'd moved into. After they'd started their new school, their mother had started saving to buy a home so they could be closer to their school. It took almost two years before Beatrice came home one day and announced: "I found us a house!" It was a welcome announcement that meant Sam would no longer have to share a room with her sister. They would have their own house, and she her very own room. Now, she lay in the middle of the tiled floor, a fierce cramp rising from her belly, threatening to invade her. It was the third time that morning that she had come into the bathroom and stretched out on the floor.

Her mother had made plans for them to go to a barbecue at Aunt Nellie's, but there was no way she could go. No way she could fake her way out of the dizziness in her head, and especially the scarlet red that seemed to keep coming.

She had thought about telling her sister, just calling her into the bathroom and showing it to her. But Sadie Mae seemed less interested in her nowadays, often ignoring her. As soon as they had turned thirteen, it was as though Sadie Mae had drawn a dividing line, forced a wedge between them.

It was months before Sam stopped puzzling over it. She figured it meant that they were growing into their separate spaces and separate lives. That's what her aunt Nellie had told her one day, the only one she could talk to. And she believed it. But deep down inside she knew it was something more.

"Sam, what are you doing in there? You've been in and out of that bathroom all morning. Open this door!"

Sam heard the knob turning. She couldn't tell her mother about the voices in her head, or the fierce cramps that rose from her belly through her whole body, or the scarlet that stained her Sunday panties.

Sam picked herself up from the floor, turned the faucet on, and quickly washed her underpants. "I'm coming out in a minute," she shouted toward the door.

"Samantha, you open this door up right now!" Beatrice turned the knob again. "Right now, Samantha!"

Lately Sam had been able to avoid her mother's watchful eye, the curious undertone of her words. Sam wondered if she had eluded Sadie Mae, too. But Sadie Mae seemed to know something was not right with her. Sometimes, Sadie Mae would catch Sam staring at nothing. "What's wrong with you?" Sadie Mae would ask. But Sam would say nothing.

"Samantha, I'm not going to tell you again to open this door!"

Sam turned the water off, and quickly stuffed the wet fabric into the hamper. "Yes, ma'am," she answered, checking around one last time before she unlocked the door.

"What in God's earth is going on with you? Hiding in this bathroom for hours at a time. What's ail' you?"

"Nothing."

"Nothing? What do you mean, nothing? You've been acting strange for a while now. Now you hide in the bathroom all
times of the day and night. I want to know what's going on!"

"Nothing, Mama. I just haven't been feeling good, is all."

"What do you mean, you haven't been feeling good?" Beatrice stepped closer to Sam and put her hand on her forehead.
"You ain't got no fever. Maybe you comin' down with a cold
or something."

Sam shook her head.

"Then what is it, Sam? Why have you been acting so
strange, hiding in the bathroom, not talking to us?"

Sam let her mother's words drift for a while, holding back.
The longer she hid her secret, the more suspicious her mother
had become. One Sunday, she had come into Sam's room to
wake her after she'd been asleep all afternoon, and she had
questioned Sam persistently, determined to get some answers.
Now, she gave Sam a stern look.

"What is it, Sam?!" Beatrice asked again.

Almost without realizing it, Sam reached into the hamper
and pulled the damp cotton from it, handed it to her mother.

Beatrice looked at it, first with confusion, and then a sudden understanding. "Good Lord in heaven. You done got your
period."

Samantha eyed her mother. It wasn't her period. Her
mother had told her and Sadie Mae about this when they were
eleven, and she had seen some of the girls at school get theirs.
But this was something else, something to do with the strange
voices. The voices started long before the scarlet. Then one
day she had a dream about it, and she knew the moment she
saw the blood, it had something to do with the voices.

"I don't think it's that, Mama."

"You don't think it's what? Your period? It is that, Sam,
what else would it be? Is something else ail' you?"

Samantha stared at the damp cotton, tried to say something. "No, Mama," she finally said, and looked away.

𝒜

The band brought the room to life—playing Motown to Mozart to Frank Sinatra. Emma and Johnny danced in the center of the room with every pair of eyes glued to them. Emma looked ravishing, beaming as brilliantly as the carat on her left hand.

Agnes smiled at Emma and Johnny, moving so fluidly together, the same way she and Morris once moved. She looked around the room, sipped her cocktail. Their family, everyone was there—Morris's mother, his sisters, his brother, Ben, even his best friend, Vincent, and Vincent's father, her father, and nearly two hundred other relatives and friends and acquaintances—had responded to her handwritten invitations, a personal note inside for each of them. *A Celebration of Love,* she had titled the invitations. And on the inside, they were left blank for Agnes to write a special note. It took a lot of time, but it helped chip away at the long hours she sometimes had to herself now that she was no longer working. She had told Morris she needed time off. In reality, she just couldn't face Joan, Janet, and Annette, the three nurses who worked the early morning shift with her—her best friends. The ones with whom she shared everything, except for the *secret*. Telling them would be like tearing down the walls to the perfect home she had worked so hard to build.

"You look so beautiful," Morris mouthed to his daughter as she took the seat across from him.

Emma smiled. "Thank you," she said, and nestled closer to Johnny.

The chiming of metal hitting glass brought the room to a

hush. Johnny's best man stood. "May I have your attention, ladies and gentlemen." Everyone looked at the wedding table, at Carl. "It gives me great pleasure on this beautiful evening to wish my best friend and his lovely bride all the best for their future. I would have never imagined the day that Johnny, my buddy since second grade, would tie the knot, in a big way, a big *knot*." The room chuckled. "But he and Emma are like salt and pepper, they belong together." Carl tipped his glass to Johnny and Emma. "May God bless this marriage, your family, and your life together." Carl raised his glass, and waited for everyone in the room to raise theirs.

Morris stood next, more out of love for his daughter than out of duty. "Sweetheart, you look stunning. My little girl. All grown up, and happy." Emma smiled at her father, teary-eyed. "May God bless you, honey. And, Johnny, may Emma make you as happy and proud as she's made me and her mother." He raised his glass to them, a look of tenderness on his face.

Agnes watched her husband, torn between love and disdain. She took in the smiling faces, the way they all revered him, the war hero, unaware of his secret, their *secret*. She despised that she had allowed it to go on for so long, pretending to be the perfect family, the perfect wife. Protecting him. She had managed to keep her repugnance at bay with her own secret, her habit, softening her pain. The loose, contorted smile hung on Agnes's face, and she was filled with a familiar warmth. She knew she should slow down, but she couldn't seem to stop drinking. She waited for Morris to finish.

From the moment that Agnes stood, Emma knew her mother was in trouble. Emma noticed the odd expression on her mother's face and held her breath. Morris settled into his seat, startled by Agnes's sudden interest in speaking.

Agnes looked around the room, held the wineglass in her hand, an unsteady smile on her face. She took her time. "So where do I begin?" she started, her voice deliberate. "Emma, darling, you are my life," she said, tearing up. "I've loved you deeply from the moment you were conceived. You are my greatest joy, and today I'm so very happy for you." Agnes fell into an almost trancelike state. Slowly, the tears clogged her throat. Everything that she had held in for so long, all the secrets, the shame, rising. "I have loved my husband more than anything. More than my life," she said suddenly, her words slurring. "I've given him everything. All of me . . . but apparently that wasn't enough. It was never enough!" Alarm fluttered across Morris's face. He reached to take Agnes's hand, to guide her back to her seat. Agnes pulled away. "No! I will not be silent anymore! I've been silent for far too long. And what has it gotten me?!"

The room felt airless, the guests unanimously shocked by the turn of events.

"How?" Agnes slurred, finding her balance. "How do you go on living after your marriage has fallen apart? When your husband doesn't love you anymore?" And in one sudden move she tilted her glass and hurled the liquid in Morris's face.

Morris hadn't seen it coming. It happened so fast that the cool, pungent liquid hit his face before he had time to think about what Agnes had said. He calmly stood and reached for Agnes's arm. Agnes struggled to pull away, until she finally gave in, and allowed Morris to escort her from the room.

Johnny looked over at Emma, saw the shame, the sheer embarrassment. He quickly stood, broke through the eerie silence.

"Ladies and gentlemen, Emma and I would like to apologize for Agnes. She's been a bit under the weather with all the planning and preparations for the wedding. But please continue to celebrate this special moment with me and my beautiful wife." He turned and raised his glass to Emma.

Whatever embarrassment Johnny might have had could

not be read on his face. He took his seat, and reached over and grabbed Emma's hand. He could feel her trembling. "Are you okay?"

Emma sat quietly. To speak would risk tears. She could feel *their* eyes on her. This could not be happening to her. Not here. Not now. Suddenly, she stood and gathered her dress, her legs giving way as she steadied herself. "I need some air," she said, and rushed from the room with Johnny following close behind.

44

Sam

Sam lay on her back staring at the ceiling, the tears sliding onto her pillow. She could smell the rain—crisp, fresh, clean, unlike her own smell. The rain drumming against the window was the only sound, a welcome respite from the sounds that usually went on inside her head. It was Easter vacation, and she had been unable to do much of anything except for the piano lessons that her mother insisted she and her sister take. She loved playing the piano, the sound of the chords, the way the music calmed her.

One minute she would be all right, feeling like the fifteen-year-old spirited girl she had grown into, and other times she'd become lost in her thoughts, her mind burrowing deeper into the abyss. She tried to steady her mind against the incessant string of faces and figures and fantasy that suddenly appeared like dark, lucid crystals, floating: that horrible man and what he had done to her, his face so vivid; and those contorted faces that hurled tomatoes, and bottles, and eggs; and now those mean, ugly girls at school who made her feel weird, telling her that she didn't belong.

Sam's only familiar dreams were of those faces, their meaning beyond her reach. She thought about telling her mother, but the more she tried to puzzle it out in a pattern that could be explained, the less sense it made. It was Sadie Mae who had come into her room, trying to pry open the cocoon that shelled her. But there was nothing that Sadie Mae, or her mother, or anyone could do.

Sam tiptoed out of her bed and pressed her ear against the closed door. She could hear her mother and Aunt Nellie downstairs, their voices an army of whispers.

"*I'm worried about her. I know something's wrong. All of a sudden she just stopped talking as much, like something's bothering her.*"

"*Has she said anything to you?*"

"*No. She refuses to talk about it.*"

"*Have you told Morris?*"

"*Not yet. I thought I would try to talk to her first.*"

"*But you're going to have to tell him. Maybe he could talk to her, get her to open up.*"

"*Sam is not as close to her father as she used to be.*"

There was something in the tone of her mother's voice that made Sam want to snatch open the door and run downstairs and tell her everything. But instead, she went to her closet and pushed her hand deep into the narrow corner and grabbed her notepad, hidden away.

Outside, the rain drenched the streets and trees, made shadows that danced around her room, like the waltz that danced in her head—strong, weak, weak; strong, weak, weak. The rain seeped through the cracked window as she opened her notebook and emptied her thoughts onto the page. When she was done, she tucked the notepad back into her closet, walked over to her dresser, and looked at herself in the mirror. The face that stared back at her was not her own—sandy hair, blue eyes, a round chin. Every time she looked in the mirror, her heart twisted with confusion.

As a little girl, she used to imagine dancing in her princess dress for her father, making him so proud of her. Often she thought of what it would be like to have her daddy with them all the time. It was their turn—hers and Sadie Mae's—to have

him now. They were his family, too, she had told her father
one day when he came to visit and she asked him why he
couldn't spend more time with them. And when he told her
the same story that he had been telling her since she was old
enough to understand, she changed beyond the fanciful little
girl, and thought less and less about her father. What still ate at
her were the times he would show up at her school, revealing
to everyone that they were different.

She was different.

She despised looking like her father, a telltale indication
that she was different. She had tried to identify her mother in
herself—her olive skin, the roundness of her body, the tangles
in her hair. But her mother's features more closely matched
Sadie Mae's—and were the polar opposite of her own. For a
long time, she had tried to overlook the mismatched kinship
to her mother, satisfied to be more like her father, until things
had shifted, signaling a change in their fragile relationship.
Now, as she listened to the rain pounding against her window, she couldn't stop the images and the voices that flooded
her mind.

⚘

The bus glided down Washington Street and crossed Dud-
ley Square. Sadie Mae watched the people, the quaint
homes and shops. She had thought all week about making this
trip, had even emptied her small pink clay pig bank that she
kept hidden for a rainy day. Today was a *rainy day*.

Just that morning, she heard Sam sobbing, and when she
finally went to Sam's room and knocked and Sam didn't answer, she let herself in.

Sam sat in the corner, her eyes lost, her face wet with tears.

"What's wrong, Sam?" When Sam didn't answer, Sadie Mae turned to leave. "I'm going to get Mom!"

"Noooo! Don't! Please don't, Sadie Mae. Please," Sam cried.

Sadie Mae tried to recognize the frail girl who squatted in the corner. She had seen Sam like this before, noticed how one day Sam seemed like the vibrant girl that she sometimes envied, and then the next, how she would transform into someone Sadie Mae barely recognized. She had thought to tell her mother, but had gone against her better judgment, refusing to break the kindred pact that she had always shared with her sister.

"Then get up, Sam, and come lie with me on the bed." Sadie Mae reached out her hand for Sam to take.

Sam slowly took Sadie Mae's hand, allowed Sadie Mae to lead her. They lay there for a long while, not a word between them, until Sadie Mae heard their mother calling.

"Let's go eat, Sam," Sadie Mae said, sitting up. She looked over at Sam, and noticed that she was sleeping. She sat there, taking in how peaceful Sam looked, nothing like the broken girl in the corner. She slipped quietly out of Sam's room and went downstairs without her, making up an excuse for Sam. And now, the bus driver called out: "Cambridge Street," as Sadie Mae waited for the doors to fold open, then stepped off the bus. She collected herself, and took in the quaint shops and brick sidewalks, rows of federal homes, a tin street sign that read BEACON HILL EST. 1795.

Sadie Mae pulled a crumpled piece of paper from her tote and read the address again before she crossed to a narrow cobblestone street. She had changed her mind a dozen times about going there. But she knew she had to do it. *For Sam.*

Sadie Mae finally came to the strangely familiar house and gazed at the red door, the flag suspended high above the window swaying in the breeze, planted boxes adorned the window's ledge. She checked the paper again to make sure the address matched the brass numbers on the door. Her heart beat against her chest as she rang the bell, stepped back, and waited.

When the door opened, Sadie Mae froze, her eyes locked on the woman who had hurt her and Sam.

"Yes?" Sadie Mae stared at Agnes.

"Is Morris Sullivan home?" Sadie Mae said timidly.

At first, Sadie Mae could tell that Agnes didn't recognize her, didn't remember the pain she had caused. Then she saw Agnes's composure change as she placed the sheepish little girl who had grown into a young woman—Sadie Mae—an extension of the betrayal, the pain. Sadie Mae watched Agnes taking her in—her tan jacket, her white cotton sweater, her denim jeans, the face that reminded her of her husband.

Agnes's mood turned crimson. "He's not here," she said.

Sadie Mae was ready to dart away, but thoughts of Sam made her go still. "Would it be okay if I waited for him?" she asked.

Agnes gave her a strange look, and then begrudgingly stepped aside to let her in.

Sadie Mae followed Agnes into the familiar living room. Everything still looked the same, the room tidy and tempered. She took a seat on the settee across from Agnes and stole glances at her, and she could feel Agnes looking at her, too. She gazed at an imaginary speck on the wall, thinking back on the first time she and Sam had been there and the way Agnes had sat across from them in that very same seat and tossed them away. The thought of it conjured up all the times that Sadie Mae wanted to come back here and give Agnes a piece of her mind. She remembered the time that she almost got the chance to do it. They were twelve years old, and out

of the blue one day, Sam said: "Let's go see Daddy." Sadie Mae
had given Sam one of those *No, Sam, we better not* looks and
told her that their mother would kill them if she ever found
out. "How's she ever gonna find out unless one of us tells?"

Sadie Mae finally agreed.

They took the bus to Beacon Hill, and when they got there,
they walked around trying to remember the right street, the
exact house. They were surprised when they turned down the
same street that Sadie Mae had turned down today, and spotted the red door. They stood across the street, just watching
that red door, wondering what was going on inside, if their
father was home, and moments later, when they saw the door
open and Agnes step out and walk in the opposite direction,
they both stared at her, watched her move gracefully down
the street—so beautiful, so in control, as though she had not
a care in the world. It wasn't until Sadie Mae felt Sam pulling her that she realized they were following Agnes. They
followed her, stealing glances at the woman who had hurt
them. Through the narrow streets, down brick sidewalks,
past quaint shops and restaurants, past places and people that
were a distant life from their own. And when Agnes finally
turned into one of the restaurants, they stood outside, peering through the glass window, watching her sip her tea, never
knowing that they were there, that they despised her.

Sitting across from Agnes now, Sadie Mae could feel herself trembling. She no longer hated Agnes. Hating Agnes was
counterproductive, and she had long since let go of the hate, and
replaced it instead with another emotion. She sat still, avoiding
Agnes's eyes until she heard the front door open, and they both
quickly turned and looked toward the foyer. She could see the
shock on her father's face when he saw her sitting there.

"Hi, Daddy," she said, her voice small. She saw her father
give Agnes a nervous look, then turn back to her.

"Hi, honey. What are you doing here? Are you okay?"

Sadie Mae rushed to stand. "Yes, but Sam needs help, Daddy," she blurted, then told her father about how she had found Sam in her room that morning and about how Sam often stayed locked in her room, refusing to talk for days, and the blank stare that sometimes showed on Sam's face. "Something's wrong with her, Daddy," Sadie Mae said.

Sadie Mae watched her father turn to Agnes. "I have to go," he said.

Silence filled the room like an elephant, big and stark and voluminous. Agnes stared blankly at him, a slightly perplexed look on her face, as if for a moment her maternal instincts had surfaced, betrayed her.

She felt torn.

She couldn't help but wonder if he was with them every time he did not come straight home from work, or when he would disappear for hours, sometimes a whole day. She always *knew* he was. She could see it on his face. Over the years, they hardly talked about it anymore, and she had thought to leave him, a thousand times, but she just couldn't bring herself to do it. A ripple rushed through her, and she had to still herself as she thought about what he had done to her and Emma, to their family. Emma had been furious at her for months about her outburst at the wedding, even though she blamed her father for putting her mother in that state of mind. Emma had been willing to forgive her only if she promised to cut back on the drinking. She was trying, if not completely succeeding, and this very moment threatened to break that promise.

She wanted Sadie Mae to leave, disappear beyond the same fate that had brought *them* into their lives in the first place. She searched Morris's face, his eyes pleading with her. She could sense how much he loved those girls, the same love he had for Emma. And in some strange way, it made her heart soften toward him. In a moment of ambivalence, she walked away and left them standing there.

Sadie Mae watched her father follow Agnes into the kitchen. She could barely make out what they were saying.

"Please, Agnes. Try to understand, I need to go see about Sam. Why won't you at least try to understand?" Morris said, trying to keep his voice low.

Agnes's face flushed with hurt, a look Morris had brought to her face so many times. He understood the source of her pain, and of his own. As the years passed, he had allowed himself to believe that things had gotten better between them. But looking at Agnes now, he knew that it had only been camouflaged by the artificial life they had contrived. For a moment they stood there, just looking at each other.

"If you leave, I want a divorce!" Agnes said, her voice quivering.

"Agnes, you know you don't mean that. They are my daughters. What do you expect me to do?!"

Agnes stared down the man who had grown soft around the middle. She still loved him, there was no denying it. But she was tired. So very tired of trying to undo what had already been done.

"Look, I need to go, okay? I won't be long," Morris said, searching Agnes's eyes, and when she turned away and refused to look at him, he left her standing there, and walked out the front door with Sadie Mae, never seeing the crystal vase that Agnes flung at the door behind him or the bottle of gin that she retrieved from the cupboard to dull her pain.

The moment Beatrice saw Morris and Sadie Mae, she knew something was wrong. "What are you doing here? And, Sadie Mae, where in God's name have you been? I've called around everywhere looking for you."

Sadie Mae's eyes darted from her mother to her father and back to her mother. "I went to see Daddy. I took the bus to his house." Her mother looked at her, confused.

Of all the people Beatrice thought to call, Morris never entered her mind. The girls had not stepped foot on that side of town for years, as far as she knew.

"Why?!" Beatrice demanded.

Sadie Mae looked nervously at her mother. "Something is wrong with Sam, Mama. She didn't want me to tell you. She made me promise." Sadie Mae sounded like a child again.

"Sadie Mae came to see me because she thought I could talk to Sam," Morris said, butting in.

"What do you mean, something is wrong with Sam?" Beatrice had known for a long time that something was not right with Sam, had even taken her to the doctor, but they just said that it was puberty. *Many children go through this,* the doctor had told her.

Morris gave Beatrice a troubled look. "Sadie Mae said Sam's been crying a lot, and when she went into her room this morning, something was wrong with her."

Beatrice rushed past Morris and Sadie Mae, and up the stairs to Sam's room. Morris and Sadie Mae followed her. When she opened the door, the room slumbered in the faint dusk light, everything was in disarray—Sam's bed, her books, her clothes—and Sam hovered in a corner, her knees folded to her chest, her head tucked into her arms, sobbing.

"Sam?!" Beatrice gasped.

Morris pushed past Beatrice and stooped down to Sam. "Honey . . . are you okay?"

Sam rocked in silence, her head heavy. She didn't seem to hear them.

"Honey, talk to me," Morris said as Beatrice watched in

disbelief, and Sadie Mae stood frozen in the doorway, on the brink of tears.

Slowly, Sam raised her head to her father. "Daddy, I don't feel so good," she said. "My head hurts."

Morris hastily grabbed the blanket from Sam's bed, wrapped it around her, and carried her down the stairs and out to his car, with Beatrice and Sadie Mae following closely behind.

45

In the three years since her father had rushed her to the hospital, the voices in Sam's head had quieted, albeit with a daily dose of colorful pills. At first, it took three doctors, all skilled in their own right, to try to get her to open up, but she would not until a twenty-eight-year-old, first-year psychologist, Dr. Abbie Faulkner, came along.

The moment that Sam entered Dr. Faulkner's office and saw photos of Dr. Faulkner with her parents—a white mother and black father—Sam knew she liked her.

"Call me Abbie," Dr. Faulkner said to Sam. "I want you to feel comfortable, like you can tell me anything."

Sam took a seat on the sofa across from Abbie.

"So, I hear we have something in common." Abbie gestured toward the photos. "I wonder if it was as hard for you growing up as it was for me?"

A shy look came over Sam.

"Sam, I want you to be able to tell me as much or as little as you like. Anything we talk about will stay between us. You can trust me. I don't want to just be your doctor. I want to be your friend. We have a lot we can learn from each other."

Those words would spark a very special relationship. In time, Abbie earned Sam's trust and Sam told her things that she never told anyone. "The kids hate me," Sam had confided. "Even my own sister."

"Why do you think Sadie Mae hates you?"

It took Sam some time to think it through. "She hates me because she's not me, because things are much harder for her," Sam said, surprising herself.

Abbie jotted something down in her file. "Did you ever talk to your sister about it? Ask her if she really felt that way about you?"

Sam shook her head. "No. She would never tell me, no way."

"I see," Abbie said. "I talked to Sadie Mae and she told me something very different." Abbie paused, watched Sam's face go flaccid. "Sadie Mae is so proud of you, Sam. She said that you are her best friend. She loves you, Sam. Very much."

Sam felt her chest tightening, the tears coming. All this time she had thought her sister hated her the way the other girls hated her. They always called her *white girl* and made her feel bad about the way she spoke, always telling her she sounded stupid trying to *talk white*.

"I'm not trying to talk white!" Sam would respond. Then she would go home and keep it to herself, never telling her mother or Sadie Mae. And it didn't matter anyway because she wondered if even her own parents were ashamed of her and Sadie Mae—the odd-looking pair, one black, the other white, a mismatch that always brought stares. Talking to Abbie about it was as painful as talking to her about what that awful man had done to her in the park, and the way those mean people treated her on the bus, and about Agnes. "Agnes hates us," Sam told Abbie about a year later, when she found the courage to finally talk about her father. "All he really cares about is his other family," Sam said, breaking into tears. Abbie reached for her and held her, rocked Sam in her arms until she stopped crying.

"Sam, I'm sure your father is doing the best he can. It's a very difficult situation. It must be very hard for him, too."

"But we're not even allowed at his home!" Sam blurted, suddenly feeling angry.

It was hard for him, Sam knew. She often wondered how her father could split his heart between two families, sometimes showing up at their home to just sit there, watching her mother cook in the kitchen while she and Sadie Mae sat at the table doing their homework. Sam imagined it gave him peace to be near them, even if for a few stolen hours. He loved them deeply, this much Sam knew. But it wasn't enough to mend the brokenness she and Sadie Mae felt from wanting their father to have a permanent presence in their lives—to tuck them in to bed at night, or to take them out for ice cream, or to send them off to their first dance. And they weren't the only ones who wanted more. Sam saw the same longing in her mother's eyes, and heard the sobs coming from her room sometimes after her father left.

"My mother and father are both very sad," Sam confided in Abbie. "I don't ever want to be like them, stuck in something I can't get out of."

"Why do you think they are stuck?"

Sam closed her eyes. She remembered when they were still living in their apartment, and how their neighbors would look at them. About the time her mother had taken her and Sadie Mae to the park to meet their father, and how two men called him a *nigger lover*. About the time when she and Sadie Mae were only nine years old and her father had taken them for ice cream, and she saw how the woman had looked at her father, and then turned her back to them and spit on Sam's cone. Her father didn't see it. Sadie Mae didn't see it, but Sam saw it. She saw it as clear as she could see it now. Tears rose up inside Sam. "They are stuck because people won't let them be unstuck," she said, and turned and stared out the window.

Sam heard Abbie take in a breath. She could feel her thinking. "Sam, we can't change what other people think and do, but we can change our own thoughts and actions," Abbie said, looking straight at Sam. "I know things have been very difficult, but you are the one in control of your life. You are the one who gets to decide if you are going to allow other people's actions to stop you from living."

Sam considered what Abbie said, and she knew she was right. It was up to *her*. She left Abbie's office that day, and she decided that she was going to take back her life. If it had not been for Abbie, she would not have had the clarity of mind to take part in her high school graduation in less than eight weeks.

46

Morris

A mixture of rain and fog had drifted through the night, in the same way Morris's mood drifted this morning. He could not shake the chill that had kept him awake most nights—probably more to do with his old bones and age than the weather. He had slept fitfully the night before, and he moved around the room stiffly, laying out the things he would take with him—Agnes's medical records, her health insurance cards, the book he would read while he waited with her. When he was convinced he had everything, he checked himself one last time in the mirror, and then made his way across the hall to Agnes's room.

Agnes lay with her back to him. He moved quietly to open the draperies. The gray light poured in, brightening the room. He grabbed Agnes's robe, lay it on the bed beside her.

"Are you hungry?" he said gently.

Agnes just stared out the window, not answering him.

"Would you like me to start a bath for you?"

Still no answer.

"It's very chilly outside. We have to be sure to dress warm."

Agnes lay stiffly, holding the blanket up to her chin, her body rolled into a ball. She could smell herself and she knew he could smell her, too. She hadn't showered in two days. There was a silent moment between them, a warning that this day would be like the day before, and the day before that, and the many days before.

"You have to get through this, Agnes, you have to do what the doctors said. You can't just lie there and wither away. We can beat this."

Morris moved closer to the bed. "Come on, Agnes. You have a doctor's appointment today. Let me help you get dressed."

Agnes tried to listen, but the news had knocked the wind right out of her. She remembered it vividly—the ringing phone, her doctor's voice on the other end. *I have some bad news,* he said.

Agnes went numb.

She had hung up the phone, then sat alone in the living room for hours, the soft glow from the street the only light fading in.

When Morris came home, he found her sitting in the dark. He rushed to turn on the lamp. The light shadowed her pale face. "Agnes, what's wrong? What happened? Is it Emma?"

Agnes didn't answer right away. She finally looked up at him. "I . . ." She paused, her voice nearly inaudible. "I . . . I have breast cancer."

She remembered the way he reached for her, took her in his arms and held her. Held her like he hadn't for years. And she could feel her heart throbbing against his chest. And she cried, her face pressed against his shirt. She cried.

Now, she lay there, unable to face another day.

Morris picked up the robe and held it in front of her to step inside. "Come on, honey. You'll feel much better after you bathe and eat."

Agnes finally let him lead her by the hand, like a small child. He helped her into a warm bath and took his time gently washing her. And when he helped her out of the tub, he already had a gray turtleneck, black slacks, and a silk headscarf picked out for her.

After he dressed her, he helped her downstairs to the kitchen. "I made oatmeal and toast and fruit, your favorites."

Agnes tried to smile, tried to open her heart to him. Ever since they'd first learned of her disease, the course of their relationship had shifted, as if they had gone to sleep one night, separate and shattered, and awoke the next morning unified by a common enemy.

They adjusted.

Agnes wanted to just lie there, let the disease take her. But Morris refused to let her slip away. He did everything for her now—took her to every doctor appointment, made her meals, even bathed her. They were closer now, in a strange and unusual way.

Agnes worried about the way Morris fussed over her and couldn't help but wonder if he felt an obligation to stay with her now. Just before she'd been diagnosed, they had talked about divorce. Something they'd periodically talked about in the past, but this time was different. It no longer mattered to her, his other life. The hurt had cut so deep it couldn't wound her anymore.

Agnes stared at the oatmeal that Morris set before her, and her stomach turned. The chemo and radiation treatments stripped bare what little was left of her.

Morris sat across the table from Agnes, waiting for her to eat. He wanted so desperately now for her to return to the way she had been for as long as he knew her, making the same sounds that he had listened to all the years they'd been together. He knew Agnes just as well as she knew him, a familiarity that came naturally with time. Habits asserted themselves—good and bad—his more predictable than hers; like the way he folded his shirts and socks, the way he read the morning paper from back to front, or the way he took his coffee, black with just one teaspoon of sugar, unstirred.

He had come to know his wife better than he knew himself, watched her form her own habits. But even he was surprised by one nasty habit that had revealed a side of Agnes he didn't know existed. The first time he discovered it, years ago, was after he brought Sadie Mae and Sam to their home. And when he refused to turn his back on them as Agnes had expected him to do, she closed down one side of herself, only to open up another. At first she drank on occasion, a glass here and there, a substitute for her dinner beverage, a nightcap to help her sleep, a habit that soon grew over time. Morris suspected that no one knew, except him and Emma. And Emma never told until after her wedding. Emma was mortified by the way everyone gawked at her mother. Then came the whispers, the speculations, the utter embellishment of the truth.

Morris checked his watch again: 12:45 P.M. "Why don't you go upstairs and get the rest of your things? We have to leave soon for your appointment. I'll clean up quickly, and maybe we'll grab a late lunch at the hospital," he said, noticing how little she ate.

Morris watched her leave the dining room. He moved around the kitchen slowly, his joints aching, reminding him of how quickly his life had slipped through his hands. At sixty he had reached a perilous age that had forced him to examine his life. He had spent a lifetime loving two women, being a father to three daughters, serving his country. By rights, he was a simple man, a man who had done all that he knew how to do. He had spent so much time trying to fix what sometimes proved futile. In the end, he had hurt two families—Agnes and Emma, so dear to him, the kind of family men longed for, a loving, beautiful wife and a daughter who made him proud. And Beatrice, a love that cost him everything, including her.

He often tried to understand it, but there was no script, no explanation to make sense of it all. It had been more than forty years since he first met Agnes, and in those early days he thought he would never look at another woman. But time had changed the course of his life, revealing a path that he still didn't understand.

When he was done putting the dishes away, he walked to the stairs landing, listened. The only sound came from the last chunk of the wood that slowly burned in the fire, the windows shivering against the chilly temperatures. He climbed the stairs. When he reached the last step, he turned and walked the few paces to Agnes's bedroom, knocked on the closed door. "Agnes," he called out, leaning his ear into the door. "Agnes, honey, we need to go. We're already late."

Morris knocked again, and this time he turned the knob and let himself in.

Agnes sat in the chair, staring out the window. "I'm not going," she said.

Morris looked at her, confused. "What's wrong?"

Agnes gave Morris a long, contemplative look, her tone hard and coarse. "I just can't do it anymore. The chemo. The radiation. The doctors. None of it!"

"Agnes, we can beat this thing. Please, you have to try."

"What good is it, huh? Really? The doctors already told us that I have less than a fifty percent chance to live!"

"But, honey, you've only been doing the treatments for a few months now. Already, the doctors said you're showing some signs of improvement. It's going to take some time."

Agnes sat very still, lulled into thoughts of her own mortality. Suddenly, she flashed back on her life, thinking of all the time she had spent catering to her husband, her daughter, her family, and very little time catering to *herself*. Sometimes she envied Morris's secret life; at least he had known something beyond the mundane frigidity of their lives, an existence that she had never known. She might have wept then, but she had long stopped crying, long since surrendered her tears for a time she could no longer alter. All the jagged pieces they had built over a lifetime. The puzzle now scrambled, amiss. She no longer envied her husband, that had become too broad a burden to bear. And she had kept these feelings to herself, dreading that anyone she might have told would have thought she had lost her heart alongside her head and health.

Agnes finally looked over at Morris. "I know you want what's best, but I just don't want you to have to take care of me for the rest of your life. It's only going to get worse."

"Don't say that, Agnes. We're going to get through this. Together."

Agnes gave him a perplexed look. She had never heard him describe them, in almost anything, as *together*. She couldn't help but wonder if he pitied her, if he was doing all this to absolve the pain he had caused her. She knew he often regretted hurting her, this much she could tell in the way he was now so very protective of her. There was a tenderness, a warmth in his voice, and against her better judgment, she felt the tears coming. "But why?" she said, anguish in her voice.

"Why what?" Morris asked.

Agnes's teary eyes pressed into his. She was remembering the day they had sat in her parents' yard—so young and so very naïve—and he had given her the chain with the butterfly, its wings so perfectly shaped, the way she had thought their lives would be shaped. *For you,* she remembered him saying. And she knew then, as she knew now, that he would always take care of her. No matter the cost, the pain, the indiscretions. They would always be together.

But somehow time had managed to break the whole into two halves, equal parts separate from the other.

"Why are you doing this? It would be easier for everyone to just let me go so you can go on with your life." Agnes held his gaze.

"We're going to get through this together, honey. We can beat this."

Morris reached out his hand for her to take, and this time, she didn't shun him or question what little of the future was still left for her. She just took his hand and allowed him to guide her where she had no choice but to go.

47

Sadie Mae

Sadie Mae had planned this moment many times in her head, but still she couldn't help but wonder if something was amiss. She had always been very meticulous, making sure that not one detail went awry, a habit she had formed as a little girl. Sadie Mae excelled at everything she put her mind to, embracing every task and challenge with ease. Her first few years had gone beyond her own expectations. She was reminded of her first day, her mother and Aunt Nellie and Sam by her side, all of them blown away by the picturesque brick buildings, the immaculate grounds—the very air exuded prestige.

"Welcome to Harvard," an eager, young white woman said to her when she walked up to the admissions desk. It had all seemed so unreal to her, that she—and not Sam—was standing there. She thought back on the endless days she had spent studying, trying so hard to do her best. It was never as easy for her as it was for Sam. But everything had changed, and she remembered the *day* that got her to Harvard. It was September 1974, the day she sat on that bus, watched the rocks, the eggs, their ugly faces.

Go home, niggers! Niggers, go home!

She tried to close her eyes and ears to them, and listen, instead, to her own silent words: *I will never let them treat me like this again. I'm going to try harder so that they never look at me the same.*

After that day, she never told anyone—not her mother, not her father, not even Sam. She didn't have Sam's skin, Sam's hair, Sam's eyes. Pretending that she would be treated like an equal was futile and foolhardy. Sitting on that bus had shown her just how very fragile she was, that she had one thing that could change things for her—her brain—and she intended to use it.

Sam, however, turned from a spirited, adventurous girl into a frightened young woman. She hardly talked anymore, and the medication that kept the voices at bay softened her mind. There had been brief bouts of aliveness for Sam. Like one Christmas morning when they were sixteen and she and Sam sat cross-legged near the tree, and they giggled and laughed and gossiped. Or the time Sam went to her first dance with a boy who never *knew*. And the time Sam learned to drive, sitting behind the steering wheel looking so grown-up, so normal.

Sadie Mae often thought about her life, the one that was meant for Sam. Now every time Sadie Mae looked at her sister, she was reminded that it was Sam, not her, who was the adventurous one. It was Sam, not her, who was to become the most popular girl in school. It was Sam, not her, who was supposed to go to Harvard.

Sadie Mae sprinted across campus toward the bus stop. It was seven thirty and the test was to start at 9 A.M. sharp, no excuses. Since her freshman year, she'd attended every lecture, every special event, every workshop, consuming as much and as often as her hectic schedule and boundless mind could absorb.

Her first year was tough overcoming all the obstacles that were stacked against her. Sadie Mae struggled with her class-work, despite having studied twice as hard as her classmates, and took extra classes. Had the assistant dean not summoned

her to his office to inform her that she was being put on proba-
tion for *marginalized performance,* she may have never pushed
herself. It wasn't that she didn't already know that she had allowed her own fears to impede her progress. It was the way
he had looked at her, the way he had said it: *marginalized performance.* She had met his eyes, and something in that moment
reminded her of all the other *moments.* She felt the heat rising
to her face. "I will do my best," she said, and then stormed out
of his office. What he didn't know but would soon find out
was that her *best* meant *the best.*

By her sophomore year, Sadie Mae excelled at every class
she took—biology, chemistry, physics. She even volunteered a
few hours a week at a local medical center, and that summer,
she decided to stay on campus and take extra classes while she
worked part-time at the medical center. Whenever her mind
was too overburdened with work and she couldn't sleep, or
fleeting thoughts threatened to rob her of her own sense of
self, she would roam the campus in awe of the magnificence
of Harvard, the mere thought that she was there. Her mother
had come to check on her several times, but Sadie Mae knew
when she showed up with a pot of soup, or stewed chicken, or
a basket of fresh-baked cookies, she came to bask in the very
idea that her Sadie Mae had *made it.*

Now, having just completed her junior year with exemplary marks, Sadie Mae stood in the registration line ready
to take the MCAT, to apply to medical school. When she approached the registration table, she said her name with clarity and confidence: *Sadie . . . Mae . . . Sullivan.* The sound of
it rolled off her tongue like she had studied saying her own
name. The woman looked up at her as though she expected to
see someone else standing there. "Your ID?" she asked. Sadie
Mae pulled her license and social security card from her purse
and watched the woman check her information against a long

list. The woman looked up at her and back at the photo ID to ensure that the photo matched the person who was standing in front of her. She handed Sadie Mae a number 2 pencil and two sheets of blank paper. "You may be seated," she said. Sadie Mae nodded and then walked into the half-filled room and took the first seat she came to.

She'd come to think of the test as a kind of penance, the final step to prove that she was just as good, sometimes better, than most had given her credit for. Secretly, every time she was confronted with a test, a challenge, or an obstacle, she thought about Sam. Reminded herself that she and Sam had come from the same genes, shared a similar acuity. And now, it wasn't the clock on the wall that she watched ticking down to the last second; or the rumblings in her belly that she always got when she was nervous; or the faces that sat around her, so much different from her own, that she thought of. It was Sam.

She was going to ace this test for Sam.

48

May 1985

Beatrice reached for her teal satin dress, a choice that matched her mood. She liked the way the color enlivened her skin, bringing out her best features. She hung the other dresses back up in the closet and laid the chosen dress on her bed alongside a pearl necklace and matching earrings. She took a seat at her dressing table and looked at herself in the mirror. Sitting allowed the memories to unveil themselves, some subtle, others bursting to full revelation. She would be sixty-two on her next birthday, had carved out a life of her own—rooted in three generations that blended the lines, evident now in her girls: Sadie Mae, a clearheaded young woman, who used life's heartaches to stretch herself. And Sam. It broke Beatrice's heart to remember eight-year-old Sam, so full of life . . . before all the trouble. She would have done anything to see Sam's face shine like that again. It seemed only yesterday that they were little girls, running bare-legged, so carefree. How quickly life had passed. Now, Sadie Mae was being honored by Harvard.

Beatrice wrapped the shawl around her shoulders and checked herself in the mirror one last time before she walked down the hall to Sam's room.

"Sam," she called out. "It's time for us to go." She leaned into Sam's door, listening.

Sam opened her door. She was beautiful, had grown into a

lovely young woman. Nothing like the illness that once consumed her. When she looked at her, Beatrice felt the love that she had for her daughters since they were first born.

"You look very pretty," Beatrice said. She reached out and brushed a wisp of hair from Sam's face. "Are you ready?"

Sam's face softened into a smile. "Yes, ma'am."

Beatrice, Sam, and Nellie sat in the row closest to the stage, behind a line of empty seats. To the right of the stage four men sat silent, all impeccably dressed. Finally, a tall, gangly man, the assistant dean, stood and crossed the stage to the podium. He adjusted his tie, cleared his throat, and leaned in to the mike. "Ladies and gentlemen, we are ready to start our program. Please take your seats swiftly."

The crowd eased to a quiet hush. Beatrice smiled, felt Sam take her hand and squeeze it. They all watched the assistant dean.

"Today is a very special day for some extraordinary students who have made Harvard proud." He paused, timed his next words. "These students will be graduating with honors."

The audience burst into a thunderous applause. The man raised his hand to silence them.

"We here at Harvard have nothing short of the finest. Our students possess exemplary skills, both in talent and academics. But every now and then, there comes a student who exceeds our expectations, who reveals exceptional aptitude, even among the elite. Harvard is a fine institution that looks for the very best, and today, we have found them."

The crowd cheered as he looked out over the audience.

"Ladies and gentlemen, I am pleased to introduce you to eight students who have mastered their fields of study and have raised the bar for those to follow. Please hold your applause as I call each student's name and ask them to join us."

Beatrice felt her heart fill with joy as she waited for him to finally announce: *Sadie Mae Sullivan, 3.98 GPA, pre-med, graduating with honors.*

Sadie Mae crossed the stage, a smile lighting up her face. She looked briefly out into the audience, spotted her family. She could see her mother's face, the joy on it; and Sam, her twin sister, always there for her, never a single strand of jealousy; and Nellie, their faithful auntie, as proud of her as her own mother. This was why she had stayed awake until the wee hours of the morning, studying. She reveled at the joy on her mother's face and the proud look in her sister's eyes. But as she took her seat, a singular heartache struck her. She didn't see her father sitting with her family. She had hoped he could make it, but his presence was never a guarantee. Then, her eyes were drawn to someone moving quickly through the aisle—it was her father rushing to take a seat. Their eyes met, hers now brimming with tears as he gave her a thumbs-up.

M orris found his way to an empty seat. He was very late, but at least he had made it. He had planned to leave the house earlier, but Agnes wasn't feeling well, and he had called Emma to come and stay with her. From where he sat, he scanned the crowd looking for Beatrice and then he spotted her with Sam and Nellie. He thought about making his way up there, but decided to just stay put, not wanting to disrupt the ceremony any more than he had already. A smile came on his face, stayed there.

Morris felt a swell of pride, radiating in waves. Sadie Mae looked so lovely, so astute, sitting on the stage. Her hair was pulled back into a ponytail, accentuating her beautiful face and eyes. She wore a tan cardigan jacket and black skirt and shoes; the outfit he guessed that she had bought with the money, a gift that he had given her.

Morris settled back and listened.

"Ladies and gentlemen, as I invite these eight outstanding young people to all stand, let's give them a resounding applause for the discipline, courage, and commitment they've demonstrated to excel at our fine institution."

The crowd erupted in applause. Morris stood and clapped hard, and looked up at the stage, at Sadie Mae waving at her mother, and then at him, a wide smile on her face. After the cheers faded and the students took their seats, the assistant dean approached the microphone again.

"Ladies and gentlemen, before we close, we have one last order of business." He paused and reached under the podium and pulled a plaque from below, then looked back out into the audience. "Every year, we honor one of these exceptional students who we believe not only met the expectations of our honors program, but also exceeded them. This student not only graduated at the top of her class, but excelled in every class she took. In fact, she was recently honored by a local hospital for the exemplary work she provided. One physician at this hospital wrote a personal letter to me expressing his sincere appreciation for her sheer commitment. Moreover, she has served or been a part of many academic opportunities and curricula associated with her field of study. And what's even more notable is that during her freshman year, I personally met with her to deliver some wrongheaded advice that she might consider withdrawing from the program for marginalized performance. Well, let me say to you today, ladies and gentlemen, from the moment that this young lady left my office, she defied all the odds by not only reversing her performance from marginalized to remarkable, but also abundantly surpassing and exceeding every challenge that was put before her. It brings me great personal pleasure to present the 1985 John Adams Award to Ms. Sadie Mae Sullivan."

When the assistant dean called Sadie Mae's name, Morris watched her once again walk across the stage. He couldn't help but wonder how it had come to be that Sadie Mae, the once shy-faced eight year old, was standing on the stage of one of the most prestigious educational institutions in the world. He quickly rose to his feet, his eyes clouded with tears, as he clapped feverishly again. A deep sense of joy rose up in him, so forceful, woven with so many emotions.

Morris turned to the lady who sat next to him. "That's my daughter," he said. "My little girl."

The lady smiled. "Good for you."

Morris was still clapping when Sadie Mae looked out in his direction. He anxiously waved at her, and watched Sadie Mae nod to the enlivened crowd, then walk back to her seat.

"That concludes our program today, ladies and gentlemen. Thank you all for coming."

Morris stood, looking in the direction of Beatrice, Sam, and Nellie; and now Sadie Mae, who had left the stage and joined them.

Morris made his way over, stopping briefly to listen to the praise he could hear about *his* Sadie Mae. When he finally reached them, he greeted Beatrice, Sam, and Nellie, then reached out to embrace Sadie Mae.

"Daddy. I'm so glad you came."

"I wouldn't have missed it for the world, honey."

For a moment they all stood silent. He caught Beatrice's eye and smiled, and Beatrice smiled back.

"Well, we are going back to my house. I made a nice dinner to celebrate. Would you care to join us?" Beatrice said.

Morris looked at her. "I can't. I need to get back . . ." A faint sadness was on his voice. He saw the way Beatrice looked at him, noticed his tired eyes.

Since he had told Beatrice about Agnes's cancer, and the

way he was now caring for her, their relationship had changed into an amicable arrangement, like an old pair of comfortable shoes. They hardly talked. Except during those times when he'd show up unannounced, looking deflated, and she just listened. Age mixed with a solid dose of wisdom had humbled them both.

"Well, I guess I better get going," Morris finally said. He gave Sam a hug, and then Sadie Mae. "I'm so proud of you, honey."

"Thank you, Daddy," Sadie Mae said before he left to return to Agnes.

♪

Emma watched a bird peck at his nest, using great skill to build it just right. She guessed from the look of him that he'd probably spent whole days putting so much love into caring for his family, the same way she tried to care for her mother.

Emma tried everything—reading to her, showing her photographs of herself as a young woman, taking strolls with her whenever her mother could muster the energy. It worried Emma that her mother was losing her will to live, had distanced herself from both of them—Emma and her father.

When Agnes had first started the treatments, Emma would come every Sunday and stay the whole day cooking, cleaning, caring for her. Until one Sunday when her mother had held Emma's eyes with intensity, and said: *Go home, Emma.* It wasn't the words that broke Emma's heart. It was the look on her mother's face. Emma cried. Then reluctantly left. But every hour she stayed away, she hurt. It was her father who had come to her one afternoon. "She didn't mean what she said, Emma. She needs you." She listened to her father but told him that she could no longer watch her wither away; just could not go back there again. After her father left, it was Johnny who told her: "You'll regret it for the rest of your life if you don't." And Johnny was right.

The next time her father called and asked her to come and stay with her mother for the day, Emma jumped at the chance.

Once Emma arrived, she went straight to her mother's room. Agnes was sleeping. Emma stood there for a long time, just watching her. Agnes seemed frail, shrunken. The yellow-and-pink headscarf accented the features in her face. She was still a beautiful woman.

Emma sat in the chair by the window, and when Agnes finally stirred and opened her eyes, Emma rushed to her.

"Good morning. How are you feeling?" Emma said gently.

Surprise clouded Agnes's face. She looked around the room for Morris.

"Are you hungry? What would you like for breakfast?"

Agnes closed her eyes again, said nothing.

"Mom, please. I know you don't want me here. But I want to be here. I missed you and I want to be here for you. Please, Mom, let's not do this again."

Agnes didn't open her eyes.

"Mom, please," Emma begged. "Why won't you just let me take care of you? Why do you have to make this so hard?" Emma thought she might cry or scream or fall apart again. She briefly glanced out the window, at the bird nest that was now empty. "Mom, I know this is hard. I understand that now. And I know you don't feel well, but please talk to me. Please, Mom."

Agnes finally opened her eyes and looked at her daughter. "Why did you come back? I thought I told you to go home."

Emma drew back and reconsidered. She came back because she needed her mother as much as Agnes needed her. The time away had made her realize just how much she missed her. "I love you, Mom," she said. "And I don't know what I would do if you left us. I need you. Please, Mom . . . Please."

Agnes turned away from Emma and then started to cry, slow and deliberate sobs.

Emma got into bed and held her, her own eyes now filling with tears. She understood why her mother felt the way she did. It was not only the sickness that consumed her, but the thought of losing her family. On those rare occasions when her mother would open up to her, she would say things to Emma that at first Emma didn't understand. *Never love someone so hard that you lose yourself in that love;* and Emma understood it now, more than ever.

After Agnes fell asleep in her arms, Emma quietly slipped out of bed and went downstairs to call Johnny. The moment she heard Johnny's voice on the other end, she broke down again. "She's so frail, and so sad. I can't believe I stayed away for as long as I did. I feel so bad," Emma sobbed into the phone.

"It's not your fault, Emma. You needed some time away. And maybe your being away helped your mother see just how much she needed you, too. Don't beat yourself up over this."

"I know, but I should have been here. And what about when we leave for vacation? I won't be here again if something happens to her. I don't think I should go."

"Emma, you need this vacation. The doctor told you it was the stress that is causing the migraines. Honey, you can't keep doing this to yourself, working and worrying about your mom all the time. You need this time off. I've been planning this trip to Italy since we got married. It'll help you feel better, like the doctor said. Your mom will be fine with your dad while you're gone, and when we get back, you'll be refreshed and better able to care for her."

Johnny was right. She did need some time away. Her work

as a teacher exhausted her, and worrying about her mother made the migraines worse. Her doctor told her that since her last test results revealed early stages of an aneurysm that was at risk of erupting, and that if she didn't take some time off to relieve the migraines, he would have to put her on bed rest. The three-week vacation in Italy would help her to rest and relieve the pressures, the doctor had advised. Her father had taken care of her mother for the previous time that she had stayed away, and he could manage for another three weeks while she was gone.

"You're right, honey," Emma said. "My mom would want us to take this trip since we never had a honeymoon, and I haven't told her about the migraines because I don't want her and my dad worrying about me."

"There you go. See, I knew it would all work out."

Emma nodded into the phone. "I gotta go. My dad should be back soon, and I want to spend some time with my mother before he returns."

"Okay. I'll see you soon. I love you."

A smile broke on Emma's face. "I love you, too," she said, and then went back to her mother.

49

Morris

Morris had slept restlessly in the chair next to Agnes's bed. The fear that she might slip into another high fever worried him. Two nights before he had rushed her to the hospital with a 103-degree temperature that made her sweat with chills. The hospital had kept her overnight, and the next morning, they sent Agnes back home with two more prescriptions to add to an already hefty cocktail of drugs.

Agnes refused to take the medication, or eat, or drink anything. She was so tired, he could tell, from all the medication, and the chemo and radiation that made her so sick. Morris sat wondering how it was possible that one fateful call from her doctor could change the course of their lives. He hated what cancer had done to Agnes. It reminded him of how he had felt years ago when their son was born, and he had sat next to the tiny incubator, willing him to live. And when he died, Morris grieved like nothing he had ever felt before. He couldn't bear the thought of that grief again.

Morris looked over at Agnes, spoke softly to her. "Honey . . . are you hungry?" He waited for her to respond, but Agnes said nothing. "How about we get you washed and dressed, and you can come downstairs with me and eat some breakfast, then maybe we can go for a walk. It's going to be a beautiful day today. It'll do you some good to get some fresh air."

Still Agnes did not move.

"Honey, I know you don't feel well. But you need to eat. It's not good to just stay in this room all the time, just lying here. Come on, honey, let me help you get cleaned up and get something to eat."

Agnes still didn't move. Then finally, in a flat, whining voice, she said: "That food makes me sick. And I hate taking all those pills. They just make me feel worse!"

Agnes looked so gaunt, seemingly thinner and more ghostly each time he looked at her. In the two years since her diagnosis, Agnes had aged ten years. Morris had never felt more helpless, and so painfully alone. Nothing he did was right. Nothing he said mattered. And the more he did, the more useless he felt.

It had been only two days since Emma left for her trip to Italy, and already Morris could not imagine getting through the next few weeks alone. He had thought to call one of Agnes's friends to help. But he knew that Agnes would never forgive him if he did.

"Agnes, honey, I really need you to try harder," Morris continued. He tried to look her in the eyes, but Agnes turned away. "Honey, look at me, please."

After a moment, Agnes faced him.

"Will you please let me help you get washed up so you can come downstairs with me to eat?" His eyes pleaded with her.

"Why do you and Emma keep pushing and pushing and pushing? PLEASE GO AWAY AND LEAVE ME ALONE!"

"Fine! If you want to just give up, then go right on ahead!" Frustrated, he stormed out of the room, quickly made his way downstairs, grabbed his keys, and left. Agnes heard the front door slam shut.

She hated them always pulling at her, taking turns the way they did. It was humiliating to be treated like a child. They tried to make her eat. Bathe her. Force her to take those horrible pills that only made her feel worse. And she dreaded going to that cancer center, where they dosed her with more chemo and made her lie on that narrow table and beamed that light into her body. Every moment of it was humiliating. It was just too hard, too much. Everyone talked at her like she was an invalid, incapable of caring for herself. But what they didn't understand was that she didn't want to be taken care of.

All the things that were once familiar to her had vanished, replaced now by the skeleton of a woman she no longer recognized. Eating or even looking at food made her sick. And the fatigue. At a moment's notice, it would just deplete her. The exhaustion was her respite, a reason to stay folded up in the blankets. She did not want to talk. She did not want to eat. She did not want to take that god-awful medicine.

Her bitterness had become like the open sore that blistered on her backside.

M orris looked flustered when Beatrice opened the door to let him in. She led him into the living room, and when he took a seat, and didn't say anything for a long while, she just waited until he finally looked at her and said: "Agnes refuses to eat or take her medication. She just lays in bed all day waiting to die."

Beatrice was surprised that he came to confide in her about Agnes. Seeing him look so lost, so miserable, made her feel sorry for him. "She's going to pull through. It's normal for her to feel this way. Her life has suddenly changed. And it's really hard . . . feeling sick all the time. I went through the same thing with my mother."

Morris remembered her telling him about how she had cared for her sick mother, also stricken with cancer. He knew she would understand. She was the only person he could talk to. "How did you get through it? You know . . . taking care of your mother?"

Beatrice closed her eyes for a moment, mulling it over. "Well, it was hard. Back then, the treatment options were very few, and Mama refused to take her medication, too . . . said the Lord was gonna see her through." She chuckled. "We used a lot of prayer and homemade remedies to help her get through it."

"I've never felt so helpless in my life. Seems like anything I do isn't enough. I try cooking for her, feeding her, bathing her. It's just too much. I don't know if I can do this anymore, and it seems like she's gotten worse since Emma left for vacation."

"What about your other family and friends? Can't they help?"

"Agnes doesn't want anyone to see her like this, and she would never forgive me if I asked any of her friends."

They were quiet; the weight of the situation hung over them. There was as much being unsaid as said, and they both could feel it.

"Why don't I do it?" Beatrice said.

Morris looked at her, an odd expression on his face. "Do what?"

Beatrice thought for a moment about how ridiculous it sounded. They stared at each other. "Help you take care of Agnes . . . just until Emma returns."

"No. I can't ask you to do that. We can't do that!"

"Why not? No one has to know."

The room filled with an awkward silence. Morris thought about the countless hours he spent nursing Agnes, the sleepless nights filled with worry. He had come to realize that it wasn't just the cancer that had made Agnes sick—it was more than that. Something much deeper that no chicken broth or chemo could cure. He had managed to keep *his* secret for decades, but still the truth asserted itself, all the stronger for being ignored. Now here was Beatrice saying things he couldn't even fathom. He stiffened at the thought.

"All I'm saying is that since I took care of my mother, maybe I can help with Agnes." Beatrice braced herself at the way Morris was now looking at her. She chose her words carefully. "Look . . . I know this sounds crazy. I realize that."

"It just wouldn't be right, Beatrice. She'd much rather have a stranger caring for her."

"A stranger? Don't you think that's an odd way to put it?"

"You know what I mean."

Morris turned away then, a moment of truth and tragedy—all his transgressions laid bare. Earlier, he had sat by Agnes's bed and watched her sleep, thought about their life together. And he and Beatrice had been through a lot together, too. He trusted her. After a moment, he turned back to Beatrice. She looked different. *Maybe it could work,* he thought. *Just until Emma gets back.* He looked carefully at Beatrice. "Are you sure?" he said.

Beatrice knew in her heart that it would be the right thing to do. Surely, she would have never considered this under any other circumstances. But it was the least she could do, a sacrifice for all the hurt she had caused Agnes. If she did it, it would not be because she was filled with shame or guilt. It would be a choice, a courageous, loving choice. "Yes, I'm sure," she heard herself say, more confidently than she felt.

The next day, when Morris opened the door, Beatrice stepped inside, stunned that she had come. All night she had lain awake, thinking about it. She had even picked up the phone several times to tell Morris she'd made a mistake. How could she think to do such a thing? But each time she tried to phone him, something pulled at her. Now, there she was standing in *their* living room—his and Agnes's—everything so immaculate and tidy, a distant reality from the secret life they'd shared. She still loved Morris, but it was not the kind of love that brought flutters to her belly. Time and truth had replaced that with a more genuine love, rooted in care, camaraderie, and compassion. She stood there for a long while, struggling with her own emotions.

"Is she upstairs?" Beatrice finally asked.

Morris nodded, looked vaguely toward the stairs. "Yes, the last bedroom on the left."

"Maybe it's best if I go up on my own."

Morris watched her put down her things and head upstairs. When she reached the top, he saw her pause to catch her breath, and then slowly disappear down the hall.

Beatrice stood outside the door. Her legs felt suddenly weak, her stomach twisted in knots. She closed her eyes and took a deep breath before she turned the knob and went inside.

Agnes lay in the bed, buried in blankets. The room was dark, shadowed against the heavy draperies. A litany of little brown bottles—different shapes and sizes with white caps and labels—sat on the nightstand next to a glass of water, untouched. The room was bare, raw with suffering. There was a loneliness to this house, whetted by so much pain. Beatrice felt it more than she saw it, evident the moment Morris opened the door and let her in. It wasn't the beautiful home with its matching furnishings and drapery that Beatrice noticed first. It was the sheer emptiness, the hollowness, a home devoid of life.

Beatrice stepped closer to the bed. "Agnes . . . ?" she muttered.

When Agnes didn't budge, Beatrice gently pulled back the blankets, tapped her on the shoulder. "Agnes . . . ?"

Agnes finally shifted, turned to look up at her.

"My name is Bea. I'm here to help care for you while Emma's away," Beatrice said, surprised that she had used a name she hadn't heard in so long. Her father was the only one that would ever call her that—his little bumble Bea. She shivered at the thought.

Agnes returned the stare. A perplexed expression hung on her pale face, accentuated by the lilac scarf tightly wrapped around her bald head, bringing life to her green eyes and the pink nightdress she wore. "Bea, is that your name?" Agnes said.

Beatrice stepped closer to the bed, nodded.

"Well, thank you for coming. But I don't need any help. Please leave." Agnes turned her back to Beatrice again and pulled the blankets over her head.

Beatrice had a mind to simply walk out, but she halted, stopped by her pity for the frail-looking Agnes. "Well, I know you don't want my help. But I'm here anyhow. Besides, I got plenty of time with nothing else to do, so might as well spend it taking care of you." Beatrice walked over to the window and flung back the draperies, letting the sunlight pour in.

Agnes lifted from below the blankets, squinted against the bright light. "I don't need you or anybody else caring for me. Please leave!"

Beatrice cocked her head, considering. "Really? . . . Is that why you're lying in that bed feeling sorry for yourself?"

Agnes sat up at once. "How dare you? Who in the hell do you think you are coming into my home, talking to me that way?!"

"Don't dare me, I'm already here. I dare you to stop all this nonsense and let me help you. Now, I done made a promise that I intend to keep. So you might as well get used to me being around."

"I want you out of my house right now!" Agnes said with a force that sent her into a hacking cough, small, dry outbursts that grew incessantly and then suddenly, strangely, turned into sobs.

Beatrice grabbed the glass of water and put it to Agnes's mouth. She rubbed Agnes's back gently as she watched her drink the water.

"Are you all right?" Beatrice said.

Agnes wiped her mouth, embarrassed.

Beatrice felt a strange sadness, an overwhelming sympathy for the small-boned white woman. A peculiar anguish gripped her heart. As if her own dark cloud had parted, in an instant, she was sitting on the edge of Agnes's bed, holding her. "It's going to be all right," she said as she stroked Agnes's back. "It's all going to be all right."

Agnes held fast to Beatrice, putting up no resistance, just allowed herself to fold into this stranger's arms and cry.

50

Agnes

The first time she cried in Beatrice's arms was just a moment of sheer anguish. Agnes thought nothing of it. But the next day, when Beatrice brought her some homemade chicken soup that she'd stayed up all night making, and told her, "This is gonna help your healing," Agnes started sobbing again, for reasons she didn't understand.

It seemed bizarre that this stranger, this woman Bea, could extract an emotion that she had kept locked up for so long. It was the way Bea spoke to her, with such delicacy and patience, as if she knew Agnes was only moments away from giving up. There was something different about Bea, an understanding that surpassed what everybody else didn't quite get. Bea understood her beyond the measure of her sickness. She wasn't just trying to *save* her from this terrible disease. She was trying to help Agnes save *Agnes*.

The long hours alone had allowed Agnes too much time to think about her life. One minute, she was battling for her marriage, and the next minute, she was battling a disease that threatened to devour her. There was little hope and terrible fear in what was left of her. The picturesque life that she had protected for years—of her and Morris and Emma—had vanished, dissipated over time. She wondered if it would be easier to just let go of the life that had betrayed her—both her family and her body. Still, despite her defiance, she clutched to a scrap of hope. A conviction that seemed to deepen since Bea showed up.

Beatrice arrived early every morning, with a new batch of soup, or fresh bread she'd baked, or a book she planned to read to Agnes. And when Agnes refused to eat or take her meds or listen as Beatrice read to her, Beatrice never lost patience. Sometimes, Beatrice would just sit there for hours with a stubbornness that matched Agnes's own.

Some days, Agnes just waited for the misery to consume her. It felt to Agnes as if her days melted from one to the next, and her nights burst with the silent grief that nurtured her isolation. Every day that Agnes sank deeper into herself, Beatrice yanked the rod harder to keep her afloat.

By the next week, Beatrice had made up her mind: *she was going to save Agnes*. It was a Monday morning, rain poured in droves, and the rich gray morning sky had turned the city into a giant soak, drenching everything. But Beatrice didn't let the rain stop her. She made a pot of chicken soup and loaded everything into her car. This time when Morris opened the door, she whisked past him into the kitchen, put the chicken soup on the burner to heat, boiled some water for tea, put everything onto a server, and took it upstairs to Agnes.

When Beatrice went into Agnes's room, she set the tray on the nightstand. Again, Agnes just lay there, looking out at the pouring rain.

"I made you some more soup," Beatrice said.

Agnes ignored her.

"Agnes, you can't just lie here and die. Sit up so you can eat something, then I'll run you a hot bath. You'll feel better."

Agnes held the blanket up to her chin, still facing the window, her once lustrous hair now gone, her body unwashed, dirty. She watched the rain, sheets of it soaking the trees outside her window.

Beatrice sat in the armchair next to the window, watching the rain with Agnes. They sat that way for some time until out of nowhere, Beatrice turned to Agnes and said: "When I was a little girl, my mama loved to comb my hair. Part it right down the middle, grease it with petroleum jelly, then press it with a hot comb until it became stiff and shined like wax." A wide smile broke across Beatrice's face as though she could see her mother standing there with the hot comb. "When she was done, I looked so pretty with my two ponytails, all done up just right. . . . 'You the prettiest little girl on this side of town,' my daddy used to tell me. And Lord knows I believed him. I'd run out that front door and jump on my swing, and I'd swiiiinnnng. Raise my legs in the air so high I thought I was going to touch the sky." Beatrice chuckled. "Those were the good ole days," she said. She looked over at Agnes. "I lost my daddy when I was a little girl. Then my brother. And later my mother." Beatrice's eyes welled with tears. "I didn't think I was gon' be able to go on. I lost everything. My family, my will to live. I couldn't see past my pain, couldn't see past all the terrible things that had happened to me. But somehow, some way, God gave me the strength. In time, I got stronger, and the pain started to fade, and my life changed. Things didn't seem as bad." Beatrice looked straight at Agnes, her voice more gentle. "You believe in God, Agnes?"

Beatrice saw Agnes's eyes water. A full minute passed without either of them saying a word. Then Beatrice stood, went over to Agnes, and sat on the edge of her bed. She grabbed Agnes's hand, held it. "Let me help you, Agnes. Please, you got so much to live for," Beatrice said. "I'm going to run you a bath, and you'll feel better. Then you'll eat something."

Agnes teared up like she was trying to get her body to respond, to feel her way through. The tone in Beatrice's voice made her feel like she could see past the fog. This stranger gave her hope.

Beatrice squeezed Agnes's hand tenderly, then went into the bathroom and filled the tub with warm water. She gathered the towels, placed one on the basin and another on the edge of the tub, and found the shampoo and a fresh bar of soap.

This time when Beatrice returned to the room and reached for Agnes, Agnes took her hand and held on to it like she was clutching a life raft. Beatrice wrapped her arms around Agnes's fragile waist and guided her into the bathroom, taking small steps. When they entered the bathroom, Agnes looked away from the mirror, not wanting to see herself. Beatrice led her into the bathtub, and Agnes wrapped her arms around her knees, her thin body curled into a ball. The warm water felt tantalizing against her skin, reviving the muscles that had been dormant for so long. Beatrice sat on the floor next to her, lathered the washcloth with soap, and with gentle strokes, with the love she would give her own child, with all the mercy she felt, she washed away all Agnes's grief, her agony, and her pain.

51

Beatrice made Agnes better, in every way. Little by little, Agnes's cheeks pinked again, and for the first time in more than two years, Agnes began to see beyond the life she had come to know.

"What would you like to do today, Ms. Agnes?" Beatrice said when she walked into the familiar contentment of Agnes's room. She put her things away in their usual place in the closet and sat next to Agnes on the bed.

Agnes thought about it. "Well, let's see. How about we go downstairs and sit by the fire? I miss sitting by the fire. Maybe you can tell me another story about your life growing up in the South. That story about your mother combing your hair was so touching."

"Awww, my life wasn't all that fascinating. I just wanted to tell you whatever I thought would get your puny butt out of this bed!" Beatrice chuckled, and then the broad grin on her face gradually turned serious. Since the day she first met Agnes, not a day had gone by that she didn't think about her life. Every day that she cooked for Agnes, bathed her, or read to her, she couldn't help but wonder how she was able to keep a straight head and heart, knowing that the very care she gave to Agnes was the same deception that could hurt her. It pained Beatrice every morning when she awoke to face another day with Agnes. There were times that she thought she was going to go crazy, trying to keep it all straight, careful that she didn't slip and say something that she would regret.

The thought of Agnes ever finding out made her heartsick. She liked Agnes, had even begun to think of her as a friend, a companion. It sometimes made her forget that Agnes was Morris's wife, the woman she once envied. Agnes was nothing like what she once thought of her, especially after she hurt her daughters. Every day she spent with Agnes softened her heart, made her feel more ashamed.

"Bea," Agnes said, interrupting Beatrice's thoughts.

Beatrice went still at the musing in Agnes's voice. "Yes?"

Agnes's serious tone broke into a gentle smile again, then went back to nostalgia. "I'm so glad you're here . . ." she said, holding Beatrice's gaze. "I know I was a pain in the ass when you first came, and I gave you an awful hard time, but I just want you to know that I didn't mean it. I was just . . ." Agnes's eyes clouded with tears; she looked away from Beatrice, suddenly embarrassed. "Well . . . I was in a different place. You understand, don't you?" she said, holding Beatrice's eyes.

Beatrice felt her heart squeeze at the same measure that she now squeezed Agnes's hand. "No, don't. Please, don't apologize. I know you weren't well. So, please don't you ever feel like you need to apologize to me or anybody for how you feel. It's hard. I understand, believe me, I do. Besides . . ." Beatrice teared up, too. "I wanted to be here. This has meant more to me than you could ever imagine."

Agnes squeezed Beatrice's hand, then wiped the tears from her face. "Gosh, I think I've cried more in the last year than I have in all my life."

A kindhearted smile came on Beatrice's face. "It's okay to cry. My daddy used to say tears were God's way of letting us know that we still living; that the day we stop shedding tears

would be the day that our soul done left us. There's nothin'
better than a good cry sometimes. Heck, I cry sometimes just
to make sure I'm still breathin'." Beatrice chuckled again.

"You're so special, Bea. Really. I've never met anyone like
you."

"I reckon you haven't! Ain't that many black folk on this
side of town. I was beginning to wonder when the police was
gonna come knockin' on your door for me."

Agnes snickered. "Well, they would have to get through
me before I let them take you away from here."

Beatrice smiled, watched Agnes conjure up another thought.

"Bea, do you have any family that live here?"

Beatrice's breath skipped. Until now, she had managed to
keep their talks fixed on Agnes, seldom talking about herself.
In fact, whenever Agnes would ask about her, she found a way
to skirt around it, drawing on the moment to deflect Agnes's
questions, never talking overmuch or about anything that
would trigger more questions. She felt terrible about the blatant deception, the deceit.

"Yes, I have family here," Beatrice finally answered, then
stood abruptly. "How about I go and get that fire started, and
then I'll come back and get you when it's nice and ready?"

"All right, then," Agnes said.

Beatrice made her way downstairs. When she went into
the living room, she was surprised to see Morris sitting there.
Since the very first day she came, they had tried hard to avoid
each other, seldom being in the same room at the same time.
Once, when she and Agnes came downstairs for breakfast,
Morris had quickly made an excuse and left. In fact, oftentimes, he would leave as soon as Beatrice arrived, and stay
away most of the day, or hole up in his room, where he still
worked on his ships.

Beatrice stopped in her tracks when Morris turned and saw her.

"Is everything all right?" Morris said. They looked intently at each other, feeling somewhat awkward.

"I didn't know you were here. I thought you left," Beatrice said. She saw the same surprised look on his face.

"Yes, I did leave, but I had to come back to get something, and I was just sitting here resting for a minute."

Morris looked empathetically at her then. "How is she? I mean . . . I noticed that she's doing much better. You two seem to be getting along very well. She's really become fond of you, I see." There was an uneasiness on his face.

Beatrice walked over to the fireplace and stacked the wood, prepared to light it. "She's better," she said, her back to him.

"And you? How are you doing?"

Beatrice turned around to face him, held his gaze. "As well as expected under the circumstances. We're making it work."

"Do you need anything? I mean, is there anything I can do to help?"

Beatrice looked around the room as though she was searching for something that she could just neatly tuck back into place the way she wanted to tuck back into her life in Roxbury. Yes, there was something he could do, she thought to herself, something they could both do. They could tell Agnes the truth.

"What are we going to do when Emma gets back?" Beatrice watched him flounder uncomfortably.

"I don't know," Morris finally answered. "I've thought about it, but I'm not sure what to do. Maybe I can talk to Emma."

Beatrice was trying hard not to worry about it. "I need to get back upstairs to Agnes."

"Beatrice . . ." Morris said as she turned to leave.

Their eyes met, and, for a moment, she thought she could read the pity in his.

"I just want to thank you for doing this. You know, being here. I know it must be hard for you."

Beatrice could tell he understood why she was doing it by the way he was looking at her. Agnes needed her, this much she had come to understand. Being there gave her a sense of belonging, forgiveness. But most of all, it helped Agnes. She held his eyes. "You're welcome," was all she could manage before she turned to go back to Agnes.

52

Beatrice

Beatrice stared out at the picturesque view—the fifty-two-foot white spruce, covered in festive lights; men, women, and children gliding across the ice-skating rink; the park blanketed in snow, a light dusting still drifting. "There's something magical about the Boston Common in December," she said.

They sat on the park bench, bundled in their coats, scarves, and hats. The freezing air was almost warm enough to be pleasant. "You come here often?" Agnes asked, staring ahead.

Beatrice gave this some thought. "Yes," she said slowly. "I used to come here all the time. Spent many days here just watching people. My mama used to tell me that there's so much you can learn from people, just watching them—the way they walk, talk, even the way they look at you. Mama was right. Sometimes, I'd come here and sit for hours, just taking it all in." Beatrice thought about something and smiled. "One time," she said. "There was this woman. She was very tall with long red hair and freckles. She couldn't have been more than thirty. Pretty as she can be. She sat next to me. And she must have sat there for almost thirty minutes before she said something. And you know what she finally said?" Beatrice turned and looked at Agnes. "She asked me if I had a dollar, then she told me that she'd lost her job and her home and had been living in the park for almost a month because she didn't have no one to help her." Beatrice shook her head, thinking back on it. "From the looks of her, you could tell that she come from a good family. And when I asked her about her family, she told me that she and her parents hadn't spoken in more than five years. Now, the thing I didn't understand was that she'd rather live in a park than call her parents and tell them she needed help. What's the sense in that?!"

"In many ways, I'm like that young woman, I suppose," Agnes said, giving it some thought.

Agnes watched the trees, the snow, the life that surrounded her. She felt grateful, the very gratitude she had been feeling since the moment she sat in that tub and felt Bea's hand on her back. Bea wasn't like anyone else. She had a special way of talking to her, reaching her. At first, Agnes was distrusting, distant. But in time she realized that Bea just wanted to help, to inspire her to live. And she *did* want to live. Just not with the cancer and the treatments that made her sick all the time; or the pain it had caused her family—Emma, so brave, so desperate to save her. Agnes saw the way her daughter often looked at her, as if the look alone could cure her. And her husband, so eager to atone for his sins. She was no longer angry at him, but that didn't mean it would just all go away, it could never go away—the infidelity that led to two children, now grown. Agnes often wondered about them; she hadn't seen them since the last time one of them came to their home—Sadie Mae. She remembered that day as vividly as the snow that now fell from the gray sky.

"I haven't always been this way." Agnes shifted her thoughts. "You know, quiet," she said. Beatrice turned and looked at her. "I used to love to talk, about almost anything." She paused. "I lost a baby once. A baby boy. We named him after his father. He was only six days old."

Beatrice felt her heart crush. Morris had never told her.

"That was the first time I ever thought I wouldn't be able to go on. I shut down. I stayed in bed for months, couldn't even take care of Emma. I wanted that baby so much. Had planned my whole life for it. Two kids. A boy and a girl. A beautiful home. A dog. Emma came first. Then later Morris Jr."

Agnes's eyes became sad.

"I felt as if I died inside. Thought nothing could ever hurt as much as that hurt. But . . ." Agnes paused, looked lost. "That wasn't the worse pain. The worse came years later when . . ." Agnes heard her voice become ragged. "The worse came when I discovered that my husband had been unfaithful, fathered two children. Twin girls. I never knew about them."

Beatrice froze.

Of all the times she imagined this moment, of all the times she pictured it in her mind, never had she thought it would happen like this. It was easy to defend her relationship with Morris when his family was just a distant thought—another side of *his* life. But when she decided to step into their home, it all changed. She changed.

"I met them," Agnes said, her voice low. "When they were little girls. He brought them to our home. I needed to see them. For a long time I couldn't bring myself to believe it. I thought I'd done everything right. Thought I had a good family, the perfect home. Then one day there he was standing in my foyer with them holding their hands." Agnes chuckled, an odd expression on her face. "They were just standing there! Looking at me."

Beatrice felt her heart quicken, ready to free herself of forty years of shame. But instead, she turned away from Agnes, looked out at the tree, said nothing.

Nothing at all.

Later, when they returned home, they were both surprised to see Emma waiting, sitting with Morris in the living room. Beatrice stared at her.

"Mom, look at you. You look great!" Emma said, and embraced her mother. She hardly noticed Beatrice.

"Hi, honey. What are you doing here? I thought you weren't due back for a few more days?"

Emma released her mother and stepped back to take another look at her.

"I know, but we came back a few days early. I missed you!"

"Oh, honey, you should have stayed and enjoyed those last few days. Why didn't you just call?"

For the first time, Emma noticed Beatrice. "Hello, I'm Emma. My dad told me that you came to help while I was away." Emma reached out her hand for Beatrice to take.

Beatrice looked coyly at Emma, and then her eyes met Morris's.

"Bea, right?" Emma said, smiling.

"Yes." Beatrice said, finally taking her hand.

"I can't thank you enough for caring for my mom while I was away. She looks really great. My dad told me that you have experience with caring for people with cancer. Is that right?"

Beatrice tried not to look at Morris. "Yes, you could say that, I guess."

"Well, it's obvious you know something, because my mother looks one hundred percent better." Emma smiled at Beatrice.

Beatrice glanced back over at Morris, saw the distress on his face. They all stood facing one another—Emma smiling at Beatrice; Agnes taking in her daughter, so pleased to see her; Morris shifting uncomfortably, his eyes on Beatrice.

"Well, it was nice to meet you, Emma, but I should get going," Beatrice said, not taking her coat off.

"No, Bea. Please don't go. Why don't you stay and have dinner with us?" Agnes seemed genuinely disappointed.

Beatrice did her best to smile calmly, as if she wasn't dying inside. "No. I really need to get going. I have church this evening."

"All right, then," Agnes said. "But I'll see you tomorrow, right?"

Beatrice stood there, a stroke of time passed. "Yes, of course. I'll be back tomorrow," she said at last before she walked back out the front door.

53

Morris

M orris had fumbled around all morning, trying to keep his thoughts from intruding. At some point, he had gone into Agnes's room to check on her, and Agnes was still sound asleep. He stood there just watching her, quiet, careful not to wake her, amazed at how much better she was doing. Since Emma returned home, he had managed to avoid facing Agnes. Somehow, he had not expected to feel as befuddled as he did when he stood in the living room with all three of them—Agnes, Beatrice, and Emma. The time that Beatrice had been there had allowed him to suppress his guilt. It was strange, somehow, how easily he had come to accept the way their lives had cozily come together. In fact, it almost felt *normal*.

Later that morning when he peeked into Agnes's room again, Agnes was sitting in the chair.

"You're awake," he said, and stepped awkwardly into the room.

Agnes turned from the window to face him. "It's really beautiful outside today. I think Bea and I will get out for another stroll. I enjoyed our time at the park yesterday."

Morris stood there, feeling a bit rattled.

"So what do you have planned today? Maybe you can join Bea and me?" Agnes said.

Morris looked uneasy. "No, honey. You and Bea go on without me. I have some things to take care of today."

"Maybe another time," Agnes said. "Bea should be here soon, so I'm gonna get my things together and get ready, but I just need to rest a little while longer."

"Of course, honey. You get some more rest and I'll see you when I get back later today."

Morris kissed Agnes on the forehead, made his way back downstairs, and sat in the living room. He remained very, very still as though to move would destroy his equilibrium. He thought of Agnes again, how different she looked, how very much she had changed in the past few weeks, beyond the color that now flowed in her face. Agnes seemed to flourish around Beatrice. How very odd, he thought. What he had managed to keep a secret had unfolded, the perverse and bizarre untangling of his deceit. What was he to do? How could he have allowed it to come to this? And Beatrice, what extraordinary measures she had to take every day to put aside her own heart and hurt. He longed desperately to talk to someone, anyone. But who could he tell? How absurd would it sound, trying to explain the unexplainable, a past that had melded together by utter fate and fiction. The only person he thought to talk to was his longtime friend Vincent. But Vincent had grown as cynical and skeptical as he in their old age. Vincent, or anyone else, could never be told the very thing he was still unable to confess to himself.

Morris heard the front door open and he listened to Beatrice's familiar footsteps. Slowly, he stood.

"I was hoping we could talk," he said, looking fixedly at her.

Beatrice took a seat on the sofa, across from him. It was as if she expected him to be there.

Morris seemed troubled, didn't say anything for a long while. Then he looked at Beatrice. "I'm sorry about what happened yesterday. I was as surprised as you to see Emma.

And . . ." He paused, careful with his next words. "I'm sorry if I did anything to offend you. I didn't know how to handle it."

Beatrice felt something flow through her then, a familiar emotion. She had not stopped thinking about them—Agnes, Emma, Morris—all standing in the living room with her. Morris's face showed the same affliction as hers. They sat for a time in silence.

"We need to tell Emma," Beatrice finally said, as though she was talking more to herself than to him.

Morris hesitated for a moment, and looked away. When he looked back at her, his reaction was as if he had suddenly realized what they must do. "I know . . . when Emma comes today. I will tell her."

Beatrice sat there for a little while longer, then gathered her things and headed upstairs to Agnes. There was nothing more to be said.

An hour later when Morris heard Emma's key in the door, he was still sitting in the living room. He didn't even wait for Emma to make her way fully into the house or even take off her coat. He met her at the door.

"Honey, we need to talk."

"Dad . . . what's wrong? Is Mom okay?" Emma asked.

Morris looked bothered. "Your mother's fine, honey. Come, join me in the living room."

Emma followed her father into the living room and took a seat across from him. Still she hadn't taken off her coat.

Morris looked attentively at her. "Honey, there's something I need to tell you. And first I want you to know that I love you and your mother, and I would never do anything to hurt either one of you again. I know I've made some mistakes in the past, but I hope you were able to forgive me."

Emma stared at her father, unmoving. Ever since she was

a little girl, she had come to learn that whenever her father had to tell her some bad news, he always started in the same way: *Honey, there's something I need to tell you.* She braced herself. "What is it, Dad? Please *tell* me."

A weary look settled on Morris's face. He got right to it. "Honey . . . while you were away, I was having a really hard time trying to take care of your mother until Bea offered to help." He paused, held Emma's eyes. "Bea is Sam and Sadie Mae's mother. She wants nothing but the best for your mother. Only to help."

Emma looked at her father, trying to understand. It took a full minute for it to sink in. "What? . . . You can't be serious!"

"Honey, I know how it must look, but I didn't have anywhere else to turn. Bea is a good person. I trust her."

Emma stared fixedly at her father. "How could you?! . . . How could you do that to Mom?!"

"Honey, please. Please try to understand!"

Emma stood up, her face fastened into a sneer, and stormed toward the stairs.

"Emma . . . don't!" Morris called after her, but Emma quickly made her way to her mother's bedroom, and when she pushed open the door, Beatrice was sitting in the chair reading a book to Agnes.

Agnes's face lit up when she saw her daughter. "Hi, honey. I've been waiting for you. Come, sit next to me. Bea's reading me a wonderful mystery by Agatha Christie. She reads it so beautifully. Come sit with me and listen." Agnes patted a space on the bed next to her.

Emma's heart quickened. "Maybe another time, Mom," Emma said, and turned to Beatrice. "Can I speak with you in private, please?"

A concerned look came on Agnes's face. "Honey, what's wrong?"

Emma looked back over at her mother. "It's nothing, Mom. I just need to speak with Bea about something."

Beatrice put the book down on the nightstand and slowly rose from the chair. "I'll be right back," she said to Agnes, and followed Emma into the hallway, careful to shut the door behind her.

"How dare you come into our home, pretending to be someone you're not!" Emma's mouth grew tight. "I—want—you—out—of—here—this—very—instant!"

Beatrice stepped closer to Emma. "Emma, I know how you must feel. But please. I only want to help."

"Help! You want to help by coming into our home and deceiving my mother? You have some nerve!"

"I didn't expect you to understand. But we need to do what's best for your mother."

Emma shoved her finger at the stairs again. "I want you out of here right now!" she shouted, a little too loudly.

Beatrice stared at Emma, letting Emma's words sink in. "Have you taken a close look at your mother? Do you remember what she looked like before you left?"

Emma wrapped her arms against her chest, furious. She refused to answer her.

"Now, I know that this is not right. Trust me, I've thought about it every second of every day. But I've put aside my own personal feelings to help your mother. She's doing so much better now, and I'm not leaving her. So, you can be angry and bitter toward me all you want. I deserve that. But I made a promise to your mother, and I intend to keep it."

Beatrice turned to go back to Agnes and left Emma standing there.

54

Emma

Emma had stormed out of her parents' home without speaking another word to Beatrice or her father. It was Johnny, as usual, who calmed her. But how could she be calm? She had thought about it all night, unable to sleep; and by the next morning, she had made up her mind about what she would do.

Beatrice and Agnes were eating an early supper when Emma walked into the dining room.

"Hi, Mom," Emma said. She kissed her mother on the cheek. She hardly looked at Beatrice.

"Hi, honey. Are you hungry? Bea made a wonderful soup and fresh bread. Why don't you join us?"

Emma stole a contentious look at Beatrice. "I'm not hungry, Mom. I just came to see you on my way home from work. How are you feeling?" Emma took the seat opposite Beatrice, next to her mother.

"I'm feeling good. Bea and I went for another walk today," Agnes said, and smiled at Beatrice.

"Where's Daddy? I didn't see his car out front."

"Your father had some errands to run, honey. He'll be home later."

I bet he did, Emma thought, but didn't say it. Nothing her father said or did rang true to her. She didn't trust him or Bea.

"Are you sure you're not hungry, honey? Bea makes the best soup. Why don't you try some?"

Emma met Beatrice's gaze. There was no way she was going to eat that woman's cooking. She wanted to jump out of her skin, sitting across from her. "No, Mom. I'm not hungry."

"All right, then, honey." Agnes looked over at Beatrice. "Bea, you haven't touched your dinner. Are you okay?"

Beatrice could feel Emma's eyes on her. "I ate a good amount with all the tasting I was doing when I made it. I guess I ain't as hungry as I thought," she said, and looked at Emma, the way she glared at her.

Agnes didn't seem to notice the dissention, the silence.

"Well, I guess I'm going to turn in now. I'm a little tired after all that walking we did today." Agnes stood and smiled at Beatrice and Emma.

Beatrice stood, too. "Let me help you upstairs and I'll get your bath started."

"I can help her," Emma snapped.

Beatrice held Emma's stare. "All right, then. I'll come and see you before I leave," she said, then watched Emma help her mother from the dining room.

After Agnes had fallen asleep, Emma came downstairs to find Beatrice sitting in the kitchen. "We need to talk," Emma said.

"I suppose we do." Beatrice led the way into the living room and took a seat on the sofa.

Emma sat across from her and took in the youthfulness of Beatrice's face. She had often wondered what Beatrice would look like, whether she favored the colored woman that worked at the local grocery store, or the one who had often come to clean their home. Beatrice wasn't at all what she expected.

"I need to know how you could do what you've done to my family!" Emma said, her voice unsteady.

Beatrice felt momentarily taken aback by Emma's blunt

words, the way Emma looked at her. "I never meant to hurt anyone," she said. "I didn't mean to hurt you or your mother. I can't take back what's been done, but I am so sorry for hurting you." Beatrice's soft voice disarmed Emma.

"My mother's never been the same since she learned about you . . . and your daughters. My father hid it from us for a long time. It tore us apart. And now . . ." Emma's voice cracked, her face wide open with grief. "And now, you're here in our home pretending to be someone you're not!"

Beatrice felt her heart sink. Without a second thought, she went to Emma and held her in her arms, rocking her like she would rock her own daughters. "It's all right. Everything's gon' be all right," she whispered.

Emma leaned into Beatrice, felt her arms close around her. She could smell her, a familiar scent. But somehow that didn't bother her right now. Somehow it comforted her in ways she had not been comforted in a long time.

"I'm so sorry. I know it hurts. Let it all out. Let it go," Beatrice said.

And Emma did. With her face pressed against Beatrice, dazed by the force of what was happening. And after a while, she pulled back, slightly embarrassed.

"Are you all right?" Beatrice said.

Emma nodded. "Yes. I'm sorry."

"Nooo. You have nothin' to be sorry for. You have every right to feel what you're feelin' right now. I'm the one who's sorry. I never meant to hurt anyone, especially you and your mother."

"Do you love him?" Emma blurted, her eyes searching Beatrice's.

Beatrice wasn't expecting this question. She hesitated. Morris was the only man Beatrice had ever loved. Yes, there was Charles for a time, and there were a few men that she dated over the years—one from church, one from her school, and another that Nellie and Clifford introduced her to. She had even considered a marriage proposal or two. But she didn't love them. Not the way she loved Morris.

"Yes," Beatrice finally answered. "Yes, I do." She turned quickly to Emma.

Emma nodded. Then out of the blue, she said: "What are they like? . . . Your daughters?"

Beatrice thought about it, smiled briefly. "Well, Sadie Mae is the oldest, only by six minutes, but you would think that she's ten years older than her sister. She's so protective of her. Sadie Mae ain't the most trusting person. But she got a good head on her shoulders. She graduated from Harvard and now she's in medical school. And Sam . . ." Beatrice's eyes became sad. "Sam is very smart, too. She was once the more brazen of the two. But that all changed years ago," Beatrice said. "Sam loves children. She's a teacher's aide at the same school where I once taught."

"You're a teacher?" Emma asked, surprised.

"Yes, I was. But I'm retired now. I taught for almost forty years. I loved it. And I suppose the children loved me, too. But some of them feared me somethin' awful. I didn't take no stuff when it came to my lessons," she said with a wide grin. "I wanted to make sure that every child left my class with honor. And they all did. All but two."

"I'm a teacher, too," Emma said.

"Really?" Beatrice smiled.

For a moment they stared at each other, everything between them coming together. Emma felt Beatrice's hand still on hers, and Beatrice saw the beginning of tears again in Emma's eyes.

"My mother wanted to die before you came. Now she's so much better. I don't know what my father and I will do if we lose her."

"I know it's been difficult for you and your father. But your mother is getting better. And maybe if we keep doing what we're doing, she'll get even better," Beatrice said.

Beatrice's hand was smooth and warm against her own, and Emma felt her hurt fading, the moment bringing them closer together, growing, as if they had been connected all their lives. She remembered feeling this way long ago when she was a little girl, sick with the measles, and her mother had held her, slept with her in her arms all night long. And the time she fell off her new bicycle and scraped her knee, and her mother nursed it until the pain went away. And the time her mother stood shoulder to shoulder with her in the mirror, telling her how beautiful she looked in her prom dress. The thought of losing her mother was unbearable. She just couldn't imagine her life without her—the fleeting moments, the telephone calls, the Sunday dinners.

Emma suddenly felt Beatrice's arms around her, her head against Beatrice's chest, pressed so close that she felt Beatrice's heart thumping. She thought about the countless hours she spent nursing her mother, the sleepless nights filled with worry. In a moment of revelation, something came to her, full in its meaning. She pulled away from Beatrice, looked at her.

"Bea, I'm sorry for the way I spoke to you. I guess I was just surprised to learn who you were."

Beatrice squinted like she was trying to understand. "I know. There's no need for you to apologize."

Beatrice turned away from Emma, thought about what Emma said, and in that moment, she knew she had made the right choice.

T he next day when Emma came to visit, she was surprised to find Agnes in bed. Beatrice stood next to her, rubbing her head with a damp rag.

"What happened? Is Mom okay?"

"She's not feeling too well today. She has a fever," Beatrice said.

Emma sat on the bed next to her mother and watched her sleeping. "I'm really worried about her. She looked so good yesterday, and now today, she's so sick."

"Sometimes she has good and bad days. The medication makes her weak and sick."

Emma studied Agnes's sleeping face. "How long has she had a fever?"

"Your father told me it started late last night, and by the time I got here, she was burning up." Beatrice removed the rag and touched Agnes's forehead again. "Good, the fever seems to be down. I guess the cool bath I gave her helped."

Emma was heartsick, watching her mother, so frail and weak. "Has she eaten anything today? Maybe that'll help."

"She forced down a biscuit and some tea earlier. I'm gonna make her some soup, and see if she can keep that down. She likes soup."

There was a warmth, a peacefulness that Emma noticed immediately when she first stepped into her mother's room. And it wasn't the fresh-cut flowers on the nightstand next to her mother's bed, that Bea had put there, she suspected, or the sunlight that beamed through the window, or the candle burning in a lantern that sat atop a side table, emanating scents of cinnamon. No, it wasn't any of those things. It was Bea, the gentle warmth that radiated from her, the way she watched over Agnes.

Emma had a sudden urge to talk to her mother, and as if Agnes had read her thoughts, her eyelids fluttered open.

"Hi, honey. What are you doing here so early today? Didn't you have school today?" Agnes sounded groggy.

"Yes, Mom, but I decided to take the day off and come spend it with you."

"Oh, honey. You didn't need to do that," Agnes said. Emma noticed how weak she seemed.

Emma touched her mother's cheek. "How are you feeling, Mom?"

"Not so well, honey. But Bea's going to make me some of that homemade soup. I always feel better after eating Bea's soup." Agnes forced a smile, glanced over at Beatrice.

Emma took in her mother's pale face, and then turned to Beatrice. "Is there anything I can do to help?"

"Maybe you can sit with her while I go and start on that soup. She'll also need to take her meds in about an hour, but I want her to eat something before she takes them. They always make her feel so sick if she doesn't eat something first."

"Of course. You go on and I'll stay with her."

Emma watched Beatrice step closer to the bed to touch Agnes's forehead.

"Now you stay put and rest while I make that soup you love." Beatrice smiled at Agnes, and patted her hand when Agnes tried to smile back.

A little while later, Emma joined Beatrice in the kitchen. "Is she sleeping?" Beatrice asked.

"Yes," Emma said, watching Beatrice move gracefully around the familiar kitchen with her mother's apron wrapped around her, chopping the vegetables that lay freshly rinsed, an array of celery, onion, potatoes, bell pepper, green cabbage, and zucchini.

"What kind of soup are you making?" Emma asked. She watched the way Beatrice chopped the celery with such precision.

"A vegetable soup. It's a recipe that I learned from my mama long ago. She used to make it for me and my brother whenever we got a cold, or the chicken pox, or the measles, or just when she thought we needed an extra dose of vegetables."

"It smells delicious." Emma looked over at the stockpot on the stove, its aroma drifting through the whole house.

"Yes, it does. I used to just sit there in the kitchen watching mama make it. The smell alone made me feel better," Beatrice said, smiling at the thought.

"Where is home for you? I mean, were you born here in Boston?"

"I was born in the South. Jackson, Mississippi. Didn't come this way till I was college age."

Emma looked curious. Suddenly, she reached inside the drawer and grabbed a paring knife and a carrot, and started helping. "I'm worried about Mom. I mean, I know she's much better now, but seeing her so sick today . . . scared me."

"Don't you worry, she's gonna be just fine. She just needs her rest."

Emma looked over at Beatrice. She wanted to believe her. "Does my dad ever stay around . . . I mean, I noticed that he's not here today."

Beatrice kept at her task. She didn't look at Emma. "He leaves before I get here every morning. I guess it's strange for him to be here with us. It's his own way of dealing with this, I suppose."

Emma got quiet again. She had planned to talk to her father today, to tell him that she was still conflicted about the whole thing. She wasn't sure if she could forgive him, but at least she was willing to try. And seeing the care Beatrice gave her mother, not to mention the companionship, made it easier.

"How did you and my father meet?" Emma suddenly asked.

Beatrice put down her knife and walked over to the stove to stir her pot. She took her time before she answered.

"My brother, Robert, saved your father's life at Pearl Harbor," Beatrice said, her face a mixture of emotions.

Emma's hand went to her heart. "Really?"

"Yes. Robert later died, and your father . . ." Beatrice paused. It had been so long since she talked about it to anyone. "Well, your father wanted to show his respects, so he found me. I was living in Roxbury by then, attending college."

"My God! I had no idea! My father never mentioned any of it."

"I suppose it's difficult for him to talk about the war . . . and what followed isn't something he's proud of," Beatrice said. Then she caught Emma's eye. "Nor am I," she added.

Emma held her gaze, and something passed between them in that moment that even they didn't understand.

Since then, Emma had come every day, and she and Beatrice banded together to take care of Agnes. They both nursed her, taking turns as though they had been doing it all along. Doing anything that kept their minds off what was passing between them—an uncanny friendship that no one would understand. Beatrice hadn't told her daughters, nor Nellie. Not because of what they would say or think, but because of how she now felt. The guilt. The blame. Thoughts of how she had allowed herself to hurt another family.

"That's not so," Emma had said to Beatrice one afternoon as they talked. "You're a good person. You've raised two beautiful daughters. You come from a good family. My father needed something to give him hope, and your brother's memory did that for him. And if things hadn't gone like they did, my father might have died at Pearl Harbor. The two of you meeting was beyond your control. I understand that now. And someday, my mother will, too."

Still, Beatrice felt guilty. For the past weeks, she had changed her mind a dozen times about telling Agnes the truth. It just wasn't right to continue to be in that woman's home knowing what she had done. But she had to. She couldn't see herself leaving now.

And Emma had finally softened toward her father. One day, she got there very early, before he had time to leave. "Dad, I know you've noticed that Bea and I have been taking care of Mom together," she said.

Morris nodded. Sometimes when he got home each day, Emma was still there, and the three of them—Emma, Agnes, and Beatrice—would be upstairs in Agnes's room or sitting in the living room together. He'd just rush in and quickly make his way upstairs to his hiding place. He went out of his way to avoid seeing them together.

"Yes, honey. I'm glad to see that your mother's doing so well, and that you're spending more time with her." Morris avoided the part about Beatrice.

"Dad, I've been spending time with Bea, too, and . . ." Emma looked her father straight in the eyes. "We've become friends."

Morris looked at his daughter, befuddled.

Emma told him about the times she and Beatrice spent together, getting to know each other, the way they took care of Agnes. "I know what you must be thinking, Dad. I really like Bea, and . . . and I know how you and Bea met." It was mostly what she and Beatrice had talked about for the past few weeks—things her father had never shared about Pearl Harbor. Robert. The letters. And the twins, the way her father had taken care of them, refusing to abandon them. As strange as it was, Emma respected her father for that. And somehow, her love for him had deepened, knowing that it must have been agonizing for him to love two families.

Morris walked over to the window, looked out, tried to clear his head. After a while, he turned back to Emma. In that moment, she looked just like her mother. "What do you hope to gain from this?" he said, a wary look on his face.

"I don't expect anything. I just wanted you to know that I know everything, and I know you don't want to talk about it, but if you change your mind, I'm here to listen."

Morris stared at Emma. "All right," he said, lost for words.

So it began that Morris, Emma, and Beatrice each did their part to make Agnes well, despite the uneasiness that swelled whenever all three of them were together. In time, they adjusted. Morris still left most mornings and didn't return until late afternoon or early evening. When leaving wasn't a choice, he stayed upstairs in his room, his thoughts drawn into the delicate piecing together of one of his ships.

Emma and Beatrice took turns caring for Agnes, as they had so often tended to her since the time Emma returned.

"Mom has gotten so much better," Emma said one after-noon as she and Beatrice stood shoulder to shoulder in the kitchen, concocting Beatrice's homemade chicken stew, while Agnes napped in the living room by the fire.

"Yes, she has, hasn't she?" Beatrice smiled back on thoughts of what Agnes looked like the first time she met her; how the color in Agnes's face now bloomed, the way her mood had changed; and how Agnes ate almost every meal Beatrice made for her.

"The doctor said that her blood count is up and she seems to be stable. He said we should keep doing whatever we're doing. . . . I told him that we've been fattening her up with some good old southern cooking."

Beatrice chuckled. "Yeah, I reckon southern food would do that."

"Bea," Emma said, now contemplative. "What do you do

when you're not here? I mean, you never talk much about yourself . . . and, well, I was beginning to wonder about your family. Your daughters?"

Beatrice was still not prepared to talk about her life with Emma. She looked toward the kitchen doorway that led into the living room, wondered if Agnes was still sleeping. "Well, my daughters lead their own lives now," she said quietly. "I cook Sunday dinner for them every week, rain or shine. I love to cook."

"I'd like to meet them someday," Emma said. She noticed how Beatrice looked at her, seeming uncomfortable with the thought.

"Well, maybe one day," Beatrice said.

"Bea . . ." Emma said. Beatrice stopped stirring her pot, turned to her. "I know we got off to a rocky start, but I just want you to know that I'm glad you're here."

Years of guilt and shame and betrayal had filled her, for as long as she could remember. And now she felt peace in hearing someone beyond her own imputing voice; Emma— her words—giving her all that she had prayed for: *forgiveness*. Beatrice held Emma's gaze. "I'm glad I'm here, too," she said quietly, and quickly turned back to her pot before Emma could see her eyes fill with tears.

55

Agnes

Agnes waited patiently for Beatrice. When Beatrice showed up, she announced: "It's beautiful outside today, feels like spring. Let's go to the zoo."

"The zoo?" Agnes gawked. "Why in the world would I want to go to the zoo? We can find something better to do."

"Don't you know that the zoo is the tunnel to the soul? My mama once told me: *'God created the animals before He created man. Whenever you feelin' weary. Whenever things don't look so good. Go to the zoo, baby. The zoo is the tunnel to the soul, to God.'* "

Agnes looked at Beatrice, perplexed. "The tunnel to the soul? I've never heard such a thing!"

"Ain't no need for you to have heard it. You just need to trust me." Beatrice pulled a pair of slacks, a white turtleneck, and a jacket from Agnes's closet. "Come on now, let's get you cleaned up. Oh, one other thing." Beatrice remembered, and grabbed a box that lay next to her purse. "I want you to have this."

Surprised, Agnes opened the box to a layered mid-length auburn wig. "Oh my! What am I to do with that?"

"You're gonna wear it. That's what you gonna do with it!"

"I can't wear that thing. I've never had to wear anything like that, and I'm not going to start now!"

"You are as stubborn as a mule. It's no wonder it's taken all this time to get you out of that bed. Now, what sense is it to keep prancing around here in that scarf when you can look like yourself? I saw pictures of you. This wig is almost an exact match to your own hair!"

"If you like it so much, then why don't you wear it?"

"You're right!" Beatrice pulled the wig from the box and plopped it on her head.

"So, how do I look?"

Agnes burst into laughter. Beatrice laughed, too.

"So are you gonna put this wig on before I start trying to fit in those little clothes of yours?"

Agnes sauntered into the bathroom behind Beatrice, slowly removed the scarf, and stared at her bald head. Beatrice stood next to her, watching her in the mirror.

Agnes flipped the wig inside out and slid it over her head, pulling it down to the back of her neck.

"My, my, my . . . look at you! You been hiding yourself from me all this time."

Agnes tried desperately to see past the wig, her frail face, her sunken eyes. "I can't do this!" she said, snatching the wig off.

"Agnes, please. Stop feeling sorry for yourself! You're ready to give up on yourself before God's ready to give up on you! Now I know it's hard. But you got too much to live for. Your family needs you. I need you!"

The moment the words were out of her mouth, Beatrice noticed that the hurt she usually felt whenever she thought of Morris and Agnes and Emma—as a family—didn't gnaw at her. Her pain was replaced now by the genuine care that had grown for Agnes.

"Look at me, Bea! I look like a monster!" Agnes tore open her robe, revealing two long scars that marked the places where her breasts used to be.

"You hush up with all that silly talk! The only monster in this room is the one you been creating! Now God don't like ugly, and you making yourself ugly with all that silly talk! We gonna get you cleaned up and dressed, and put that wig back on you, and we're going to that zoo and look at all those beautiful animals, and you're gonna feel better." Beatrice grabbed a towel and washcloth from the linen closet and placed them on the basin. She laid Agnes's clothes on her dressing table next to the wig. "Now I'm going back in that room and wait for you, and when you come out of this bathroom, I expect to see you all dressed and ready to go. A little lipstick wouldn't hurt, either."

Agnes glared at the lipstick. "Well, if you insist that I must put on this god-awful wig and pretend that it's gonna help to go and look at animals all day, then I guess I better try to make myself look as best I can so they don't think I'm one of them." Agnes grabbed the lipstick from Beatrice.

A smile broke on Beatrice's face. "Don't forget to put these on, too." Beatrice placed a box with a pair of gold cubic-studded earrings on the basin, and walked out of the bathroom, closing the door behind her.

B eatrice and Agnes strolled arm in arm, taking in the sights and sounds and smells. When walking became too much for Agnes, they sat on a bench and talked, immersed in the moment. Beatrice noticed how happy Agnes looked, so resilient and carefree. Agnes glowed in her wig, and when they returned home hours later, Beatrice helped Agnes out of her coat and started a fire. "My mama always told me that a good meat loaf and corn bread can heal almost anything. You sit here by the fire, and I'm gonna make you some."

Agnes could see glimpses of Beatrice moving around in the kitchen, the scent of meat loaf and fresh-baked corn bread lingering. The sun glimmered through the frosted February windows, bringing currents of warmth into the living room.

Agnes gazed at the blazing fire and smiled at the thought of the wig, the earrings, the zoo. She hadn't been to the zoo since Emma was nine years old. Bea was right. It was the tunnel to the soul. Her soul had been lifted ever since the day Bea came into her life, and there was something magical about that wig, too. Now she couldn't imagine leaving the house without it.

Beatrice came into the living room. "Try this," she said, scooping a spoonful of the meat loaf into Agnes's mouth.

"Ms. Bea, I think you've outdone yourself today," Agnes said, reveling in the taste. "Is dinner ready yet?"

"Yes, ma'am, it is. I'm about to set the table now."

"Let me go and find Morris so he can join us."

An unsettling feeling came over Beatrice. She watched Agnes leave, then she took her time setting the table until Agnes returned from upstairs.

"Morris will be joining us. I told him how good your meat loaf was, and he seemed not that interested, but I think I changed his mind. Anything I can do to help?"

"No, I think everything's ready. Just need to grab the corn bread." Beatrice rushed off into the kitchen, nauseated at the thought of Morris sitting across from her. She pulled the corn bread from the warmer, took her time spreading a thin layer of butter over it. She looked around the kitchen; with little else to do, she straightened up and walked back into the dining room.

"There you are. I was about to send Morris in there after you." Agnes smiled at Beatrice.

Morris sat in the seat next to Agnes. Beatrice placed the corn bread in the center of the table and took the seat across from them.

"How lovely," Agnes said, admiring the spread.

"Honey, why don't you slice the meat loaf?" Agnes handed the knife over to Morris.

Morris took the knife and carved the meat. "Would you like this piece?" he asked, turning to Agnes.

"Oh no, that's much too big for me. Give that one to Bea."

Morris placed the meat on Beatrice's plate. Then he carved another, smaller piece and served Agnes. "Now, I guess I'll have a nice piece. It looks delicious, Bea."

Beatrice nodded coyly. She thought about the first time she had made a meat loaf for him, a Sunday afternoon. The girls were ten and Nellie had taken them to the circus. "A day for you to just enjoy some time to yourself," Nellie had told her. And she was glad for that time, especially when she heard the knock on the door, opened it to Morris. He would often disappear for weeks, then just show up, surprising her. She had just taken the meat loaf out of the oven, an early start to Sunday dinner. And he had relished the meat loaf in the same way he relished the time with her after he'd been away for a while.

"It's really good, Bea," Morris said.

"Yes, Bea, it is," Agnes followed. "Do you make this often?"

Beatrice dropped her chin. "Yes, I've made it a few times."

"Well, I know your family is happy to have you as a cook. I wouldn't be able to get enough of it."

Beatrice glanced quickly at Morris. The room became quiet, silence illuminated by metal hitting porcelain.

"Bea, tell Morris about your family. Bea has two daughters and she lives in Roxbury," Agnes said, breaking the silence.

An awkward look came on Morris's face.

"Go ahead, Bea, tell him about your family."

A terrible nausea swept over Beatrice as Morris stared at her.

The door opening and closing made them all turn and look toward the dining room entry at Emma.

"There you all are," Emma said, smiling. "I'm sorry I couldn't get here sooner. Johnny isn't feeling well. I wasn't sure I was going to be able to make it when I spoke to Dad earlier, but I decided to come and stay just for a little while.

"So what's for dinner? I'm starving." Emma rushed into the kitchen, grabbed a plate, and returned to the dining room. She took the seat next to Beatrice and scooped a hefty serving of the meat loaf and corn bread onto her plate. "You look good today, Mom. You're feeling well?" she said, finally slowing down to eat.

"Well, yes, I am. I feel very good today. And Bea made this wonderful meal for us. She was just about to tell us about her daughters."

Emma took a bite of the corn bread, absentmindedly. "Oh, about Sadie Mae and Sam?"

The room went still.

Agnes looked at Emma, confused. "What did you say?"

Emma put down her fork, glanced nervously at her father and then at Beatrice.

"Nothing," Emma said quickly.

"No, I heard you. You said *their* names."

Emma held her mother's eyes, glanced over at Beatrice again.

"You said Sadie Mae and Sam. I heard you," Agnes said.

A long moment passed before Emma could speak again. "Yes, Mom, I did say their names. Bea . . . Bea is their mother," she said slowly.

Agnes furrowed her brow in confusion, trying to understand. Emma watched her mother, the way she looked at Beatrice, held her gaze.

"Get out of my house and leave my family alone!" Agnes finally said, her voice strained.

"Agnes, no . . ." Beatrice said in a low voice.

"GET OUT! GET OUT NOW!"

"Mother, no! It's not her fault. Please!"

Agnes eyed Emma, appalled. "How dare you!"

"Agnes, please. Calm down. Let's talk about this," Morris said, reaching for his wife.

Agnes forcibly pulled away from him. "And you! Bringing your bastard children's whore of a mother right up under my nose. Don't you touch me! Don't you ever touch me again!"

Agnes pushed her chair back from the table and stood. "I SAID GET OUT OF MY HOUSE NOW!"

Beatrice stared intently at her, the tears building. She placed her napkin on the table, pushed her chair back, and stood unsteadily.

Emma grabbed Beatrice's arm. "Bea, don't go. . . . Mother, please don't do this!"

"No, she's right," Beatrice said, prying Emma's hand from her arm.

Beatrice held Agnes's eyes for a long while. "I didn't mean to hurt you. I never meant to hurt you," she said, and then glanced at Morris before she grabbed her things and left.

56

Beatrice

Beatrice sat on the sofa across from Sam, waiting for Sadie Mae. She said very little. She had been that way for more than a week, full of so many emotions—fury at Morris and even Emma for letting Agnes find out that way, anger at herself for not being honest from the start . . . even hurt at the terrible words Agnes had said to her. She knew it was ridiculous to expect anything else, but she couldn't help how she felt. She had played the look on Agnes's face over and over again in her mind.

Beatrice's thoughts were interrupted by the sudden opening of the front door. Sadie Mae had used her key to let herself in.

"Mama," Sadie Mae called out.

"We're in here," Beatrice answered.

Sadie Mae was surprised to see Sam already there. "Mama, is everything all right?" She looked from her sister to her mother.

Beatrice gave her daughter a cautious look. "Take a seat."

Sadie Mae had last seen her mother at church that past Sunday. Beatrice had barely noticed Sadie Mae, just kept her eyes on the pastor. And when Pastor Gilbert invited anyone to come up and pray, Beatrice had slowly risen from her seat and walked up to the altar. Sadie Mae watched her mother, and noticed there was something different about her. It wasn't the way her mother had walked up to the altar, or how she had kneeled and bowed her head. It was the look in her eyes.

"Well, it's no surprise that your father and I have had a special relationship for a very long time," Beatrice began, looking at her daughters.

Light spilled in from the windows, casting down on the two oversized photo albums that lay on the coffee table, open to pages of a young Sadie Mae and Sam. Beatrice could feel her daughters watching her.

"Mama, what's wrong?" Sam asked. She looked at her mother, waiting for her to answer.

Beatrice took in Sam's face, her blue eyes, the way her mouth curved like her father's. She turned and looked over at Sadie Mae, her features so different from Sam's.

"All my life . . . all my life I tried to do the right thing," Beatrice mumbled, her voice distant. "I was so happy when y'all were born. I promised myself that I would do right by y'all, that I would make sure y'all had everything I had, everything my mother gave me."

Sadie Mae felt a tightness in her stomach. "Mama, what's wrong? What happened? Is it Daddy? Did something happen to him?"

Beatrice looked pensively at Sadie Mae. "I haven't been completely honest with y'all about your father's situation. . . . For years I tried to act like his other life didn't exist. I told myself that I could deal with it, that as long as he was good to my girls, as long as he was a good father, that that was good enough. I never thought about all the people it hurt."

"Mama, what are you talking about? Please tell us what's wrong," Sam urged.

Beatrice stared straight at Sam. "Agnes . . . your father's wife . . . has cancer. For the past several months, I've been taking care of her. I didn't think I could ever face Agnes knowing what I'd done. But your father was having a hard time caring for her on his own, so I offered to help."

Beatrice's voice cracked.

"Me and Agnes got to be friends. It was hard at first, but in time, things started to smooth out between us. I think she even started to enjoy my visits. And I started to enjoy our time together, too. As strange as it sounds, it just felt like we had always been friends."

Beatrice stared off in the distance.

"Mama, did something else happen?" Sadie Mae asked, alarmed.

Beatrice looked steadily at Sadie Mae. "Agnes found out who I was."

Sadie Mae and Sam stared at their mother. "What happened when she found out?"

Beatrice looked away from Sam, shame chiseled across her face "She told me to get out—and to leave her family alone."

"Oh, Mama." Sam walked over to her mother, put her arms around her.

Sadie Mae joined them. "It's going to be all right. Things will work out. You'll see."

Beatrice leaned into her daughters, powerless to halt another round of tears. She thought about all that had happened, all that she had done, the years of deception and betrayal and hurt. And as her daughters held her, their contact comforting and familiar, she thought of them, and of Emma and Morris, all the lives that she had changed. So many lives. And she cried as she thought about Agnes.

57

Agnes

Agnes kept her eyes shut, listening to Morris's every move.
There was a brief moment between sounds and the smell
of fresh air that flooded the room as she felt him come closer
to the bed, tower over her.

"Agnes, you have to eat and take your medicine," Morris
said gently.

Agnes didn't flinch, didn't open her eyes. She had not gotten out of bed again, for the second week.

Morris stood there for a minute, then touched her back.
"Agnes, I know you hear me. You can't go on like this."

Agnes held the blanket up to her chin, her body rolled into
a ball, her back to him. The cool air felt tantalizing against her
bald head.

For the past several weeks, those shocking words, that terrible image, played in her mind—*Bea is Sam and Sadie Mae's
mother*—the shamed look on Morris's face, the hurt in Bea's
eyes, the way Emma looked at her. She had not spoken to any
of them since, refusing to give in to their pitiful apologies.
Bea had tricked her into thinking she was her friend; and the
nerve of Morris to allow that woman into their home; and
Emma? Her own daughter taking part in such irreverence!
How could they?

Emma had pleaded with her. But she just wanted them
to leave her alone, her isolation like a raft, keeping her from

drowning in her own misery. She was surprised each morning when she'd awake and find herself still alive. Each day brought fleeting moments when she'd think about those little girls, and the years leading up to now. She even found herself crying when she thought about Bea—all the time they'd spent together, the way Bea had cared for her, and all the things they'd shared. How could Bea do that to her? She had trusted her.

There was comfort in living in solitude, not having to face another miserable day. But she couldn't help but wonder if her life would end like that, with so much unresolved anger and hurt.

"Agnes, please talk to me. Please just talk to me."

Agnes was too afraid to open her eyes, say anything for fear that she'd regret it. But the familiarity of Morris's tone, the way he had cared for her even when she didn't want him to, the way he showed her kindness and compassion, she could no longer avoid. He wanted her to get better, and he loved her, this much she knew. She slowly opened her eyes but kept her back to him. She wasn't quite ready to let him see her face still raw with pain.

"Agnes, please, honey. Please at least eat something."

Agnes felt him take a seat on the edge of the bed.

"Agnes, I know how you must feel, believe me. And I'm so sorry, honey, for what happened. There's nothing more I can say, but I never meant to hurt you. Me or Emma or . . ." Morris paused, braced himself before he said her name. "Beatrice. She only wanted what was best for you, too. You have to believe that. I know what I've done isn't right, but we have to get past this, Agnes. We all love you. And I know it's hard, honey. I know that. But please try to understand. Please."

Morris moved closer, touched her delicately on the shoulder. "Talk to me, Agnes. Please."

Agnes hadn't spoken to anyone in so long, she'd forgotten the sound of her own voice, the way her words formed, found meaning. Morris had come to her room daily, two sometimes three times, trying to get her to talk. The fact that he was here again, his voice more contrite than before, signaled a change in his remorse. The puzzling thing was that he had chosen today, *her birthday,* to ask for forgiveness. *Why now? Why today?* She closed her eyes again and thought back on the day that she had told Bea everything—about the *other woman* and her children—and Bea had asked her if she believed in God. She had looked at Bea and said, "Of course I do." The very next day she asked Morris to take her to church, and she had kneeled in that tiny booth, the darkness covering her, and she had told the priest everything—their secrets, the heartbreak, her *pain*—and when she was done, she looked through that distorted grid, a glimmer of light shimmering, and she listened to him whisper: *You must forgive, my child. You must forgive to release your soul from bondage.*

And now, she felt the tears sliding onto her pillow. She wanted to forgive. She wanted to release her soul from bondage. The bitterness at Morris and Emma and Bea was taking its toll. She opened her eyes finally, and looked at Morris. "I need to see Emma. Please get Emma," she heard herself say.

She saw the surprised look on Morris's face. "I'll get her right away." He patted her hand and rushed from the room.

When Agnes heard the door close behind him, she cried, each tear a subtle reminder of the anguish that threatened to swallow her. She needed solace. She needed to forgive. And when she finally saw Emma, she opened her arms to her, and all those powerful emotions—anger, resentment, hurt— thrashed her like gusts of wind. She lay limp in her daughter's arms. After a time, she looked up at Emma.

"I don't want to live like this anymore. I don't want to be

angry anymore," she said. And Emma held her, rocked her, and cried, too.

They stayed that way for a long time, unabashed in their own contrition.

"Can you do something for me?" Agnes said, finally pulling back from Emma.

"Anything, Mom, please just tell me."

Agnes looked dazed. "I need to see them. I mean . . . Bea's daughters. I'd like to see them."

Of all the tears she had shed over the past few weeks, the ones she shed the most were for Sadie Mae and Sam—two innocent little girls whose names she once refused to utter; the ones she had thrown out of her house and heart all those years ago. It was them that she thought of most of all.

"Are you sure, Mom?"

Agnes knew how she must sound to her daughter. She looked hauntingly at Emma. "Yes, I'm sure," she said.

"Okay," Emma said, then held her mother like she had never held her before.

When Emma called and told Beatrice that her mother wanted to see Sadie Mae and Sam, Beatrice asked Emma to come see her right away.

"I was so glad to hear from you, Emma," Beatrice began when Emma came to her home on Sunday. "I know things have not been easy for you and Agnes. I've prayed daily that she would get better. I know I've hurt her, and for that, I'm so very sorry."

Emma embraced Beatrice before Beatrice turned to Sadie Mae and Sam. "I know it's been hard on you two as well. The way this family came about isn't the way it should have been done. But your father and I love you both dearly, and as strange as it may sound, when I spent time with Agnes, there was something special between us. A kind of connection that goes beyond understanding. I've prayed that she will forgive me."

Beatrice turned back to Emma, smiled through her tears. "Emma, I have come to love you like a daughter, and it brightens my heart to see the three of you finally together."

Emma looked over at Sadie Mae and Sam. They were young women now, so different from the little girls she had met in her parents' living room all those years ago. "Gosh, where do I begin," she said, fanning the tears from her eyes. "I'm so sorry about the way we treated you that time you came to our house. I was hurt, but I should have been kinder to you." She looked at Sam, smiled at her. Sam smiled back, tearing up.

"Your mother and I have grown very close," Emma said. "She is such a beautiful woman. I knew that the moment I met her . . . and my mother knew it, too. She's very fond of Bea, and although it's been rough for her, for all of us, she's grown to love Bea, and she wants to get to know you, too."

Sadie Mae looked away from Emma. She hadn't seen Emma since the time Agnes had thrown her and Sam out of their home, and she didn't quite trust Emma or Agnes. Yes, she understood what their mother had done, and now that she and Sam were older, she understood the complication of her mother's relationship with her father. But still, that didn't give Agnes any right to treat her and Sam the way she had. She could tell Emma was sincere, but she wanted Emma to vanish as if she and Agnes never existed. She didn't trust herself to speak.

Sam spoke for her. "This means a lot to us. I think I can speak for Sadie Mae, too, when I tell you that we are so happy to finally get to know you." Sam glanced uneasily at Sadie Mae. Sadie Mae didn't move. "And we've been praying for your mother, too, and we can't wait to see her again. You're our sister, a part of us, and we want nothing more than to have you in our lives."

Emma stood suddenly and embraced Sam, and they both cried. After a long moment, Sam, still holding Emma's hand, turned and reached out her other hand to Sadie Mae.

Sadie Mae looked hard and long at her sister, and then glanced at her mother. And after a long moment passed and she saw the look on Emma's face, she stood, and took Sam's hand, and allowed herself to be pulled into their embrace.

The next day, Morris was surprised to see Sadie Mae and Sam standing at his door.

"Hello, Daddy, may we come in?" Sadie Mae asked her father.

"Yes, please come in," Morris said.

They followed their father into the living room, and they were pleased to see Emma there.

"Hello," Emma said, standing.

Sam walked up to Emma and hugged her.

Morris watched his daughters. There they were at last, all three of them. Emma had told him about her visit to see Beatrice, and about their talk and that Sadie Mae and Sam had agreed to come to see Agnes. But still, seeing his three daughters all together, in his living room, made him wonder.

"How's Agnes?" Sam asked, after she embraced her father.

"She's not doing too well. The doctors said there's nothing else they can do for her." Morris looked distressed. Emma's face turned down as soon as she heard those words again.

"I'm so sorry," Sadie Mae said. She embraced her father again, and this time, she was the one who reached for Emma to embrace her, too.

It comforted Morris to know that Agnes had asked to see

Sadie Mae and Sam. But as much as he was pleased that Sadie Mae and Sam had come, he couldn't help but worry that seeing them might make Agnes drift back into an even more delicate state.

"Can we go up to see her now?" Sam finally asked.

Emma wiped her eyes, looked over at her father, and back at Sadie Mae and Sam. "Yes, please," Emma answered.

"I don't know," Morris said, shaking his head. "I know Agnes asked to see you, but I don't think it's a good idea. She's so sick."

"Daddy, I want to see her. I need to see her," Sam said.

"Daddy, I know this is hard. It's hard for everyone," Sadie Mae reasoned.

Morris looked over at Sadie Mae.

"We're no longer little girls, Daddy. We can handle it."

"I know, honey. I just don't want to upset Agnes. She's already been through a lot."

"Daddy, please. Let us do this," Sam said.

Morris looked at his daughter. Sam looked six again, his brazen little girl, so full of life.

"All right," Morris finally said.

Sadie Mae led the way.

They walked slowly up the stairs, taking notice of the oak wood, the floral motif runner, the white spindles. Sam had imagined that staircase a million times. She had never forgotten the first time she'd seen it.

When they reached Agnes's door, Sadie Mae hesitated, her hand froze on the doorknob.

Sam reached around her and turned it.

The room, brightened by the natural light, was quiet, eerie. Agnes lay with her eyes closed, propped up on two pillows, her complexion milky, her bald head bare. A portable

oxygen machine sat next to her bed, forcing air from the tank
to her mask. She took slow, measured breaths, oblivious to
Sadie Mae and Sam.

Sadie Mae walked up to the bed. Sam followed her. They
both took in the sickly old woman.

"Ms. Agnes . . ." Sam uttered. "Ms. Agnes . . . can you
hear me?"

Sam reached out to touch Agnes's frail hand. "Ms.
Agnes . . ."

Agnes shifted slightly, pushed through the grogginess,
forcing her eyes to flutter.

"Ms. Agnes, Emma told us that you wanted to see us."

Agnes brought the muted figures into focus, straining to
hear against the oxygen snarls.

"We want you to know that we're praying for you," Sadie
Mae said.

"We are worried about you," Sam said gently.

Agnes lay still, her body frail and stiff.

"Ms. Agnes, I know how you must feel, but I want you to
know that we still love you, no matter what," Sam said.

Sadie Mae looked at Agnes as though she was looking right
through her.

Sam reached out to grab her hand again. Agnes took it.

"You know, that day we first came to meet you, I'd written you a letter," Sam said. "I was only eight years old. I never
told anyone, not Sadie Mae, not even my mother. It was only
meant for you. I used to imagine what you looked like. When
I learned that our daddy had another family, I cried for days.
I thought that he was only our daddy. But then I had a dream,
and in my dream, there was this beautiful woman, and she told
me that I should feel special that my daddy had two families,
that it would mean that now I had more people to love me. I
remember waking up the morning our daddy was coming to

get us, and I tore up all the horrible stuff I'd written about my daddy's other family, and I wrote another letter. To you." Sam pulled the old wrinkly paper from her purse, the letter Agnes had refused to read all those years ago.

Agnes held Sam's gaze as she took it and then slowly unfolded the letter.

> Dear Ms. Aknes,
>
>   I know you don't know me. My name is Sam. I am 8 years old and my daddy comin to get us today. Me and my sister Sadie Mae to take us to his house. We never been to his house but my mommy told us that he has a big house. We don't have a big house. But we have a family, and now, mommy say we gonn have 2 familys. I like havin 2 familys. Mommy say me and Sadie Mae gonn have another sister. Her name Amma. Amma can be my sister but she can't be my twin. I already have a twin. I can't wait to meet you Ms. Aknes. I know I already love you. And I know you already love me too.
>   Love Sam

Agnes folded the paper and removed the mask from her face. "You misspelled my name," she whispered, her face soft. A wide smile broke on Sam's face. She reached out and grabbed Agnes's hand, and she cried when Agnes squeezed it.

58

Beatrice

"I thought that was you," Agnes said. She looked frailer since the last time Beatrice had seen her.

Beatrice quickly dried her eyes, and stepped closer to the bed. "I've been here for most of the morning. You've been asleep the whole time."

"Sam and Sadie Mae came to see me the other day," Agnes said, straining to speak. She had been in and out of sleep for the past few days, but she remembered them. She saw Beatrice in them both, and in a way they reminded her of Emma, too—in ways an untrained eye would miss. Like the way Sam was easily flustered, coiled in her own emotions. And Sadie Mae, the strong-willed one, so ready to fix things, the way Emma wanted to fix her.

"I know. They told me," Beatrice said.

"They are very special. I regret I didn't get to know them."

"Shhh," Beatrice encouraged. "Let's not talk like that. You know them now. That's all that counts."

Agnes's eyes watered. "I just wish I had known them earlier. I'm so sorry."

"No. Don't. You did as anyone would have done. I know how painful it must have been. I've spent most of my life thinking about what I would do if I were in your shoes, and no matter how hard I try, no matter how many ways I play it

over and over again in my head, I don't think I would have
handled it any better."

Agnes covered Beatrice's hand with her own, started to sob.
It felt liberating not to cover up her emotions. She had lived
that way for most of her life, and she was not about to live her
last days like that now. She had finally come to terms with her
life, had found a deeper level of understanding. In the end, it
wasn't the life that she tried so desperately to perfect, or the
pain she had carried for so long, or the memories that mattered.
It was the people who had opened her heart to forgiveness.

Agnes locked eyes with Beatrice. "I'm dying, Bea," she
said suddenly.

"No! Don't say that . . ."

"Help me sit up. I need to sit up."

Beatrice gently grabbed Agnes's bony arm, propped her up
on two pillows.

"I feel so tired."

"I know. But you got to fight. You can still beat this."

"No. I can't. Look at me." Agnes slowly opened her pajama
blouse to show the lesions and the charred blotches that covered the place where her breasts used to be.

Beatrice looked at the scars, at Agnes's translucent skin.
She rushed off to the bathroom and filled a basin with warm
water and peroxide, found a washcloth and bar of Ivory soap,
and came back into the bedroom. She set the basin at the foot
of the bed, then delicately helped Agnes remove her pajamas.

Holding Agnes against her, Beatrice leaned in and rubbed
Agnes's back with the warm washcloth. Then she washed her
chest, the lesions, her charred skin and scrawny legs and arms;
Agnes sank into Beatrice like a rag doll.

Beatrice found a fresh pair of pajamas, carefully slipped
them on Agnes, and rubbed Agnes's bald head with Vaseline.

Then she pulled a chair up to Agnes's bed, took the Agatha Christie book out of her purse, put on her reading glasses, and opened the book to the dog-eared page. Beatrice slowly began to read as Agnes closed her eyes and drifted off to the sweet sound of her voice.

A few days later, Morris took Agnes to the hospital and called Emma and the rest of the family. They all piled into Agnes's room, made uncomfortable small talk, and watched Agnes with a sadness that made them think of their own lives. Once everyone had gone home, Morris called Beatrice. "She's asking for you," he said quietly into the phone.

"I'll be right there." Beatrice wasted no time getting to the hospital, made her way there as quickly as she could.

"I knew you'd come," Agnes whispered when she awoke and found Beatrice sitting there.

"Of course I was comin'." Beatrice forced a smile, rose stiffly and went to her; and they looked at each other for a long while.

Agnes reached for Beatrice's hands, took them into her own. "Bea," she said, her voice low. "Promise—me . . . Promise me . . ."

Beatrice leaned in closer, braced herself.

"Promise me you'll take care of him. Promise me . . . Bea," Agnes whispered.

Beatrice closed her eyes, felt grace come over her. "I promise," she finally heard herself say, unsure of her own words.

A gnes died that morning with Morris and Emma by her side.

Beatrice cried when the call came. It was Agnes's last words to her that made her think back on her life. She waited until the next day to call Sadie Mae and Sam.

Sadie Mae didn't cry, didn't weep for the woman she had never known.

Sam cried like someone had torn the scab off an open wound. "I wish I had known her. I wish things had turned out differently," she sobbed, unsure about the source of her pain—if the tears came for Agnes or for her father or mostly for Emma, because she couldn't bear the thought of losing her own mother.

Morris made arrangements for the funeral that Agnes told him she wanted.

The funeral would be held at the same church where they had wed.

No open casket.

Purple and white lilies.

A beautiful photo of a younger Agnes.

And she was to be buried next to their son.

Emma came every day to be with her father.

On the second day, she lay on the same sheets where her mother had last lain, the implicit emptiness of the bed twisting her into unfathomable grief. And when she was done pouring it all out, she smelled the things her mother had last touched—the headscarf, a robe, her Bible.

Emma held the Bible for a long time, and when she placed it back on the nightstand, she noticed a box inside the drawer, and opened it.

Letters.

Countless letters addressed to her mother from her father. Letters he had written while he was at Pearl Harbor.

Emma took a seat in the chair near the window and allowed the natural light to guide her as she read the letters and cried.

59

Morris

The letter came three months after Agnes's funeral. It wasn't the official envelope with the perfectly printed letters, or the Department of the Navy seal, or even the custom military stamp that caught Morris's eye. It was his name.

Petty Officer Morris Sullivan.

An identity he had all but forgotten.

Since the war, he had seen many things that reminded him of that time—ships docked at the Boston Harbor, an occasional card from one of his shipmates, old photographs. But nothing had intrigued him the way the envelope did.

The morning was cool, a crisp chill making the house feel colder than the sixty-eight degrees on the thermostat. The turtleneck, heavy corduroy pants, and wool socks, along with the crackling fire and the steam heat from the radiator, did nothing to warm him. Now that he was alone, the house seemed even more lifeless and cold.

Morris made his way to the living room with his walking stick, the envelope in hand. He settled into his La-Z-Boy and put on the reading spectacles that hung loosely around his neck. He studied the envelope, then used his forefinger to delicately unseal it.

> *Dear Petty Officer Sullivan,*
> *The Department of the Navy, including the Navy*

*and Marine Corps, invites you to attend a special
ceremony to honor the survivors and our fallen soldiers
that were aboard the USS Oklahoma at Pearl Harbor
on December 7, 1941. We would be honored to have
you attend . . .*

Morris took his time reading it once, then twice, and a third time. He carefully inserted the letter back into the envelope, and then leaned back into his La-Z-Boy, remembering his last days at Pearl Harbor—the day before he was due to return home, his duty to the navy finished. He and Bernard had taken one last stroll to their usual spot. *We gon' stay in touch, right?* Bernard had said. *It not gon' be easy leavin' this place. Ain't no fondness in what done happened, but we still got some good memories here.* Morris had nodded. They stared out at the blue waters, the waves crashing against the shore. *We gon' stay in touch. I promise. And when I marry LouAnn, I want you to come. I want you to meet my family.* But that would be the last time he would see Bernard, the last time they would talk. He had often thought of Bernard, had even written a letter, sent holiday cards, tried to call the number he was given. But his letters went unanswered, calls unreturned.

And then there were the countless holiday cards and occasional letters or invitations he received over the years from other men he had come to know, working alongside them for days on end. A few would reach out to him over the years, inviting him to this ceremony or that gathering, but he never went. Could never bring himself to be reminded of a past that he had learned to conceal.

No one would ever again refer to him as Petty Officer Sullivan.

He had left Pearl Harbor, and returned home to live a quiet enough life. Had managed to put it all behind him, except for the random dreams that occasionally awoke him in the middle of the night, and the model ships that served as a subtle reminder of the ships he once loved.

Since losing Agnes, he'd had plenty of time now to think back on his life, the way it unfolded like grains of sand slipping through his clenched fist. The markings of his life were woefully clear now. It pained him that his memories of Agnes were bound to a blemished past. He missed her, felt a huge void, a hollowness in his home and heart. For years he'd walked through that door to find Agnes in the kitchen cooking his meals, or in the living room reading a book, or upstairs in their bedroom, the sweet smells of her nightdress mushrooming through the house. Never once did he think about what it would feel like to lose her.

Somehow, he had allowed himself to believe that he could have the best of both worlds—the one that Agnes gave him, and the one that he contrived with a woman who had confiscated his heart. Inevitably, in the end he had lost them both. And now receiving the letter from the navy was an omen, he supposed.

Morris stared into the blazing fire, listening to the quiet sounds of the empty house. He turned and looked out the window, filmed with ice, the view to the street covered in a light dusting of snow. He watched the snow cascading outside his window, blotches of it covering his home. The snow, so unbearably beautiful, reminded him of the times when he was a young boy and he'd spread his legs and arms in it like wings. How so very innocent he was then, his young mind and heart incapable of knowing what the future held. He longed for that innocence again, in the same way he longed for his loneliness to fade. He missed Agnes . . . and he missed Beatrice, too.

Without a second thought, he checked his watch and then

made his way to the foyer and grabbed his coat, scarf, and hat. He quickly bundled up, looked around one last time, and checked his pocket for the letter before he walked out into the frost.

He had thought to take this drive many times over the past few months, but he just couldn't bring himself to do it. It was just too soon. So much time had been wasted thinking back on all that had happened. These past few months were unbearable, agonizing over what had passed. But what did it matter now?

Morris slowly eased down the familiar street and parked the car. He sat there, just watching the house. The lawn and trees and bushes glistened in the white snow, reminding him of a Norman Rockwell painting. Impulsively, he opened the car door and slowly made his way up the path. He dusted his feet on the WELCOME mat, and then rang the bell.

Morris could tell that she was surprised to see him when she opened the door. They had not seen each other since her last visit to see Agnes in the hospital.

"Hello, can I come in?"

Beatrice looked uneasily at him, then led him into the living room.

"How have you been?" Morris said cautiously after he sat on the sofa across from her.

"I've been okay. Can't seem to keep warm." Beatrice pulled her sweater close around her.

Morris looked at her, noticed the long gray strands in her hair, the way her face had matured. Moments lingered and stretched into an awkward silence.

"How are you doing?" From the looks of him, Beatrice could tell that he had not been sleeping well.

"I guess I'm okay," Morris finally said. "It's been a little rough, I suppose."

Beatrice felt a pang of sadness. She thought of Agnes, and of Emma, and she imagined how he must be feeling, too.

"How are the girls? Sam's called a few times, and we talked briefly, but I haven't heard from Sadie Mae."

There was another silence. He could tell when he spoke to Sam that things were difficult for them. He suspected that she and Sadie Mae both blamed him for the way things turned out.

"They're fine," Beatrice said. "They are young women now. They'll be just fine." She said it as though she knew he needed to hear that.

"Agnes . . ." Beatrice paused, looked straight at him. "Agnes was really special. I mean, I wish I had known her under different circumstances."

Hearing Beatrice talk about Agnes made the past months feel more real. He looked at Beatrice, his eyes sad and serene.

"I suppose you came here for a reason," Beatrice said after a while.

He looked back at her again, held her gaze, he touched his shirt pocket to check that the letter was still there. "I got a letter from the navy," he said. "They are holding a ceremony at Pearl Harbor. It's going to be next month." He pulled the letter from his pocket and handed it to her.

Beatrice read it, then suddenly walked over to a desk, pulled an envelope from it, and handed it to him. "I got the same letter. They want to honor Robert after all these years."

Morris read the letter, and when he was done, he looked up at Beatrice, and Beatrice saw his eyes water.

Beatrice became still, and after a few moments, Morris looked at her, held her eyes. "Maybe we can go together," he said.

"I can't go with you," Beatrice said at once.

Morris looked perplexed. "Why not?"

"Because it's not right."

"Beatrice, please, I think it's time to let that go. Don't we deserve to do this after all these years? If for no other reason, we should do it for Robert."

A serene look appeared on Beatrice's face as she imagined what Robert might think of the world these days, of how far things had come—that she and Morris could hold hands in public if they wanted, that the navy would finally honor his sacrifice.

"I've never gone back." Morris seemed to be lost in his thoughts. "I could never face it. But with you . . . it might make more sense. It's where we started, and it would mean so much to me if you would come."

Beatrice could sense that he needed her to go with him for more reasons than he revealed; and she thought of Agnes, Agnes's frail face when she had held her hand and made the promise to her.

"All right," she said slowly. She would do it for Robert, and for Agnes.

A feeling of peace came over Morris's face. "Thank you, Beatrice," he said, sheer gratitude on his face. "You have always been more generous than I deserve."

60

Pearl Harbor, 1986

When Morris set foot on Pearl Harbor's soil again, there was something surreal, amiss about it. It wasn't the Pearl Harbor he remembered.

The ceremony would be held on the upper deck at 09:00 hours, commonplace for such an honorary event. Fully decorated officers, navy men and women, and a slew of families, friends, and spectators had come to take part in the momentous occasion. Morris was in his full dress whites, decorated in ribbons, honors he received for his unwavering dedication to his country. But today he did not dress for himself. Today, he dressed for Robert.

The morning breeze felt good on Morris's face as he made his way down the pier with his walking stick. The last time he took this walk, he was a much younger man, and his bad leg ached the same as it did today. He was mesmerized by what had become of Pearl Harbor—old battleships berthing the shore, the cemeteries, the museums, the USS *Arizona* Memorial, marking the sunken remains, the final resting place for more than 1,100 sailors and marines.

He cut across the docks, a shortcut he used to take, and immediately he could see it in the distance—the beach, the limestone rock. When he reached the rock, he thought back on the last time he and Bernard had sat there, their last words, and the countless times he had come there to read Beatrice's letters. A tranquil moment passed over him, and though he would never tell a soul, he felt an overwhelming peace, a presence. He reached inside his breast pocket and pulled a withered envelope from it, and unfolded the first letter he had ever received from Beatrice.

> *I've thought about you, too. But I just didn't think it was*
> *proper for me to write to you. . . . You are so different.*
> *I know Robert would have really liked you; and for that*
> *reason, I find myself liking you, too.*

Her words disarmed him every time, making him feel both lonely and sad. He had kept the letter all these years, not knowing what would become of them. He had always loved Beatrice, and he would give anything to do things differently. He knew Beatrice had risked her own happiness to oblige the love that had taken them both by surprise. He never meant to hurt her, any more than he had meant to hurt Agnes.

And Agnes. The pain he endured these past months since she passed was unending. There were days that he couldn't face the man he saw in the mirror, knowing how much he had hurt her. Just yesterday, before he left for Pearl Harbor, he had gone to the cemetery, the place where Agnes and their son had been buried, and he had asked for forgiveness.

Age and the clarity of hindsight had humbled him.

A sea hawk flew over Morris and headed out to sea. He sat there for a while, sealing the moment in his memory. The saltwater breeze carried bits and pieces of a life that he once knew. He looked down the beach and saw two young sailors walking with ease in the distance. They couldn't have been more than twenty, Morris guessed—one white, the other black. When they neared him, they slowed and saluted, acknowledging that he must have been one of the men who were being honored today. Morris stood and saluted. And when they passed, he smiled with memories of him and Bernard, and he couldn't help but wonder if he had made a difference.

A small difference, he thought as he slowly made his way back to find his family.

B eatrice looked out at the calm seas. Hawaii was so breathtaking, a far cry from the world that she imagined long ago. She had always wanted to come here, to be in the place where Robert spent his last days. She had never imagined this paradise—so beautiful even heaven might have suffered by comparison. She hoped Robert had found happiness here.

The USS *Missouri* was beginning to fill with people, some dressed in navy attire, and others in their best clothes. They had all come, she suspected, for the same reason as she. From where she stood, she could see the USS *Arizona* Memorial, such a heartbreaking site.

Until now, she had seen the massive ships only in the old books that Robert had shown her as a child; and once, she had stumbled into Morris's room across the hall from where she took care of Agnes and seen his model ships, miniatures of the ship she stood on now.

They were beyond her comprehension—so massive, so mighty. She understood why Robert and Morris were fascinated with them. To Beatrice, just being there, in the place where Robert once lived, among the ships that he so dearly loved, warmed her heart. Beatrice closed her eyes, thinking back on the times that Robert had shared his dream with her. *I'ma be a seaman,* he had said. And now, standing there, breathing in the splendor of the ship, she closed her eyes and thought of him. "*Yes, Robert, you were a seaman,*" she whispered to herself.

"This is an amazing site, isn't it?"

Beatrice opened her eyes and turned to see a black woman, about her age, neatly dressed and proper.

"Yes, it is," Beatrice answered.

"Who would've guessed that this place was once destroyed by such blasphemy. My, my, my . . . It's almost too much to imagine," the woman said, almost to herself. "Are you here for the ceremony?"

Beatrice nodded. "Yes, I am."

"Then we are probably here for the same reason. My husband served on the USS *West Virginia*. Thank God he survived the attack, but he never could put it out of his mind. He came to pay his respects and to honor his best friend who was lost."

"My brother . . ." Beatrice paused. "My brother is being honored today, too. He died here during the attack."

"I'm so sorry to hear that, but I know you must be so very proud of him."

"Yes," Beatrice said, then looked back out at the waters.

"I'm LouAnn, by the way." The woman stretched her hand toward Beatrice.

"I'm Beatrice."

"Well, it's a pleasure to meet you, Beatrice. May God bless you and your family."

"And I wish the same for you." Beatrice watched LouAnn head back over to her family.

The ship's horn blew, spilled into the sunlit air, and Beatrice felt a sensation breeze right through her. It was hard to believe that forty-five years ago Robert was here, in the midst of it all. She closed her eyes and tried to imagine what it must have been like. In her mind's eye, she saw Robert, so young and carefree, walking this very land—a colored man, in the navy, doing what he always loved to do. His love for the ships was what gave him the strength to withstand all that came against him. And she suspected that it was that same courage that carried him through in the end. She said a silent prayer for Robert, and when she was done, she unpinned a white flower from her white dress and gently kissed it and threw it over the deck. "*I miss you, Robert*," she whispered, and watched the flower feather away.

"There you are."

Beatrice turned to see Morris approaching her. At first glance, she recognized the young man from decades ago who had shown up at Mrs. Baker's house in his dress whites, so confident, so self-assured. She took Morris in intently, the way his gray hair, his wise eyes, his face, still reminded her of that same young man from so long ago.

"Where's everyone?" Morris asked, looking around for Sadie Mae, Sam, and Emma.

"They went ahead. I wanted to spend a few minutes alone."

Morris nodded, his eyes catching hers. Standing there with Beatrice took him back to all the times he had spent thinking of her in this place.

"It's about time for the ceremony to get under way. We need to go and join them," Beatrice said.

"Wait. I have something I need to talk to you about. We still have a few minutes."

Morris looked out at the open water, as if to steady himself. And when he spoke again, he seemed calm, absolute.

"I just wanted to tell you that I appreciate all that you've done, you know, through the years and . . . for Agnes. I know it must have been hard for you, and I wish I could take back the difficult times and the wrong decisions I made. I've never

really told you how sorry I am for hurting you and that I
know you sacrificed your whole life for me."

Beatrice stood quiet, confounded.

"Beatrice . . ." Morris said as if sensing her mood. "What
I'm trying to say is that I still love you and I hope that you can
forgive me. I know things have been especially tough for you,
but in the end, Agnes was grateful for you, too."

Another horn blew in the distance, and Beatrice could
hear people moving around them. She was remembering, for
some odd reason, the time she was sitting next to Agnes reading her a book and Agnes suddenly interrupted her and asked
her what she thought about forgiveness. She remembered it
as vividly as though Agnes was standing there between them
now. *Forgiveness is about honoring your own heart and soul,* she
had said to Agnes. *It's about letting go of the past and breathing life into the future.* Agnes had smiled at her then, and they
never spoke about it again. It was only now, when she closed
her eyes, that she knew her own words to Agnes were meant
for her.

Morris reached into his jacket and pulled something from
it. "I have something I wanted to give to you," he said. He
handed the tattered paper to Beatrice.

Beatrice unfolded the worn paper and stared at it.

"That's the first letter you wrote to me. I kept it all this
time."

Beatrice gazed at the writing, her words, so neatly displayed
on the page. The writing reminded her of the young, spirited
colored girl who had taken the bus to Boston so long ago.

"Beatrice, your letters helped me to get through all the
tough times while I was here. And I know what we did wasn't
right. I realize that, and believe me, I've paid a huge price for
it. I'm still paying for it. But I've loved you, Beatrice, from

the first time I met you, and I hope that you will find it in your heart to forgive me."

Beatrice didn't respond. Morris watched her, staring out at the water.

At last Beatrice turned to face him. "I forgave you long ago," she said.

Morris glanced out at the water, over toward the memorial, and then turned back to Beatrice.

"There's something I want to give to you." He undid the ribbons from his dress jacket and handed them to Beatrice.

"I want you to have this. For Robert. He's the one who deserves these ribbons. He was the true hero."

"I can't take that," Beatrice said. "You deserved them as much as Robert."

"No, please, Beatrice. I should have done this a long time ago. It would really mean a lot to me. Please."

Beatrice nodded, remembering the last time she had seen Robert, and the way his face lit up whenever he spoke about Pearl Harbor. That moment was so meaningful to her, an endless memory she always kept in her heart. She closed her eyes and imagined Robert in his full dress whites with ribbons.

Beatrice took the ribbons from Morris, smiled through her tears. "Thank you," she said, and looked back out at sea as though she expected to see Robert.

Another horn blew in the distance, calling.

"I guess we better make our way over there before we miss out on the most important part," Morris said, making light of the nostalgia.

Beatrice smiled again and followed him.

The USS *Missouri* was similar to the USS *Oklahoma,* the last ship Morris had served on. Her giant hull, the scale of her heavy artillery, and her massive decks reminded him of the last time he had walked her. He was proud to be walking these decks again with Beatrice by his side.

They walked the stretch and they could now see Sadie Mae, Sam, and Emma standing together looking out toward the USS *Arizona* Memorial. As they approached them, Morris suddenly stopped and stared at an elderly black man.

Bernard.

Morris searched the man's face. "Bernard?"

Bernard turned, and they stared at each other, trying to find the younger versions of themselves.

Without another word, they embraced. Beatrice, Sadie Mae, Sam, and Emma watched them for a long while and smiled blithely at the people who surrounded Bernard. Beatrice recognized the woman she'd met earlier, LouAnn.

"Man, it's been a long time. A long, long time," Bernard said, still taking in his friend.

"Too long." There was anguish in Morris's voice. All this time, he thought that Bernard had forgotten about him, and for years, he wondered if he had lost his friend forever.

"This hea' my wife, LouAnn," Bernard said. He reached for the elderly, handsome, stout woman, her short layered hair silver gray, her eyes as bright and beautiful as her smile.

LouAnn reached out to embrace Morris. "My God. We've waited for this day for years."

"Let me introduce you to the rest of the family," Bernard said.

A middle-aged woman stepped forward. "Hello, sir. I'm Mary Carolton, Bernard's eldest daughter." She reached out to shake Morris's hand. Morris embraced her.

And when she finally let him go, Bernard reached for an almost identical version of himself, a young Bernard dressed in his full whites, his lapels and chest decorated in medals and ribbons, honors from the navy.

"This hea' is my son, Commander Bernard Johnson Jr."

Bernard Jr. stepped forward and saluted Morris.

Morris returned the salute, their stances and postures marking the respect and admiration they had for each other.

"And this is my youngest daughter, and my grandson Simon," Bernard said, smiling at the fussy toddler and a younger woman who favored LouAnn.

"And over hea'"—Bernard reached for a young man— "this is my youngest son."

The young man came forward and extended his right hand. "How do you do, sir? My name is Morris Sullivan Johnson."

Morris gave him a peculiar look. "Morris Sullivan Johnson?" he repeated, astounded.

"Yes, sir. I guess you left an impression on my father."

Morris didn't take his hand. He embraced him for a long while. And when he let him go, he smiled through misty eyes and finally turned to his family. "This is my family, my oldest daughter, Emma," Morris said, reaching for Emma.

Bernard reached out his hand to Emma. "How do you do? I'm so pleased to finally meet you. I still have a photo of you when you were just a little thing. I always kept it," he said, smiling.

"It's an honor to meet you as well, sir. My father has told me so much about you."

Bernard embraced Emma.

"And these are my twin daughters," Morris continued. "This is Sadie Mae." Morris pulled Sadie Mae close to him. "And this is Sam."

Sam stepped forward and embraced Bernard and his family, and when she embraced Morris Sullivan Johnson, her eyes moistened.

"And this," Morris finally said, reaching for Beatrice.

"This is Beatrice." The tone of his voice revealed just how very special she was to him. "Robert's sister."

Bernard came forward and took Beatrice in his arms. "Robert was my best friend," he said, holding Beatrice; when he let her go, Beatrice embraced LouAnn, too.

The ship's horn blew.

"I guess we need to take our seats," Morris said.

Bernard and Morris took their seats alongside their families in the front row.

The band began to play "The Star-Spangled Banner" as sixty-four men stood in perfect formation while twelve men marched—some with flags, others with guns, not one breaking his stride.

Beatrice watched with awe, and when the band stopped playing and an officer stepped to the podium, she reached inside her purse and held the ribbons Morris had given her.

There was silence, a moment of honor, and after some preliminary remarks he began the ceremony.

"The Admiral, on behalf of the president of the United States, will now present the Navy Cross posthumously to the family of Seaman Robert Dobbins.

"The Navy Cross is our nation's second highest award for valor and personal courage in combat, ranking second only to the Medal of Honor. The president of the United States is pleased to present the Navy Cross to the family of Seaman Robert Dobbins, the United States Navy, for extraordinary heroism during the Pearl Harbor attack on the seventh of December 1941 on board the USS *Oklahoma*. During the Japanese assault against U.S. fleets, Seaman Dobbins put his life in danger when he retaliated against the enemy as his squad came under heavy and relentless fire from the enemy force, manning a gun he had never been trained to use and bringing

442 · L. Y. MARLOW

down one of the enemy planes, and then rescuing and retrieving more than twenty wounded men. By his demonstra-
tion of outstanding leadership and unadulterated courage in
the face of an enemy attack, and utmost dedication to duty,
Seaman Robert Dobbins upheld the highest traditions of the
United States Navy. Signed by the president and the secretary
of the navy."

Admiral John McMurthy stepped forward and presented
Beatrice with the Navy Cross.

"He was a great man, and demonstrated courageous leadership," Admiral McMurthy said to Beatrice, taking her hand.

"Thank you," she said. Tears streamed down her face. She
looked out at the crowd, saw Morris and Bernard and the
other uniformed men take a moment of silence to remember
Robert, and she closed her eyes and said a silent prayer for
Robert, too.

When Admiral McMurthy walked back to the podium,
she turned to Morris.

"Thank you for allowing me to share this moment with
you," he whispered, and reached for her hand.

Beatrice felt a surge of compassion, the way he now looked
at her. Suddenly, she could see their family differently. The
very essence of Emma and Sadie Mae and Sam; and Robert,
his presence as real as the grown children that stood before
her. They each reminded her of the choices she had made. She
couldn't regret anything that had led to her loving family.

Even a secret they had kept for nearly a half century.

The past was merging with the future. That first letter she
had written to Morris, now tucked away in her pocketbook,
a subtle reminder of the young, carefree girl who craved a
life that was beyond her own knowing; and the Navy Cross
and ribbons clutched tightly in her hand, a sacrifice that had
started it all. A brief cloud passed across the sun, striping the

ship like the ones that rippled across the flag fluttering in the breeze, and for the first time in decades, she felt at peace.

A smile came on her face as she looked over at Morris and then quietly slipped her hand in his, a lifetime of love passing between them, as she squeezed it.

Acknowledgments

I would be remiss if I did not pay homage to some very special women who have been a part of this journey.

To Shana Kelly, who brilliantly guided the careful orchestration of this book and helped me to navigate and craft what I truly believe will be amongst my best works. Without your fierce guidance and untiring commitment, I could not have done it.

To Suzanne O'Neill and Anna Thompson, my editors at Crown, who challenged me to dig *deeper*—unearth the meaning and moxie of a story that was beyond my own comprehension. Had it not been for your diligence, *A Life Apart* would not be the book it is today.

To Suzanne Gluck, my agent. Thanks for believing in me from the beginning when I showed up on your doorstep with nothing more than hope and a dream.

Finally, I want to give much gratitude to four very special women who touch my life in every facet of its being—my grandmother, my mother, my daughter, and little Promise. You are the reason I do all that I do.

And last but not least, to my greatest friend and confidant—God—for giving me the courage to stay the course, especially during those most difficult times of my life. It was because of those moments that I have come to understand, I mean *really believe,* that once I surrender, put my faith in you, ALL is possible.

About the Author

L. Y. MARLOW is the author of the award-winning *Color Me Butterfly* and the founder of Saving Promise, a national organization dedicated to raising awareness and preventing domestic violence. She lives in Maryland.

Saving
Promise·

A Note on the Type

This book was set in Bembo Book, a digital version of Monotype's Bembo, which was inspired by Aldine, a typeface cut by Francesco Griffo and used by Aldus Manutius in 1495 for Cardinal Bembo's tract "De Aetna." As there was no italic in the "De Aetna" work, Monotype drew on one found in a publication produced in Venice circa 1524 by the writing master Giovantonio Tagliente.

B\D\W\Y
BROADWAY BOOKS
Available wherever books are sold